The Bridge to Isla Sofia

A GENRE-BENDING MYSTERY/ROMANCE WITH SOUTHERN GOTHIC FLAIR

JENNIFER DANIELS NEAL

SemiTone
BOOKS & MUSIC

I dedicate The Bridge to my
cousins both here and gone.

I love you very much.

Contents

An Unexpected Guest

THE RAIN DANCES in puddles and explodes upon stones along the front path. It falls from the steep tin roof and occasionally gusts onto the porch, but it can't quite reach me where I'm snuggled in Mammaw's old quilt. Sometimes the wind rocks my chair, and I imagine it's her, reaching out to soothe me.

I always liked days like this when I was a kid. I rarely got to enjoy them, though. There were cousins everywhere you turned, always looking for action, and we'd end up at the river more often than not.

Jake would inevitably come home caked in mud, and if he did, I did. Sometimes all you could see of him before Mama or Aunt Rose could hose him down was that big, toothy smile.

That's how I like to remember him.

Jake died the day I turned eighteen, like some evil price of admission. *You are now an adult, and you are required to surrender your heart.* I can't believe it's been four years. And Mammaw gone three. I'm sorry the numbers weren't reversed. I'm sorry she lived to see it. Her toughest part, she'd said, the reason she'd break down and cry, was the worry that in those last moments he'd felt afraid.

That's not why I cry. Jake wasn't scared of shit.

Nothing much about the old cabin has changed. The wrap-around porch appears just as it has my whole life, though my sister has replaced some of the worn-out things—that swing, for instance.

Around back, there are spectacular views of mountain peaks. Well, not today. Today, everything is shrouded in delicious gloom. It's the middle of June in Tennessee, but it's downright chilly this evening.

I stay Mammaw's quilt and reach for my favorite mug. There's a sketchbook too, but I don't reach for that. About a quarter of the pages are smothered with words from the days leading up to my eighteenth birthday. The rest are blank.

I used to fawn over those large, empty pages. I'd even caress them. I really would. Just to feel the happy potential, like the anticipation I felt at the start of every summer once we got to the bridge, or like Mammaw's welcoming wave from this front door. Now the stark white of the pages is jarring like the door slammed shut. Nobody to open it for me.

All three of these items—the quilt, the mug, the sketchbook—were positioned for me when I arrived, all Sissy's doing. She brought her kids last month. It's my month now and the first time I've used the cabin since Mammaw left it to us.

Sissy has attached an old-fashioned fountain pen to the sketchbook. Her way of encouraging me to write. And writing is number two on the list of goals my therapist and I have set for this trip. But to write means to think, means first to have something to say, means to make myself vulnerable to—all of it, all over again.

Rather than consider that, I twist my birthday bracelets so that the leather knots line up. They're strung with stones panned from the water here. I may go down to the river, but I may not. My therapist said I should take someone I trust. I certainly can't go alone then. I do not trust myself.

The wind throttles the trees and taunts me like we have an appointment. It must have been one hell of a hurricane down there to cause so much action hundreds of miles north and this far up into the mountains. The river will rise—has surely done. It will cover the bridge, and here I will be.

I knew I'd get stuck. I intended to. I brought a few groceries. And more than tea for the mug.

When the thunder rolls across the sky, I lay my head back and close my eyes. I never did have any time to myself, so there's one silver lining. There were a ton of us when we could all get together, and more as Sissy and Wren had kids of their own. Always, Jake would instigate something reckless. Always, I would follow his lead. I can almost hear him shouting at me to *drop the book, dammit, and come on!*

No, I can *actually* hear him shouting. I open my eyes and scarcely have time to cognize what monster is upon me before seventy pounds of soaking, yellow hair is panting in my lap. I instinctively wrap the quilt around it.

In response, the dog works to rub its face dry on my tank top.

"No, Lucy!" a deep—and deeply mortified—voice shouts.

At first, I don't know what to do. And it's not just the shock of the unexpected visitation. It's the small fear that perhaps it is a *spiritual* visitation. Except that the dog is truly heavy, and cold, and wet. Dreams don't feel like that. I bet ghosts don't either.

The dog's father, whether real or apparition, drops his massive, camo duffel and rushes onto the porch, bypassing the steps the way his dog did. He wrestles the friendly beast off of me and scolds her, not harshly, more out of embarrassment, I think, with, "No, Lucy. No, Lucy."

When he turns his attention to me, his hands are raised in silent apology. Lucy barks a proper hello. Or maybe she's encouraging her human to use his words. He throws her a look and then fixes me with sharp, grey eyes on a face as handsome as it is confounded. Still, he does not speak to me.

I heard him talk to the dog. I know he can. Maybe he wonders if *I'm* a ghost. Maybe I am.

Also, if I can come up with all of these fanciful thoughts on the fly, why can't I write anymore? There used to be a never-ending supply of storylines to explore—and the enthusiasm with which to craft them. But I digress. There is a strange, attractive, and probably corporeal man standing in front of me on Mammaw's porch.

I rise to my feet and say—wait for it—"Hi."

OK, so I'm not much better at making conversation than he is. But this cabin sits on two hundred acres and is bordered by the Great Smoky Mountains National Park. Surely this guy has not just stumbled out of the backcountry hauling that enormous duffel. Speaking of which—"Your bag is getting waterlogged. You should bring it up."

He glances back, sees the sense in this, and lugs the bag onto the wooden floor. All three of us—I'm including the dog here, as she seems to be the most effective communicator—simply stare at it. It appears to be leaking.

"Did you bring your fish as well?" I ask. "There's a tub." I point a thumb toward the house. "If that will help."

"What?" the man says. He doesn't get my joke. To be fair, it wasn't a very good one.

"Are you OK?" I ask. "You seem...addled."

The man draws a breath which also draws him to height, and now I can appreciate the contour of his broad shoulders beneath the sopping t-shirt. I swear he looks like Jake. If Jake had let his beard grow thick like that. I bet it would have been the same barley-wheat color.

"This is Wren's place, right?" he asks.

"*Whew.* I am so glad we got to speaking terms. Yes. Well, it belongs to all of Mammaw's grandchildren. Wren is my cousin. Each one of us gets it for one month a year, and we rent out the rest."

By the size of his duffel, this guy brought enough to stay all summer. "It's my month," I declare. "Did Wren rent it to you?"

"No. I've been slogging through the evacuating traffic from the coast." He backtracks to explain that—"There was a hurricane in the Gulf."

Have I already begun to take on the appearance of a hoary-haired, hermit woman who has no access to the news? "I'm aware," I assure him.

"Of course." He pinches the bridge of his nose and tries again. "I've been driving in this for over twenty-four hours. I was heading to my parents' place in Indiana, but Wren called to check on me and told me to shelter in here. He didn't say it would be so far off the beaten path. Or that cell coverage would disappear. Or that my dog and I would be intruding upon his—beautiful cousin." He drops his eyes to mutter the last and cringes to see my tank top, which his dog has used for a bathmat. "Sorry," he adds.

I can now make out the black truck that's parked on the far side of the house. It's only just visible through the fog. I guess the storm masked its sound. More importantly, did he just call me Wren's *beautiful* cousin?

He's speaking again. "The bridge back there is all but underwater. I barely made it across."

"Well, you're stuck now," I tell him. "It'll be impassable for days."

"Sorry," he says again.

He looks it. He looks exhausted too. And just uncomfortable. His jeans are sticking to him. He's shivering. I feel bad for the guy.

"Don't be," I say. "Let's get you out of those—" I shouldn't say it that way. I don't even know his name. "Come inside and get warm. We'll go from there."

His face relaxes some. "You're gonna let me in."

"Well, you've invoked the sacred right of familial connection, so I sort of have to." I'm only half joking. I can't recall the number of times I've walked in on a stranger who simply called out something like, "Friend of Wren's," or "Jake's baseball team."

This stranger offers his hand. "I'm Banner Kirk."

"Isla." I over pronounce the E sound. "*Eesla*, like the Spanish word for island. No, I do not speak Spanish. Yes, my parents conceived me on an island."

"Which one?" he asks, which makes me blink twice and shrug one shoulder.

"I try not to ask too many questions. One of the Virgins."

"That's ironic."

A laugh escapes me in what feels like the first genuine expression of mirth in—forever. "You'll fit right in here," I tell him.

Banner looks pleased with himself. He hefts his huge bag, and a mini waterfall flows from one end. "Did I bring my fish," he says. "I get it."

"It was dumb. I'm out of practice."

"I should leave it here."

"Well, grab anything you want to throw into the dryer. Will your dog stick around long enough for me to be back with a towel?"

Lucy is lying on the welcome mat like she owns the place.

"Yeah, but let me," he says.

"No. You're freezing. It's nothing."

"You'll get soaked."

"Banner." I lift my hands and frown at my shirt which, as we have already established, is a colossal mess. "I've got it."

So, he dips his head with a cute half-grin and gathers some things from his bag. Once his arms are full, he nonetheless reaches for the door handle. "*Allow* me?"

With the emphasis on *allow*. Like it's a question. Like it means more than he's asking. In a good way—not in the way a vampire gets you to invite him in so that he can maintain his evil powers.

He doesn't appear to be a vampire. He's got a nice tan, and his teeth are all even. The longer I study those teeth the more I hope I'm wrong about that. Honestly, I can't think of a better way to go.

This is Kind of Fun

UNFORTUNATELY, this is not a vampire story. It's my real life, and I lead Banner into it through the front door.

Having breached the threshold, he scans the place and says, "Wren called this a *cabin*."

Kitchen, dining, sitting, hearth—they're all gathered into one vast, open space under high ceilings and a loft. You have to walk twenty yards to hit the first wall—which is mostly windows onto the back decks where, on a clear day, you can see Sissy's new outdoor fireplace and the Great Smoky Mountains beyond.

"But it's still charming, right? Still homey?" I keep moving, and I assume he does too. "You're an Army guy?" I ask.

"Does it show?"

His voice comes from further back than I expect, so I turn to find what's keeping him. Someone—one of Sissy's girls I imagine—has left Pap's old guitar propped against the hearth, and that's what caught his attention.

"Well, you're friends with Wren," I say, "and I couldn't help but to notice the camo luggage."

"Four years active duty, two in reserve. I'm out now. But my dad's a lifer. My sister too. You play?" He motions to the guitar.

"I used to. It's actually on a list of goals I have for this trip, but —see?—it's missing a string."

"What I *see*," Banner prods, "is that you're the kind of woman who makes to-do lists for vacations."

That is so far from the truth, it makes me smile. "Not usually. It's a—whole story." I wave the subject away.

"Well, I'll get you some new strings, OK?" he says. "And change them for you. That's the least I can do."

I don't know what it is about Banner's offer that touches me, but I find myself ducking his gaze. "Yeah, that would be nice." I guess it's been a while since I allowed someone to share a burden, even a small one.

He watches me in what I take for a moment of connection until I remember that he simply can't do anything else because he doesn't know where to go.

Right. "Keep up, Banner Kirk."

At the end of the room, we veer through the Hall of Heights, so named because every cousin has been measured and marked at the beginning of every summer since forever. I smile to see that Sissy's kids and Wren's have kept the tradition going. Banner wants to stop to inspect it—I can tell—but I usher him on.

A flip to light the laundry room and a tug to open the dryer, and I move aside while he deposits his things. When he steps back, it's with a quirky, pursed-lipped grin.

"What?" I ask.

He just shakes his head, innocent eyebrows jutting into his hair-line, but when I start the machine, I come face to face with the lacy, yellow bra and matching thong I've hung to dry.

Click. I close the laundry doors and narrow my eyes at him, which only causes him to snicker like he's used to ribbing me.

"Come along," I sing. "This is the boys' side of the house— which is clearly where you belong."

That's how we always divided things—boys over here with a row of twin beds, and girls on the front of the house with a full bed for Sissy and me. Whatever younger cousins showed up was catch as catch can.

"Shower's in there," I point. "And you can sleep in here. I'll lay out some clothes for you." I size him up. Asher and Wren are too tall and slender for theirs to work. I'll have to go through Jake's, smell Jake's, remember things.

I guess Banner reads the reticence on my face. He says, "Don't go to any trouble."

"No, it's no trouble. Go get warm. Take your time."

He hesitates, scrutinizes my face.

I want to ask what conclusions he's drawing.

"Thank you, Isla," is all he says.

With a jaunted nod, I go to retrieve the keys to the closet where we keep personal items separate from the space we allow renters to use.

I'd thrown a fit when Aunt Rose said it was time to get rid of Jake's things. Wren intervened, said I could go through them on my own time. That was three years ago, the last time we were all here together—for Mammaw's burial. I'm not sure my dad and Aunt Rose have spoken since then. There was an argument. I heard my name tossed around. I've never had the heart to ask, but I know that Aunt Rose blames me for Jake dying. Doesn't matter. I blame myself.

I return with the key and stare at the closet like it's the enemy. Inside is a box full of whatever Jake deemed necessary to bring that summer. *What did I bring? Why did I get to grow older and not him?* I'm paralyzed until I hear the shower clunk on and the pipes complain as the water heats them. It sort of kicks me into drive. I unlock the closet, locate the box with Jake's name, and drag it into the room. The first thing on top? Jake's favorite Atlanta Braves t-shirt. I cradle it, lift it to my nose. I don't have time to get lost in emotion, though, because Banner's voice reverberates from the bathroom.

"This shower head is off the charts!"

"It's great, isn't it?" I call back. "Sissy got it. My sister."

"What?"

"Nothing!"

The bathroom door opens and, along with a puff of steam, Banner's wet head emerges. "Did you say something?"

Hands flying to my mouth, I laugh in surprise because the

naked man is talking to me face-to-face. "I was just answering you. About the shower head."

"It's like having your own adjustable raincloud."

"Why don't you go enjoy it, then?"

"Yeah, I am." He disappears, and I catch a glimpse of my own bemused face in the mirror. *What am I supposed to do with this guy?* Crap. His dog. I hurry through Jake's box, pull out a few nostalgic items for myself and select some comfortable clothes for my guest.

You know, sorting through Jake's stuff isn't that hard—not with another living human in the house. I think I isolate myself too much.

My step is lighter as I walk outside. "Lucy!" I call. The rain is loud, and the thunder is louder still. *Oh, gosh. What if she ran away in fear?* For just a moment, I glimpse what at first I see as a human form. A person cloaked in white. But it's too hard to define through the weather, and then a crashing sound reaches me and a bark-bark-bark. Now Lucy comes bounding out of the shadows.

"Come, Lucy." I clap. "Are you OK?"

She gallops onto the porch and performs a massive shake while I hold up the towel to shield myself.

"I'll take that as a yes. What happened out there? Did you knock something over?"

Lucy does not answer me, and she does not readily submit to the drying process. She thinks I'm playing tug-the-towel, and I *do* get soaked. Banner was right about that. But eventually, we work it out, and I invite her in.

By the time Banner rejoins us, I've changed into something Lucy has not molested, and I'm chatting her up on the impractical, but comfortable, shaggy, white, living room rug that my sister bought. It's possible that the clothes I've chosen are not the most hideous I own, and that I've released my hair from its messy bun prison.

Banner is wearing Jake's white waffle henley. He fills it up the way Jake did too, better, actually. He's solid. His biceps. His chest and shoulders. It's a nice look.

"Did you find everything?" I ask.

In response, he floats his arms to present himself dressed. Now that he's comfortable, he exudes an easy kind of confidence, and he pushes each sleeve to the elbow as he browses the decor.

"I like this place," he says. "It's rustic, but it's nice too."

"My sister spruces it up with the rental money it generates. She keeps it true to Mammaw's ideals, but just, you know." I motion around. "She's good at stuff like that."

"What are you good at?"

The question takes me off guard. I silently run through the list of my most recent accomplishments. Brooding. Drinking. Survivor's guilt. Aloud, I say, "I'm good at living inside my own head. I'm phenomenal, actually. If there were some kind of award for it, I would put it..." I swivel to choose the perfect spot. "There." I point at the trash can.

Banner doesn't miss a beat. "So, you're good at being hard on yourself."

After allowing my eyes to drift around the ceiling, I say, "That's a fair assessment. What are you good at?"

While Banner considers the question, he roams the room. "Assimilating. I guess. Army brat, remember? We moved around every few years. Sometimes every few months. I'm good at deciphering the unspoken rules of a place. This is you?"

He's found a photo of possibly the longest, dang kingsnake in the history of Earth. Within the frame, I'm gripping its head and Jake is gripping its tail so that Asher can measure it. My mousy-brown hair is a mess around my face and Jake looks like he's been dipped in mud.

"You're a wild child, aren't you?" he asks. It sounds like a compliment.

"That snake flipped and twisted and threw a stink bomb so musky I could taste it for days. Totally worth it, though. It was over five-feet long."

And now he's roving again. He spies a poem framed over the huge, family table like a blessing. It's written in kid's handwriting.

"Oh, don't read that." Before the words have left my mouth, I know they're just going to insight him.

"Oh, but now I have to." Banner nods to convey the inevitability. "*Cousins,*" he reads aloud. "*By Isla.*"

I hurl a pillow that hits him in the back, so he clears his throat, turns to procure it, and sends it back at me, basketball-style. Then, he proceeds to read the first verse of my poem with lighthearted gusto.

> *"We jump together on the count of three*
> *I cry out when you skin your knee*
> *The wind blows and knots your hair to mine*
> *But we don't even notice till it's dinner time.*

"Ah, that's sweet," Banner says. "You played so close you didn't know your hair was tied together." He continues with increasing gravity.

> *"One day our children will eat dinner here*
> *While we untangle the wind from their hair*
> *And the line of your smile will extend on my face*
> *And the leaves from the same tree will cover our graves."*

Banner finishes the poem quietly and turns to search me out. "Damn," he says. "How old were you?"

I shrug. "Ten? Eleven?"

"It makes me homesick for a family I don't even have."

His words pull a hum of longing from me. "Me too, now." I change the subject. "So your place took a beating?"

He nods.

"Were you in it?"

"Oh, yes. Like an idiot, I thought I'd ride it out. Wind took half the roof before the actual storm even made landfall. And still, I hunkered down, but it's like the damn thing was out for me personally. The weather reports kept getting worse. The wind kept getting louder. A few days ago they weren't even going to give it a name! It sprang up out of nowhere. I stuffed my bag with whatever would fit while Lucy let me know how dumb I'd been."

Lucy lifts her head at the sound of her name. Banner says, "Gas stations were running out of fuel as far north as Atlanta. Folks lined up. I guess I'm lucky. I had a full tank in the back of my truck, and I just kept driving."

"Have you eaten since you left?"

"Beef jerky and Red Bull, baby. I was going to pick up some food for Lucy once I got settled."

"Yeah, that's not gonna happen." I trek to the pantry. "We can make her something though. There's plenty of rice for a few days." I grab the bag of rice and rummage around to find something else that would make a dog happy. "Also, there's this eccentric neighbor who raises chickens. He might sell us some eggs. But for tonight..." I come out with two cans of tuna. "How about this?"

"Perfect. I'll pay you back. How eccentric?"

"Like, if you don't come with me? I won't go—eccentric. And that is how much more I trust you, a perfect stranger, than I trust him. If you *do* come with me, I can give you a whole hillbilly education."

I open the tuna with a rusty, not-so-easy-to-operate can opener. It squeaks every time I turn it. "We have an electric one," I explain, "but this one reminds me of Mammaw."

When I look up, Banner's grey eyes are smiling at me. "This is kind of fun," he says.

"I'm glad you think so," I laugh.

It could be fun, I guess. I just thought I needed to be alone. Move on from the idea that they buried me in Jake's grave too. I came to say goodbye—one way or the other. I'm sure Banner sees the cloud that darkens my face.

"I'm sorry, Eesa," he says. "You had this whole solitary getaway planned, and—"

"What did you just call me?" I ask.

He has to think back.

"You called me *Eesa*," I prompt.

"Ah—I'm a nicknamer. Part of my assimilation skills. Was it too familiar?"

"No, I love it," I gush. "Somebody else used to call me that."

"Old boyfriend?"

"Noooo. One of my cousins. Jake. When we were little, he couldn't say my name. *Eesa* was as close as he could get, but then he never called me anything else." I lower the heat beneath the rice. "A *boyfriend*," I mutter thickly, but then I remember—"We did kiss once when we were fourteen."

"*Kissing* cousins!" Banner claps as he exclaims it. "Let the hillbilly education begin!"

He continues to goad me while I set him to work buttering a loaf of French bread for us. He makes me laugh. "Let's go, then, Eesa! Hillbilly 101: How to know which cousin is the one."

"It was not like that!" I shriek. "My eighth-grade boyfriend had kissed me for the first time, and then he *immediately* broke up with me. I was extremely worried about my skills."

Banner snorts while I crush garlic. "Jake got sick of hearing about it. Told me he'd give me a non-biased assessment."

Now Banner is howling, and it's contagious.

"Shut up!" I laugh. "I know it sounds dumb! So, we kiss, though. And Jake coughs and sputters like it's the most godawful thing he's ever had to endure."

I have to stop what I'm doing to wipe my eyes where they're tearing from the sheer, unexpected joy of sharing this stupid memory.

"And then he grabs his heart and pretends to—" I suck in a breath and stall out as real tears flood my eyes. Just like that.

"What just happened?" Banner asks.

I try to blink them back. "I'm sorry. He pretended to die. But a few years later, he actually did. He drowned here on the property." I can't swallow down the emotion. My face gets screwed up, and my voice comes out higher-pitched as I go. "I haven't been back here since then. Not really. And that's why I'm here now. Nothing's been right. Not for me. Not for our family."

Poor Banner—who met me less than an hour ago—on accident —after escaping a hurricane and driving all night—bless him—tries to console me. He says, with some uncertainty, "I'm gonna hug you."

And that makes me laugh even though I'm crying. He snickers too, but with eyes that are full of concern. Gingerly, he encircles me like he's testing the waters, and slowly pulls me close. Also, he rocks with me like we're dancing. It's all very odd, and sweet, and comforting. I lay my head on his shoulder, take a stabilizing breath, and allow him to guide me. He takes a breath too. I feel it expand against me, and I swear it fills me up as much as it does him.

When the stove's timer chimes, Banner switches off the burner and moves the rice so it can rest, but he's holding me all the while.

I sniff as I pull away. "I'm sorry."

"No need. Humans cry when they need to cry. This is Wren's little brother who died?"

"He told you about it?"

"Yeah. The first thing he ever said to me was that I reminded him of that brother. Of Jake."

"There is some similarity," I say. "I noticed it too."

"He has another brother, right?"

"Asher," I tell him. "Asher's the middle one. Jake was the baby. He was my age." I stir Lucy's food together and stoop to offer it to her. "So, *how* do you know Wren? Did you go to West Point? You couldn't have gone through at the same time unless you're older than I think."

There's a slight hesitation that makes Banner's answer feel too long in coming. "I never went through Point. My sister did."

"So, you know Wren through your sister?"

"No."

OK…

"We met in Florida. We had a—class together."

Wren finished law school ages ago. He's a successful attorney now—for the Army, but I don't see how—"What kind of class?"

Another hesitation. "Why don't I let him answer that?"

Huh.

"It's just that—I'm not at liberty to say." He rushes to add, "It's nothing nefarious."

"No," I agree. "Wren doesn't do nefarious. He's the strait-laced one of us."

He doesn't do sloppy either.

"He didn't mention that I might be here?" I ask.

"Said the house would be a welcoming respite is all."

Interesting. "He knows it's my month. Maybe he assumed I wouldn't use it. I haven't in the past." A funny thought crosses my mind. "Did you curse to yourself when you found out someone was already here? You can tell me. I won't be offended."

"Are you kidding me?" Banner flashes his eyebrows as he pops an almond into his mouth. "I thought I'd won the lottery."

He's pretty damn cute.

"Let's eat," I say and head for the couch with the platter we've made, but Banner says, "Do you mind if we eat at the family table? I just like the idea of it."

His suggestion opens a trove of memories. The first dinner without Pap. Sissy's announcement that she was carrying twins. That time we *forgot* to add sugar to Asher's lemonade and he spit it all over Mammaw. Jake's body lying there overnight.

"Sure," I say slowly. "We can eat there." I say it more to myself. "It's actually number three on the list of goals." It's possible that Banner thinks I'm joking, but I mean, how can I feel at home again if I can't even eat at the table? I make my feet walk over to set the platter down.

To Flooded Bridges

IT'S AN ENORMOUS TABLE. I don't know why we couldn't just have laid Jake's body on the bed. Why did we have to approach it like an old Irish wake? I didn't question it then. I was numb with shock. I hung around the body like one ghost searching for another. Occasionally I would raise my head to see the same haunted expression on Aunt Rose.

Banner brings me back to the present. "Where do you sit?"

"Depends on who's around, but anywhere I want to."

"Except here." Banner butts in to occupy the seat I'm pulling out for myself.

"Oh my gosh." I thump his head. "You *do* assimilate. You act just like one of us."

Once I'm settled around the corner from him, he raises his water glass. "To flooded bridges."

"To flooded bridges," I repeat. And with that clink, we consummate his stay.

"What do you do on the Gulf?" I ask. "Are you a professional beach volleyball player? 'Cause, that would be cool."

He's building some kind of sandwich contraption. "Sorry to disappoint. I *dive* a lot," he offers. "Which is also cool. 'Cause sharks.

And shipwrecks. And you have to be all courageous. and manly, and stuff."

"No, you're right." I nod solemnly. "That's cool. Just—those volleyball players are *mmh*." The face I make emphasizes how *mmh* they are.

"Hey! I'm *mmh*. Why do I always have to convince everybody how *mmh* I am?"

He doesn't. At all. And I'm pretty sure he knows it.

"I can play volleyball," he mumbles.

"I'm sure you can." Feels good to joke with him. Feels good to flirt with him.

A gust of wind causes the lights to flicker, and Banner roams the air with his eyes.

"I'm surprised it's stayed on as long as it has," I tell him. "If it goes out—"

Before I can complete the sentence, a huge clap of thunder sounds and an almighty crash. The electricity fails. The house goes silent. I hadn't realized how many soft currents were humming until now. The absence of them, especially the dryer's noise, leaves only the outside sounds of wind and rain. It's magical. I sort of hate to offer to turn it back on.

"There's a generator," I admit. "It's easy to rev up. If we want to."

Although Banner is close to me, he's little more than a shadow. "No way," he says. "Let's do this."

"OK, I'll grab some candles!" I hear myself, and I sound as eager as a kid.

Three lit pillars later, I walk them back, triangled in my hands.

"What's your real gig, then?" I ask. "If not volleyball."

Banner watches me all the way to the table before he answers. "I hate to tell people. It never sounds legit."

"Oh, that's not intriguing. OK. I bet I can guess it in three."

He likes that. He flips his hands to invite me to try and sits back in his chair, looking cocky as hell.

"You don't believe me?" I say. "I got this. *Ummm*, well, I think we can rule out dog trainer."

He laughs good-naturedly. "Decidedly not. But you're never gonna guess what."

"If I do, you have to cook breakfast."

"Deal."

"You're a pancake chef!"

"Because that's what you want for breakfast?" he asks.

"And bacon."

"Keep trying, then."

"Is it something you have to live in Florida to do? Like a fishing charter?"

"Is that a guess?"

"No."

"Florida's just a base for me. I live on the road most of the time."

"*Ooo,* something sketchy you have to be on the road to accomplish… Drug smuggler!" I shout.

"No. But I'll give you an extra chance because you're actually quite close."

"Really?"

"No."

I like him.

"Fuck it, just tell me."

"I write a travel blog," he says.

"You're a writer? Where all have you been? How'd you get started? What's the site?"

His expression catches somewhere between amused and overwhelmed.

"Sorry. That was a lot."

"No, I'm glad you're interested. It started while I was on active duty. We had the freedom to interact with locals in this rural town in Afghanistan, and I kept a journal of things."

"Like what?"

"Like the way the women wouldn't make eye contact but found ways around the cultural norms. They'd perform songs and stories but pretend they weren't meant for us to enjoy. They'd sit just around a corner or behind the couches where the men sat. And the men—you'd expect what you hear, all the hype about domineering severity. But in reality, at least in that small town, they treasured their families. They were tender with them. Playful."

I mean to respond, but only the tiniest sound comes out. Who *is* this man?

"There's a motto that governs the blog," he says. "An old proverb. 'Whoever goes hunting for what is right and kind finds life itself.'"

"That's—that's beautiful, Banner. I can see it. The way you take everything in. The way you ask questions. There's a kindness to your curiosity instead of a spotlight. I bet it's really popular, isn't it? I bet tons of people are attracted to you—to your work, I mean." *Oops.*

The candlelight shines in his eyes. "I resisted showing anybody at first, but my friend Sayeed—he served with me—he stole my journal one night in the barracks. Brilliant guy." He pauses. There's something he doesn't say. "Anyway, he encouraged me to put it out there."

"Do you see yourself doing it long term? I mean, is living from a *hub*, as you say, going to be enough for you?"

He shrugs. "It's what I know."

The reserved quality of his response causes me to search him, but I'm also trying to clear our plates, and I knock over a candle in the process.

"Careful," Banner laughs and quickly rights it, but the lingering tension in his shoulders betrays his relaxed tone of voice. "Wren won't let me visit you anymore if we burn the family homestead to the ground."

"I could be wrong," I retort, "but it sounds like you think I'm gonna ask you to come visit again."

"*Well,* I've decided to take up volleyball, so you'll probably want me to."

"*Well.* Wren's not the boss of me."

There's this pregnant pause while our eyes meet, and we don't say anything. I break contact first, smiling down at the plates in my hand, and Banner helps me carry the rest to the kitchen where he immediately stations himself at the sink and begins to wash them.

"You don't have to do that," I tell him.

"Volleyball?"

"The dishes. I'll get them tomorrow."

"That's impossible. Army brat, remember? You'll probably grow to hate me for it."

"For being a neat freak?"

"It's a curse."

"Not for me," I say. "Have at it." I place a candle on the window sill and head for the couch. "So, there's no *Mrs.* Kirk, then?" I ask. *I'm not digging. You're digging.*

"Um. Yeah. There is. She's a writer too."

Well, that blows. Was he not just flirting with me?

"She mostly writes about Army living, encouragement for spouses. That sort of thing." Having finished the dishes, Banner strolls over to sit down on the other side of the couch. "Is there any way to call her from here? Let her know I'm safe?"

"Sorry. No. Once the bridge opens up, you can go into town. There's plenty of cell service there. Where is she? Is she safe from the storm?"

Banner looks confused. "She lives in Indiana."

"Your wife lives in Indiana?"

"Oh—no—my mom. *Mrs. Kirk.* I'm not married. I don't have anyone. I'd like to. I just...don't. I don't stay anywhere long enough."

Is it wrong to rejoice because someone has no one to love?

"What about you? Your boyfriend was too much of an asshole to come keep you company?"

"That's not nice," I reprimand him. "He *wanted* to."

Banner's upward nod of acknowledgment seems just a tiny bit disappointed. Maybe even pissed. Wishful thinking?

"But he doesn't exist," I add. "So, it's hard to take him places."

"Probably embarrassing too," he offers, regaining his smile.

"You don't know the half of it."

We talk some more, but my new friend's kind eyes are growing heavy. He laces his fingers behind his head. "Why don't you have a boyfriend, Eesa?"

"Gah, I don't know. One of the hazards of growing up in a tight-knit family, I guess. Outsiders tend to feel like—outsiders. Nobody gets me. Nobody knows how to joke."

"You want him to come worn-in."

"Is that too much to ask?"

He shakes his head. "He'll be a lucky man."

Awwww. What am I supposed to say to that? *Um, want to make out?* "Thanks."

I catch him yawning more than once. That settles it. He's not nocturnal enough to be a vampire. "Don't stay up on my account," I say. "I'm gonna go to bed."

I'm gonna go drink. But in private. And hopefully enough to fall asleep.

While Banner lets Lucy out for the last time, I move the candles to the boys' bedroom and search for extra blankets. I'm feeling around in a trunk when the lights blaze back to life, and I can tell that Banner is switching them off as he and Lucy make their way back through the house.

"The electric's on," he calls out.

"Are you sure? How can you tell?"

Was that a snort? I think he just snorted at my obvious sarcasm.

"There was a big limb on the line," he says.

"Banner, you got it down?! You could've been fried!"

When he finds me, I'm kneeling between two of the twin beds, having procured what I was searching for.

"I used another limb to throw at it," he explains. "What do you think you're doing in my room?"

"I'm retrieving warm covers for Your Highness."

I glance over my shoulder to find him shrugging out of another wet shirt and I am suddenly very grateful for the electric lights. He flashes his eyebrows and snaps off the overhead.

"There's no one else on the property?" he asks.

"No. Not for miles. Why?"

Banner shakes his head and breaks a chocolate bar that he must have rescued from his truck. "It's nothing. Lucy acted funny. I thought I saw something. It's just the storm. Dessert?"

"Yeah, man." Once I'm criss-cross-applesauce on top of Wren's bed, I cup my hands, and Banner fills them. "We have rain slickers," I say around a bite. "And umbrellas."

He mirrors the way I sit, but on the bed next to me. And with no shirt. In mock sincerity, he says, "Really? Maybe you could offer me that fifteen minutes ago."

"Smartass."

His smile is wily and—damn, he's adorable. And—damn, he's ripped.

"Where's your room?" he asks.

I point down the hall. "Just on the other side. We used to make blanket forts that reached from this very thoroughfare"—I slide my hands between our beds—"to Sissy's and mine."

"Oo, can we do that tomorrow? If it's still storming?"

"We can blanket the whole house."

I can't say how many times I've done this very thing. Snacks and chats in the middle of the night, plotting the next day's activities, and no reason to go to sleep.

Except that Banner is going to fall asleep whether there's reason or not. He rubs his eyes. I kind of want to hug him. Would that be weird? I swing my legs over the side of the bed and blink a good-night instead. "Thanks for dessert," I say. "Rest well."

"Hey," he calls, and when I turn, it's déjà vu. Banner is Jake sitting there, calling me back as he did more often than not. "Don't forget to blow out that candle."

"OK," I say thickly, but now I think he's serious. "I won't. You're really concerned about getting to come visit me again, huh?"

He just grins. "Thanks for letting me in, Ees. You're a lifesaver."

The statement, kindly intended, solidifies my decision to knock back a few. If I were a lifesaver, Jake would be alive. He'd be *here*. Along with all the others. "See you in the morning," I manage.

Alone in my room, I pour up a whisky and sit against the headboard to consider the swaying trees. The window itself is plenty big enough to walk through. Sissy and I used to beg Mammaw to install swinging, French doors, but for some reason, that made the whole thing *unladylike.* "Why in the *world* would two young ladies need their own private entrance?" So, instead, we pushed out of the window and scaled the retaining wall like fugitives.

I'm thinking about this and sipping, not chugging, my measured glass of bourbon—a feat for which I am also congratulating myself —when I decide to have one more and try to sleep. I'm feeling pretty good. The second one goes down faster. I look at the bottom and frown.

"Shot glasses are for pussies," I say aloud. It's something one of my mistakes said to me while he poured freely. What the commercials show is true. When you drink, you feel like you're a part of things. You laugh. They laugh. You feel good. You hook up. What they don't tell you is that even as uninhibited as you may become, reaching orgasm is increasingly elusive. So, it's like adding insult to the self-injury of idiocy and shame that won't creep up until it punches you in the face the next morning. They should have one of those fast-talkers to record that information for the end of the ad. Drinking-too-much-can-lead-to-embarrassing-bouts-of-stupidity-and-acts-of-degradation-that-cause-further-self-loathing.

But hell, at least you're not thinking about your four-year dead cousin who you feel responsible for killing. I should have jumped. I should have jumped when he told me to. I should have at least climbed up to find out what I couldn't hear over the sound of the waterfall. I should have died—*stop. Stop with the negative self-talk. It doesn't serve you. Remember?*

Sometimes I have dreams where I can finally make out what Jake was trying to tell me. But when I awake, the message is gone.

It's not until my fifth drink that I forget all about the fast-talker's disclosure and wonder what Banner would do if I tip-toed into his room. I've never kissed a guy with a full beard before. I bet it's soft. He doesn't let it cover his whole face like an animal but keeps it trimmed so that you can see the dip below his cheekbones. That's where I would start.

I'm looking out the window, enjoying this new train of thought way more than the others, when it occurs to me that I am staring into the face of a man who is outside staring at me. And now, here is another foolish, foggy-brained effect of liquor. A silhouetted shadow of a man is leaning against my enormous bedroom window, and I just peer back, dull-witted, only vaguely aware that this is not OK. I blink hard. Now there is no man outside my window. There are only trees.

This is Me

ALL. OUR. Lives. That is how long we studied how each rapid behaved—*especially* in flood state—*especially* that particular section, the one we called The Hydraulic. *Don't fight it. Let it drag you down, chew you up, spit you out. No matter how counterintuitive it feels or how every cell in your body stings for oxygen. Don't. Struggle. To the top. You will never get there.*

I wake in the dark with a pounding heart and a sick headache. I suck it in, but I can't find the air. I can't fill my lungs. Panic builds. I start to squirm—when I feel a warm, solid body pressing back against me through the bedclothes. It's not Banner, in case that's where your mind went. It's his dog, Lucy—who is supremely unmoved by my plight. She simultaneously stretches all four legs, licks the air, and relaxes back to sleep.

And I am miraculously able to breathe. *This is the best! I should totally get a dog.* I stroke her soft fur and kiss her sleepy head. "When did you come in?" I ask. In response, she thumps her tail twice on the mattress without much conviction.

When I open my eyes again, the sun has risen. It's gloomy, but it's daytime. I splash my face, stumble into the living room, and *hallelujah* the smell of coffee wafts over me like a song.

"Banner?"

He *is* a neat freak. The dishes have all been put away, the counter wiped clean. And *bacon* is waiting to be made. The pan is loaded. The oven is preheating. Also, there's a mixing bowl with pancake ingredients standing by, measured independently, and ready to be mixed. *That is so nice! I didn't even win the bet.* I sniff at what appears to be milk, and it's sour. "Is he creating buttermilk with the vinegar?" I ask Lucy. But Lucy nudges her bowl, so I feed her some of our homemade doggy breakfast.

The dryer is running. What are the chances that Banner has already dealt with the rest of his wet clothes? A glance at the oven's clock tells me it's only six-forty-seven. I gawk at Lucy. "If he starts playing *Taps,* I'm out."

Rifling through the usual cabinets, I cannot locate my usual mug. I suspect that it has found a new companion and I suspect that that new companion is enjoying his coffee on the front porch. I would be. I fill Sissy's mug and open the door to tease him. "There are a few ground rules," I begin, but Banner raises a hand to keep me from advancing.

He's seated on one of the rockers, staring straight ahead with a rather formidable expression that puts me on alert. I race his gaze to one of our resident black bears.

This particular bear has been described to me in a note my sister left tied to the shotgun. *Sam,* as we have dubbed him, is a seven-year-old hooligan, larger than most, and he's been hanging out too near the house. Now, here he is in all his glory, standing on his hind feet with his muzzle raised like he's trying to decide from a sniff test if Banner has—or is—a yummy treat for him.

The shotgun hangs over the door. I haul it down in case I have to make some noise.

Lucy makes noise too. She starts barking like a maniac. She nearly knocks me down in a bid to get past with her hackles raised, and I barely catch hold of her collar. Shoving her inside, I step onto the porch. "Get on out of here, Sam! We don't have anything for you this morning!" I pump the shotgun and raise it to my shoulder. "Go on! Shoo!"

Sam seems to take my word for it that he's not getting a hand-out. He lands on his front paws rather hard, gives a snort, and ambles away. Inside, Lucy is running from window to window sounding her alarm. "And you chill out in there, Luce!" I rap on the door while I unload the gun. Once I locate my brew, I take a seat in the rocker next to Banner.

"I see you're meeting the locals," I say. "He's a *big* boy. Hey, thanks for making coffee and for getting breakfast together. This is great. Are you planning to use buttermilk as an egg substitute? My mammaw taught me that trick."

Banner slowly swivels his head to me but does not respond to my statements. Instead, he exhales a breath that puffs his cheeks. I think it might be the first time he's been able to move air since Sam showed up.

"How long was he here?" I ask.

"Long enough to take several years off my life. Has my hair turned white?"

I grab a fistful to check and yank his head sideways when I let go. "Nah, you're good." Now he's peering at me like he's trying to recall what I look like. *Yep. There's that beard.* My cheeks warm under his scrutiny.

"What is it?" I ask.

He doesn't say the thing that's really on his mind. I can just tell. He goes a more playful route. "You stole my dog last night."

"I did not steal your stinky, old dog. She came to me. She prefers my company."

The wind kicks up. The rain is falling in gentler showers this morning.

"You didn't look too upset about it, all cuddled up around her."

I whip my head around. "You saw us?"

"Yeah, well, I woke up smelling smoke—don't ask—and I went to find my dog, but you were asleep, so I left you alone. Can we visit the eccentric chicken man today? If the rain lets up?"

"Hang on. You watched me while I slept?"

"No, I didn't *watch* you. I'm not a creeper."

"But...I was asleep."

"That's what I said. So, I left you alone."

"But...I wasn't wearing very much."

"You weren't shutting your door either."

"I was so," I protest. "Your dog pushed it open. What did you see?"

"Honestly, Isla. Nothing. It was dark."

"So you trekked across an unknown house in the middle of the night without a light?"

The side of Banner's mouth quirks, and he looks away.

"What did you see?"

Banner rolls his eyes. "I saw the back of one beautiful bare leg and the curvy beginning of an extremely well-sculpted a—"

"Banner!"

He laughs out loud. "I was just trying to keep Lucy from bothering you. I didn't mean to see anything. But you certainly don't have anything to be ashamed about."

I cross my arms and huff.

"Come on, Ees. I'm sorry. I'd never just ogle you like that." He hesitates. "I mean, without your permission. I'd totally—" He shakes his head. "Not important. Will you forgive me?"

Arms still locked, I sulk. It's really more of a pretend sulk. "Maybe," I say at length.

He chuckles. "While you decide, can we go visit the chicken man?"

It's hard for me to care about visiting the chicken man right now, what with the subject at hand, but I try. "We'll have to bike there," I say. "It's not that close, and the trails will be a mess. Are you up for that?"

"Absolutely."

Also—I don't say—we'll have to ford the river at the bottom of The Hydraulic. Am *I* up for that?

"Lucy couldn't get used to the place," Banner is saying. "She must have been sensing a thousand new animals. She kept pacing to the door like a sentinel."

I sit forward having remembered the man outside my window. "Did you go out after I went to my room?"

"No."

"There *was* someone here. A man was looking in at me."

"What? Why didn't you get me?"

Um, 'cause I was drunk. "I couldn't see him that well. I blinked and he was gone. Maybe it was Sam, the bear. Maybe I dreamed it."

Banner stands decisively, then sits back down—just as decisively.

"What was that?" I laugh.

"If anyone was here, there's a good chance he left some footprints because of how wet the ground is."

I drive my eyes from side to side. "Buhhht, we're not going to check because..."

There's a certain answer behind the way Banner focuses on me, but he doesn't voice it.

"Sam," I guess, and try not to smile too much.

"I thought we could give him another minute to move along."

"He didn't go that way."

Banner bumps my knee. "OK, let's go look."

It's chilly this morning. Banner's wearing a fleecy jacket that turns his eyes blue. I'm still wearing the tank top I slept in—although I have managed to pull some joggers over my extremely well-sculpted ass.

While Banner lets his dog out, I stand on the steps wondering if I really did see someone while subconsciously rubbing my arms to keep warm. I rejoice to feel Mammaw's warm quilt being draped around me from behind. Banner doesn't hang around to receive thanks. He marches onto the grass and we traverse the yard with Lucy sniffing everything in sight.

"That's my window." I point. "What will we do if we find footprints?"

"No idea."

We peruse the ground, but where there's no grass, there is mulch, and I don't see anything that I'd call a footprint. Lucy keys in on something, though, and digs into the earth beside the brick retaining wall—the same wall my sister and I used to climb to get into our room. If someone *was* looking in at me, he would have had to climb that wall too. I scramble up to scan for clues.

The window dwarfs me. I've never seen another one like it. It hinges at the top, so you have to push the bottom—from the inside —to open it. It's nearly impossible to open from the outside unless it's already propped. I try it now, but I'd have to have a crowbar or something.

"No one could have been here," I decide. "Where would they have come from? I think I dreamed it."

"I don't think you did," Banner says solemnly. When I glance down, he's staring over my head, so I slowly lift my eyes, aware that I don't want to encounter whatever it is.

The not-so-recently dead bodies of three adult rattlesnakes have been stretched into a line and placed on a thin ledge where the sloping roofline protrudes to protect the window's woodwork. The first serpent's rattle has been inserted into the mouth of the second, and the second's into the mouth of the third.

"What in the hell am I looking at?" Banner asks. He gorilla-hops up beside me, stretches his arm, and stands on his toes. "I can't reach it. If I were to jump I could, but then I wouldn't be able to place them so...artfully. Whoever did this was one tall mother —person."

"Or used a ladder. Those snakes have been dead for a while. I don't think this happened last night."

"They couldn't have been here long. They would have blown off. Or been eaten."

"The wind is strong right now," I argue, "and they're fine. This part of the house is guarded."

"This does not creep you out?" Banner asks.

"I mean, it's not my thing, but Jake and Asher used to do crazy stuff like this all the time. They'd hunt things and display them like they were trophies from a safari or something. I don't think anyone came last night for the sole purpose of decorating Mammaw's house with snakes. What would be the point?"

"It's not the whole house. Is it?" he asks. "It's your room."

We walk around searching for footprints and other orally fixated window serpents, but although we circle all the way back to my room, we find nothing out of the ordinary.

"Some kids probably stayed in my room," I downplay it. "And thought it would be cool. I think Sissy gave up one of her weeks last month. Let me check on who stayed."

Banner scowls doubtfully. "You can't check. You can't get a call out. What if you're being targeted?"

"What do you mean, *targeted*, Banner? Someone killed three poisonous snakes and laid them on the roof. I'm not into killing things, but I'm not going to mourn these guys. When I arrived, I had to release a live turtle that had been stashed in a cardboard box. Nature's all around us, begging to be explored."

"Nature's not coming out in droves of rattlesnakes," Banner counters. "Who finds three fully grown rattlesnakes in the same time period? This is strange."

The rain reasserts itself, so we jog back to the porch, and now Banner's eyeing me with that quizzical stare.

"Why do you keep looking at me like that?" I ask.

"I don't know. I get the same feeling about you as when I find someplace I want to add to the itinerary. Someplace I want to explore."

"You want to...explore me?"

He thinks for a second and says, "Yeah."

I don't think he's joking.

"I need to make notes," he says. "Maybe a map. You have paper?"

I have the *Wh* of the *What?* shaping my lips, but I'm not sure what to follow it with, so there it stalls.

He wags his fingers to urge me on in his quest for paper. "My laptop isn't charged. Anyway, I like to draw."

"Um. Sure," I say. "I have three-quarters of a sketchbook."

"You're an artist?!" He asks it like it's important news. "See? I need to write that down."

"I'm not an artist. I just like the potential of big, blank pages. I used to write my poems and stories there. But I haven't written much since Jake died. Thus, the reason it's three-quarters blank."

Banner's eyes go wide with all the intel. "I need it right now. Go get it."

As we step inside, I'm snickering to myself, and when I present the book to him, it's with a bow, hands outstretched like it's a crown on coronation day. He snatches it, finds the first empty page, and starts scribbling.

"What in the world are you writing?" I ask. "You've only known me for sixteen hours."

He holds up a finger to me and, as he writes, he mutters, "very well-sculpted—"

"Extremely," I say.

"What?"

"Before, you said *extremely* well-sculpted."

Banner bites back a smile, vigorously scratches out the *very*, and writes, "Exxxtreemely…"

"You are such a goofball."

When I try to look over his shoulder, he blocks me. "Stop it. I have to work. You can see it later." He paces the floor and continues to jot down all the thoughts—about me—that he has in his head.

"I suppose *I'm* going to have to cook now?" I don't really mind. I just like to egg him on.

"Hang on. What's your middle name?"

I deposit the bacon into the oven and lean back against the counter. "Every question you ask, you have to answer," I say.

"Fair enough. Ellison. My mom's maiden name."

"Banner Ellison Kirk," I recite.

Apparently, his own details don't interest him. He wags his fingers again impatiently.

"Isla Sofía."

"That's pretty. Payne?"

"No. Payne is Wren's last name because his mom is my blood relative. I'm a Miller."

He writes it down. "You're what? Like five-eight?"

"You're writing my height?"

"I need all the facts," Banner insists. "If I'm going to live with a sexy badass who wields shotguns and yells at bears and isn't freaked out by creepy snake voodoo, then I need all the facts. Who will believe me otherwise?" He comes over to compare the two of us, thumping my back to get me to stand up straight. "I'm six-one," he volunteers.

"I'm gonna have to call bullshit on that. *Maybe* six-even."

"Get a measuring tape. Right now."

When I laugh out loud, a look of triumph spreads across his face. "Six-and-one-half-inch," he says. "There. I can compromise. Can you?"

"No. No, I can't." I seize him by the collar and lead him to the only section of house that has not been marred with new paint. In fact, it has been lovingly framed.

"The Hall of Heights," I declare. "Every cousin, and now second cousins, get measured every summer. Here's me."

Banner scans the whole of it. "How cool is this?" There's a longing in his voice that surprises me. Before I can comment, he says, "Is Wren really that tall? He and Asher both."

"Yeah. Jake wasn't. Look. I was taller than Jake until the summer we turned fourteen. He hated it." I show Banner, on the wall, how Jake trailed me until that year, and then I lovingly rub the line that marks the last time we measured. The summer he died. "Did you grow any after you were seventeen?" I ask.

"A little bit," he says gently.

I nod my head.

"Well, get up there then," I tell him. "Heels to the wall."

He submits to my instruction, stands tall, and awaits judgment. Once I mark it, we step back to observe. "Far closer to six-one," he says.

"You think? You may be right."

"Your turn." He physically muscles me into place and then cries out a mournful, "Oh, nooo."

I spin around. "What is it?"

"You're shrinking." Using the length of the pencil to evaluate whether or not this is true, he then scratches his head.

"I probably had on shoes last time."

"That is unacceptable. The rules of height management are clear. There can be no—"

I interrupt him by stepping my feet onto his, and when I grasp his shoulders, he wraps an arm around my waist, uses the other to brace us against the wall.

"Measure me now," I say.

I've surprised him. It's becoming my life's ambition. He waddles us into position where he has to press himself against me to free his hand and place a mark above my head. His beard is soft against my face. When I reach up to comb my fingers through it, he stills, looks down at me. His eyes roam my features like he's memorizing them. My cheek. My lips.

"Now write our names," I whisper because he makes me nervous in the delicious, tingly way that volume would ruin.

"You want me to add *my* name?" he asks. He's quiet too.

"Yeah. You're here."

Banner reaches up again. He smells like—like I'm in trouble.

Once he's finished, he bows his head again, and I become aware of his thumb tracing my collarbone. "It's good?" he asks.

I can't see what he's written, smushed between him and the wall as I am, not that I mind, but he slowly—reluctantly?—frees me.

Isla standing on Banner's feet. And the date.

"It's perfect."

With new energy, he says, "Climb onto my back," and he presents said back, stooping so that I can comply. When I have a roost, Banner hands up the pencil, and I shift my weight to find the wall, but I nearly topple us. He's chortling. He's telling me to settle down. Telling me to keep it together.

"Move back, though," I say. "I can't reach it."

After some jostling and stretching, I make our mark.

Banner leans so that I can label it.

"Lean the other way," I tell him. "I'm left-handed."

"Shit, *fuck*, Isla! I have to write that down."

"Hang on, you idiot." *Oh my gah, I love his sense of humor.* "Move that way." I write *Isla and Banner, #1 tallest of all time, world record holders.* And the date.

When I slip off of him, we step back to view the wall as a whole.

"I feel like we just did something," Banner says. "But I'm not sure what."

"You made a memory for me," I tell him. "Here, where I'd stopped making them."

"We made a mark of us," he adds. "Now we exist."

I hum my agreement. "And I can check off number four."

"From your vacation to-do list? It's about Jake, isn't it, your list? Things you stopped doing when he died?"

"Something like that."

Lucy rounds the corner to check on us, and we eye one another with identical grins. "Come, Lucy!" we both call and proceed to measure the dog.

When we reenter the living area, the oven's timer can be heard, and Banner mixes the pancake batter while I heat the griddle. We breakfast together, chatting the whole time, and it is just *great*. How can this feel so natural?

After that, Banner grabs his phone to take pictures of the measurements we've recorded and sits down to fill my blank pages. I watch how effortlessly the words spill out of him.

What all the man could possibly be recording, I have no idea, but after he catches me admiring him from across the room, I walk outside. Soon, my feet are trudging up a familiar path.

I can hear the swollen river. I can smell the wet earth. And now I come to the old tree, the hollowed-out storehouse for our found treasures. I reach in to touch them, but before I can explore, I run right back to Banner and throw the door open wide. When he jerks his head up in question, I motion for him to follow, and I run before I know if he will. He's on my heels within seconds, though, and I lead him to the tree.

"This is me," I say and offer one of the many blue bottles we unearthed through the years. He's only just had the chance to observe it when I swat it away and press his hand to my chest. With a deep sniff, I say, "That scent? It's what the trees drink. It's what the river moves. It's what beats through my heart. Or it used to. Back when I was alive."

I start to give his hand back, but Banner holds it in place and secures me with his other hand on my back. "You *are* alive," he says. "You're irrepressible. And funny. And generous." He opens his mouth to say more, but thinks better of it and simply ends with, "You're very much alive." He lifts my palm to his lips and plants a soft kiss there.

What I want to say in response, I don't trust myself to articulate. That he makes me able to feel again. That he gives me back myself, just by searching for me. "I'm glad you're here," I manage.

"Me too. Show me what else you have in there."

We remove things one by one—a turtle shell turned musical instrument, a Cherokee-fashioned arrowhead, a slingshot. Each of them calls to mind who found it and why it was kept. "We all fancied ourselves expert whittlers," I say. As proof, I offer several misshapen animals and a few totem poles.

"What the heck is this?" Banner asks. "A spine?"

"Oh, man! So, the chicken man? Our land goes to the river, and on the other side is his land. One time we were all swimming and Jake was about to swing from a vine on the chicken man's side when he freaked out. 'Come up! Come up! Come up!' So we climbed to the top and there was this huge pit, like deeper than a man is tall, and it was full of—"

"What?"

"Rattlesnake carcasses."

Banner doesn't comment.

"I do realize the coincidence," I say.

"Coincidence," he repeats. "That your next-door neighbor, the eccentric chicken man, has an odd fascination with rattlesnakes. Oh, and some guy tacked three to your window."

"He's not next door. He's miles away."

"But miles that can be crossed without access to a bridge."

"Well. Yeah."

"OK. Keep going."

"The next day, three of the carcasses appeared here in our tree. You should have seen us gaping. Asher turned white! But he was the first to catch on that Jake had done it. At first, Jake denied it, but he couldn't keep from bragging for long."

Thinking back, I wonder if Jake *did* bring the snakes or if he just couldn't resist taking credit for it.

"I like this Jake," Banner says. "I'm sorry I didn't get to know him."

"I'm glad you said that. Look at this." I find another skeleton whose rattle is still attached and shake it ominously. "They can rattle like fifty times in a second. Did you know that?"

"Whoa. How many were in the pit?"

"I don't know. Twenty-five. Can you imagine the noise of all of them alive?"

"How did they die? Was it a mass murder pit?"

"No, they died of old age."

Banner regards me. "Yeah, that's more probable. Or maybe Chicken Man makes boots." He takes the rattle from me and gives it a shake. "You think he knows these were stolen?"

"I've wondered that, but I mean, anything could have snagged them, right?"

"I'll ask him when we see him."

"No, you will not!"

"Oh yeah, I have questions. We're gonna have a heart-to-heart." Banner reaches in for more artifacts. "Isla, don't you want these?" He comes out with two bracelets like the two I already wear, strung with river stones.

"I didn't know about them."

"They have your name etched on them." He shows me.

"The first two showed up for my eighteenth and nineteenth birthdays. I think it was an effort to comfort me. Every person in the family denies it was one of them."

"Like the tooth fairy. Here are years twenty and twenty-one."

Banner takes his time to tie both bracelets around my wrist, rolling them softly over my arm, perhaps more than necessary. It tickles in the best way.

"I like this one," he says. "It's got all the stones: orange, gold, that smoky blue…"

When I don't respond, he cocks his head to catch me studying him and I quickly drop my eyes to locate the bracelet he means.

"Yeah, that's a good one," I say too late.

Banner hooks a strand of hair behind my ear and brushes my cheek with his fingers.

"When I was fifteen," he says, "we lived in Arizona for a while. Two whole baseball seasons." A wry smile tells me how precious two short baseball seasons must have been. "Dad came home in uniform one day, informed us that we had to move again, and I had a complete meltdown. Just lost it. He walked out the door."

"Wait. For good?"

"No-no. I'm sure he was just damn sick of me whining every time he had to do his job. It was hard on all of us. But anyway, Bekah—my sister—took me to a local copper mine where she bought us necklaces strung with turquoise stones that had been mined there. She said it was so we could hold on to that place. I think it was so that we could hold on to each other. That was the last time she lived with us. From there, she went to West Point, became an officer."

He pats the treasure tree. "Do you have any idea how precious this is? I'd give about anything for your roots, your traditions."

"This is you, then," I offer. "Like the Hall of Heights. All you have to do to be part is to make a contribution."

He thinks about that, his eyes roaming.

I listen to Banner's stories. He listens to mine. And in this way, I am able to safely access the memories I've locked away.

"What's the story with the rock?" he asks, having divested a plain, flat stone.

"*That* is Jake's perfect skipping stone. He was saving it for just the right time. Seems like a shame now." I pocket it. "We're gonna skip it."

"I'm in."

Banner's stomach roars.

"Did you eat Sam?!" I exclaim and grab hold of his torso to find out for myself. He's such a good sport. He lets me do whatever comes to mind. I daresay he enjoys it.

"How can you be hungry already?" I silently number the food items I brought. I was depressed. I haven't been eating much. I only brought the bacon as a prayer to find my appetite. "You any good at fishing?"

His eyes light up. "Yeah. You?"

"I guess I know what we're doing next."

As we trek back to the house, the trees baptize us with sporadic raindrops, and the breeze sounds a parental hum through the branches. It reminds me of Mammaw's calming shushes and her lullabies. I feel Banner's fingertips against my palm, coaxing my hand into his, and we walk that way like we're family. Like we want to hold on to whatever this is so that it won't blow away. When we get home, he squeezes before he lets go. Gives me a shy smile. Doesn't use any words.

After that, we have a lovely afternoon. We never do make it to the chicken man's house, but we do go fishing. We trade music. We dance. I teach him an old family board game that my sweet mammaw would become ruthless to win. And Banner works on his map of me.

I feel happy. I feel light for the first time in ages. I'm on the couch gazing out the window. It's not raining now, but the clouds are swirly and grey. The sun has set. And just like that, a sliver of dread wedges into my heart. The sky will grow dark. At some point, I'll have to sleep.

"I'm gonna go to bed," I say.

I'm gonna go drink. I just—I can't do it. I start feeling so anxious I can't sit still.

"*OK.*" Banner sounds surprised. I was abrupt. I want to say more, but also I don't. I feel his eyes upon me as I fill a water bottle at the sink.

"I'm crowding you," he says. "I haven't given you any space at all."

"No. It's not you."

"It is. I'm sorry."

"Banner, I've enjoyed every minute with you. But in a few days, that bridge will open up, and you'll go back to your life, but I'll still be stuck here in mine."

"You don't seem stuck."

"Well, I'm not when you're around." My shoulders fall with an exhale as I realize the truth of what I've said. "You help me."

"Come here." He tugs me to himself. I'm afraid I'll cry all over him again if I allow myself to sink into his hug, but it sure is tempting. "Get some rest," he says. "If I'm up first, I'll make the coffee."

I nod against his shoulder. "It was a good day," I tell him, and my heart physically aches. I don't want to be alone anymore.

"It was a perfect day," he says.

I'm almost to the hall when he calls, "Ees? Close your curtain, OK? Humor me?"

"I will," I call back.

"And come get me if anything is weird."

"Like your dog choosing me over you?"

"I never thought I'd be jealous of a dog," he mutters. "But here we are."

In my room, I pour a drink and double-check the lock on the window. I guess the snakes are stationed right above me, but they're hidden from this angle.

At our other house, the one where we lived during the school year, there was a mirror at the end of my hall. I could see it as I rested on my pillow, and whatever it reflected at night looked like two menacing eyes. I was able to re-envision it, though, into a royal guard who was vigilant for my safety. I do the same now with the snakes, imagining them to be protective gargoyles.

I close the curtain, as Banner requested. But I leave the door open.

You know…for Lucy.

The Chicken Man

I DIDN'T DRINK AS MUCH last night. After Banner's long hug, I didn't feel the frenetic compulsion to numb myself, and I fell asleep considering how much I enjoy hanging out with him. He's a good man, genuine, deep. I woke up thinking about him too. I wish I could feel the weight of him beside me right now, the way I do his dog.

When I hear the cabin door creak slowly open, I can tell that Banner is trying to be quiet. His boots are barely audible upon the wooden floor, and Lucy raises her head.

"Maybe Lucy's not an early riser," I call out. "And she sleeps with me because she's sick of you waking her at the crack of dawn."

The boots pad down the hall, and Banner peeks in with smiling eyes. He looks cozy in his fleece. His cheeks are pink. Windblown.

"You may be right," he says and proceeds to lie down on the other side of his dog—on my bed.

"I like seeing you there," I say, then bite both lips after the words have slipped out.

"Oh, yeah?" His roll toward me is disrupted by a lick to the face—not from me. He pushes his dog toward the foot of the bed. "I could learn to sleep in," he says. "If I had a good teacher."

"*Tch.* Stupid, worthless English degree. I *knew* I should have pursued Education."

Banner cups my neck, traces my cheekbone with his thumb. I'm pretty sure the longing on his face mimics my own.

"You don't have a trumpet here do you?" I ask.

"Why?" he laughs in surprise.

"Because Lucy keeps warning me that you're going to break into *Taps* to get us out of bed."

"*Taps* is the one they play at a funeral. You mean *Reveille*. And it's a bugle call."

"Oh lord, do you have a *bugle*?"

Banner's big laugh is a beautiful sound. "No. My sister has one. Do you know the difference?" As Banner explains to me the difference between a trumpet and a bugle, he uses his masculine hands to demonstrate the shape of each one's bell and the darker tone that the bugle makes. Then he threads his fingers through mine. "Too much information?"

I shake my head where it's still lying on the pillow.

So, here we are chatting face to face like lovers.

"Have you already been hiking this morning?" I ask.

"I went to check on the bridge."

Aaaand the lovely, romantic music in my head screeches to a halt. *Hello, Reality Check, you son of a bitch.* "Right. Of course." I push to sit. "How'd it look?"

"Don't know. It was completely submerged."

"It won't be for long," I assure him. I don't know why I'm faking like it doesn't bother me that he's watching the bridge for his first chance to get out of here.

"You ready for some coffee?" he asks.

I nod. He waits. "Come on, then," he prompts me.

"I should probably put on some pants."

"No, don't do that," he teases. "It's *your* house."

"Yeah, well, when I'm *alone* in it, maybe I'll run around naked."

"Right." He sits up, having received my passive-aggressive rebuke, stands, and says, "Well, the coffee's ready when you are." And walks out.

I feel like an ass. Because I acted like an ass. I roll my eyes, jerk on my joggers, and pause beside the nightstand while staring at the wall. Inside, the whisky is waiting. On impulse, I smack it open, tip it up, and suck some down. 'Cause fuck it. I'm sick of being miserable. I pop the top back on and shove the bottle out of sight. I already regret it. And yes, I am aware that I'm behaving with the maturity of a three-year-old.

I didn't use to get irritated so easily. Or so intensely. I'm pretty sure the alcohol, instead of alleviating that kind of thing, is creating an endless loop that keeps me from moving through it. Why can't I just cope like a normal human being? I sit back down on the bed in defeat.

It doesn't take long to feel a little better, though, so the alcohol does work in the short term. That's what makes it so tempting. I brush my teeth to get rid of the harsh scent and wash my face to try to start over.

When I show up in the living room, Banner is sitting forward in a corner chair reading the visitor's log which Sissy leaves out to invite guests to record details of their stay. He looks up from under his eyelids to say, "I'm sorry for suggesting you—this sounds so dumb—I'm sorry for suggesting you not wear pants." He nods once, having choked out his apology. "I thought we were both enjoying that kind of banter, but I offended you, and I'm sorry I took it too far."

"No, you didn't. I changed the rules on you. We *have* been enjoying that kind of thing, and I guess I started to—but you're leaving, so—I just have to remember this is on a deadline." I try to lighten the mood. "I do have one real grievance, though."

"What's that?" he indulges me.

"You're not from around here, so, no harm, but that is the coffee mug *I* use." I indicate my favorite mug on the table to his right.

"Impossible," he says, matching my tone. "Because that is the coffee mug *I* use." He dismisses me by flipping to another page in the guestbook, leaving me to exhale my feigned aggravation while Lucy trots behind me into the kitchen. Now she's sitting beside her food bowl, wagging her tail for breakfast.

"Fat chance, you traitor," Banner mutters.

"I'll feed you, Lucy, you poor, hungry beast."

He snickers and watches me feed his dog, but when I check on him, his countenance hasn't quite caught up to the joking. Once I pour coffee into Sissy's mug, I cross the room to offer it to the usurper. "This one is fresh and hot," I croon. "*Mmmm.* I'll trade you."

For a moment, he regards me and then his own mug—*my* mug—before he makes a show of bringing it to his mouth, where he pauses, challenges me with his eyes, and takes a long, deliberate sip that doesn't end until he finishes licking his lips in what seems like slow motion.

I don't guess he means to leave them parted like that, and wet, but can the man be any sexier? Yes. He can. He swallows, and I watch his Adam's apple bob with the effort. I drag my eyes away, chuckling under my breath, and he seems to take it as a win.

"Hey, check this out," he says.

A number of the guestbook's pages have been tabbed with small, orange Post-It Notes.

"What in the world are you marking in there? Is it that interesting?"`

He flashes his eyebrows, peels back the first Post-Itted page, and reads, "'*Thank you, Asher, for turning us on to this place! This is the first time we've gotten away in ages. We partied so hard I forgot how old I was.*' There's a smiley face," Banner adds. "'*The weird thing is that, while we were in town, a few of our crew were approached by a man who berated them about the way we were behaving here at the cabin. Things only those of us here could have known about. My girlfriend was all creeped out. Said he was quoting Bible verses at her. Apocalyptic shit.*'"

Banner finishes reading and waits for my reaction.

"Banner, what? There's always going to be some Bible-thumping weirdo accosting the public. Especially down here in the South. I'm sure they weren't doing anything here that was that hard to guess."

"Hang on." He flips to the next Post-It. "'*This beautiful, remote, old house is not without its ghosts. I admit I am sensitive to the supernatural, but in this case, my husband and I BOTH saw a man peering through the** *windows on two separate occasions. He was a huge man in life, and he wore a long, old-fashioned, white smock. We went out to him, but he had vanished. We'd love to know if anyone fitting that description lived or died here. And don't worry! As far as we're concerned, your ghost only adds to the charm of the place.'"*

I deadpan my new friend. "I mean, they couldn't come up with something more original than that? An old-fashioned smock? Did he make weird moaning noises too? And die young? Did he nail snakes to the building?"

"I'm glad you asked," Banner says. He reads another. "'*When we first arrived, there was a large man here releasing live snakes around the house. He turned his back to us when we questioned him and walked right into the woods. All he said was that they were good snakes.*'" Banner slows the words and annunciates: "'*A gift for Isla.*'"

"OK, that one's weird," I say. I think about it. "Whoever wrote that could have known my name. You found it right away, in my *Cousins* poem." I point to the poem above the table.

"Isla, what would anyone gain from making that up?"

"That's what this place is *for.* Imagination. Inspiration. Stories. There *are* ghosts here. And faeries, and witches, and really hot vampires with full, thick beards."

He all but ignores the last, though it does briefly snag him. "For you, Baby," he says, "because that's who you are. These people don't have your creative mind." He indicates the book. "Disturbing things happened to them here, and they made note of it. Things revolving around a large man and snakes."

Sorry, what? I got distracted when he called me *Baby.*

"What does that even mean, *good* snakes?" he's asking. "They control the rodent population?"

"They eat the bad ones. Like kingsnakes. Mammaw practically cuddled up to kingsnakes. She hated copperheads and rattlers. What else have you read?"

"That's as far as I got. But there's this." Banner shows me a swatch of flannel cloth that is taped to the page he just read. It boasts a blue background with crossing red lines. "The large man who released the snakes wore a shirt like this. Apparently, in his hurry to get gone, the shirt caught on something and this patch was torn from it."

I stare at the patch. Banner stares at me. "That's a believable detail," I admit. "Of course, the first rule of a scary story is to stack it with believable details."

"Isla, this is factual."

"You just keep tiny Post-It Notes on hand?"

"I found them in a desk."

"Banner, give me the mug."

"*Nuh-uh.*" He sets the book down and moves next to me on the couch, where he grips my thigh at the knee, seems to *realize* he's gripping my thigh at the knee, and pulls his hand away to cross his arms like he's all of a sudden worried he's being too familiar.

"Please don't be weird," I tell him. "Everything's been so natural between us. Let's just enjoy the time we've got."

Banner doesn't answer, but he does re-establish his grip on me, and when I respond by leaning my head onto his shoulder, he kisses it. Now I want this for real.

"Ees, if some guy is showing up here stalking you, we need to address that."

"No one has ever bothered me here. I haven't even been back in three years."

"OK, but—leaving you out of the equation—if someone is spying on your guests or your family, we need to stop that from happening. Could we call the guests who wrote in the log? Get more details?"

"Yeah, that's no problem. We have their numbers. Sounds like Asher knew the one guy personally."

Banner lifts his eyebrows at me expectantly.

"Well, we can't do it right *now,*" I remind him. "The bridge..."

"Oh yeah. I really have to get across that thing. My mom worries enough about my sister and my dad. She's probably sick that I haven't told her I'm safe."

Oh, that's a good reason to hike to the bridge early in the morning. You could just pop into town, tell Mom you're fine and that you'll be living with me from now on.

"What about the security cameras on top of the house?" Banner is saying. "Can you access those?"

"I have no idea what you're talking about."

"The small surveillance cameras over each porch and the one in the corner where your room is."

I shake my head.

"Let me show you." Banner takes my hand and walks me out the door to point out a small protrusion in the flashing near the chimney.

"Banner, how did you even see that? How do you know it's a camera?"

"Army has specialized schools for that kind of thing. It's good to know when you're being watched."

I whip around to face him. "Is *that* where you met Wren? Something specialized and secret?"

"Something secret, yes. But not what you think."

"Tell me. Tell me."

"Will you focus in, please? Sissy? Wren? Nobody told you they were installing cameras? Don't you guys make decisions together?"

"Yeah, but sometimes I don't pay attention." Because sometimes I drink to get ready for those meetings. "I'm the baby. I don't really have to do anything."

Banner pulls out his phone and points to a WiFi network it finds. "I bet this belongs to the cameras. I bet I could access the information if I had the password."

"Well, when I can call out, I'll—"

"This is ridiculous," Banner interrupts. "I'm getting you a landline. I've served in the middle of Nowhere, Off the Grid, The End of the World, and we could still communicate with the outside."

"Sorry," I say. "Maybe the chicken man has a phone."

Banner's mind is racing ahead. "Can I snoop around the house? Try to find out if those cameras have a monitor or any hardware to store information?"

We spend the next hour searching the house—closets, cabinets, furniture—to no avail.

Back in my room, Banner says, "Show me how your window works."

I unlock it, push it out, prop it open, and he climbs onto the retaining wall to check the angle of the camera. It's small, like the others. I don't know how he spotted it. While he scours the area to discern what it's able to frame, it occurs to me that what it's able to frame is the inside of my room. Honestly, Sissy couldn't have given me a heads up? I wonder if the same thought is occurring to Banner. He eyes me through the glass and then takes a picture of the dead snakes that I can't see from here.

"If that camera is recording, it caught whoever hung the snakes. We just have to figure out how to access the footage. I should remove them. You have a ladder?"

It's not raining today. The sky is still cloudy, but the fog has lifted. Summer is going to reassert itself. After Banner and I get rid of the snaky artwork, I say, "Can we take a break from detective work? I have things to show you. Go change into something you can ride a bike and swim in."

Banner salutes me with all the strict angles of a good soldier and turns on his heel to obey. This leaves me pondering what he looks like in uniform, but I shake it out of my head to focus on my own clothing needs.

We're going to bike past The Hydraulic. This is good. I need to do this. When I rejoin Banner on the porch in my shortest brown cut-offs and my pushiest white swim top, he scans me head to toe. I don't expect a big, huge reaction, but his complete *lack* of a reaction is slightly disappointing. I'm attractive. I mean, I may not be a model, but—

"*Holy shit,*" he finally says.

OK, that's better. I do realize that I break into the smile of an idiot. I don't have cheek muscles strong enough to fight it. I enlist my fingers to help push it down.

"Am I allowed to react to how gorgeous you are, or is that crossing another invisible line you haven't told me about?"

"I don't have any lines I haven't told you about. I just don't want to get my heart smashed up."

"I'm not gonna smash it up. I love your heart." He takes another look at me and—"Help me," he says under his breath.

"OK, that's enough."

He offers his arm. "I'll try to keep it to myself. How much will it bother you if I keep stealing glances?"

"It won't bother me." Again, with the goofy smiling.

We find the bikes and check the air in the tires while Lucy bounces around us, ready for adventure.

"I've warned you that the chicken man is eccentric, right?"

"That's what you said."

The trail's a little soft, but only super messy in spots. Even so, our legs are speckled with mud by the time we get there, and Banner tells me that the tire has painted my back like a sexy Jackson Pollock.

The water is roaring incessantly. Inescapably. Even through the smaller rapids.

I don't give in to the memories.

I give in a little.

Jake had been so full of himself that day. He woke me up at the crack of dawn. Said we had to get my birthday started.

We ate pancakes, failed to get anyone else out of bed, and biked to the swimming hole. The water was up like it is today. He dunked me, got too rough. It's how he was sometimes. High on his own strength. It's why I have such a great left hook. I told him to stop it. Told him it was his worst quality. He said he was sorry, hugged me while we were treading water, and then shocked me by kissing me on the mouth.

I kicked him away from me hard. "Jake, if you ever do that again, I'll break your jaw. What has gotten into you?"

"Up there," he said and pointed just with his eyes to the top of the rock wall that bordered the pool. I craned my neck in time to see someone pull away from the ledge. Jeremiah. The chicken man's son. "I'm just taking a piss," Jake said. "You know he has a thing for you."

"Whatever. Act normal. Why you gotta treat him like that?"

After that, things were fine. We lay like lizards in the sun on a massive rock island and talked about what the next few months would hold. I'd be moving to college for the first time. Jake was taking a gap year. He was restless. Felt like he lacked purpose. Maybe felt like he was being left behind. Anyway, he got through talking before I did. "Time to ride The Hydraulic," he said.

"I don't want to do it this year. The water's too high. Let's go home and eat cake."

"No, we're gonna do it," he declared. He climbed the river wall and trotted up the trail. As usual, I followed, but I tried to talk him out of it.

"It's *my* birthday, asshole! Come home."

But it's like he and the water were of the same mind that day. Rough. Reckless. Ready to prove themselves.

He climbed the rock behind the waterfall. It was so loud I wanted to cover my ears. He disappeared for a few minutes, making me think he'd changed his mind. But suddenly he was at the top again shouting down at me and pointing at something I couldn't see.

I crossed my arms and cocked my head in defiance. He yelled something else. I couldn't make out what it was. He cupped his mouth, but I just shook my head. And then he made a sign he used for whenever Jeremiah was around.

Jake leaped while I wasn't looking. I saw it from the corner of my eye and then watched him go down like he was water in the falls, but I couldn't spot him once it pummeled him under. "Jake?" I called his name and leaned over as far as I dared. He didn't come up.

He's waiting. He's allowing The Hydraulic to do its thing. Chew him up. Spit him out. Don't swim to the top.

"Jake?!"

I scrambled around to try to get a better view, but it was like being snow blind. The water broke white. The mist rose to my face.

We had a hypothesis. If another body were to dive in, it would interrupt the flow, and the hydraulic would release the first. I jumped.

"Isla?!" Banner's voice booms. We're standing with our bikes between our legs. I'm not sure at what point I stopped talking to Banner and started sinking into my own head.

"It's so loud!" he says.

I nod and lead him further away. When we've put some distance between us and the falls, I point to the overhang. "He jumped from there. It never let him out. I don't know why it let me out, but not him."

"It's not your fault," Banner says. And I know it's not. I really do. But also, it is.

"It was the chicken man's son who found him," I say. "His head had a horrible gash." I touch my own and take a steadying breath. "I guess he'd hit a rock."

"Well, it's not your fault he jumped, or that he hit his head, or that somebody else found him. And it's not your fault for being alive."

I nod, but I don't agree. "We're here," I tell him. "The chicken man's property is up on the other side. Let's tie Lucy till we get back. I don't want her to mess with his animals." We leave the bikes, ford the river, and climb the rocky trail out of our property. When we exit the noisy wood and set foot into the quiet fields, I relax.

I throw a t-shirt over my swim top.

"No, don't do that," Banner says.

"I don't want to offend anybody. They're pretty...conservative."

"You're offending me. Right now."

"Shut up." I punch his arm, which makes him laugh, and he rubs the site of impact while he takes a look around. Gently rolling hills serve as a pasture for white cows, and over the hills are magnificent views of more distant mountain tops—which we can see because the sun is burning off the clouds and stringing them like a garland across the vista.

"It's a beautiful way for the land to behave," Banner says.

"That's a great line, B. You should put that in your blog."

"Yeah? Alright, remember it for me. I don't see any snake pit."

"Oh, it was over there in the woods near the top of The Hydraulic." I'm not ready to tackle that yet. I get sick just thinking about it.

Banner reads my mind. "Surely staring down that waterfall ranks on your list of goals for this trip."

I display my index finger. *Number one.* "Let's keep going."

We traverse the soggy, green fields, pass between two long, narrow, walk-in chicken coops, and approach the farmhouse from the back. There are twenty or so other cages set upon makeshift tables spaced three or four feet apart. I can't tell what they house, but the wire mesh is made to contain smaller creatures than chickens. Mice?

"Hello?!" I call. I don't want to startle anyone by coming up unannounced. "Hello?! Mr. Ridley?! It's Isla Miller. Mossy Miller's granddaughter."

My mammaw had a cordial relationship with everyone around here. She was well thought of. One of those ladies who would come help out, deliver food, deliver babies—mostly animal babies. She was tough too. She'd fight for what she thought was right. Everybody used to say I was just like her. Though, nobody has said so lately.

We walk a bit further. There's a white pickup truck next to the farmhouse. Mr. Ridley exits the large opening of a grey barn. I begin to greet him, but when his eyes fall upon Banner, he goes white and becomes highly agitated. He turns on his heel and reenters the barn, then wobbles out again. He's mumbling something.

"Is he speaking to us?" I say under my breath.

"I think he is *preaching* at us," Banner says.

"Fornicators," the man says. "The righteous will stamp out the wicked, the impure, the drunkards, the self-mutilators." He says other things that sound too fire-and-brimstoney for me. Then he comes back to, "Fornicators."

Mr. Ridley paces in and out, in and out. He flaps his hands. I'm beginning to regret that we've come.

"Maybe we should just—" Banner begins, but from directly behind us, a threatening, low voice stops us cold.

"You shouldn't be here."

It's Mr. Ridley's twenty-something ox of a son, carrying a massive sledgehammer.

"Jeremiah," I greet him, and although I'm unnerved by his abrupt appearance, I work to keep my voice friendly. "You certainly grew up. It's Isla, remember?"

There were times, over the years, when Jeremiah and I had cause to interact. Once, I visited with Mammaw when his mother was ill. Mr. Ridley wouldn't take her to the doctor. Said the Lord would cure her if she remained faithful. She must not have. She died from something that Mammaw griped could have been cured in a day with medicine that the good Lord enabled people to make. "Every good and perfect gift comes from above," she'd argued. But Mr. Ridley wouldn't budge.

Jeremiah sought me out some after that—if the boys weren't around. He was odd, but I always remember him as kind. He took care of a lamb once whose mama had died birthing it. He nursed it from the very beginning, and it followed him everywhere. I don't know what became of it.

"Our bridge is flooded over," I tell Jeremiah now. "We were hoping to buy some eggs from you. It's Isla." I say this again because I'm not sure he's tracking.

"Yeah, I know who you are," he says gruffly. "You shouldn't be here."

He does not sound as kind today.

Jeremiah's sleeves are rolled up to the elbow, revealing a plethora of punctures and scars. "Jeremiah, what happened to you?" I blurt out.

His face morphs and through clenched teeth, he says, "You. Should *not*. Be here."

"We'll go," Banner volunteers and takes my arm to steer me away.

But Jeremiah thrusts the sledgehammer out in front of us. "Get your hands off her," he hisses. His voice is as chilling as the mountain water.

Banner regards him and seems to be weighing his options. He takes the high ground by simply lifting his hand from my person, but he gestures for me to keep moving, which I do.

Banner says, "We don't want any trouble. We're sorry to bother you." He stares into Jeremiah's scowling face without moving, and Jeremiah glances toward the barn where his father is now brandishing a fist our way and screeching about filthy whores and damned fornicators. I guess he means us.

"Come on, Banner," I plead. Now Jeremiah's eyes flick to me. Banner still doesn't move an inch. He's tensed and tall, and even so, Jeremiah dwarfs him.

They stare each other down until Jeremiah finally nods Banner in my direction. Banner waits another second before he slowly steps my way. His expression is not unlike the one he'd worn when Sam, the bear came to call. Formidable. Calculating. Concerned. I watch Jeremiah over his shoulder, the question thick on my face. "Jeremiah, what happened to you?"

He doesn't answer. Just watches us go.

Banner urges me on, and when we put some distance between ourselves and our neighbors, he mutters, "More than eccentric."

We pass the chicken coops, where Banner subtly points out a shirt that is hanging from the water pump. A familiar blue flannel with red stripes that cross each other to make plaid. I don't comment.

In my haste, I bump into one of the smaller, mesh cages and am met by the sudden eery sound of vigorous rattling. Cage after cage of multiple aggravated snakes catch on and join in.

Banner yanks me back. "Let's get the fuck out of here."

We run for it. The fields seem to have quadrupled in length since we arrived, but we haul ourselves over them, and when we make it into the woods and across the river, I brace myself on my knees to catch my breath.

"You saw the shirt?" Banner asks.

"Like the swatch in the guestbook," I answer.

"He's been to your house. He was there the other night."

"Which one of them?"

"By the size of the shirt? Jeremiah."

"He's harmless. He's just a bit odd."

"Isla, did that sledgehammer look harmless to you?"

"He'd been working with it. Or something."

Banner makes a face that says he strongly doubts it.

"He did use to show up sometimes," I admit. "And just watch us without joining in. To be fair, Jake and Asher were horrible to him. Wren wasn't much better. They always chased him off."

"I don't think he cared about joining *them*. Seems pretty intent upon *you*."

We untie Lucy and pedal up the trail. The further away we get, the less dangerous it all seems to have been, and the funnier it becomes. We arrive home hot and sweaty, but trading one-liners about the whole bizarre scene.

"Now what?" Banner asks. "That one's going to be hard to top."

"Ah, but I can," I tell him.

"Does it involve any more characters from *Deliverance?* 'Cause I think I've met my quota."

"Cute. No, it does not. And we don't have far to go. Follow me."

Mmh

*Whoever goes hunting for what is right and kind finds life
itself.*

PROVERBS 21:12

MY ACCIDENTAL TRIP TO THE SMOKY MOUNTAINS

[Here is a picture of Sam, the enormous, resident black bear.]

*[Here is a picture of three snake skeletons that guard an oak
tree that is a trove of childhood treasures.]*

*[Here is a picture of a mushroom that my host cannot identify
by name.]*

*When a hurricane dismantled my Florida apartment, I drove north to shelter at a
friend's place in the Great Smoky Mountains of Tennessee. Though the cabin
was already occupied, the beautiful tenant turned out to be a good-natured host
with a great sense of humor.*

[Here is a picture of her mud-splattered back on the bike in front of me. Trust me, I am always trying to keep up.]

Isla is tied to the land through an umbilical cord of summers spent with her extended family at their homestead, which bridges seven generations. For me, an Army brat who is more used to relocating than staying put, Isla's sense of home, her family traditions, and her deep desire to hold on to the Lost command my soul. It took me about three days and a scary-as-hell, backwoods snake handler to realize I need to belong to her as much as she belongs to this land. (B. Kirk, working draft)

"YOU STILL UP FOR A SWIM?" I ask. Since we returned from our encounter with Jeremiah Ridley, Banner has been standing at the kitchen island typing into his laptop.

"Yes, Ma'am. I just wanted to throw down a few quick thoughts."

"Like what?"

"Like how your eccentric chicken neighbor raises rattlesnakes and cranky, giant sons."

I peep around his shoulder. "Why's there a picture of my back?"

Banner grins, swats the computer shut, and gulps down the rest of his water. "Because you got in the way of my shot."

"*Hm.*" I narrow my eyes at him, but he sticks to his story.

"Lead on, my queen."

"Alright, well…" I can't resist revealing what I read. "Keep trying to keep up."

He swats my backside as I'm hopping from the porch, and I take off running, knowing he'll be right behind me.

"What's the hurry?" he calls.

"You're gonna want to be hella hot when you hit the water."

We run for ten minutes or so and come to an open pool where, despite the high water level, the current isn't a big factor. How much I have missed this place is hard to communicate. I leap from rock to rock with Banner on my heels, and then we scramble up one enormous, overhanging boulder where I offer my hand, and we jump. No hesitation. When he surfaces, though, it's with a "*Woooooo!*"

"I told you!" I smack the water in front of his face, and he makes a grab for me, tosses me sideways, and then chases me down to pin me close because now I have to "keep him warm." He's as playful as Jake ever was, but without the bent for being too rough. In this manner, we find ways to explore the boundaries of the pool. But mostly, we just find ways to explore each other.

"Get back here, Eesa. What have you got in there?"

He fingers the pocket of my cut-offs and digs out Jake's perfect skipping stone.

"Do you want to do the honors?" I ask.

"I'd never." To prove he has no intention of stealing the moment, he relinquishes the treasure with his hands upraised. I rub that smooth stone between my fingers. I kiss it. And I fling it across the surface of the water. It skips all the way, striking a boulder on the other side with a satisfying clack.

"That is the perfect skipping stone," Banner confirms. He's got his arms crossed, his biceps flexed beneath his now-translucent sleeves.

I throw my arms around his neck and plant a kiss on his cheek. I'm rewarded with a surprised smile and those biceps around *me*.

"Maybe some other kid will find it now," he says and grips the hem of my t-shirt. "Skin the cat."

I'm not sure what that means, but I raise my arms in response to his guidance.

"You've never heard that? My mom used to say it." Banner strips off the shirt and tosses it onto the land, leaving me only in my swim top. "I was sick of that thing," he says with the spreading smile of the Cheshire Cat.

"Well, I'm sick of that one."

"That's fair." He stretches his arms upward—for me to undress him.

Oh, yes, please. I take the hem and guide it over the hood his back makes. *Gah,* he is beautiful. He has to bend down for me to get the thing over his head.

"Are you trying to one-up all the hot, beach volleyball players with the whole washboard abs thing?" I ask.

"Is it working?"

"It is."

"You want to touch them, don't you?"

I nod my head. I really do.

"Go ahead," he sings like he has to make this concession all the time.

"Yeah?"

"If you want to."

"I do."

"Then go ahead." Now he's laughing, and he swings his arms wide to give me access.

OK, then. I run my fingers over each contoured muscle down to where his dripping shorts hang heavily from his hips. I *am* biting my lip. "*Damn.*"

"Can I get an *mmh*?" He *mmhs* with the pained expression I'd done describing the volleyball players.

But I shrug and say, "Don't push it.

Banner closes in on me, bends to my ear, murmurs, "What's it gonna take, Ees?" His breath is warm as he grazes my cheekbone with his lips. He journeys to my mouth, teases me with little nudges that never land a kiss. And then he just stares at my lips while he licks his own the way he'd done over my coffee cup. My heart rate climbs with every moment he simply hovers. When he tilts his head and pushes in, I close my eyes, open my mouth to receive him—but the kiss never happens. I look up to find him wearing a smug smile that leaves me sucking in an injured breath. "That was so *wrong!*" I protest. "That was *way* worse than how I snubbed you."

He's laughing his ass off. "You are so much fun to fuck with." He combs my damp hair back and leans in again, but—"Nah!" I slap his arms away.

"No, please! Let me kiss you. I've been dying to."

"Too bad."

"Come on, Ees. I was just playing. I'll do it right." I'm slapping his hands away as he works to get them around me again. "You know you want to," he says.

"I'm not listening!" What I *am* doing is bouldering up the rock to jump into the water and swim away, but he's right behind me. Before I can leap, he spins me around and traps me between the 'ceps.

"Truce," he says. "Take me back."

"I never took you to begin with." Raising eyes to the sky, I spout, "Bridge will be open soon." And Banner physically recoils with an, "*Ouch.*"

I went too far.

"I didn't mean it," I tell him, but I don't get much of a response.

"I didn't mean it, Ban. I'll make it up to you. Here. Close your eyes." He gives me a funny look like maybe he's still got a shot and shuts his peepers submissively. But he's too tall. "Um, sit down," I instruct him. "*Don't*—open your eyes—or we do not have a truce."

To his credit, Banner plays along. He feels around for a perch and silently lowers himself to the rock.

Now, what? With the help of my teeth, I untie two of my birthday bracelets, the ones that hold the stones he likes best. I've been plotting this since he told me about the necklace his sister gave him.

"You still there?" he asks. "Just abandoning me out here is not that good of a—" He leaves off when my knee crosses his thigh, first one and then the other to straddle him where he sits.

"No peeking," I say.

"No peeking," he agrees. His voice has gone dark. He secures me to his lap, and his chest rises.

Good.

When I lengthen my spine to reach the bracelets around his neck, he pulls me against him, begins to direct my movement.

"Hang on," I tell him. "I'm not doing that." Even though it feels damn promising.

"You're not?"

"No."

"*Feels* like you are."

"Feels like *you* are," I counter. "I'm working on something else for you."

"Maybe you could multitask."

He makes me laugh. I turn the tables on him and use my hips to create the friction he wants. But the joke's on me when his hands clamp down on my thighs, and now I don't want to stop.

"Give me my eyes back, Ees." It sounds like a warning. "Let me watch you do that."

"You'll get to. Just—damn, that feels good."

Banner kisses my neck while I work. The man is distracting. I finish knotting the bracelets the way Sissy and I used to make jewelry as kids. The last knot secures them around his neck. "OK. You can look."

His eyes fly open and find mine while he traces the beads on his neck. Then he lifts my wrist to confirm the number of bracelets I have left for myself. Two. Not four.

"You're giving them to me?"

"So you can keep this place," I explain. I want to add, "so you can keep me," but he looks stricken. Apologetic? "When you go, I mean. You don't have to wear them."

I wonder if I should get off of him. I back away to give him space, but he instantly follows my movement, cups my head, guides me to his mouth—and kisses me so deeply I lose myself. His fingers in my hair. His chest crowding mine. His—

"*Mmh.*" I genuinely, self-forgetfully make the sound.

We are mid-kiss. He pauses. His lips tighten, and I swear he's trying not to laugh.

"Dammit, Banner. I was really into that." One of my knees is already off of him, but he quickly pins it back into place.

"Woman, you are so *mmh*, I can't think straight. *Please* keep going." The hungry look he gives me brings me back to point. So, we continue and we cross some invisible line between spin-the-bottle and playing-for-keeps.

It's Banner who slows us down. He rolls us over and uses my bare belly as a pillow, grips my sides like he's holding himself back. This is new for me. I've had a few boyfriends and a number of drunken mistakes, but nothing that ever felt like this. I want to urge him on. Instead, I lie here wondering what he's thinking as we catch our breath.

Finally, he scales the length of me, kisses my sternum, growls between my breasts, and continues to my throat, where I lift my chin to make room for more kisses. The sky is blue above the green leaves as I enjoy his ministrations. The sunlight causes me to see rainbow bursts. Too soon, Banner pushes up to brace himself with elbows on either side of me.

"What is it?" I ask. I'm raking my fingertips through his beard—I know. I've developed a fully-fledged thing for the beard. I can't help it.

Before he speaks, he sighs. "I have a trip starting Saturday."

"*This* Saturday?" I say with alarm.

By Banner's own admission, he never stays in one place for long. I stifle the urge to protest, but this *sucks*. I'm gonna miss him. And I'm gonna be alone. I don't *want* to be alone.

"Where will you go?"

"St. Lucia."

"It didn't get hit by the hurricane?" I ask (hopefully).

He shakes his head.

Why does this man have to feel like my favorite pair of blue jeans? The ones that are soft and worn and sit just right on my hips.

"I don't suppose you'd want to come," he says.

I'm so taken aback, that I don't respond at first. "*This* Saturday?" I ask again.

"I know. It's crazy. But—or you could join me later. I'll be there three weeks."

I slide out from underneath him to do the math. "Are you this spontaneous with everything?"

Before he answers, his eyes slide from side to side. "I've been told that I lack certain skill-sets necessary for being grown up."

"No, you're the best kind of grown-up."

"It's not *that* spontaneous," he says. "The plane doesn't leave for four days."

"From where?"

"Orlando," he admits.

"You'll have to drive out Friday."

"That's a valid point. We could fly from Knoxville."

"We don't even have a way to book it."

I guess he feels like I'm shutting him down. He drops it with a decisive, "Yeah."

"Banner, I would love to come play with you in the Caribbean, but—I've got shit to work out. That's the whole reason I'm here. My real, everyday life is not working that great. Me tripping off to St. Lucia won't help."

"Yeah. No, I get that." He fingers the necklace I gave him.

It's not like I didn't know he was leaving, but now the timeline is set. We get two more days. The sun ducks behind the trees like a stage light shifting with the mood, and a chill causes me to quiver. I don't know whether it's from actual cold or the reality that this sweet meeting is so short-fated.

"Let's go see about dinner. You want to?" I suggest it like I'm fine. Like I'm not even a little torn up.

"If that's what you want." He doesn't sound as fine as I do. Maybe he's not as good of a liar.

Why does this hurt so much? I wish we'd gone ahead and made love so that I'd have that to keep.

As we trek back, Banner asks a seemingly random question. "How good a shot are you with that shotgun? "

Uhh, why? "I'm OK. I wouldn't starve if I had to hunt."

"Could you defend yourself? Against a human?"

"You're worried about me staying here by myself."

"I'm not in love with the idea—now that I've met Jeremiah. I'd feel better if we could access the security cameras and know for sure that he wasn't at your window. My sidearm's in the truck. I could leave it with you."

"I'll be alright. If something happens to me, it won't make much of a ripple anyway."

Banner stops walking. "Isla, what is that supposed to mean?"

That was probably a weird thing to say out loud. "No, I just mean—I'll be alright."

When we round the front porch, we both stop and stare at a large bucket that has mysteriously occupied the welcome mat. "It's full of eggs," I say. Which is obvious. It's so full that a few of them have spilled out and cracked.

Banner glances around the yard. "Walk me to the truck." He marches me in that direction.

Once there, he procures a sandy-brown lockbox from which he extracts a tough-looking pistol of the same color. He expels the magazine from the handle, checks the chamber, then reinserts the magazine with a hard click. When he tries to holster the gun in the back of his shorts, the material is too flimsy, and the gun thumps to the ground.

"So much for my Jack Reacher fantasies," I mutter, making Banner chuckle as he scoops up his firearm and takes my hand. Even so, he's vigilant. We retrace our steps, and he cautiously opens the front door to peer inside. He scans the living room like we're on a covert military operation, and he waves me inside.

The egg bucket is surprisingly heavy. I lug it to the kitchen while Banner bolts the door and then proceeds through the whole house room by room. He keeps asking Lucy to "check it out." Once he's back, he lifts his hands in question.

"We said we wanted eggs," I offer.

"I don't get it. You think Jeremiah came all this way carrying that huge bucket because you said you wanted some eggs?"

He carried Jake that far—all while I tripped and wailed and grabbed at the body. He practically carried me too.

Before I can search my memory about that, the entire egg bucket lurches across the counter. I jump to steady it without first considering *why* an inanimate object would do such a thing, but I'm too late. The bucket clatters to the ground, and eggs thwack against the floor, vomiting their gelatinous guts onto the hardwood. Yellow yolks ooze into clearer, goopy parts.

But the most bizarre piece of the action—the piece that is slightly nauseating—is that in the center of the slippery debacle, two snakes are engaged in a wrestling match.

Lucy, who at first stoops to lick the icky egg-yum, is now cocking her head to gawk at the snakes. *What am I looking at?* she seems to be asking. Good question.

Only one of the snakes' heads is visible, a black kingsnake, and its mouth is open wide, wider than you'd think possible. That's because the second snake's head, a timber rattler, is already several inches down its gullet—if snakes have gullets. The kingsnake is swallowing the rattlesnake whole, bit by bit, but the rattlesnake is still thrashing and fighting even while it is being digested.

Lucy barks once and throws a glance back at Banner. *What exactly is the game plan for this one, Boss?*

"I have seen some weird-ass things," Banner says. "But this ranks." He's wearing a slight snarl. "Please come to St. Lucia. Whatever you've got to work out, you can do it just as well lying next to me on the beach."

NOW IT'S MORNING. I guess. Sunlight is streaming through my window. I come to life—or maybe this is hell—with a groan and push myself to sit, wearing nothing at all—which isn't *necessarily* odd, but I can't remember how I got this way. I work to assimilate the events of last night.

We got eggs. We got snakes. Banner took a hundred pictures of the snakes, then we threw them outside—which was hilarious because neither of us really knew how to approach the task—and then the sun went down. We ate together. Not eggs. That makes me want to throw up. *Ow, my head.* We danced. I remember that. It filled me with all kinds of longing. We have two days left. I can't waste this one on a hangover.

But then what happened? We argued. I came to my room, poured a drink, shot it, poured another drink. I should really go back to measuring the shots. Maybe I should get beer. Beer lasts longer. Maybe I should stop drinking altogether as I promised myself I would.

I'm squeezing my eyes shut and trying to vice-grip my bursting head when I hear the click of the front door and the sound of Banner's low, dulcet tones as he talks to his dog. Lucy's claws click in the hallway louder and faster until she rounds the doorway and launches herself onto my bed. "Good morning, sweet girl," I rasp. I wrestle the covers over my breasts, not that the dog cares, but a soft knock on my door makes me glad that I did.

"May I come in?" Banner asks without breaking the plane.

"Just a minute." *Where is my shirt?* I sweep the floor for another one and pull it over my head (inside out) before righting myself and propping up the pillows. "Yeah, you can come."

"Good morning," he says with just a glance before he averts his eyes.

"Good morning," I reply cautiously.

"It's after nine. Are you OK?"

"Yep." I search his face for any sign of knowing. *I didn't...we didn't...did we?*

"Good. Great. Want me to bring you some coffee?"

"No, I'll come in. Thanks."

"OK." He hesitates. "Um...are we good?"

Oh, shit. "Yeah, of course."

"OK." He exits sort of haltingly, and I pinch the bridge of my nose.

"What the hell happened last night?" I mutter.

It is Lucy who answers with a bark.

"I don't suppose you could tell me in English?" I pet her pretty yellow face.

She doesn't tell me, but a disembodied t-shirt (yes, the same I'd changed into for dinner and dancing) comes soaring through the door and hits me in the face.

Oh, dear. I heave myself up, swallow three Ibuprofen, drink all the water in my large bottle, and take the world's longest shower. Not to be gross, but there's no sign that Banner and I—you know.

I feel a bit better as I step into the living room if a little bashful. Banner's in the corner chair like he was yesterday morning, reading the visitors' log. He lifts his eyes, and maybe he's bashful too.

"What will you record in that log before you go?' I ask.

"Best. Evacuation. Ever." He uses his hands to emphasize the three words. His kindness sounds forced, but he surprises me by saying, "You look beautiful."

My eyes are puffy. I've only towel-dried my hair, and it's dripping. "Are you teasing me?"

"No."

"I don't feel beautiful." I pour a glass of water just so I can turn my back.

"You don't think I'm a dick, right?" he asks.

"What? No, I think you're great. Why?"

He gives a quick half-smile. "It's in the past."

I didn't call him a dick. I don't even use that word. Aloud I ask, "Did you and Lucy have coffee on the porch?"

"We went to check on the bridge. It's nearly passable."

I swear the thought pinches my heart. "You're ready to get going."

He shrugs a shoulder. "I just want you to be happy."

There's an uncomfortable silence after which Banner says, "I found another entry in the guestbook." When I give him my attention, he lowers his gaze and begins, "'*This cabin is the perfect respite. We swam and relaxed beside the river for hours.*'" Banner falters, then, ploddingly he continues, "I need you to know that when I leave this place, I'll leave a piece of myself behind."

"That's what they wrote?"

"That's what I'm telling you."

The sorrow on his face troubles me.

Just ask him what happened. I draw a breath, but Banner says, "You need to hear this. '*We were about to cross the bridge on the way back from town, when a white pickup truck*'"—he emphasizes that part—"'*who had been trailing us from the main road, passed us and crossed in front of us, barring our way. My husband got out to see what was the matter, but the truck crept back toward us, and the driver rolled down his window, only to glare. We asked what the problem was. Asked the man's name. He told my husband that the unrighteous are thrown into the lake of fire. Told us to leave. It was unnerving, to say the least. I make note of it here so that you have a record, in case this same man disturbs other guests.*'"

Banner keeps talking. I think he has been planning what to say.

"Here's what I think: These neighbors of yours are deluded zealots. They have a white pickup truck. They have a shirt that matches the patch from the guestbook. And the snake fascination? Maybe that's enough to go to the authorities. God knows I can't tell you what to do,"—*what is that supposed to mean*—"but I think you should drive out of here when I do and let Wren know what is going on. I'm going to call him whether you do or not."

"You're talking like you're already gone."

"Isla, don't do that," he says sharply. "I'm just trying to honor your wishes."

"What wishes, Banner?" I am at a total loss. From the way he's gaping at me, he is too.

"You have no memory of last night, do you?"

The dread in my chest tightens into a knot. "What happened?" I can't meet his eyes. "Just tell me."

"We ate. We danced. We argued over whether or not you should stay here by yourself. Is this ringing a bell? You went to your room."

"Yeah, I remember all that part. Then what?"

"You tell me. I assume it has to do with you knocking back about a fifth of something hard."

When I don't respond, he continues, "You came to my room. I thought something was wrong, that somebody had shown up at your window or something. But you were crying, started apologizing. Started—I didn't realize how messed up you were." Banner checks in with me to see if I understand what he's saying.

"Did we, um..."

"No. You—wanted to." The way he says it makes it clear he's trying to protect me from the humiliation of how strong I came on to him. Blitzed.

"Oh *gah*," I blurt out. "I must have been a sloppy mess. Please don't remember me that way."

"You were a gorgeous mess, but yeah, you were pretty drunk. And when I realized that, I trudged you to your room where you threw a big, fucking pity party. Turned on me. Told me I was a dick. Told me you didn't want me to stay here any longer than I had to."

I groan into my hands. "No wonder you went to check the

bridge. You probably started building a boat." It's all coming back to me in embarrassing snapshots. I was a wreck. "I'm so sorry, Banner. Will you please forgive me?"

"For wanting to sex me up? How could I blame a woman for that?"

I roll my eyes. "For being a mean, drunken asshole! And it's too soon for comic relief."

"Hey," he says seriously. Concern carves lines into his face. "It's got a hold of you, doesn't it? It's the reason the flip gets switched in the evenings. The reason you go off to your room by yourself."

I've never told anyone. I don't know what he'll do with the information. I swallow past the lump in my throat and nod my head. "I can't sleep without it. It's too hard. All the junk that goes on in my head gets so loud. All the trying to figure out what Jake was trying to say in those last m—" Instead of finishing the sentence, I shake my head.

Banner settles beside me on the couch. I'm as stiff as a board. I'm sitting forward, locked up. My shoulders, my neck. Even my eyebrows are tense.

He tugs me back, but I resist him.

"I've been in recovery for three years," he says. That gets my attention. I turn to face him. "Took causing a wreck to admit it had me beat. Hurt the woman I was with. Got a DUI. Ruined my relationships. Not because of fights or anything. Just sheer neglect. I didn't hang out with people who cared about me. I hung out with people who wouldn't hold up a mirror."

"Like you're doing for me right now," I say.

"Eesa, if you saw what I see when I look at you, you'd sleep like a baby every night."

"I don't know how that could be true."

"Well, it is," he says emphatically.

He makes me smile despite the mortification. "I don't know how it got this bad. It was just one or two on occasion. Helped me get out of the house, helped me not to think. But now I'm honestly afraid not to have it on hand. Like I'm scared I'll—I don't know—

explode or something. Every time I try to quit, I get so anxious. It's unbearable. It sounds pathetic, but it's true."

"It's not unbearable."

"Yes, it *is.* It *feels* like it."

"I know," he's quick to say "I really do. But you dull everything when you drink, so when you don't, everything feels supercharged. There are things you can do to tolerate the anxiety until it subsides. If you're willing. It won't always feel like biting the bullet. Ees, you took a huge hit when you lost Jake. But you can't waste the best years of your life dodging your own story."

I know he's right. It's why I'm here. "Do you think I should be in a program?"

"I can't answer that."

"Would you be my sponsor if I was?"

"No," he says flatly.

"*Ow.* Why not?" I demand.

"I'm pretty sure they'd frown upon me sponsoring the woman I'm in love with."

"Are you?" I ask.

He exhales a laugh, issues a rumbly, "Please come here," and pulls me to his chest, wraps his arms around me. I relax into it. Gah, I love it. He says, "I can walk you through these first few days if you want to test it out. They're the hardest. They feel the most vulnerable, the most out of control."

"That sounds fun," I say brightly. But I don't care right now, because he's playing with my hair and honestly, this whole situation has taken a lovely turn.

"When's the last time you woke up without a headache or sense of regret?"

"I can't remember."

"And *that's* fun? Feeling ruined before you're twenty-two years old?"

I don't answer.

"Give me these two days alcohol-free," he says.

"It's the nighttime that's the hardest," I mumble into his t-shirt.

"I'll stay with you. We can sleep right here."

"Do I get to fall asleep on top of you like this?" 'Cause, for real, I could live and die right here listening to his heartbeat.

"Yes, please."

"Will you keep playing with my hair like that?"

"You like that?"

I nod against his chest. He settles in further.

"Wasn't it even a *little* bit hard to turn me down last night?" I ask.

He *pffs*. "Let's just say that most of our clothes hit the floor before I talked myself out of it. But you weren't in any condition to make that decision. Even though you were very...compelling." He shifts underneath me. "Stop talking about it if we're not gonna do it." He changes the subject. "What message do you think the damn snake circus was meant to send?"

"I'm not sure. It could have been a coincidence. Both snakes trying to score an easy egg meal once the bucket was left."

"Isla, you know good and damn well that that was no coincidence."

"Probably not."

Lucy steps to the couch and rests her head on my back. Maybe she senses my need for consolation. "No, Luce. *I* get to cuddle her for a while."

Maybe we could just spend the rest of our time entwined like this.

That reminds me of how little time we have left. "There are things you should see before you go," I say. "Things I need for you to witness."

Chasing Fireflies

"EES, WHAT *IS* THIS PLACE?" Banner turns full round three times. I knew he'd love it.

We drove the go-kart to get here. Well, Banner drove it—*well*, if you can call it that. He sped about, careening wildly to test the turning radius and nearly the roll bar as well. Meanwhile, I did my best to keep his dog from going airborne.

My throat hurts from screaming. My cheeks hurt from laughing.

Now we're on foot in this lush, green glen where the trees grow further apart than in any other area of the wood. Sunlight filters through the branches, turning everything yellow. The river is swollen, but it rolls in smooth, gentle mounds beside us, not in turbulent, hammering falls.

"Mammaw used to say that it was a place like this where King David wrote the twenty-third Psalm. You know the one? The LORD is my shepherd?"

"He leads me beside quiet waters," Banner says and turns around yet again. "He restores my soul."

"He restores my soul," I echo.

Several stacks of large, moss-covered stones surround us. In this secluded landscape, they seem to have grown as organically as the trees, and yet there is no natural explanation for them. Banner inspects each one with his usual curiosity. He walks between them, measures the distance in steps, and finally gives his attention to me. "Burial ground?" he guesses, and he's right.

"Cherokee. Mammaw turned it back over to the tribe, but they've only used it once that I'm aware of. Of course, most of the Eastern Band live in North Carolina."

I find the newest stack of rocks which is still over a decade old. "This is the grave of a little boy named Onacona. I didn't know him, but I chanted his name about a million times during his funeral."

I can practically see Banner creating a new headline for his notes. "What was *that* like?" he asks.

"It was long. It lasted for seven days. Jake and I got to go because this neighbor girl, Inola, asked us. She used to come to play at the cabin when her grandmother would visit my mammaw." I search my memory for details that Banner would find intriguing, while I brush the tops of the tiny, white flowers that grow among the graves.

"How are you doing that?" he asks.

"Doing what?"

"The flowers—they're following your fingers. They reach for you when you move away." He tries it himself, but I just laugh at him and brush them the other way. They do appear to be reaching for me.

"How are you doing that?" he asks again.

"I'm not doing anything."

"*Huh.* OK, this boy's funeral."

"Right. A holy man cleansed the body right here on a blanket." I show Banner where, beside the grave, the little boy was laid. "He used some kind of lavender-scented oil and wrapped him in a white cloth."

The scent of that oil is as strong in my memory as it had been in reality, and I swear it hangs in the air now, allowing me to view the event like a photo gallery.

"The trees provided a sparse canopy, as they do today. Ferns speckled the hillside and those tricksy, little flowers grew all around where the body lay."

Before Banner can ask, I say, "No. I do not know the name of the tricksy, little flowers."

"How can you not know that?" he laughs.

This has become a thing. He wants me to identify and deliver details on every wildflower, every bulbous mushroom, every twisting tree root.

"I don't know the names of most of the streets I drive either, Banner, but I get where I'm going because I grew up on them. You know what I mean?"

I look up to find that he actually does not. He has no experience with a place from sheer exposure. Very seriously, he says, "I know the names of every major road in every single city I have ever visited. I start learning them before I go. Driving *here* without that information nearly gave me a panic attack. I have a phobia of getting lost."

"Isn't it kind of your *job* to get lost?"

He grins like he's been caught. "In my desire to get you to come with me to St. Lucia, I may have led you to believe that I'm more spontaneous than I am. I plan all my trips well in advance. I also make backup plans. I used to have nightmares that I'd forget the way to my house, and my family would have packed up and moved out by the time I found it."

"That is so sad!"

"They wouldn't have," he assures me. "But still..."

"You need more than a *hub*," I tell him. "You need something permanent."

"Woman, I am painfully aware of that, all the more as I follow you around this place. What's wrong?"

I'm sure I look stricken. After what he just revealed, it physically *pains* me that I ordered him out of my house last night.

"Banner, you are welcome here anytime you want to come. I am truly sorry I said anything different while I was drunk. It wasn't me."

I'm never going to drink again. I'm not sure how yet. But I'd rather suffer the debilitating anxiety than make this man feel abandoned.

He's watching me in a way that makes me think he can read my thoughts. Maybe he can. He has his own drunken regrets. He cups my neck. "Don't think about that anymore. I forgive you. Is that what you need to hear?"

I nod. My naked shame stings the back of my eyes like a dagger.

"I forgive you," he says again.

My question—"Do you still want me?"—is met by his mouth on mine, clever as those tricksy flowers. He teases my lips with the tip of his tongue, deepens the kiss. But when he draws a thumb across my wet cheek, he pulls back to confirm that I'm crying. "Am I that bad at this?" he whispers.

I shake my head. "You're that good."

And now he encircles me in the steadiest, strongest hug of my life, making me inhale a sob.

"You're gonna be OK," he says. "Do you hear me?"

I nod into the crook of his neck. "I'm sorry I cry all the time." *Sniff.*

"Why?"

"I don't know. I thought I was supposed to be." *Sniff.* "It can't be that much fun for you."

"Humans cry when they need to cry." That's the second time he's told me that. He looks down at me in his arms and winks as he says, "It's not such a bad arrangement for me."

Banner finds a fallen log overlooking the river, and for a long time, we just sit. It doesn't feel like a waste, even though we don't have much time left. I think I'll remember it the way I remember being confined to the couch that winter I broke my leg. Mom tended to me the whole time it took to convalesce. Maybe I *can* do Recovery. I just can't do it alone.

"We slept out here most nights," I say at length. "At that boy's funeral. Jake and I only went home to eat—and only then because all the mourners fasted. Mammaw said it would be rude to eat in front of them. But otherwise, we joined in as if we were part of the tribe. It was beautiful and eery. Prayers and songs were offered continually, even through the dark. The moon came up through the clouds like in a werewolf movie, this moment hidden, this moment revealed. And Inola and I chanted the boy's name for hours. All the women did. In these low, long mournful tones." I perform it for him. "Ohhhnaaacohhhna. Over and over until we had no wisp of breath left in our lungs. And then we would draw new breath and begin again."

"It must have been transcendent."

"I'll never forget how the sound became part of the scene, drifting heavily over the ground like mist. Jake went off with the men for a while, and came back with ashes drawn on his face."

He wasn't the only one.

"*Jeremiah* was there," I say as I recall it. "He and Inola were friends."

"I can't imagine that guy being friends with anybody."

"He wasn't always so hulking as he is now. He fostered a little lamb once. Did I tell you that? It followed him around like a puppy."

Banner considers that while he continues to watch the water.

"*What's* the tagline for your blog?" I ask, even though it's obvious that I'm only asking to lead him to my point of view.

Now he turns my way with a suspicious grin that means he's willing to follow. "Whoever searches for what is right and kind finds life itself."

"I'm telling you there is righteousness and kindness in that boy."

"I hear you," Banner says.

"On the seventh day, the holy man took us all to the river where we filed in one after another as silent as could be. We were told to immerse ourselves seven times, lifting hands to the east and then hands to the west. It must have been a sight, tens of us rising from the pool like we were rising from our graves. They call it 'going to water,' and it was meant to release Onacona's soul to Creator. The Cherokee have no word for religion, did you know?"

He shakes his head.

"Their spirituality is just built into everything they do."

"Take me to that pool."

"I did. Yesterday."

"That was where?"

"Can you imagine? You and I are going *that* way, though, away from the river. You ready?"

He is. He always is. Banner does the thing where he coaxes my hand into his as we walk.

"Keep talking," he says.

"You know, up till then, nothing had frightened me. I mean, yeah, there was a body and it all felt weighty and sacred, but then the elders built a fire to cook these birds to eat. When Jake and Jeremiah went to get theirs, the fire crackled loudly and popped in their direction. This frightful murmur went up from all around, and it scared me. I asked Inola what it meant, but she would only say it was a bad omen. Years later, though, at Mammaw's funeral, she told me that the elders watch the funeral fire to determine if any other beloved son is going to die. She said the fire had picked Jeremiah, not Jake. She said something wasn't right about the way Jake died."

"Well, no shit," Banner says.

"Yeah," I laugh. "No shit. That's all I remember. The dead boy's family was given new clothes and leather strands of sanctified stones from the river to protect them."

"Like these?" Banner tugs at the bracelets around my wrist.

"Very much like these. Banner, will you stop for a second?"

He shakes his head. "Sorry, no. I only stop for kisses at this point."

"I have some."

He consents, leans down for me to pay up, and weaves his fingers behind my back. "What is it?"

"Thank you for honoring these memories. For being present, for asking questions. You make me able to access them."

"I'm not sure how much I help. I think you're just ready to remember them and I got lucky enough to be around for it."

"No, listen. I was bogged down. I was afraid to leave the front porch or to think on anything at all—even though that's why I came. It's like an invisible force kept me glued to the rocker, and all I had for memories were dead things inside me. But you unlock me.

You shine a light, and I find that they're still alive. So, *I'm* still alive. Does that make sense?"

"I think so. You feel your heart as a vacuum of loss when in fact, it is teeming with life." He motions around us. "How could it not be? I can't wait for you to start writing again. I want to watch the world fall in love with you. You are just so wildly attractive." He steps back and folds his arms to stare down at me like he's trying to determine how it is that I can be so wildly attractive, and, while I know that no real human being is as captivating as all that, I think my soul is actually taking up more space from being sent the message.

"How do you come up with shit like that?" I ask. "Do you think of it ahead of time?"

"Woman, have you not been listening to yourself? You gush in poetry."

"I do?"

Banner rolls his eyes. "Yeah," he says like I'm slow to catch on, but then his demeanor takes an abrupt shift. He thrusts out a protective arm and goes still.

"Do you smell that?" he asks.

"Smoke."

"It's really there, right?'

"What is your deal with fire?"

He ignores that. "Somebody's here. Or they have been."

Ducking under a low-hanging branch, we move past several more graves before we get to the thing Banner noticed: a ring of rocks with ashes from a recent fire and a whole pile of firewood waiting to be used. The wood is stored inside a human-made lean-to. Banner examines it. A tree limb has been placed into the crooks of two standing trees like a beam. Other branches lie against that beam to create a sloping wall, and bark has been mudded into the cracks.

Banner stoops to check out the inside. "It's been standing for a while," he says. "And it's in good shape after the storm. Somebody knew what they were doing."

"Thank you," I say brightly.

"You built this?"

"I built all of them. All of us did."

Banner pivots around to find more structures but when there are none to be seen, I thrust an index finger upward and he slowly raises his head to search the treetops. "No. Way." And he's off. He jogs under the triangle of rope bridges that connect three tree huts. "Are you an Ewok?!" he exclaims and regards me like he's never seen me before.

"Asher turned out to be an architect," I tell him. "And Sissy went into interior design."

"How long did it take?"

"A whole summer. Thatching them took longer than anything else."

"They've been well-maintained."

"Probably Asher's doing."

"Can we go up?"

"Of course."

I start to show him the way, but he spouts, "I'll find it!" and takes off like it's a choose-your-own-adventure. Once he locates the ladder, he chatters the whole way up, with the glee of a kid. "This is fantastic!" he says over the railing, and then gasps because there's a slide. Now he's gone. "I love it!" And now he's climbing the ladder again. I follow him this time. "Can we stay here tonight?" he asks.

"Sure. We may want to go grab some—"

"What?"

"Sleeping bags."

"Yeah, all the better."

"No. I mean, there are sleeping bags." I point to two cinch sacks in the corner. "Hit the lights."

"There are lights?!"

I reach across him to do it myself. "Solar," I tell him. "Asher ran the receptors so far up the tree we didn't know if we'd ever get him down."

"Um...Ees?" When the warm string lights come to life, Banner is staring at a portion of the wall where we've all signed our names. Wren, Asher, Sissy, Jake, Isla. But someone has chiseled Jake's name away, and around my name, there's a circle. Two long arrows seem to be shooting my name from opposite directions. It has no chance of escape.

"Who did this?" Banner asks.

I shake my head and rub the ghost of Jake's signature, feeling wounded because something else of him was taken. "*Why* did they?"

Banner is more interested in what is hanging above *my* signature: a wooden mask, a crude carving of a man's face with ghoulish, wide-spread teeth exposed from a gaping mouth. Encircling the mask-man's head like a crown is a carved rattlesnake, its rattle raised high.

"What is it with you people and snakes?" Banner asks.

"It looks *ancient*," I say. "It's a booger mask."

Banner waves his fingers the way he does when he wants more intel but is too impatient to ask.

"The Cherokee have a traditional dance in which the men sneak off to get into character. They come back wearing masks like this. Inola's grandmother had one."

"What does it symbolize?"

"I don't know. They linked rattlesnakes to evil spirits, though, to the storm gods." I open one of the cinch sacks. "It *is* a sleeping bag. Smells like it's been smoking weed."

Banner takes a whiff. "It's herbal, but more like...sage?"

"Maybe? It reminds me of something. I can't put my finger on it."

Banner empties the second sack. Another sleeping bag. "Same smell. Look." Wrapped in the bag are several bundles of dried herbs tied with twine. He stuffs it all back into the sack. "Let's look through the other houses."

The strange discoveries have done nothing to derail Banner's enthusiasm. But they have had the opposite effect on me. While the snakes that were placed above my window didn't disturb me too much, these feel ominous. Threatening. Why would someone have destroyed Jake's signature and targeted mine? Is that person trying to pick us off one by one? It's a ludicrous thought. Paranoid.

We trek across the rope bridges and search the other two tree huts, but there are no more sleeping bags or symbols, and trust me, we would know if there were, because Banner searches every side of everything. There is, however, that same heavy, herbal scent hanging in each room.

Below us, Lucy lets out a bark. "We're up here, Lu—" I begin, but Banner shushes me.

"Someone's down there," he whispers.

"I don't see anyone."

"There. Through the trees. About twenty yards." I lean over Banner's shoulder and can only just make out a figure. "Turn off the lights," he says. "It's a woman. Do you see her now?"

"Yeah. Among the graves."

"I was getting worried that I was the only one."

"Lucy sees her."

True fact. Lucy has jogged over to introduce herself. As the woman pets Lucy, she cranes her neck, probably to locate the dog's owner. I keep shifting my position to see her better through the leaves. She's slender. She has dark-brown hair, straight, but pulled into a short ponytail. She's wearing hot-pink shorts and a navy t-shirt with capped sleeves.

"She'd make a very preppy ghost," I remark.

As the woman moves in our direction, I become aware that we're spying on her. "Let's go talk to her."

Banner nods his head but scans our surroundings. "There are two sleeping bags," he reminds me. "She's coming to meet someone."

He gently pushes in front of me. "Let me go first." As if he can't resist, he adds, "I'm still using the slide." And hurls himself down it.

I take one more look around. What would Jake say if he saw this? He'd probably stick the mask on his face and dance around in it for the rest of the day.

I don't have long to enjoy that thought, because a shriek rips through the air.

Banner must surely have startled the woman when he came barreling down the slide, but that scream went way past startled. I see through the window that the woman's eyes are round as plates. Her hand is covering her mouth and it's trembling. "Jacob?" she stammers.

Banner is shaking his head, trying to introduce himself, but as he takes steps toward her, she takes steps away and holds out her other hand to block his advance. In this manner, she continues slowly backward like she doesn't want to trigger his prey drive.

Lucy looks from Banner to the woman and back again. It would be comical, except that the woman is truly terrified.

"Inola?" I call from the window. "Is that you?"

But the woman has turned and is now sprinting away, leaving Banner to gaze up at me. "Probably should have used the ladder," he says.

"I don't think that's what scared her. I'm coming down." Banner meets me at the bottom of the slide. "I think it was Inola. And I think she thought you were Jake."

"If the bridge is closed," he begins.

"How did she get on the property," I finish. "Right."

"She was already on-site?" he suggests.

"And she's been camping here?"

He shrugs.

"There are other places you can cross the river," I note. "You just can't drive over."

"Like where Jeremiah lives."

"Sure," I say. "They could still be friends."

"They could be more than that."

"No," I say, but then think better of it. "Maybe? They were together a lot at Mammaw's funeral."

"Maybe they have to keep it secret because of all the fornicating."

"Stop," I laugh. "That is gross."

"We know what his dad thinks of filthy fornicators. He probably tests their holiness in the snake pit."

The laughter dies on my lips. What if that *is* what he does? "Did you see the way Jeremiah's forearms were scarred? Punctures."

"No. Do you know what you're saying? You think that man would put his own son's life in danger like that?"

"He's already responsible for the death of his wife!"

"He *killed* her?"

"He denied her medical attention. It ended the same."

"Did she *want* medical attention?"

The question steals my thunder. "No. Mammaw asked her. Made sure Mr. Ridley wasn't around. Told her she'd take her to the doctor herself and Mr. Ridley would never have to know. She wouldn't go."

"Well. Then that's hard to hang on Mr. Ridley."

"It was sad, though. Jeremiah was still so young."

"This place has seen a lot of funerals." Banner frowns at me. But I smile. "Why in the world would that make you happy?" he asks.

"Because that is a great segue. I have one more thing to show you before we go home for the night. You don't still want to sleep here, do you?"

"Uh, no. Not with the booger man."

"Come on. You're gonna love this."

I've been avoiding the family cemetery, number five on the list of goals, but now that Banner is with me, I think I can do it. Anyway, it's the best place, by far, to introduce him to one of the Smokies' greatest treasures, and who knows if tomorrow night—our last night—don't think about that—will be temperate enough, like tonight is turning out to be.

We ride on and come to a broad field, at the end of which is a round knoll dotted with stone monuments. It was grandfathered in with the property since it was in use long before laws were set up against burying folks out back. There are twenty-two stones. They go back seven generations.

When Jake died, and the bridge was flooded as it is now, we buried him quickly and privately without embalming him—an act for which I am forever grateful. He can just go into the earth. He doesn't have to remain down there, falsely preserved, turning more zombie-like with each passing year.

I have dreamed, many times, that I would go lie upon Jake's grave and sleep. Or die. I half want to now. But the much alive man beside me simply states, "It's another graveyard."

"Yes. But it's more too. It's an open piece of land where we'll be able to enjoy a thing that is special about the Smokies."

"Ghosts are everywhere, Ees."

"Indeed. Come meet the fam." Banner follows me from grave to grave. "This is Mammaw," I say. "This is Pap. And this is Jacob Miller Payne." I nod my head once. "Jake." I dust off his name and plop down on top of him, my back to his stone.

"Four years ago," Banner says as he reads the date. "Almost to the day."

"My birthday," I say.

"Are you kidding me right now?" Banner asks.

The corner of my mouth quirks to say, *Nope. It's true.* "He thought he was invincible. It was just as fucking loud that day as it is now. *Ass*hole. I *begged* him not to do it."

Banner sits beside me. "Would he have liked me?"

"Most assuredly. But not before a time of great testing."

"I'd expect nothing less. You said your family hasn't been the same. But you speak about your cousins like you're thick as thieves."

"Oh, we are. It's more Aunt Rose. She and my dad argued at Mammaw's burial. She blames me. She won't come here anymore."

"Isn't this *your* first time back?"

He knows it is, so I don't answer.

"Is it possible that you and your aunt Rose were just so wounded that it's taken all this time to even think about reconnecting?"

It is possible. She lost her son. "I couldn't feel," I say. "Couldn't reach out. She looked like I felt, though. Like she'd lost so much that her own life was forfeit. I should have comforted her. She kept wanting to know all the horrible details, though, and I couldn't."

"Why can't you reach out now?" He rolls his head to look down at me, Jake's gravestone supporting us, and I wonder if I can.

"I like how we're sitting on his grave," I say. "Like we're piled on his bed or something." Even Lucy plops down. "What are you gonna do with Lucy while you're in St. Lucia? I could take care of her if you want."

"Oh my gosh! Is it not enough that she sleeps with you? Are you trying to *keep* her now?!"

I laugh, but half-heartedly.

We spread out a quilt and on top of that, our picnic. The sun sets while we're eating, and the world grows dark, but I'm not plagued by the usual dread of the coming night. Banner keeps asking me what we're waiting for, and his guesses are getting more ridiculous as time goes by. A meteor shower. An alien invasion. A festival of possums. But since neither of us got good rest last night, he dozes off using my thigh as a pillow. I comb his hair with my fingers and welcome the phenomenon that he's at risk of sleeping through. "Wake up, B," I whisper. "You're gonna miss it."

It's dark now. We're far from any electric lights. We never lit a fire. I can tell that Banner has opened his eyes when I hear his intake of breath.

Although I have a small flashlight on hand, wrapped in red cellophane as the rangers instruct, I don't turn it on. All around us —in the field, among the gravestones, between the trees—millions of lightning bugs flash at once like a fairyland palace. After a while, as if a conductor has signaled them, they all go dark. Until, all at once, they blast their lights again.

"They're synchronous fireflies," I say. "There are only a handful of places in the whole world where you can see them."

Banner pivots all around. "How can there possibly be so many of them?" he asks. "Where do they hide all day? How do they know when to blink?"

Having exhausted his questions, he falls silent to enjoy the show. Occasionally, one of us will beg the other to notice something—a firefly that lights bluer than the rest, or one right up close.

"It looks like *you're* directing them," Banner says. And I realize that I've been swishing my hand as if I'm the conductor, so I raise both hands at once. "*Shh!*" I command, and they all go out. "This one needs a solo. Go ahead, Little Guy."

The little blue one I mentioned glides this way and that in lovely arcs. I find myself giggling, and when I drop my hands all the bugs light up again.

"Isla, how are you doing that?"

"Isn't it funny? You try."

Banner doesn't meet with the same success that I do, but he has a hell of a time trying.

I don't think he's going to sleep for the rest of the night. I feel utterly gratified. I know he's thrilled with nature. It's why he does what he does. But *I* got to reveal this to him. My part of the world. My home.

He nuzzles the side of my head and says, "Babe, I am never going to forget this. You are one-hundred-percent awesome. I think you were made for me."

Here we are under the tiniest sliver of moon, sitting less than twenty feet from Jake's grave, and I am as content as a fat, little baby. "I wish we'd brought the tent," I muse.

"I know where some sleeping bags are."

"*Ack!* I can't wait to visit Inola."

We roll up in the quilt like a date-night burrito, but we finally give up and call it quits when it gets too cold. I deny Banner the keys to the go-kart, so he scoops Lucy onto his lap and I drive us home, concentrating on what small part of the path the headlights can illuminate.

It's not until we walk through the front door that the first dark thoughts flit through my mind. *You can't sleep without it. You just need one.*

"Eeees?"

"Whaaat?"

"Go get ready for bed and meet me back here. I'll get blankets."

He knows what it's like. He must because he can spot it in me.

WHEN I WAKE in the middle of the night, I don't have a headache. I don't feel depressed. Or confused, or defeated, or ashamed. I remember lying on Banner's chest. I fell asleep like that. And Banner is with me still, here on the couch, his breathing smooth and deep. He's got a knee in the air and a forearm resting on his head. He doesn't look as much like Jake as I thought.

When his sleepy eyes flutter open, he finds mine and rasps, "S'matter, Ees?"

I just shake my head and lie back down, so he rolls to face me, brushes my hair from my face.

"You sure?" he asks. "You want me to take you to bed? I mean, and then I would go to my own bed."

I laugh through my nose.

"In case you were concerned about my intentions," he says.

"Well, now I'm concerned you don't have any."

Banner growls the best, low, gravelly, "Careful." It shoots a dart into my spine. "I have no qualms taking you sober."

Hmmmm. "Are you uncomfortable here?" I ask.

"Me? Yeah, awful. I'm just taking one for the team."

"Can we stay then? Without any intentions for tonight?"

Banner lifts an arm in invitation, opening himself for me, and when I snuggle in, he drapes that arm over me, kisses my head. "Sleep," he whispers. And I do.

Today Is All We Get

"YOU'RE HAVING A DREAM, Babe. Wake up."

I hear Banner in my ear, but I see Jake on top of the falls. My eyes come open with a shuttering breath, and now Banner is kneeling before me, pressing a solid hand to my chest, which I grip to reset my bearings. My heart rate is through the roof.

"It's just a dream," he soothes.

Scrambling to a seated position, I spew words rapid-fire. "He said to go get Wren! He was telling me to go. He wasn't telling me to come up. He needed my help. Something was wrong up there."

"It's OK, Babe. It's just a dream."

"Stop saying that!"

"Listen, your dreams can be more vivid when you're not drinking."

I ignore him, go inward. *Jake wasn't aggravated with me. He was unsure what to do. He was...afraid.*

Banner tries to reach me with a different tack. "What could have been wrong?"

"I can't imagine. I never knew Jake to be scared of any damn thing, even when he *should* have been. But he *was* just now."

"Just now," Banner repeats.

I throw him a look. "I know that's what I said, but what I mean is—" I interrupt myself with a frustrated sigh. "I don't know what I mean. Jake made this sign he use to make for when Jeremiah was around." I twist my finger in the shape of a J. "In real life, he did that—and in the dream too."

"Would he have called for backup because of Jeremiah?" Banner asks. "If Jeremiah had tried to pick a fight or something?"

"Decidedly not. And I can't imagine Jeremiah trying. And I just can't imagine what in this world could make *Jake* that afraid."

"Was he really that brave?"

"He was that idiotic!" I laugh despite myself. The dream is fading. My heart rate is returning to normal. "I sometimes see myself up there behind him in the dreams, which shows you how badly I've wanted to know what he was trying to tell me. Or how badly I wish I'd climbed up." I silently plead with Banner to let the new information be a clue, but then admit that—"I guess it was just a dream."

"Would it help you to go up there and take a look around? We could mark it off the list."

The list of things I have to do to move on. Number one actually reads like this: *Look over the falls without any magical thinking and ask what you, as an eighteen-year-old girl, could possibly have done to keep that bull-headed jackass from jumping. Check this one off only when you can forgive yourself for not being able to save him.*

My therapist has advised me not to go alone. She said, more than once, that that would be beyond foolish.

I've shown her the letter.

"So, is that our plan today?" Banner asks.

I should let him read it. I have it with me—for some bizarre reason that I am not ready to unpack—and Banner is hard to shock.

I don't mention it. Instead, I say, "Let's play it by ear."

We study each other for a long moment. He's so handsome. Damp hair. Bare chest. My beads crowning his collar bones. I reach out to touch them. "Have you already showered? The sun's not even up."

He must take this to mean that the crisis is over. He kisses my head and glances out the window on his way to the kitchen. "It's trying," he says about the sun.

"Seems early, even for you."

"It is," he agrees. Now he's strolling back, a cup in each hand, basketball shorts slung intriguingly low.

When I reach for what we have clearly established to be *my* mug, he makes a show of sipping from it, but then hands it over and takes a seat on the coffee table facing me.

"At least I don't have to ask if we slept together," I offer.

"Oh, we did, though. In my mind. In about five different ways."

I consider the possibilities. "What's the fifth?" I ask, causing him to choke.

"I hadn't really—you came up with four?"

"My imagination is unrivaled," I say.

"Or maybe you just find me that inspiring."

I concede as much with a lift of my brow.

"No, we did not sleep together while I held you in my arms all night wondering what was going through your beautiful head and whether or not you were wearing the things I saw hanging over the dryer on the day I arrived."

It's my turn to cough and work to swallow the coffee down, but Banner plays it straight. "Which is why I had to get up before the sun to take a cold shower."

"Did that help?" I ask, trying not to smile.

"No, it did not. I kept envisioning you walking in on me."

"And *then* what?"

He blows out a *whew*. "Serving *me* coffee for a change."

"Banner!" I *ugh* at him loudly, and he chuckles into his cup. I adore the way his eyes crinkle when he riles me up.

"What?" he asks innocently.

"Your fantasies suck is what."

"You've got a better one?"

"Yeah," I assure him.

"You did sleep, though, didn't you?" he asks. "Aside from the dream?"

"Very well."

"So, you can."

"Yeah, if I can borrow your heartbeat all night."

"I'm at your service." This time Banner's smile doesn't reach his eyes, and I wonder if he's recognizing the fact that tonight is the *last* night he can be at my service. Maybe we could just pretend all day that he doesn't have to go. "Also," he says, "I should probably point out that you yourself have a heartbeat."

I think about that. "I do." I say this like it's news. But I do. My heart beats round the clock. I should draw comfort from that. Most of the time, when I'm aware of it, I'm just running three a.m. pulse checks to make sure it's still working.

"Because you're alive," Banner says. "A fact for which I am growing ever more grateful." He offers a hand and tugs me up, motioning toward the outside. "Sky's off the charts. Come see."

He's right. When we walk out back where the trees have been cleared, we can see the land drop away, exposing both vertical falls and mountain climbs. The dawn stretches in layered clouds that glow with bands of orange and pink, puckered by grey shadows. "Off the charts," I agree.

Today is all we get. It's going to chorus through my mind like an earworm from the stickiest pop song ever.

He leans back against the railing to enjoy the expanse above. He's so comfortable in his own skin that I want to feel what it's like to wear it. He turns his attention to me, reaches out, draws me in. "I'm gonna miss you," he says.

"Maybe it will storm some more," I mumble against his bare skin, which is warm, though the air is cold. A large breath expands his ribcage beneath my cheek, and it contracts just as slowly. I guess it's good to know the sorrow between us is mutual. But I'm not ready to be sad, so I bite into his pec—pretty hard.

"*Ow!*" he laughs. "You did not just do that!"

"It was only a nibble. Don't be a baby."

He stretches the skin. "You left teeth marks."

"You're delicious."

He chuckles, squeezes me, and then his smile recedes as quickly as it sprang up. "Let me make love to you," he says.

"Oh, is that how you like it? With the biting?"

"I'm serious." He looks it. Full-on brooding.

I barely nod my head before he's kissing me.

Let me tell you, I missed out the other night for not remembering. The man acts ravenous for me. It locks out every other thought except his hands and his mouth on me.

"It's OK?" he asks while he tugs at my shirt.

"Yes."

"You trust me with that heart of yours then?" A hint of a smile.

"Yes." I can hardly breathe the word, but suddenly he goes all chatty.

"I don't want you to stay here. What if your dream is true, and this whole time your brain heard more than you realized? What if Jeremiah was done being treated badly? Or thought Jake was trying to take advantage of you and felt some sort of twisted sense of justice in pushing him over?"

"Banner, did you just jump from *this*,"—I place my hand over his, which is squeezing my breast—"to Jake being pushed to his death?"

"*This*,"—he means my breast—"is why I'm thinking about it. I want you safe and whole."

"Jeremiah is the one who found Jake and dragged him out of the water. He didn't push him."

Banner lays his face on my shoulder. He has yet to release my breast. "OK," he concedes and turns to place sweet kisses on my neck, starts to rub small circles over the sensitive flesh he's been exploring. I get lost in it all over again when he says, "You still want this?"

"Oh my gah! If you'll shut up!"

Now he laughs into those kisses and half-carries me toward the house. Instead of entering, though, he backs me against the wall.

I can't remember making love to anyone sober. This is better. It's scary as hell, but it's way better. After all the time being numbed out? This is the opposite. It's electric.

I don't say *I love you*. Only in my head. I want to. I don't know why I keep that stuff back. I'm able to flirt with him. Able to confide in him. Able to—do this. But have I been able to just flat out ask him if there is any possibility that he'd change his plans for me and stay?

Suddenly he smooths my shirt into place and goes utterly still, the same way he did yesterday when he smelled smoke.

It is not because of my unspoken thoughts. I pick up on what he's listening to. A helicopter chopping the air, growing louder by the moment, coming our way fast, now uncomfortably loud. Soon, its noise wants to implode my head.

"Get inside." There's an unfamiliar edge to Banner's tone. He grips my arm and moves us through the door so quickly I have to jog to keep from being dragged. The sound increases, if that's possible. The treetops blow wildly.

We're no sooner inside than the helicopter appears.

"Who in the world is it?" I ask.

Banner exhales in relief. "Army," he says.

The aircraft hovers over the backyard. Banner moves toward the door, but I halt him. "You were afraid before."

"It's just memories. A heli screaming in that low, unannounced —it just took me back. We're good." He pushes out, and I follow, but I'm curious about what he meant. The only thing I really know about his service is that he searched out the good stuff in the community where he served. What bad stuff did he also encounter?

A camouflaged soldier descends on a cord. Once on the ground, carabiners are unclamped, the cord tugged twice, and the soldier stomps around. Two obvious thumbs up toward the chopper, and now the soldier is climbing the deck stairs.

I am beyond shocked when Banner yips in recognition, clamors to the steps, and practically lugs the person up onto the deck and into his arms.

The helicopter is slowly landing, first one skid, then the other. Meanwhile, the soldier is calling things into a radio. When she removes her helmet to reveal a broad smile and pretty, grey eyes—not unlike the eyes I've been getting lost in over the last few days—I understand who she is.

"What the hell are you doing here?" Banner yells.

"I'm telling Mom you cussed at me first thing," she responds. "Sorry if my unplanned arrival brought back bad memories."

"It did. But I'm OK. Come inside."

And now that the helicopter is landed, the engine stops pushing, but the huge blades continue to rotate. Banner guides the soldier into the house with a hand on her back.

"Isla, this is my sister, Bekah."

She says, "How's that for an entrance?"

"Effective," I tell her.

"Where are you coming from?" Banner asks.

"We flew choppers out of Fort Rucker to protect them from the hurricane. Flying them back now. The *General*"—Bekah overemphasizes their father's title—"made a certain don't-ask-don't-tell kind of a statement about the flight path, which I took to mean I could come to check on you. The pilot—and I use that term loosely—is still in training."

"How did you know where I was?"

"The pilot is one Lieutenant Colonel Payne."

"Wren?!" we both say.

And here he is now, grinning like the cat who ate the canary.

I cross my arms. "Hello *Cousin*," I greet him suspiciously.

"Hello, *Cousin*," he parrots. "How are things?"

"*Hm*," I say.

Wren makes a face to deny the accusation I haven't made. It has nothing to do with him landing a helicopter in Mammaw's backyard and everything to do with his mismanagement of the cabin's occupancy.

"I just dropped in to make sure the two of you were thriving."

"So, you did know that I was here when you volunteered our fair cottage to your friend."

"I can neither confirm nor deny."

I close the distance to embrace him. "It's good to see you," I say.

"You too. It's been too long."

After that, my cousin and my love interest hug like they're the dearest of friends.

"You look well," Wren tells Banner. "You must not have taken too badly to the company."

"Anything's better than being stuck in a hurricane," he replies.

When I *pff,* Banner wraps his arms around me from behind and rests his head on my shoulder.

Wren is studying our familiarity with know-it-all satisfaction. The fact that Banner is half-naked probably gives him ideas. If he'd only been a few minutes later, he may have seen a lot more.

"Is that a bite mark?" he asks. Banner nods matter-of-factly. I close my eyes.

"Wren, you totally planned this," I say.

"I just offered a refugee a place to shelter. I can't help that the two of you are wildly compatible."

"You really didn't know?" I turn on Banner who holds up a hand to proclaim his innocence, but I'm narrowing my eyes at him.

"How long do we get to keep you two?" I ask. "Breakfast? Dinner? Overnight?"

Banner gives me a silent signal to stop extending the offer. Yeah, I guess that could derail our little love fest. Probably a good thing, though. I mean, he's leaving.

"They can't park a copter for a sleepover," Banner says.

"Little Brother, it's like you're not even happy we showed up." Bekah's wearing the same inquisitive amusement that Wren is. She frees a phone from a large pocket in her uniform and pushes through the backdoor where she dials a long number, listens, dials another. I don't have the heart to tell her it won't work. But apparently, it does. She beckons Banner out with, "Come, tell Mom you're alive."

He grabs his fleece and says, "Hello? Mom?" while he wrangles it over his head. "This is insane," he mutters to his sister. To his mom again, he says, "I'm fine. I'm great, actually..........Yep. Lucy too. I'm sorry to worry you. There was no way to call you from here." He adds, "Without a specially delivered, Army-issue, satellite telephone."

Bekah snickers and closes the door on him. "Yeah, I'm pretty sure the allocation of trip resources will come under review."

"At least you have a JAG lawyer," I volunteer. "*Why* are you learning to fly?" I ask Wren.

"I just want to. The Army has all kinds of schools, and—"

"Wren," I butt in. "How do you know Banner? He acts like it's a big secret."

"We spent time on the same base."

"He said you met in a class, but told me I had to ask you which one."

"Ooh, riiight." He drags the words, and his eyes flit to Bekah apologetically.

She cottons on before I do. "Isla, is there a restroom I can use?" she asks.

"Of course. Yes." I show her the way and return with my eyebrows raised. "You can't tell his sister?" I ask.

"I don't know if I have his permission. Banner and I met in AA the day Trish told me I couldn't come home till I got help."

"You?" I ask. "You're the last person I would have guessed to have a problem."

"Yeah—well—grief hurts."

"Yeah." I should tell him. I almost don't, but then I blurt out, "I need help too."

"I know."

"You do?"

"You're not as good at drinking off-camera as you think. All those online family meetings?"

Shit. "Does everybody know?"

"Nah. I think it's a takes-one-to-know-one type of thing. I'm glad you told me. We'll get you straightened out." Wren scrounges the pantry. "What's for breakfast?"

I'm still wondering who all knows when Banner opens the door, and his words make my heart jump. "I love you." I raise my eyes and, though he's looking at me, he's talking into the phone. He tilts his head quizzically, reaches for my hand, and ends the call.

"What'd you say to her, Wren? She looks ready to cry."

"Just talking about how obvious it is that you haven't been able to work out since you arrived. You should definitely keep the jacket on."

Banner observes his arms with a frown. Which is laughable.

"I love this place," Bekah calls, and now she's present in the living room. "What do you think, Payne? Should we stay all weekend?"

"Can I see you for a minute?" Banner asks, and he escorts his sister onto the deck while I laugh under my breath and go to help Wren, who is grouching about our meager food supplies.

"We haven't been able to shop," I remind him. "And, by the way, I had no heads up that there would be a ravenous man-guest to fuel —because my cousin did not inform me of his diabolical plans."

"Sounds like a devious, though brilliant and loving cousin. That reminds me..." Wren un-pockets a sleeve of thin foil squares. "I brought these just in case."

"I am not having this conversation with you."

He chuckles and tosses the condoms onto the counter.

"Anyway, he's leaving," I add. "Tomorrow."

"Ah, that's too bad." Wren sounds genuinely disappointed. "Off to the next exotic location?"

"You know it."

A twinge of loss followed by the sudden desire to swallow some liquid happiness sets in.

Wren hoists a red, woven net of potatoes. "Let's make that breakfast hash Mammaw used to. Do we have all the stuff?" He procures salt, pepper, parsley flakes, olive oil.

"I think so. There's also bacon." I travel to the fridge and hand it to him behind my back. "And butter for toast." I hand that back too. I don't even look because I know Wren will nab them. We've done this a thousand times, and I have to admit it's comforting to have him here, relating to me as he has my whole life.

"Don't we have eggs?" he asks, searching over my shoulder.

We turn when Banner lets out a gagging sound on his way back in. Wren stares at him blankly. "You're opposed to eggs?"

"I am now. *Why* are there condoms?"

"They were a gift," Wren says. "But I hear you won't be around to use them."

"I'm not having this conversation with you."

"That's what I said! Wren, what do you remember about Jeremiah Ridley? Is he...all there?"

"Hell, Isla, you know more than I do. You're the only one he ever talked to." Wren begins chopping the potatoes.

"Why'd you guys give him such a hard time?"

"We didn't do anything. He was just odd. He didn't fit in."

"He was the one who pulled Jake from the water. Did you know that? Carried him all the way back here."

I get Wren's full attention with that. "I never understood how," my cousin says.

"He just did. Set him down on the grass out there." Wren knows where I mean. Sissy planted a gardenia bush. "Carefully too. Laid him out like—" I shrug.

"You were alone when we came out and saw you holding him. You'd cried yourself dry by then. We couldn't get many answers out of you."

"I was in shock."

Wren goes back to chopping. Banner answers a few questions his sister poses about it.

"I jumped in after him to force The Hydraulic to let him go."

Wren's sharp eyes dart to mine. "You did not."

"I did. And no sooner was I being sucked down than I was released, floating downstream as safe as you please. Jeremiah came up from the water behind me, coughing his lungs out. He dragged me to the shore, tossed me down."

"What do you mean he came up from the water?"

His question gives me pause. "He must have jumped too. Is *that* why it let me go? Every time I tried to get to my feet, he forced me down again. I couldn't make him understand that I had to look for Jake. And he just kept apologizing."

"For what?"

I shake my head. "I'd like to know."

"Here's what *I'd* like to know," Banner says. "Is he dangerous or not? Isla had this weird-ass dream that he was up above the falls with Jake and that Jake was scared."

"Jeremiah isn't aggressive," I cut in. I don't know why I'm defending him. "He's a little backward. But he's not mean."

"Ees, he forbade me to touch you while wielding a sledgehammer. *But* he did come all this way to deliver eggs after that." Now he's pinning me with a stare that begs me to stop insisting Jeremiah is harmless.

"So we do have eggs?" Wren asks.

"No," Banner spits. "Because along with the eggs, was a rattlesnake. And that rattlesnake was halfway down the throat of a kingsnake. But that rattlesnake did not *want* to be halfway down the throat of a kingsnake. So, it fought and it thrashed until the bucket tipped and all the eggs broke onto the floor, creating a great, gross mess in which the snakes continued to wrestle. *Here.*" Banner snaps his wrists to indicate the floor at his feet.

"So, no eggs?"

"No eggs, Wren," I say.

"For a lawyer, you are stunningly off-point," Banner says.

"That's because I'm hungry. And I'm tired. Your sister entered the barracks at three a.m. *actually* blowing a bugle."

My hands fly to my mouth, and Banner cracks a smile.

"You are welcome," Bekah says. "You think the snakes were a deliberate contribution?"

"These people *farm* snakes," Banner says. "And Wren, listen, this is a problem. I've been chomping at the bit to tell you." Banner goes for the guestbook. While Wren and I continue to cobble breakfast together, he reads the entries he has marked. Wren helps me less, the crazier the entries become, but it's not until Banner reads about how the snakes were *a gift for Isla*, that Wren stalks over to read it for himself.

"And this swatch," Banner adds, "matches a shirt that was hanging on a water pump at the Ridleys' house."

"He released *good* snakes," I call out.

"It's still *bizarre*, Isla," Wren snaps, and Banner says, "Thank you."

"He shouldn't have been here at all, freaking out our guests. But what concerns me right now is his fixation on *you.*"

"Right. And that's not all." Banner opens his laptop to show pictures: the booger mask, Jake's marked-out signature, the arrows aiming at my name, the snakes nailed to my roof. "He was outside Isla's bedroom window on the same night I arrived. Or someone was. But we can find out."

Banner clicks to open the WiFi settings and turns his computer for Wren's ease of use. "Do you mind giving me access to the security cameras?"

In the time it takes the confusion to wrinkle Wren's brow, a shockwave slithers down my neck. He has no more knowledge of those cameras than I do.

Banner uses his thumb to motion to the door. "The little cameras on the roof," he explains. "Can we——"

Wren's shaking his head, and I watch the same sense of unease take hold of Banner. He glances at me.

"Who installed the cameras, Wren?" he demands.

"There are no cameras."

"There *are* cameras. There is a camera pointed directly into your cousin's bedroom. Who is surveilling this house?"

It's Bekah who takes charge. "Show me," she says, and off they go, all three of them and Lucy too, out the front door. "I'll just stay here and watch the bacon," I say to no one. "Season the potatoes and stuff."

Through the kitchen window, I watch Banner point upward and then stomp out of sight, presumably to the outside of my bedroom. Wren's gazing up. He says something to Bekah who dials a number into her phone and hands it over for Wren to dial something else. I guess the first number is like calling the operator.

When they return to the house, Wren has his lawyer face on. "Sissy didn't have them installed. We disabled them. I left a message for Ash to get in touch with the friend who wrote in the book. I called the sheriff. He's going to visit the Ridleys, ask them some questions. I'll follow up with him and—I have to complete this trip." He says the last by way of an apology. "I'm bound by the Army."

"I understand, Wren."

"But I'll meet you back here as soon as I can drive from Florida —if you still mean to stay."

"I do."

"OK. I can be back as early as Sunday evening."

"I'm not worried." I kind of am, but this is my house! It took all the courage I had just to come back, and I'm not going to let what amounts to a few obnoxious pranks force me to leave. Anyway, I want to track down Inola and see what light she can shed on all this.

"Promise me you'll go to town at least once a day to check in with me," Wren says.

"I will."

"I'll have the sheriff come check in here too. You remember Billy Banks."

"Awwrrr, Wren," I whine. "I hate that guy."

"Why?"

"He *stole* the middle-youth baseball tournament," I remind him.

"He *stole* a base," Wren reasons. "Legally."

"*That's* debatable!"

"A decade ago."

"And then he gloated for the rest of the summer. I still can't figure out how *I'm* the one who got grounded!"

"You punched him in the *face!*"

Banner snorts.

"I was twelve."

During breakfast, it is decided that, despite my penchant for violence, the neighbors would benefit from hearing us firing weapons, so Wren retrieves a life-size deer target and produces earmuffs and ammo.

"I forgot how invested you guys were in this whole thing," I tell him.

It's loud. Jarring. I do not love the concussive nature of the sport. Still, I'm a pretty good shot. I mean, if we needed meat, I could get the job done. As long as someone else would dress it. 'Cause *ew.*

Jake would. Jake would skin it and gut it and boil the skull and all the shit. But it's not my thing.

I aim the shot, gun to my shoulder, eye to the sight.

"She's left-handed," Banner says.

Wren smirks. "Yeah, I know."

"It's hot," Banner tells him.

I'm giggling too hard to shoot. "Will y'all shut up?" I take the shot.

"Isla, you're good!" Banner says. "Why didn't you enlist?"

I bring the gun down, rubbing my shoulder where it's going to bruise from the recoil. "Because the pen is mightier than the sword."

Wren's eyes light up. "D'you bring your Sig?" he asks Banner.

Banner pulls it from his waistband.

"She's so tough," Wren says, turning it over. "I love the brown."

"It's coyote tan," both Banner and Bekah correct him. They're not even kidding. I may as well go inside. They're going to geek out over this stupid firearm for a while. "Magazine holds twenty-one rounds." Banner pops it out.

Bekah adds, "It's already set for optics—straight out of the box —laser, night—whichever brand you want."

"How'd you get to keep it?" Wren asks.

Banner just makes a face. "Shoot it," he tells Wren.

"Yeah?" Wren asks a few questions, points it, and shoots without even meaning to. "Shit!" He engages the safety and hands it back.

Bekah steps up. She is exceedingly confident with the weapon. She raises her arms and unloads five rounds into the heart of the target, one after the other. The slide ejects the brass remnants of each bullet and rolls back into place as it chambers another round.

"Here you go, Ees." Banner takes it from his sister. He goes through the mechanics—the safety, the chamber. Surrounding me from behind, he teaches me how to hold it, with a kiss on my neck, but since I'm a lefty, he has to think it through the opposite of what he's used to. "It's going to give you some recoil. Allow it. Cage your elbows." He squares me off. "Perfect. Squeeze when ready."

I miss the target but keep shooting. My third shot hits the fake deer's rump. My fifth hits the heart.

"Nice adjustment," Banner says.

I'm feeling pretty good about myself. I engage the safety and hand him the gun. "K, I'm gonna go inside. Have fun."

Banner's voice reaches me half an hour later. "Hey Babe, you wanna go up in the helicopter? Wren's gonna show me a lay of the land."

"No, you go ahead," I call. He finds me in my room straightening up. I think I became clutter-blind from drinking. I'm more productive when I don't.

"We won't be gone long." Banner kisses me on the mouth. "Or else I wouldn't go. He has to log so many take-offs and landings, you know?"

I lift my head for another kiss. "Can I read some of your blogs?"

"Sure. Yeah." He sets up his laptop for me. Tells me the password. "Read mercifully," he says.

"I won't have to. I want to live in the world through your eyes."

"Oh, gah!" Wren interrupts.

Banner winks at me and turns to go. As an afterthought, he says, "Come lock the door behind me, OK? I'll leave the Sig."

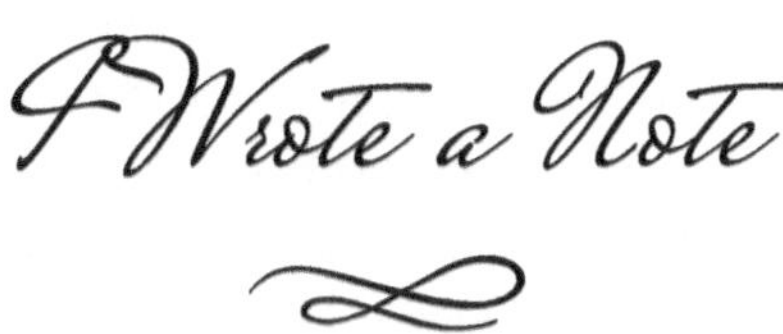

I Wrote a Note

BANNER TOLD me to read his blog mercifully because I edit other people's stories for a living (instead of having the courage to write my own as he does), but even if I wanted to judge his work, I wouldn't be able to. It's no wonder he's successful! He has a contagious excitement about every place he explores and its people. He's full of innocent wonder, and his humor makes me laugh out loud.

The more he extols the magnificence of each new place, however, the more I worry that *this* place is just another in the long line of amazing scenes he can leave for the next. I remember the way Wren asked it as if he'd half-expected as much: *Off to the next exotic location?*

Up till now, I've been reading through the digital folder of blogs labeled *Published*. It's the one he opened up for me. There are other folders: *Drafts, Pictures, Marketing, Potential Destinations*. And there is one marked *The Incinerator*.

Click.

The text here, as you can imagine from the title, is very different. It's less of a blog and more of a journal entry. It occurs to me that he wrote this during (or about) one of his tours on active duty. It starts in the middle of what must have been a horrific chain of events.

The night is dark, and the ground is hard. Sabina is crying in the corner. She thinks I'm asleep. Or she doesn't think about me at all. "Humans cry when they need to cry," she'd said. Not to me, but to a boy who was orphaned by the first attack. To save the boy's honor, Sayeed and I had stood off to the side like we weren't listening, Sayeed interpreting for me under his breath. The boy was devastated. I was too. And he was embarrassed. Anyone could tell he wanted to show the strength of a man. But finally, he gave in to Sabina's maternal affections and cried his eyes out while she held him in her arms. I wish I could have known such comfort.

I found poppies this morning. I was searching for a road out of this godforsaken place—something with the cover of trees to give us some protection, and what I found was a goddamn field of the most vibrant red poppies in existence. What right do poppies have next to the charred remains of a town that just two days ago sang with life?

Sabina calls them lalas. The flowers. I brought them to her the way Sayeed had done, but that only made things worse. She laid them on top of the shallow grave he's never going to rise from. The grave I dug.

No matter where I wander, inside or out, I can't escape the smell of smoke.

I measure my exhales to keep from breaking down. I don't know how I'm going to survive this. Even if I survive this.

I don't go to Sabina. I don't touch her. Don't squeeze her hand. Hell, if I look at her too long, she shirks it off like I'm trying to fuck her.

I half think that if I do fall asleep, she'll run away, and then she will be fucked.

And so will I.

God, help us.

But why the hell should she stay with me? What kind of man in her culture goes around clean-shaven as I do? Sayeed rocked that big, wiry beard. He'd claimed his religion demanded it, and the Army made allowances. But I'm just a baby-faced American kid who managed to get separated from his unit and keeps looking women in the eye (why aren't we supposed to again)?

Sabina's the only one of us who knows the way out. Of course, now I can't find out what she's saying, so I guess if she's going to continue to guide me, she's just going to have to point. And there's also the fact that if we ever do make it back, her only thanks will be a ruined reputation for the simple fact that she's traveling alone with a man.

Humans cry when they need to cry.

If that were true, I would be crying now, and I would never stop.

I glance around this bombed-out space that just this morning was a kitchen. I sat at a wooden table on this very spot, Sayeed taunting me from the window with a tiny cup of that jet fuel they call coffee. Taunting me with his huge, wiry-bearded smile.

Oh, Sayeed, my brother. Sayeed.

I don't even realize I'm saying it out loud, groaning it and rocking back and forth, my hands gripping my head to keep it from exploding.

My brother. My brother. My brother.

I can't stop the weeping now, and I do try. For Sabina's sake. For my own. I have to keep listening. I have to keep quiet. But I'm sobbing. Piteously. Fervently. The only strange comfort is how much the act of weeping hurts the new holes that were torn into my jawline. It should hurt. It should hurt as much outside as it does inside.

Sabina creeps over like a mouse. She doesn't face me, but she doesn't turn her back. She kneels toward the remnant of the outer wall and says quiet words—foreign words—but they are meant to soothe me. I regard her with a sniff, and she risks a look full into my face before I remember to drop my eyes. It's a weird place where humans don't touch.

She finds a cup of water, sets it on the floor in front of me, retreats to her corner.

"Thank you, Sabina."

She doesn't respond.

I pray to God that Bekah's OK. I pray for my mom and dad. I pray for a road home.

It's not until I hear the return of the helicopter that I come out of Banner's blog and realize my cheeks are wet. Is this what Eve felt like after she took that first bite, her eyes opened to the knowledge of good *and* evil? He's so cheerful, so hard to rumple. But he carries all this in his memory. I didn't *steal* it, did I? He didn't tell me not to eat from any of the trees.

I've been too focused on myself.

Wiping my eyes with the back of my hand, I scroll to see how much longer the article is, and I find pictures. A beardless Banner in Army fatigues with his arm around a soldier I imagine to be Sayeed. The fellow's beard *is* wiry. They both stand, chests puffed out, a hint of a smile in their eyes like they've been up to mischief. They were friends. Brothers.

Another picture shows Banner lying on a hospital bed, his head lifted so that the focus of the picture is the underside of his jaw, revealing jagged sets of sutures. The scars must be significant under his thick facial hair. Is that why he grows a beard now? To hide them?

"How did you get out of that dangerous place?" I ask the picture. "Did Sabina continue to guide you?"

I splash my face at the sink and walk out on the back deck, hands over my ears, to watch the helicopter land. It's not one of those huge, multi-bladed aircrafts. I'm sure they save those for career pilots. It's more like the ones they fly around here for the tourists.

I can see into the heli to where Banner is speaking with his hands, his face alight and animated. A sudden conviction plunks into place: *He's the one.*

Banner, Wren, and Bekah climb the stairs, and when Banner sees me, he runs at me without warning, tackles me onto a lounge chair, and kisses me all over my face while I'm laughing too hard to fend him off. Lucy bounces around trying to join in.

"I told you I'd come back," he says.

"And so you did."

He kisses me once more, soundly on the mouth. "Get used to it," he says and pulls me up. "I have to fix the map."

I don't know what map he means. He jogs inside and back out again with my sketchbook. When he opens it to reveal a full spread over both pages, I draw in a sharp breath. "Banner, you really are a cartographer! When did you do all this?"

"All along. I added to it while you were getting ready for bed last night." With the eraser end of the pencil, he thumps his drawing of the bridge. "It's passable now. We saw it from the air."

I knew it would be. I don't comment. Anyway, Banner is

pointing out all the other details he has sketched—from the house to the Ridleys, to the burial grounds and tree huts, to the cemetery, complete with fireflies. He has a stick figure with a ponytail waving a conductor's baton.

The river itself looks like a snake, slinking across the page.

"You even drew the treasure tree! Look at those tiny snake skeletons!" I squint my eyes to see more clearly. "Is there a little bearded man in there? Is that you?"

"That's what I drew in there for you to keep."

My heart. I raise a hand to it, but Banner begins to aggressively plow through a section of his graphite river with an eraser.

"Banner, stop it! What are you doing?"

"This isn't correct. It bends more like this. I studied it from the air."

"Wow. You are committed."

"You should see the map I've been drawing of *you.* I add more to it every time I get to explore."

Is he being serious? It's hard to tell because his head is bent in concentration. He chuckles under his breath.

Wren stomps out of the house and steals my attention with a kiss on the cheek. "Take care of yourself, Cousin. Check in with me."

"I will," I tell him. "Keep him in the air, Bekah."

"Don't worry." Bekah wraps me in an exuberant hug, which is...surprising. I almost don't hug her back. Then she smiles into my eyes in a searching way I can't interpret. "Take care," she says.

I find my voice. "OK. You too."

Banner acts half-exasperated and flicks his hands upward as if to ask, *Really?* But Bekah just laughs and hugs him as well. "See you over Labor Day?"

"I'll be there. Don't get called away."

"I serve at the pleasure of our Commander in Chief."

"Hey," Wren says to me. "Be strong, but be gentle with yourself. We'll follow up on Sunday."

Oh yeah. The reality of my...addiction? Is that what we're calling it? I just nod my head.

"It's good to see you back here," Wren adds. "We'll always have a home as long as this place is standing, right?"

"I don't know what I'd do without it. I love you, Wren. I hope you know it. I hope all of you know it."

His eyebrows dip. "Of course, we do. And you are loved by all of us. Mom included. We'll talk Sunday. Check in tomorrow, though."

"I will."

He heads down the stairs, and from about halfway, he calls, "Be nice to the sheriff when he comes!"

"As long as he admits what a big, lying cheater he is! And brings me my trophy!"

Wren waves. I don't watch them take off. I go to my room, sit on my bed, and envision the big bottle of whisky through the wooden door of my nightstand. Apparently, my cravings are triggered when the people I love leave. I don't want to be left by Banner too.

One shot would smooth out these turbulent feelings.

I'm not really a fool, though. One shot leads to two leads to five leads to eight.

A rap on the door puts an end to the argument.

"They're off," Banner says. "You OK?"

I shake my head.

"What's the matter, Ees?"

The mattress dips beside me as he takes a seat. In answer, I kick open the nightstand to reveal my stash. "I think *I'm* the one missing crucial skill sets necessary to be a grown-up."

"You want a drink."

"I do."

"It'll pass."

"It'll pass a lot faster if I drink."

He smiles at my joke, but says, "That's actually not true. You'll just get stuck in the loop."

"I know."

"Why do you want a drink?"

"Honestly?"

Banner scans the room. "That would be more helpful," he says.

Because I don't want our time to end. Because I don't want to lose all the sweet kisses, and the playful banter, and the powerful heartbeats. I don't think my own heartbeat is going to get the job done.

Instead of saying all that, I root around the closet. When I locate my beloved blue jeans, I toss them at Banner's chest.

"Because I love these blue jeans," I proclaim. "And if I could no longer wear these blue jeans, that would greatly distress me. Down in my soul. When you find a pair of jeans like this, you can't replace them. You can't pretend they don't feel great, or sag on your hips just right, or hug your ass in a way that shows how extremely well-sculpted it is."

Banner looks both bewildered and amused. "So, you want to drink for fear that you will no longer fit in your blue jeans?" He holds up the apparel in question.

"Kind of."

"Wouldn't drinking make it more likely that you *won't* fit? At some point?"

"You're not helping."

Banner gets to his feet, stalks over to me, jerks the waist of my joggers, and begins fumbling with the drawstring.

"What are you doing?"

"I want to see these fucking jeans," he declares. My joggers fall to the floor, and Banner opens the jeans, bends to assist. When I do not immediately step into them, he swats my leg. "Go ahead."

With a roll of my eyes, I comply, pulling the jeans up and buttoning them into place. I wave my hands with a flourish to let him know the task is now complete. He's chewing the inside of his cheek, studying me in the jeans. He twirls a finger in the air to direct me to spin around—which I do with an overwrought sigh because of course, this is not the real point—and I await his conclusion.

"Yeah, those are great, fucking jeans," he says, making me laugh.

He continues to examine me, tracing my bare skin with his fingers where the band rests on my hips, and he circles me to evaluate the other claims I've made. "I feel jealous now of anyone who has previously enjoyed you in these jeans. They're perfect. The shade. The length. The way they fall around your pretty, little feet. Why did it take you so long to—"

"*You* are the jeans, Banner," I snap.

"*I* make you want to drink?" I think I have boggled his mind.

"This is impossible," I say with a slap to my thighs for emphasis.

"Maybe if you would just tell me what you're thinking instead of comparing me to your pants." He grips my ass with both hands. "Not that I would *mind* being these pants. Pretty sure I'd always *fit*."

I swing my palms up. "That's all I'm saying."

"That I fit." He raises his eyebrows to ask if he's tracking. "That I fit you."

I nod. "And...I think it sucks that you're leaving. Even though I know it's your job, and I have no right to ask you to stay."

"I canceled my trip."

"What?"

"I did. From Bekah's phone. I called my agent and she's going to postpone the whole thing until you agree to come with me."

"You did?" And now my grin is spreading until I'm smiling like I'm the sunshine on cocaine.

"I did."

"Really?"

He chuckles and nods his head.

"Did you tell her why? Did you tell her you were too busy having a fling?"

Banner goes cold and sounds slightly alarmed when he says, "Is this just a fling for you?"

I make a face to show that I don't know what this is, and now he takes a step back. The silence between us is new. I don't like it. I wish I hadn't used the word fling.

"It's not just a fling," I tell him. "We have an easy connection. We have the same odd sense of humor. I've told you things I've never told anyone, and you don't seem to be afraid of them." I try to lighten the mood. "Plus, we're both just so *mmh*."

That earns me a small smile. Very small. And quickly gone.

I close the distance between us and force him to hug me by manually molding his stiff arms around me. He tolerates it for a few seconds but then drops them and falls to a seat on the bed. "My whole life has been a series of flings," he says. "I want roots as you have. I want an oak tree that keeps tokens of my story. I want *you* to keep them. And me to keep them for you."

I say, "I was just afraid that, now that the bridge to the real world is no longer underwater and you are free to go, an oak tree might prove too cumbersome a thing." I find myself itching for a pen. I do kind of gush in poetry.

He does too. He says, "All I have to do to be a part of your world is make a contribution. Right? That's what you said. Is that the rule or not? I'm giving you myself." He lifts solemn eyes and my heart about breaks. "If I'm such a good fit, then keep me."

"I don't have the right to—"

"I'm giving you the right." He stands up. "Until this whole, strange blue jeans conversation, you hadn't even said you *wanted* me to stay. You still haven't really."

"Will you stay?"

"Stop equivocating and tell me to if that's what you want."

"I want you to stay. I want you to stay with me. I don't want you to leave. That thought rips me up. You're not *allowed* to leave." I shake my head for emphasis. "You have to stay." Now I'm nodding. "How could you not know that?"

I can tell that Banner approves of the new role I'm acquiring. "Keep going," he says.

"And…I want you to kiss me," I demand. "You have to kiss me." I smile, and I expect him to, but he doesn't. He's staring too hard. The weight of his unflinching scrutiny wipes the smile off my face and stabs me with fear.

He closes the distance. If I didn't know better, I'd think he was angry. He is certainly stern. He kisses me so hard my legs go weak.

"What else do you want?" he asks.

"Um," I swallow, "would you like t—"

"Ees?" he growls.

I have to bite back a smile.

He says, "What. Do. You. Want?"

"I want you to make love to me," I declare, but I get nervous and add, "Will you?"

"Hell, yes." He pushes me onto the bed, stripping me of my perfect jeans. He's wild, but he's careful too. Loving. He fills me up. Feasts on the sight of me underneath him. And he talks to me. He tells me things he finds appealing, tells me the way I move is exquisite. Tells me to take anything I want.

I never felt all the sensations before—though, I've never been with Banner. I let myself go—chase the pleasure—which riles him up. In fact, everything I do riles him up.

When it's obvious that I'm close, he slows us down, tells me what it does to him to watch me lose it. It's the *way* he tells me that makes me come. He implores me to take it like *he's* gonna lose it. My cheeks flush. Sound goes dull. And when it swells through me I know I sound like it hurts, but it's the most beautiful feeling on Earth.

"*God,* Eesa." Banner clutches my neck until I'm through and kissing his shoulder in gratitude.

"You don't have to stop," I pant. "Let yourself come."

"Are you kidding me?" I can hear the smile through his words, though his head is buried next to mine. "Once you started whining like that? *God.*" His voice is deliciously spent. He rolls off of me and then invites me, with an upward nod, to give him a kiss, which I do. The kind of fleshy, satisfied, long kiss that means I own him.

While he tugs a strand of my hair, I watch his chest rise and fall and remember the words in his journal: *I measure my exhales to keep from breaking down.* But right now I'm the reason he measures them.

We lie on my bed, limbs entwined. Banner's stroking my arm, and I blurt out, "I love you," and promptly feel like a dope.

"Take it back," he says.

"What? No. Why?"

"I was just about to tell you that."

"I'm not going to take it back."

"Good. I love *you.* And for the record, I loved you first."

"When did you?"

"When you were explaining your oak tree treasures. Speaking of which, I want you to do something for me."

"This favor—it's the reason you seduced me, isn't it?"

"*Uh-huh,*" he confirms. "I want you to write my next blog. Show my readers this place through *your* eyes. And I'll just take pictures and ask you stuff. Maybe write a forward."

"I can't."

"Why not? Writers gotta write."

"For starters, your readers come to your blog for *your* writing. You're able to boil everything down to the most critical details. I'm too close to this place. I couldn't possibly—"

"I'll help you edit," he suggests. "We'll do a series. Isla, your passion for this place is infectious. You're a natural tour guide. They will *love* you."

Slowly, I say, "I could *try*, maybe."

"Yeah?"

"Maybe," I repeat. "You're really good."

"You dug it?"

"You transported me." My inner conflict must show on my face.

"Buuut?"

"Once I finished with some of the blogs in the published folder, I moved on." I bite my lip in apology.

"You opened *The Incinerator.*"

I nod.

"I didn't restrict you. I knew you might. Honestly, I wanted you to."

"I didn't get very far before you guys came back. But Sayeed was a very close friend, yeah? I saw a picture of the two of you together."

"You saw the pictures. Right." He knows what else I saw. He raises a hand to his jawline, and I follow the move, placing fingers on top of his.

"Were you shot?"

"Shrapnel."

"Where are the scars?"

He guides my fingers over each one, beneath his beard. Is it weird to find that sexy? "I don't know how noticeable they are at this point," he says. "I started growing a beard as soon as I could."

"To hide them?"

"No, actually. To honor Sayeed. We'd hit it off right away, back in Basic. He was brilliant. He spoke seven different languages and could master dialects and pick up the subtlest accents. You read about the days we were separated from our unit. He found Sabina —I still don't know how—or how he knew she'd be willing to guide us."

"Were they lovers?"

"No. But they told each other things Sayeed never bothered to translate for me." Banner smiles at that.

I think of how it felt when Banner said he wished he'd known Jake. "I wish I'd known Sayeed," I say. "Were you with him when he died?"

Banner nods. "A helicopter screamed in from nowhere. Same thing had happened the day before. That second time, they shot a fuel tank. Sayeed got trapped behind a burning wall of debris. I couldn't get to him. I'd been hit by then. I could hardly think. He burned to death."

"Shit, Banner. You watched it?"

"Pretty much. And heard it—which was worse."

"And smelled it," I add.

"And smelled it," he agrees. "Have been smelling it ever since." He kisses my temple, speaks against my skin. "It doesn't hold the power it used to. I took a deep dive into therapy. But it catches me off guard from time to time."

"How'd you get back to your unit?" I ask. "Sabina continued to help you?"

"Sabina was amazing. She marched us through the poppy fields and then miles of dust, though she walked about five paces behind me at all times, which my American ass found incredibly annoying. She would clear her throat when she needed my attention, and I'd have to turn around—without really looking at her, mind you, so it was difficult to read her expression—and then I had to figure out what I was supposed to do. At one point, she found a driver who was willing to take us to an Army checkpoint. And do you know who was there when we arrived, commanding her own unit?"

"Your sister?"

"My sister. I've never been so relieved in my life. I ran to her, swung her off her feet, and hugged her so tight she had to tell me to knock it off. Sabina looked shocked half-to-death. She asked if Bekah was my wife, and an interpreter told her that Bekah was my khâhar, my sister. Then Bekah realized I was injured, and I was spirited away to the clinic against my will. When that woman speaks, soldiers listen."

"What about Sabina?"

"Bekah took her back home herself so that her family wouldn't think less of her for having been with a man. I didn't get to say goodbye, and that really bothered me—not that we could have processed what we'd been through, what with all the language barriers and the damn social rules. But before I was flown out, Bekah led me to a private room where Sabina waited. She said one English word and pointed to herself to make me understand. 'Sister.' She said it twice and glared at my chest until I nodded. And then she paced over to me and hugged me and cried."

Banner's eyes are glassy. "That helped me," he says. His voice cracks when he says it.

"You ever going to publish that as a blog?"

He shakes his head. "That one's just for the inner circle."

Knowing he counts me as part of that circle makes me bold.

"There's a reason I've waited to look down The Hydraulic," I confess. "Besides the fact that it's a horrible memory."

"What's that?"

"My therapist is worried about what I might do there."

"Why? What could it hurt?"

I avoid his eyes, stare past his shoulder. "I wrote a note."

Pause.

"You did what?" Banner heaves himself onto an elbow. "You wrote a suicide note?"

"I was drunk. I couldn't stop crying. I couldn't stop fantasizing about it. Turns out, counselors take that kind of thing pretty seriously."

"And you came here by yourself anyway? What were you thinking? Are you still fantasizing about it?"

I shake my head, but the truth is I don't know. I mean, I'm not right *now*. But when I thought Banner was leaving, I worried about what might happen when I was all alone. And now instead of questioning that, I'm thinking about whisky. I roll over to face the wall.

"No way." Banner turns me back around. "Don't shut me out."

I've gone dark. I can feel it. He's right, it's like a switch gets tripped.

"Eesa, don't do that," he coaxes. "Not after what we just shared. That feels *terrible*."

His words cause me to blink back to reality. "You're right. That's shitty. I'm sorry."

He looks stricken. "Please say you would never kill yourself. You have to promise me. You'd kill me. None of the people in your life would recover."

"I would never do it. I promise."

"Come on." Banner sits up. "I want you to take me there right now. It's time to face it. That's why you're here, isn't it? Let's go. You and me. And we'll come back, and we'll make love in a hundred different ways, and you'll be OK."

It's not until this moment that I recognize the trap I've set for my love. "Banner, it's not your job to save me. Oh god, please don't think that it is. Please don't just stay here for the sake of sorting me out."

"Honestly, Woman, you can come up with more crooked paths than a corn maze."

"What?" I ask through the sudden urge to laugh.

"It's something they say in Indiana when someone's acting batshit crazy. I just want to be with you. Make love to you, cook with you, write with you. Let's go stare this waterfall down, do what you need to do, and then go do something mundane like shop for groceries."

I regard him for a long moment. "I like that my batshit crazy doesn't freak you out."

He flashes his eyebrows as if to say, *Good.* But something about the gesture makes me wonder if, to some small extent, he *is* freaked out. At any rate, he is more than willing to enter the fray on my behalf, and he has certainly been in scarier circumstances.

"You ready?" he asks.

Good question.

"Let's stay here a while longer."

A Great Big Lying Cheater

THE AFTERNOON SUN is still bright when I step out of bed naked. With Banner. Also naked. Despite the deep emotional revelations and soul-baring intimacies we've shared today, I am seized by an uncontrollable bout of giggles. It's mortifying. It's adolescent. The harder I work to suppress it, the stronger it gets until it escapes my pursed lips in wispy fits. Banner crosses his arms to wait it out with a curious smirk, but since he has no pants on, that just doubles me over.

"I'm so sorry. I don't know why it's funny." I hide my eyes. Clearly, *someone* is not used to being with a gorgeous, naked man.

"I'm not sure if I should question your sanity," Banner says, "or merely my physique."

"The former. You're perfect."

A sharp knock on the front door sets me straight but sends Lucy in circles. She barks her way out of the room while Banner pulls on his shorts and heads toward the door himself—probably because he suspects the visitor to be Jeremiah.

I throw on my blue jeans and try to quickly run a brush through my tangled hair. Wow. The things we did in bed really tied it into knots. And now I'm grinning at myself in the mirror.

It's a man at the door. I hear his deep voice. I can't tell what he's saying, but it doesn't sound like anything to be alarmed about.

My face is flushed. I press a fingertip to the apple of my cheek and pull away to reveal a white print that quickly gives back the pink. I'm vibrant. I'm freaking glowing. I need more of that man in my life.

He's staying. I can't help it, with the stupid grin. *He's staying.*

I walk lightly down the hall, and then—buzz kill. Taking up far too much space in my living room is a great, big, lying cheater. Sure, he has donned the uniform of a genuine law enforcement officer, but I see through the farce.

"Billy," I greet the sheriff with barely gated disrespect, and he performs a fake flinch, blocking his face from my potential left hook.

"That's funny," I say, walking between Billy and Banner to pour a glass of water. I do not offer it to our guest. I drink it myself and pour some more.

"Isla, you can't possibly still be sore about a baseball tournament we played when we were kids."

"I can," I inform him. "It's hard to forget the first time you were robbed. I do not enjoy being robbed. You"—I jab a finger his way—"are a robber. You're lucky Jake's not here to kick your ass."

"Jake's not ever the one I was worried about." Billy glances at Banner for backup which Banner does not give. *Cool.*

Sheriff Billy clears his throat. "Isla, I stopped by as a courtesy to Wren. It's my job to protect the people under my jurisdiction."

I *pff* and take another long drink. I drain the whole glass.

"Honestly," he grouses. "Are you having trouble here or not?"

"Not really," I say, but at the same time, Banner says, "Yes. Someone with a snake fetish has been harassing the occupants of this house. Wren said you'd look into it. Maybe take a ride to the Ridleys'."

"No one was home. I'll try again tomorrow. You can't call out from here?" He checks his own cell phone. "I guess not." Now Billy's surveying the room. He's probably casing it. His eyes snag on Banner's pistol.

"Whose is that?" he asks, and Banner raises a finger. Too bad it's not the middle one. "May I?" Sheriff Billy asks. He doesn't wait for permission but lifts the gun from the coffee table and turns it over. "It's not the consumer version. You military?"

"Eighty-second Airborne."

"Last to leave Afghanistan."

"I got out a little sooner than the rest. But yes. You're familiar."

"I'm just a fan. I joined the force right out of high school."

"Didn't you move away to be a big-city cop?" I ask. *Dammit. I didn't mean to show interest in the lying cheater.*

"I came back."

Obviously.

"Billy, is Inola still around?" I ask.

"She lives with her grandmother down Ochs Gulch. Takes care of her."

"I thought I saw her yesterday, here on the property."

"Do you want me to pay *her* a visit?"

"No. She was at the burial ground. Mammaw meant for the Cherokee to have it."

"Why don't we go there?" Banner suggests. "And we can show you the disturbing things we found."

I stare a hole through my lover and I *know* he feels it. *Why are you suggesting we spend more time with this man?* I think at him. He ignores me.

"I'm sure the sheriff has better things to do," I say aloud. "Anyway, the go-kart is only a two-seater."

"We can take my truck," Banner offers. "It has four-wheel-drive."

He knows good and well that does not solve the problem. I can tell by the impish gleam in his eye. I narrow mine menacingly.

Sheriff Billy doesn't seem to notice any of this. I'm not sure he's the best person for solving the area's crimes.

"Sure," he says. "Let's see what there is."

You can imagine my eye roll.

But we go.

Billy drives us in the police SUV, and it stinks. "What is that smell?"

"Fertilizer." Billy spots me in the rearview mirror.

"How big is your garden?" The window has no controls because where I'm sitting is made for prisoners.

Thankfully, we arrive before I suffocate and hike through the burial mounds past the quietly flowing river—which I do not care to share with Billy Banks, but there you go—to the tree huts.

"How much do you rent *these* for?" he asks.

"We don't. They're just for fun. Just a summer project Asher came up with."

When we climb the ladder to where our signatures decorate the wall, mine with the arrows aimed at it, the booger mask and the sleeping bags have been removed.

"Smells like someone's been burning incense," Billy says.

"Doesn't smell as bad as your truck," I mutter.

"We found bundles of herbs packed inside of some sleeping bags," Banner tells him.

"How many sleeping bags?"

Banner holds up two fingers. *Now, if we can just get him to put down the first one...*

Billy considers the symbol around my signature. "It's Cherokee," he says, more as a question than a statement.

"I think so. There was a booger mask as well."

"Is it threatening?" Banner asks.

Billy shrugs. "Looks that way. Makes sense, if someone is upset that tree houses have been erected over sacred ground."

"Why would my name be the only target?" I spout. "I wasn't the only one to sign our work."

Billy considers the rest of the names and rubs the gouged wood where Jake's signature used to be. Maybe he's a better detective than I give him credit for.

"There were questions surrounding Jake's death," he says, which proves to me that he *does* suspect the empty space to have held my cousin's name. "I heard he was buried without so much as a certificate of death."

It takes a length of three blinks for me to respond. "What were we supposed to do? The bridge was flooded. We weren't going to wait until his body wreaked. It was perfectly legal." I really don't know *how* legal it was—not to have the death certified—but I do know that we were allowed to bury him on the property. He was already stiff by the time our dads and Asher got the casket done. I asked them to fell the treasure tree to make it, but they said that would take too long.

Billy raises his hands in a gesture of surrender. "I'm just asking questions. Was that Jake's signature?"

I nod my head sulkily.

"Why is it marked out?"

"I don't know."

"*Who* marked it out?"

"I don't know."

"Do you know *when* it was marked out?"

"Billy, is it not clear that I don't know anything about it?" I snap. "I haven't been up here since Jake died, so—sometime in the last four years."

"*How* did he die?"

I huff. "Surely you know he was drowned in the river."

"He was a great swimmer. Strong kid too."

"He was only two years younger than you. *How* are you already the sheriff again?"

Billy ignores that. "Were you with him?" He answers his own question. "Of course, you were. Who else was there?"

"I wasn't up top with him when he jumped. Nobody was. Well, Jeremiah Ridley may have been."

That seems to interest him. "What do you mean 'may have been?' How could you not know?"

"This is *not* what you were called here to investigate. Why are you being such a pest?"

"Why are *you* having so much trouble filling in the gaps?"

Banner squeezes my hand in the same gentle way he tells me to settle down sometimes.

I get the message—and I know that Sheriff Billy is just asking questions. But his questions are riding my nerves. I stretch the collar of my shirt. Maybe this prickly irritation is what it feels like to have withdrawals kick in. I cross my arms to keep from fidgeting, and I school my voice.

"Jake climbed a waterfall. I could see *him*, but—actually, there was a good amount of time in which I couldn't see him."

I think about my scared Jake dream in light of the fact that he was out of my view for so long. Where was he during that time? And now I forget about going back to The Hydraulic to seek closure. I want to go back to investigate.

As if we're of the same mind—*ew*—Sheriff Billy says, "Let's go there. See what else you can remember."

Banner's eyes fall on me, and I know what he's thinking—he and I would already be at the top of The Hydraulic if Billy hadn't shown up.

"The place Jake died is pretty emotional for her, as you can imagine," Banner says. "Maybe now's not the best time."

"We can always go tomorrow, Isla," the sheriff suggests. And to Banner, "I hear you'll be out of here by then." He might as well have said, "I hear you'll be out of my way by then."

A few seconds go by with Banner and Billy simply eyeing one another. I'm well-versed in testosterone, as I've spent a large portion of my life in the presence of three male cousins. But I'm not sure what there is to be testosteroney about. Usually, there's something to possess. And before you say it's me, it's not. Billy has never shown interest in me. As far as I can tell, the only thing he lusts after is winning.

Banner turns his back on Billy, uses his body to curtain me off, and blocks me from Billy's view. "What do you need right now?" he asks. "What does your gut say?"

On the other hand, Banner genuinely cares about the well-being of people and the world at large. Trophies don't motivate him.

"I want to go," I tell him. "Maybe Billy, with his training, can help us make some sense of things."

I know. It hurts me to say it.

"OK. Let's go." Banner re-includes the sheriff. But from the corner of my eye as I'm walking out, I see Banner stop Billy with a hand on his shoulder, and under his breath, he says, "Just so we're clear, I'm not going anywhere. I'll be here with Isla for as long as she stays."

WE CAN'T JUST DRIVE to The Hydraulic. The path doesn't allow for it. So, we park the cruiser back at the house in favor of bikes, and by the time we get to The Hydraulic, I've had the chance to doubt every memory and every dream I've ever had about that horrible day. Especially the one where I see myself at the top. Dream or memory? Except for the fact that it's impossible for me to be in two places at once, I wouldn't be able to say.

We leave our bikes by the pool in the same spot Jeremiah had pushed me down that day. I'd watched him wade back in to recover Jake's body where the water runs fast, but eddies out onto a shallower bank. The same desperation I'd felt then stings me now, but I don't linger on it.

"Jeremiah deposited me onto the shore there." I show them where.

"So, you did know Jeremiah was around."

"Well, yeah, afterward. My memory is a bit scattered. It's possible that he jumped in from up there where Jake did." Stooping to splash the back of my neck, I say, "There's a path just to the side that leads to the falls."

Up the steep trail, we trudge. First I go, then Banner, then Billy. The last time I traveled it, I was jogging behind Jake, begging him to come home. When we get to the *middle-look*, as we dubbed it, where I'd refused to go any further, we can see both down into the pool and up to where the water makes its appearance at the top of the falls. It's not as loud today, but we still have to raise our voices to be heard.

"Jake climbed from here. He stood up top and yelled at me." We all lift our eyes to the sharp ascent and then lean over to look into the bubbling water where it crashes into the pool. I can see no less of Jacob Miller now than I could once he'd gone under, and I am seized by the compulsion to explore the place where he launched himself.

"We have to climb," I say. "We have to boulder the steep wall beside the falls. It's not difficult. The holds are good." I start up with Banner close behind. I don't know if Billy will climb or not. I don't really care.

It doesn't take long. As I said, the holds are good. Banner and I stand—and soon Billy does as well—panting a bit, overlooking the river. "A few days ago," I say, "when we visited the Ridleys for eggs, we were just across the water there and beyond the underbrush."

It's a bit anti-climactic. I don't feel the big, heavy sense of moment that I thought I would. Jake leaped from here tens of times, and I did too. He had no business trying it that day, with the water as rough as it was. But as I gaze into all the river's moving might— it's not demonic. It's just our beloved river. It doesn't wield the sinister energy or the raucous chaos it did that day.

"You see that ledge?" I ask Banner. "That's where we were just now."

"You *jumped* from there?"

"Yeah. When he didn't surface."

"What more could you have done?"

"I could have followed him up here, could have seen what he'd seen. Even if I couldn't have stopped him from jumping."

Banner slides a hand around my back and into the front pocket of my jeans. "How are you doing with it?"

"I'm good." And I really am. I give him a grateful, if somewhat crooked smile and set my mind on what secrets might be hiding in plain sight. What could have excited Jake to the point of crying out for his older brothers?

I sort of forget about Billy, but as I turn my back to the falls, he's hulking over me, and I physically start, which irritates me. "Back up," I say.

A look of scorn crosses his features, but he glances at Banner and it's gone so fast I doubt I've seen it. The muscles in his jaw flex, and he steps back.

"What was that?" Banner mutters.

"You say you weren't up here?" Sheriff Billy asks.

"Right," I answer, but I'm feeling uneasy. "Only in my dreams, sometimes, I can see myself up here. I'm not myself. I mean, I'm not inside myself in the dreams. And I'm—I don't know—able to like—fly."

Billy stares at me blankly. "OK. And then your cousin yelled something, but you couldn't make it out."

"I think he was calling for help."

"From what?"

"I don't know."

"This is what you remember or what is in your dreams?"

"Dreams," I admit.

"OK. And then he fell."

I hesitate. "And then he jumped."

"That's what I mean." Billy scans the area once more and slaps his thighs with a conclusive thwack. "Well, I guess that's that. There's nothing more to see up here. Jake always was a wild son-of-a-bitch."

"Hey," Banner chides him.

"Nah, it's true," I agree. "I mean, not about Aunt Rose. She is a lovely woman, but Jake was wild."

"Are we done here?" the sheriff asks.

Not really.

I march upstream and cross the river where the rocks make a pathway.

"There's nothing to see," Billy raises his voice to reach me.

"So, you said," I call over my shoulder. I can hear Banner tell him something, maybe to give me a second, but what Billy says in response I can't make out.

The ground is rockier on this side, and the foliage blocks the sound of the falls. I shrug between two briar bushes and into a small clearing that I vaguely recognize, though it has been cultivated with great care since I was here last.

I come to an abrupt halt. I'm not alone.

About ten yards away, Jeremiah stands with his back to me. He's wearing an old-fashioned, white smock—the kind I imagine Pa to have worn in the Little House books—the kind I imagine the ghost to have worn from the description in the cabin's guestbook.

Jeremiah holds himself eerily still with his head bowed and his hands clasped in front of him. Beyond him, is the entrance to a narrow path that has been manicured through the trees. From where I watch, I can't see where it leads.

I should turn around—should get back home or at least make sure Banner and Billy are close behind. But the wind blows through the trees and, from that narrow pathway, a flash of gold catches my eye. Curiosity gets the better of me. I try to decipher what it is. I take two steps forward, eyes uplifted, quieter than a ladybug, when I am inexplicably struck across the chest by a strong arm that checks me like a seatbelt.

I gasp and try to make sense of what has happened. At my feet, the ground in front of me falls away. I have nearly plummeted into the deep pit that Jake found all those years ago. I whip my head to identify whom I have to thank for keeping me on solid ground. But my gratitude is devoured by fear when I come face to face with the feral eyes of Mr. Ridley.

Up close like this, it's easy to see where Jeremiah gets his bulk. Mr. Ridley is far younger than I realized, and he's clutching a large, bloated, burlap bag that is writhing with its contents—one guess, right?

Ridley's lips tighten into an unsettling smile. He reaches for my cheek, but I instinctively bat his hand away. His smile dies. His eyes go cold.

"What are you doing out here, Girlie?" He grabs my ponytail with enough force to jerk my chin upward.

"Stop," I say, but I can't hear myself.

Mr. Ridley pulls harder and traces a line across my throat. Now the heavy bag full of live snakes bumps my chest, and the graying stubble of Mr. Ridley's beard scratches my cheek. I hold my breath. He smells like the chicken yard.

"Let go of me." I'm shaking so hard, that my voice sounds like it's vibrating.

"A ram caught by its horns," he says. With more volume, he adds, "The LORD has provided the very ram we needed. Is this what you were praying for, Jeremiah? A sacrifice?"

I can't move my head, but I can hear Jeremiah stomping around the pit, and then nothing except air, and I swear I think he is flying. The next thing I know I'm winded as he shoves me to the ground. At the same time, Banner yells out. He's crashing through the undergrowth.

Jeremiah doesn't seem that interested in me. In fact, knocking me to the ground may have just been collateral damage. He has barreled into his unsuspecting father and now they roll, one over the other, three times around from the force of his blow.

Jeremiah hops up and flees into the woods as soon as they stop rolling. His father is screaming at him and clawing to his feet when Banner reaches him and kicks him in the side. "Stay down!" He looks as ferocious as he sounds, and he towers over Mr. Ridley, slightly out of breath. Without turning to me, he says, "Ees?"

"I'm OK," I barely whisper. I crane my neck to try to locate Jeremiah.

The sheriff catches up to us. He gapes at Mr. Ridley who is bleeding from the corner of his mouth. His burlap bag must have been thrown into the pit when he was tackled because it is rattling noisily at the bottom.

"This man *attacked* Isla!" Banner tells the sheriff.

Mr. Ridley is glaring at Banner with what at first looks to be fear but gives way to condescension. He wipes his mouth with the back of his hand and says, "You're not a Miller."

I risk a glance. The snakes, some of which have slithered out of the bag, are now exploring the walls of the pit. I hope they're not good climbers.

Mr. Ridley spits a mixture of blood and saliva onto the ground. "Get off my land," he says and now he rises to his feet. "Billy, get them off my land."

"*Arrest* him," Banner counters. "Did you see what he was doing?"

"Looks like he answered for it," Sheriff Billy says.

I don't think Billy saw what happened. I think he suspects Banner to have fought with Mr. Ridley, and not Jeremiah.

"You're all trespassing," Mr. Ridley says.

"It doesn't give you the right to *attack* a woman!" Banner counters.

Billy raises his hands in a calming gesture. "Why don't we all take a step back?"

But Mr. Ridley says, "Why don't we all put it to the test?" The sudden silky quality of his voice makes me nauseated. "Let the righteous emerge victorious."

"Ridley, you are not allowed to use poisonous snakes to test *anything*," Billy says. "How many times do I have to remind you of that?"

"God's word is my authority."

"Yeah, well so is the actual law. And the State of Tennessee says it has been illegal since 1947."

Ridley starts spewing Bible verses—not the ones about loving-kindness. Actually, I'm not sure if they're from the Bible at all or just some deranged list of his own contrivance.

I now feel certain that Jake stumbled upon a scene like this. I have questions.

The men are bickering, but I'm searching for Jeremiah. When the wind blows again and I catch that same hint of the bright gold color I'd seen earlier. I step sideways as surreptitiously as I can so that I can gaze straight down the path. It's the form of a serpent, intricately carved, lifted high onto the arms of an iron crucifix. And there is Jeremiah's face, peering out from his hiding place between the leaves. I don't react because he's shaking his head, and I think he's telling me not to.

"Isla? Banner?" Sheriff Billy says. "Go on back. I'll call on you later."

"Are you sure?" Banner asks.

"Yep," the sheriff replies curtly.

"Stop by the house on your way out," Banner says.

"Go on, now."

We climb back down, and once I've mounted my bike, I glance back to find Banner staring up at the waterfall.

"Are you worried about him?" I ask.

"A little bit. I guess the sheriff knows what he's doing." He follows my lead and points the bike toward the path.

"Do you think Mr. Ridley tests his own son by trapping him in that horrible pit with poisonous vipers?" I'm not sure I want the answer.

Banner doesn't give it to me. "I don't know. But Jeremiah's huge. He'd be hard to push around."

"He hasn't always been huge," I say. "Can you imagine the trauma a kid would carry into adulthood if he was subjected to that kind of torture?"

"Yeah, I guess you don't willingly fight your own dad, especially when he's made your life one big mind-fuck."

"But he stood up to his dad for me just now. He rescued me. Maybe that's why he ran."

"It looked to me like he knocked your ass to the ground." Banner straddles his bike, but he doesn't kick off. "*Gah,* it makes me mad all over again."

A shiver runs through me along with the queasy remembrance of how close Mr. Ridley was to me, and how awful he smelled while I stood there helpless with my head jerked back. "What do you think Mr. Ridley had in mind to do to me?"

Banner turns his face away, but not before I see the sneer of revulsion. I guess he doesn't want to say.

I bet Jeremiah knew what his dad had in mind.

BACK HOME, Banner and I remain on the lookout for Sheriff Billy. We even make dinner for him, such as it is, having been unable to make our shopping date a reality. When he doesn't show up, we save him a plate.

"He has to come back this way," Banner worries. "His truck is here."

Banner can't sit still. He paces the porch. Sometimes he leans against the wall for a moment.

"The cicadas are loud tonight," I comment.

He hasn't heard me. "We should have waited on him," he declares.

"There are other ways out," I offer. "He could have crossed the water with the bike and found the road. He'll come tomorrow."

Banner shakes his head. "Ridley was angry. Worse. He was self-righteous."

"Billy's trained for these sorts of things."

"So was I."

Oh.

"Sayeed," I say, and Banner slowly turns to me with a furrowed brow.

"I know what men will do when in the name of God."

I hold my hands out to him. "Come to bed. Let Lucy keep watch."

From under his eyelids, he gives me a small but grateful half-smile and allows me to guide him inside. We shower and make love and fall asleep.

Sometime in the middle of the night, Lucy barks us awake, and Banner goes to the window, his pistol in hand, to see the sheriff's SUV pulling out of the drive. "I guess we'll find out more tomorrow," he says. He's relieved. I can tell.

We relax back into bed in the dark. I love the way the bed creaks as he settles in. And the feel of his breath on the side of my head.

"We can sleep in one of the rooms for grown-ups," I volunteer. "There are comfy kingsize beds."

"Am I crowding you?"

"No, not at all. I love it."

"I like your bed. Tell me more happy things about this place. Tell me about your grandfather."

So, we lie together like we have a history that predates our actual meeting, like the fact of us is true, like the future of us is certain.

"Pap grew award-winning sunflowers. They were so tall I couldn't reach them on tippy-toe. But they would bob and bow to me and would share me around like a dance partner at a ball. He grew potatoes, turnips, snap peas... One year, he grew strawberries. But only the once. He said they were too obstinate."

Banner makes a small noise that is either proof he is listening or proof he is not. It's a tired, content, masculine sound that reaches the core of me.

"Every morning," I continue, "Pap drove the tractor across the bridge to the end of the driveway to check the mail and retrieve the newspaper. He worked the crossword every night while he enjoyed four saltine crackers and two chocolate kisses. I don't think his knack for moderation fell into my share of the gene pool."

Banner's breathing deepens. He makes no more attempt to keep up with my reminiscing. I trace his features in the dark. His ear, his cheekbone, his nose. "I love you," I whisper and allow myself to feel grateful, and heavy, and full, as I fall asleep beside him.

Jeremiah's Lamb

ON FRIDAY MORNING I come awake with a deep inhale and the beautiful, swelling appetite that comes from the soft brush of Banner's beard against the inside of my thigh. He takes his time—and resists my efforts to help—building me up until he has me fisting the sheets to keep myself anchored for him. I can hardly bear it, but if he stops, I swear I'll cry.

Finally—mercifully—he enters me, soothes me until I break like a wave, and I think maybe I die. But the heavy, slow way he seeks his own small death resurrects me.

We hold each other until we can both breathe again, and Banner says, "You seemed to have enjoyed that."

I don't open my eyes. "You're gloating."

"A little bit," he smiles and kisses the side of my head. He deserves to gloat.

I press further into his arms. "I'm not at all sure I'm going to survive you," I tell him.

"The feeling's mutual."

And so, we enter Friday—the day he would have been leaving—one of us smug and both of us smitten.

"Welcome to day three," he says.

It takes me a second. "Without alcohol?"

"AF, Baby." When it's clear that the only AF initialism I recognize doesn't fit the context, he says, "Yes. Alcohol-free."

"Ah. That's me. AF AF."

"How do you feel?"

"At the moment? Fantastic." We're a tangle of limbs. "I'm pretty sure you're making this easier than it should be. I think we may have discovered a new model for rehab."

The laughter that emanates from Banner's chest, rumbles against my palm. I love it so much. I feel a sort of loss too. I'm not sure why. It occurs to me that when you do this right, you *do* give your heart away.

"Why are you looking at me like that?" he asks.

"I want this to last."

As if it is proof enough, Banner comically scans the disheveled bedclothes around us.

"Yeah, but sex in and of itself doesn't make it last."

"It doesn't *hurt*," he counters.

"What if it does? What if—"

"Hey, Corn Maze," Banner interrupts. "It's not *sex in and of itself.* It's me making love to you and you making love to me. Right? I'm here. I care about you. The only real—" He cuts himself off.

"What?"

"The only real roadblock I can't get past is if you're not ready to give up drinking because—"

"I am. I was before you showed up."

He pins me with a playful, but skeptical stare and squishes me underneath himself to reach over and fling the nightstand door open. There's the bottle. The message is clear. If I were ready to give it up, it would be gone.

"I haven't touched it since—" Since I acted atrociously. And demeaned him. And ordered him out of my house. And that was not even seventy-two hours ago. "I'll throw it out."

"And the one in the closet?" he asks.

"How do you know about the one in the closet?"

He's snickering before I'm finished speaking. "I don't. I just guessed." In a more somber tone, he says, "I'm crazy about you, Ees. But I can't commit to this long term if you're not ready to be sober, OK?"

Well, shit. "What if I fuck up? Are you just going to leave me?"

"No, Baby, just—I can't stay, though. I can't allow it back into my life. I'm no good that way."

"I'll get rid of it."

"But it has to be for you. Because *you* want it."

This is how Bilbo felt when Gandalf suggested he give up the ring. I'd be relieved to have it gone. And yet...

"I'll get rid of it," I say again. And I will. And I should. And I could right now. But I don't.

OCHS GULCH IS a place where the mountains collide, where the base of one has been rammed into another. It creates a jagged road that calls to mind the picture I saw of Banner's chin riddled with sutures. The very earth here is scarred.

Small houses dot the road, and many are falling apart. Some of the roofs collapse down into the living spaces. The carports lean sideways. There are yards strewn with appliances and the rusting skeletons of ancient automobiles.

"Are we still going the right way?" Banner asks. "I'm feeling the Deliverance vibe again."

"It's a poor place," I tell him. "It's not always easy to make repairs or to have cars towed away. The younger generations tend to move to bigger cities." I point over the dash of Banner's truck. "Take the road to the left."

"That?" he says. "Is not a road."

"Well, take it."

"Does it even have a name?"

"I don't know, Ban, but it's the way to go."

The gravel driveway winds narrowly through the woods but soon opens out onto pastures bordered by wooden fence lines. "Now, *this* is more like it," Banner says.

We pass a picturesque pond and stop to allow a family of ducks to cross the road. There's a large, red tractor slowly mowing one of the fields.

"My pap's tractor is like that," I say. "Except his is Volunteer orange."

"Is? Present tense? You still have it?"

I preempt the next request with, "Yes, you can drive it."

"Thank you."

When this lane ends, we turn left, past a golden field of wild-flowers, and we come to a small, white cottage, humble but neat, with window boxes boasting vibrant geraniums. There's a front porch with nothing but a concrete slab to make it so and a free-standing swing. It is upon that which Inola's grandmother sits.

She's aged since I saw her at Mammaw's funeral. Her grey hair is tied back with a ribbon. She's wearing a long, floral-patterned house dress, and her round eyes are hooded with deep, friendly wrinkles.

"Osiyo?" she calls in Cherokee and shades her eyes.

"Osiyo, Grandmother. It's Isla, Mossy Miller's granddaughter. You remember?"

"Have mercy," she says under her breath. "Come here, child. Who have you brought with you? Have you gone and found your-self a husband?"

I nearly stammer through the introduction, as distracted as I am by the thought of Banner as my husband. *This is my husband. This beautiful, kind, bearded man is my*—"This is Banner Kirk."

"Come closer, young man." She opens and closes her wizened hands. "You're not from around here. I don't know any Kirks."

"I'm from all over," Banner says. "My dad's an Army man."

"But now you've found Isla, and you'll want to settle down."

"Is it that obvious?" he says with overwrought concern that makes her chuckle.

"Old grandmothers know things," she says.

Now that we're on the porch, Grandmother reaches for him, and he takes her outstretched hands to brace her so that she can rise to her feet. "Doesn't he look like—" She makes a motion with her bony wrist as if snapping a whip.

"Like Jake," I remind her. "Like our Jacob. He does at first."

"You're a friend of the Cherokee," she says and taps the necklace I gave to him.

"Do you mean that those were made by a Cherokee craftsman?" I ask.

"Certainly. Whether by blood or by love."

"Do you have any idea where they were purchased?" I ask.

"I doubt very much that these were sold. If the craftsman was careful with traditions, the stones have been sanctified. Where did you get them?"

In answer, I present my own bracelets to her. "A new strand appears every year for my birthday, in the hole of a tree where we keep childhood treasures."

"Well, then you are blessed and protected."

"Grandmother, I want to introduce Banner to Inola. Is she around?"

"She's out back with the lambs. Go and find her."

As we walk around the side of the house, Banner says, "Maybe I should wait here. I don't want to startle her again."

"No, come with me. She won't be afraid of you now."

"Do you smell that?" he asks and sniffs outside an open window. "It's the herbal smell from the tree huts."

"This is where I know it from! Grandmother uses it in a cleansing ritual. And there's Inola."

We see her walking beside a shed, holding the smallest of lambs in her arms. "Inola!" I wave in big arcs to be as disarming as possible. She smiles, but I don't think she recognizes me until we get closer.

"Isla, is that you?!" She focuses past me onto my companion. "And you...I saw you in the woods."

"I look a lot like somebody else, huh?" Banner winks like they're sharing a joke.

"Oh, I'm so embarrassed," she says using the lamb to cover her eyes. "I don't even believe in ghosts. Or I didn't until you came barreling down that slide."

"I should've announced myself. I'm Banner."

Inola hugs me with one arm and then hands me the lamb to shake hands with Ban. Meanwhile, the lamb looks into my face and bleats with precious, young, lamby sounds.

"Oh, I think I need one now!" I exclaim.

When Banner pets its ears, it bleats at him too. It has a soft, black nose and a pink tongue that is wholly visible when it speaks up.

Its mother is grazing nearby, and she is spotted in a peculiar way that is familiar to me. "Inola, I swear I've seen that exact sheep before."

"You have. She used to follow Jeremiah around when she was as small as this. I tease him that he must have been a good mama, for her to have learned how to do it."

"I wondered what had become of her."

The baby bucks and, though I scrabble to catch him, he jumps right out of my arms. "Oh no!"

"He's fine," Inola assures me.

He makes a clumsy dash for his mama, but he can't get to her through the fence, so he bleats piteously until Banner strolls over to pick him up. Now Banner is making faces at him and gently bleating his own high-pitched tones of comfort.

We are definitely going to need a lamb.

When the conversation stalls out and Banner notices that Inola and I are both gawking at him, he says, "What? He's cute. Are you keeping him? It's Isla's birthday tomorrow."

He's probably joking, but I say, "You're going to help me raise him, right?"

"Yeah, I'm not the baby-daddy type. Do you think he and Lucy will get along?"

While I'm nodding, Inola says, "Do either of you know anything about raising sheep?"

Banner and I question each other silently. We both shake our heads.

"Do you have some land?" she asks.

Again, we regard one another and admit that we do not. Banner doesn't know the first thing about where I live—it does not have land—and all I know about his place is that it's missing half its roof.

Inola probably assumes that we've been together for more than —almost—a week. Why else would we be discussing the co-adoption of this creature?

"So, maybe we'll put a pin in that idea," she says, "and come back to it once you've had a better chance to think it through."

"OK, but we're really bonding over here," Banner says.

The lamb screams in his face, causing him to frown, and he lowers it into the fence to be with its mother.

"Why didn't Jeremiah want her anymore?" I ask Inola.

"Are you kidding? She's practically his daughter. His father was going to butcher her a few years ago, so Jeremiah told his dad she'd been attacked and killed. Can you imagine him having to eat her? He comes to care for her most days. And he pays for all of her food and vet bills."

I raise my eyebrows to say to Banner, *see? Jeremiah's a good guy.* He placates me with an unimpressed nod.

"You and Jeremiah are pretty tight, then?" he asks Inola.

"We were always friendly."

"Were you always sleeping-together-in-a-tree sort of friendly?" he asks.

"Damn, Banner," I pipe up. "Don't beat around the bush, man."

Inola doesn't mind. She's laughing a pretty, girlish laugh. "No," she admits. "That's more of a recent development. His dad is kind of...strange."

Banner snorts in agreement.

"And my grandmother is—well, we just don't have anywhere to hang out. I hope you don't mind, Isla."

"Hang out all you want. Hey, it doesn't bother you that we built our tree huts so close to the burial ground, does it?"

"Are you not listening?" Banner asks. "She is quite enjoying the tree huts."

"Banner!" I chide him, but Inola giggles. How does he get away with that shit?

He says "Inola, there's a symbol drawn on one of the walls. Two arrows aimed at Isla's signature."

"Jeremiah drew it. He has nightmares that Isla is being ripped apart by violent storms or scratched by a briar."

Those two threats don't seem to be in the same league. "Scratched by a briar?" I ask.

"It's a euphemism. It's bad luck to talk about being bitten by a —" Inola waves her hand in a zig-zag pattern to indicate a snake. "And worse to have nightmares about it."

"Are you sure Jeremiah's nightmares aren't fantasies?" Banner asks. "The symbol looks threatening."

"Arrows can mean different things depending on context." Inola tugs her shirt to reveal a tattoo above her hip bone. "This broken arrow is a symbol of peace. See how the sharp end is pointed at the feathers of the tail end?"

The tat reminds me of the snakes above my window, one mouth biting the rattle of the next.

Inola kneels down to draw with a stick in the dirt. "When arrows face each other like this, they do indicate aggression, and when a circle is drawn between them, like this, it stands for any evil thing we can't define. But whatever is placed *inside* that circle, Isla's name, for instance, is guarded, because the arrows are aimed at the evil surrounding her. It's a symbol of protection."

I resist the temptation to look over my shoulder for all the evil that is apparently surrounding me. "Why me?" I ask. "Why not Sissy? Or Wren?"

Inola chews her next words. "You were there when Jacob died, right?" she asks. "Jeremiah won't say a word about it. But he obsesses over your well-being like there is a threat against you. Or like—I don't know how to say it—like he believes himself to be the threat somehow." She glances apologetically from my eyes to Banner's. "He does all sorts of religious rituals. I think he worries Jacob might seek revenge on him."

I feel Banner's sidelong stare, but I ignore it. "What happened up there, Inola?" he asks.

"I honestly don't know. Something that truly haunts him. It

doesn't help that Grandmother fills his head with wild tales about the storm gods and how they punish people. He believes he should have drowned that day instead of Jacob. He wants to make it right. But how can he?"

"I need to speak with him," I say. "Do you know where I can find him?"

She shakes her head. "If you wait around long enough, he's bound to show up here, but he's not always aware of the clock. Except for church. When he's not trying to appease his father, he's trying to appease God. If you really want to talk to him, you can find him on Sunday."

"Which church? The brick one next to the old school?"

"No, the one that looks like a bomb shelter—down where those massive oak trees sprawl over the road. On the way to Elkmont."

"Does no one here know the names of the streets?" Banner muses.

"I know the one you mean," I say. "Maybe we will go. Have you ever been to a service?"

"Me?" she coughs. "No. If there's anything those old, white folks hate worse than sin, it's Indians."

"No offense taken," I say.

"Not you."

"And not Jeremiah," Banner says.

"Jeremiah loves me." Inola's cheeks pink up. "He has a good heart. Did you know he's an artist? He makes sculptures and paintings and—all kinds of things."

Like dead snake art for my window. Or the bright gold serpent lifted onto the cross.

"But anyway," Inola finishes, "he doesn't invite me to his church."

We say our goodbyes and after that, we digest the new information while I show Banner the town. At the coffee shop, we both check our email and Banner actually groans to see how many he has to answer. "I can't even begin," he says and simply re-pockets his phone.

"Come on, then," I say. "Let's take our drinks to go."

We stroll through the touristy section of town and come to the smoke shop full of old-time tobacco products and fake Cherokee memorabilia. The bells on the door announce our entrance. "It smells amazing in here," I say.

"You need a stogie?" Banner quips as he stops to contemplate a life-size manikin wearing a huge, feathered headdress.

"The Cherokee never wore those," I inform him. "The shop owners just like to play up all the stereotypes from the old Westerns."

It feels right to be so casually wandering the town with this man. I point out the place with the incredible pancakes and the window where you can watch the candy makers stretch and rotate saltwater taffy on big machines.

"This is the first time we've been off the property together," I note.

"You still like me?"

When I shrug like I could take him or leave him, he bends to my ear and—in that husky way of his—says, "Don't make me remind you how much you enjoyed this morning's torture."

Damn. He lingers inches from my face, staring at my mouth and making me guess what he's going to do next. The longer he waits, the more I replay the delicious event in my mind.

"Is the sheriff's office nearby?"

What? I snap to attention and he laughs at me. "Is the sheriff's office nearby? We could check on him."

I shake the mental game out of my head. It's not like I can take him up on it here in the street. "Uh—the *sheriff's* office," I say, "is down *Main* Street." I indicate the direction of the street as I emphasize its name.

"Oh, Babe! You learned its name. You're really growing."

So, we walk that way, but when we ask to speak to the sheriff, the dispatcher tells us that he's not in today and asks if we'd like to wait for the officer on duty to return from a call.

"No, that's alright," Banner says. "He came to the house yesterday. We were just following up."

The woman's friendly demeanor takes a slight turn. "Right.

Maybe you could take a seat for just a moment." She presses a button on the desk phone and uncaps a pen. "Could you tell me your names?"

"What's wrong?" Banner asks.

"Your names? Addresses?"

"Banner Kirk. I live in Florida. I'm staying with Isla Miller." He motions to me.

The receptionist begins to take our information when from the speaker, a voice says, "Connors."

She holds up a finger as she lifts the handset. "Isla Miller and her guest are here at the office. Would you like them to wait for you?"

She listens, agrees to whatever is said, and hangs up the phone.

"Officer Connors was at your very address, Miss Miller. He'd like to ask you a few questions. He'll be here momentarily."

"Sure. Will you please tell me why?"

"You won't have long to wait."

Banner and I take a seat. "I'm calling Wren," I tell him.

When Wren answers the phone, it's with, "You made it through the night!"

"Yes. Banner stayed. Did you know?"

"I diiiid," he sings. "I think he likes you."

"Shut up. Are you still coming Sunday?"

"Yes," he says. "Have you talked to Billy?"

"That's why I'm calling." I recount for Wren what happened at the Ridleys, how the police car pulled away in the middle of the night, and how Billy is not here today, but we are being asked to wait to answer questions.

Wren takes his time to speak. He's a lawyer, so he thinks through his answers, but it makes me anxious.

"Is that bad?" I rush him. "Should I be worried? And if so, what about?"

"Worry isn't helpful. Answer their questions with what you know. True facts. Not what you imagine. And for godsake, don't get pissy. I tried to call Billy twice already. I'll try again. Probably, everything is totally fine and will soon be sorted out. In the meantime, get in touch with Sissy. She wants to hear from you."

"I will after we're done here."

Before too long, an officer walks through a side door, locates us in the waiting room, and steps over to speak. It's all casual enough. He doesn't ask us to follow him into a small, dark interrogation room with no air conditioning. So, I guess that's good.

"Isla, do you remember me?"

Now that I take a good look at him, I do remember. "Kevin. Right? From the day camp out past Beaver Dam?"

"That's right. It's been a while. I was sorry to hear about Jake."

"Yeah, thanks."

He turns to Banner with an extended hand. "Officer Kevin Connors."

"Banner Kirk."

He motions for us to have a seat and pulls over another chair to face us.

"Billy visited you yesterday?"

I nod my head. "My cousin Wren had reported some odd things that have been happening at our family cabin."

"I read that in Billy's notes. When did he leave your place?"

I consult Banner. "Around two a.m.?" I say.

The lateness of the hour leads to questions. Pretty soon, we're divulging the whole story, even the part about falling asleep before Billy got back. The officer is particularly interested in what exactly was happening at the Ridleys'. How deep a pit? How wide? Was there a ladder to the bottom, or any way for a person to climb out without help?

Finally, he asks, "You sure it was *him* driving away in his SUV?"

"Uh—I didn't *see* him," Banner says. "I just assumed."

A text comes in from Wren: *No answer. I'll keep trying.*

"Officer," I say darkly, "why are you asking us all this?" It may have taken me a while to get there, but I am now highly concerned about Billy's whereabouts—even if he is a lying cheater. "Is he *missing?*"

"He didn't show up for work today. He's not at home. His

cruiser is nowhere to be found. I mean, nobody's officially missing until twenty-four hours go by, but this is unlike him, so I'd like to get out in front of it—if in fact there is anything to get out in front of."

Suddenly, I hear Banner's military training kick in, and he glances around the small room. "Is this your main office? How many do you have on staff here? How many to go with you? It could be a cult-type situation. You need backup."

Connors considers his words. "Are you offering? Are you trained?"

"I'm an Army guy."

"You've seen conflict?"

Banner nods without voicing a reply.

"Wait. *General* Kirk?"

"My dad."

"OK, let me get back to you once I know more. We don't have much manpower without a special request, but anyway, I'm going to need you to take me to this weird pit and help me retrace Billy's last known steps." He eyes us both with more authority than he has demonstrated thus far. "Until then, do not go back to the Ridleys. I tend to think you're right about what's going on."

Banner and I plod back through town discussing what could have happened to Billy when Sissy calls. She's worried but also thrilled that I answered my phone. She wants to know everything twice. When I start the whole story over from the beginning, Banner indicates that he's going to check out the booths in the farmers' market.

He's already back, laden with fruits and vegetables before Sissy has exhausted the subject. "Did I tell you Banner has this successful travel blog, and he's asked me to be a guest writer? To write about the cabin."

Sissy practically squeals, "You're going to do it!" It's not a question.

Banner can hear her through the phone and nods in agreement. "Tell her to come up. I want to meet her."

"Sissy, I'm putting you on speaker."

"Hi, Sissy," Banner says.

"Hello, mysterious man. Y'all send me a selfie so I can see you."

"Come up and see for yourself," Banner says.

"Yeah, bring your family, Sis. Let's get together like we used to. Wren will be here Sunday night."

"I'd love that. Let me check the calendars. Once you have kids, your life gets divided in many, many ways. Call me again tomorrow if you can. And if you caaan't,"—my sister breaks into loud singing—"Happy birthday to you! Happy birthday to you!"

"Yep!" I cut her off. "That's good."

But now Banner picks up the song, and I have to strong-arm him to keep him away from the phone.

"Happy biiiirthday, dear Islaaaaa," they both caterwaul.

"I'm hanging up!" I end the call.

"I like her," Banner says.

Throughout the rest of the day, I consider how to approach this blog thing. How to convey the essence of this place without writing a whole book—or getting too sentimental.

We're back in the cabin, and I'm staring out the window in thought when Banner, who is at the family table creating an additional map of the town, says, "You're awfully quiet this evening."

I turn to him with a bewildered expression. "I can't write this blog," I declare. "I don't even know where to start. I can't separate out the land and the water from the lifetime of suppers and games and arguments and jokes and—" I throw up my hands. "I can't just describe the magic of synchronous fireflies—even if I do that very well—and hope to communicate what this place *means*. Why does that make you smile?"

"First, because you're thinking about it. And second, because what you are telling me is *exactly* the reason you can write it. You're just out of practice."

"I was never *in* practice. I don't write non-fiction."

"There's no difference."

I deadpan him. When he doesn't seem to notice, I cock my head and deadpan him more.

"There's not," he insists. "Not in the things that make it compelling. Just brainstorm until you find the essential thing that connects this place to your soul. And write about that." He looks at me expectantly.

"If you're expecting me to jump up and grab that ridiculous quill Sissy left, it's not going to happen."

Banner leans back in his chair and crosses his arms. "You said I was a good writer. Is it because I'm so great at describing the elements of a place?"

I almost say yes, like it's a dumb question, but I end up saying, "No. That would be forgettable, no matter how well done." I think about it some more. "It's you. It's how deeply you allow the place to affect you. Your curiosity, your openness. The way you get excited and peel back the layers until you find the core. The way you enjoy learning the names of the streets. Your readers get captivated, not because the place is captivating, but because you are captivated by the place."

Banner begins to reply, but I'm not finished. "It's your heart's connection that assigns it meaning. You convince us that the place is phenomenal, that its people are beautiful. But you're the one who's beautiful. *Gah*, it could be anywhere on Earth as long as you were —there."

Now Banner is staring, and I'm slightly embarrassed about the gushing.

At last, he says, "Holy shit. Did you just validate my existence?"

I go to him and put my arms around his neck from behind. "Just find the essential thing?"

"Just find the essential thing." He rises to offer me his seat in front of the sketchbook, and I accept, flipping to the next fresh, white, blank *wilderness* of paper. This is what they call *the fear of the blank page.* This is me staring it down. This is me thinking about a drink.

When did drinking become the essential thing? Fuck that. I'm going to sit here with myself, and I'm going to brainstorm all the things that are true.

The stupid-ass fountain pen flies through the air and slides across the table, bumping into the top of my book, making me smile. I don't even look up, but I do slowly reach for it.

I sit here, quill in hand until Banner creeps off to bed, but I have yet to set it to paper. In the middle of the big, blank page, I make a dot. And now that it is no longer blank, I feel better. I have in mind to call it a night but, as though that one small kiss of ink kindled their desire, pen and paper come together hot, and words begin to flow.

They're not perfect words. They don't identify the essential thing. They probably won't appear in Banner's blog. But they remind me of something. I love to write. And I'm good at it. I command words the way Banner's sister commands soldiers. I summon this one, couple it with that one, banish others, and order them around. If I abandon my post, I abandon my power. I forfeit my purpose.

This idea is an enlivening revelation. I have power and a purpose.

I make my way to the bedroom, but stop short when I hear the nightstand snap closed. He's checking up on me. When I enter, Banner glances up with a sad smile. He doesn't say anything. He doesn't have to. The bottle is still there. The conflict is written on his face.

He simply walks out.

Fuck. "Ban?"

He reappears around the doorframe. "Yeah, Babe."

"I love you."

"I love you too. I'm gonna get some water. You want some?"

"Yeah. Yes, please."

And *still,* I do not throw it out.

The Impact of Being Human

The wet leaves came to smell like freedom
Freedom was the carpet of our peace
And patience creaked and groaned up in the oak trees
Which, in turn, bowed down and dropped more of their leaves

Seasons cycled our back trails with forgiveness
Every bluet called it forth and made it grow
And hurled us toward the cliffs of rudimentary
Solo flight into adulthood of the soul

I will one day gather all these leaves around me
When they come to plant me down in this good soil
I will sprout inside the mercy of my childhood
And remember to forgive the later toil

I will welcome heaven with the wonder
Welcoming of summer
Pouring out of schoolhouse kind of joy

"DID YOU WRITE THIS JUST NOW?" Banner asks. He returns to the bedroom in only blue boxer briefs, holding two glasses of water and the sketchbook aloft.

"Oh, Banner, why do you read the stuff? It's not anything. It's stream of conscious meanderings."

"It's great fucking poetry."

I blink a thank you. It's not. But it is something.

"What's a bluet?" he asks.

I can't answer without grinning. "The tiny white flowers that cover the burial grounds."

The fact that I researched the flower to find its name makes him laugh out loud. "You looked it up! Are the bluets the essential thing?"

"No."

"The seasons?"

I shake my head.

"What about the family table?"

"I thought about that. A whole lot has happened there. But it's a little on the nose, don't you think? The heart of the home and all?"

"I think the table would be my essential thing," Banner says.

"Your essential thing is the treasure tree."

"Oh, you're right." He re-reads my scribbles and says, "You're too hard on yourself."

"You think?"

"You need someone to remind you how brilliant you are." He tosses the book and pulls me into his arms. "How beautiful." He kisses me. "How grateful they are to be close as this." He tells me he loves me between kisses. He loves me. He loves me. He tells me so many soft, gentle times that I forget I'm driving him away.

NOW IT'S MY BIRTHDAY. I have yet to open my eyes. I've dreaded waking up on this day for months, but now that I've *partially* said goodbye to Jake, I'm ready to fully let go. Banner has unburied me, has lifted me from the dirt, and placed me back in the land of the living.

I reach out to feel for him, but my hand lands on cool bedsheets. Gah, what a whirlwind.

The smell of coffee floats to me. He's already up. Already outside, I bet.

The kitchen is clean and the coffee is hot. My favorite mug is standing by. "B? You in here? Luce?"

It's quiet.

I pour my coffee—but when I go to replace the pot, I miss completely—knock it against the maker. I nearly drop it. Banner's necklace is poised on the counter like a hitman lying in wait for his mark. Beside it is a note which I reach for slowly. Very slowly. And I read:

I've walked to the door twice already, but I can't seem to leave you. You're as beautiful in sleep as you are awake, and I cherish the vision of you, the quiet rhythm of your breath, the soft curl of your hair at the nape of your neck. This past week is seared into my heart. Thank you for letting me in. Thank you for guiding me through your world. This is how I will always remember you, at peace, at home here in your cabin. But I have to make my feet move, because I can't stay, Eesa. I have to go.

I re-read it. "Banner?" I call out.

He's not—no, he wouldn't have—

"Lucy?"

I open the front door and step out onto the porch. "Ban?" They probably went on a walk. They probably—

And now our happy little honeymoon ends.

His truck is gone. I don't even believe it. I walk over to where it was parked and feel around for it as if it is more possible for the truck to have turned invisible than for Banner to have left me.

I tear back inside. There's nothing left of him. No duffel bag. No toothbrush. His bed is made like he was never here at all. Even Lucy's bowl has been put away. He's gone.

Bewildered, I pace the house clutching his necklace, and I end up in the Hall of Heights, where I locate our names just to make sure I haven't made the whole thing up.

He meant to break with me and this whole place.

I won't let him. I'll write it all down like I'm a witness to a crime.

Everything I can remember. I don't care if it's in order. I don't care if it's in complete sentences.

The page feels voracious under my hand, gobbling up the ink as quickly as I can place it. Maybe this is what Banner felt when he wrote down every mundane detail about me like it was the most important of facts. But if it was so important, why did he go? I get that he's used to exploring a place and moving on. I just thought that exploring a person—me—would prove more difficult.

It takes an hour to put down all the things, starting with the way he showed up and the bridge to the outside world disappeared. Hell, I even try to write out the erotic stuff, but it's hard to capture it with clumsy words like, "slides his tongue over my—" And anyway, I get too hot remembering it to sit still.

Once I've given up everything I can recall, I feel very empty. And I feel very sad. I wish I had a picture of us to pine over. I wish he had stayed long enough to help me finish the task of letting go.

And now I do a dumb thing.

I open the nightstand.

My first drink in days burns all the way down like it wants to rip my throat out. I draw on it like a defiant child and swallow in great gulps. I wish it would cauterize the wound inside.

That isn't what you want, though. Feel the good. Feel the bad. Write it down.

I unplug the bottle from my lips with a *pop* and look at myself in the mirror. This is why he can't stay. And now I hate the liquor with as much intensity as I ache with the loss. I practically lunge into the bathroom and when it won't pour out of the bottle fast enough to suit me, I shake it like I'm choking it to death. After that, I race to the closet to do the same with the stash there, and I leave it upside down in the drain to sit on the toilet and weep.

It's early in the morning, and I haven't eaten. What with the combination of astringent liquor and convulsive sobbing, I throw up. Seems fitting. Get rid of all of it.

For some reason, that sends me seeking the letter that made my therapist concerned. Wow. It is embarrassing. Not the fact that I was despairing enough to end my life, but the sappy way I communicated it. It is actually addressed *Dear World*.

As concerned as I am to craft perfect phrases, you'd think that the last word I left would be remarkable. It's not. I don't want it anymore. But I don't want to just throw it away either.

Dear World,

There's no reason for me to continue this charade called life. I kept thinking that I would find the energy to fight for it, to grieve the way everyone kept telling me I should. I should want to kick and swim hard enough to break through the surface of loss to breathe the oxygen of hope. But I just don't care anymore. I have no desire left. I have no feelings at all. I give up.

On my birthday, I will throw myself to the river and allow it to swallow me whole.

Please don't hurt over my passing, but feel glad for me, that I escaped this wretched emptiness.

Isla

Reading back over it now, I wonder if all this time it was more than the grief that kept me impotent and unfeeling—if it was really the liquid depressant, which I now recognize is a worse washing machine than The Hydraulic. It keeps you trapped in a battering cycle. You never get any rest. You feel like hell. You go through your days like a ghost, unable to deal or receive the impact of being human.

Even as I think these dark thoughts about alcohol, I'm starting to regret pouring it out. What is wrong with me? I need a new letter. Fast. A letting go. A manifesto for living. I do not write it to the World. I write it to the Departed.

Dear Jake, It's been four years and I still miss you every day. I miss your bear hugs and your stupid sense of humor. I miss your crazy-ass schemes and your fearless spontaneity. I wanted our kids to grow up together. I wanted to be friends with your wife. It's not fair that you're dead and I'm not. I've begged God to take me countless times. I even wanted to end it myself. But I'm not going to.

I wish I'd seen you the moment you jumped. I wish I'd seen your glorious, wild, impish smile. Or, if that's not what you were wearing, I wish I'd seen what. I'm sorry. I'm sorry. I'm sorry. I didn't climb up. I didn't know what you needed. I couldn't save you.

I have carried that sorrow around as shackles, and I fear that, to some extent, I must.

But I need to be free, Jake. Need to feel things. Need to walk with the living. I pray to God for strength to live a sober life, to be present, powerful, and creative. And to be for our family what they need me to be. I know you'll help me too if you are able.

I love you, Cousin. If I can't have you back, then I hope we will meet again in some future life. Goodbye for this one.

Eesa

This note, I fold neatly and place in my sketchbook.

The suicide note, I roll and tap inside one of the whisky bottles. I need a token of the things I'm giving up—the Dead and the oblivion—in order to gain what I was sacrificing to keep them—my life and my calling. Maybe I'll break the other bottle into pieces, and save the shards to make some piece of art. Or bury them in Jake's grave.

I throw on my sneakers and head to the treasure tree.

The morning is brisk. The cool air perks me up and clears my head. I nestle the message-in-a-bottle into the interior of the tree, and I'm satisfied.

I haven't withdrawn my hand before shades of blue and orange and grey and gold catch my eye. Another birthday. Another bracelet. It must have been Wren.

The grace of the gift works upon my sore heart as I use my teeth to tie it to my wrist. Banner abandoned his, but even so, a new one has come to me.

I grab the note I wrote to Jake and head to the cemetery. As an afterthought, I bring the whole sketchbook. Writers gotta write. I'll swim along the way too, even though it will be chilly. I want to feel alive.

When I get to the grave, I sit back against Jake's stone and receive the bright sun on my face as a kiss. Birds are calling to one another. The woods are growing, thriving. And I am too.

I'm still going to write until I find the essential thing, even if I don't get to write Banner's blog. When I open the book, it's his words that greet me, and they sound so full of love. More than that.

They make it sound like he's in awe of me like he will never be able to—nor ever stop trying to—plumb the depth of me. *Especially* the erotic parts. *Damn.*

I let my head fall back against the stone. I just can't *believe* he left the way he did. I mean, I would have probably argued and screamed and jockeyed for another chance. But still, he owed it to me to tell me to my face. What was with all the *I love yous* last night? Was he trying to convince himself or just say goodbye? Maybe if I live sober for long enough—

My thoughts are disrupted by a brittle, deep voice.

"What is *this?*" it bellows. Jeremiah is stalking toward me, crushing a sheet of paper in his fist. "What is *this?*" His brow is riddled with fury.

Now, the pen isn't *actually* mightier than the sword. And that's all I have in hand right now. The one thing Banner did leave—on the table by the door—where it unhelpfully remains—is his firearm. Maybe if Jeremiah means to strangle me to death, as he is doing to that piece of paper, he could wait to do it back at home and give me some small chance of survival.

"Why?!" Jeremiah demands.

He's close now, but he stops short of Jake's grave. Apparently, he doesn't want to strangle me enough to tread on it. With what small protection that affords, I remain as is, seated at the headstone.

"What's the matter, Jeremiah?" I try to say soothingly. "What are you holding?"

He thrusts it out for me, and his face is so tangled with emotions that I can't identify for sure which ones he's feeling. He falls to his knees, still holding the paper aloft, and he bows his head. All I can think is that he's a prisoner presenting the charge against him as he submits to his own beheading.

My heart goes out to him. I crawl forward and place a light hand on the back of his neck. It seems to break him. He sinks onto his heels, allowing his hands to fall to his lap and tears to spill onto the paper.

"I don't want you to die," he says. "I don't want you to die. I don't want you to die."

"Why would I? You didn't come here to hurt me, did you?"

He doesn't respond.

"You saved me the other day, you know?" I say. "You saved me from whatever your father had in mind." Now that we're this close, I notice fresh bruises and lacerations on the side of his face. "Jeremiah?" I ask quietly. "Did you take a beating for what you did?"

It's absurd. He's a huge, strong man. But his father is too. And he is his father.

Jeremiah doesn't move a muscle. I grow antsier, the longer he remains still. It's not a relaxed sort of stillness. It's coiled.

"Jeremiah?"

Finally, I work the paper out of his clenched fingers.

"*Oh,*" I barely say. My own declaration of suicide stares up at me. "No, I'm not going to do this. I was very sad when I wrote this. But I want to live. Why were you taking things from the treasure tree?"

Now that his hands are free, one of them flies to my wrist, and I try to wrench it free, but I can't. "Stop. You're hurting me."

"I wasn't taking," he says and practically shoves my own wrist into my eye. "I wanted to make sure you found your stones." He lets go of me and his message sinks in while I baby my arm.

"*You're* the one who leaves my birthday presents?!"

Jeremiah shakes his head, but since I'm already coddling my wrist, I raise my bracelets to eye level.

"They're not for your birthday. They're for your protection. On Jacob's death day."

I am amazed to the point of incredulity. The shiny golden beads glint in the sunlight and seem to be winking at me like they're in on a joke.

"Jeremiah, you gave me these? Did you *make* them?"

Instead of answering, he says, "Do you think you could get off of him now?"

It takes me a second to realize he's uncomfortable with me sitting on Jake's grave. "He wouldn't mind," I laugh. "He'd be happy about it." I have half a mind to lie back the full length of the grave, but I'm not sure how scandalized my neighbor would be, so I just pat the earth.

Even so, I get a stern reprimand. "Isla."

"It's OK, Jeremiah. Look." I unfold my new letter, my manifesto for living, and allow him to read it. Then I bury it down into the dirt, saying, "I left the one you found in the tree as a token of bad thoughts that I'm letting go."

When I glance up from my task, I can tell that Jeremiah is more relaxed, and I catch a glimpse of what Inola sees in him. Even though he's a big, hulking man, he has a boyish quality, a vulnerability that draws me. "Thank you for the stones, Jeremiah. They're precious to me. And they're beautiful. Inola told me you were an artist. You're very talented."

His eyes shift. I think he's unsure what to do with my compliment. I try something lighter. "When are you going to propose to her?"

He actually smiles.

"I'm coming to the wedding," I continue. "Were you planning to invite me?"

Jeremiah does this funny thing where he tilts his head from side to side. I think it's the equivalent of an eye roll.

"Well, I'm coming to it," I say. The questions I have that need answering are foremost in my mind, but I don't want to scare him off. I try to broker my tone.

"Jeremiah?"

It makes him wary.

"Will you please tell me what happened up there that day? Not knowing it tortures me. Jake was scared of something, wasn't he?"

Jeremiah drops his head but slowly nods yes.

"What was it?"

"I have to go." He gets to his feet, and I scramble up beside him.

"Please. I need to know. I have nightmares."

"You're not the only one."

His steps are quick. I jog to keep up.

"What were you doing up there?"

"I'm sorry," he mumbles. "I'm sorry."

"*Why* are you sorry?"

He shakes his head mechanically and increases his pace. I can't make him stay. I just ask it.

"Did you kill him?"

And now he comes to an abrupt halt.

"Did you kill him, Jeremiah?"

Without turning, he says, "Yes. I killed him."

"What?" I whisper though I heard him fine. I think I'm gonna be sick again. I thrust my hands out to steady myself, but I trip over my own feet and land on my knees.

Jeremiah casts a look back at me, and his eyes have grown cold. "He was going to die anyway," he says. After a moment, he barges down the hill and leaves me there to drown in this new revelation.

My mind is a swirly mess of questions and emotions. I want to pummel Jeremiah Ridley to a pulp, but I can't even summon the mental faculty to stand.

I'll go to the police. I'll tell them what Jeremiah said. I'll call Wren. I have to get home.

And now I'm up and moving. The weather seems to be directed by my turmoil. The wind drives dark clouds into the sky. By the time I'm halfway, though it's mid-afternoon, it's like nighttime.

I drive straight to the front porch and it's not until I'm already at the door that I realize someone else is here. Inside. The cabin glows with warm light. I cautiously open to the sound of jazz along with the smell of something savory on the stove. I think I may have portalled into an alternate universe. A large vase of cheerful, yellow sunflowers decorates the table, and a bottle of wine with two glasses is standing by.

That's when Lucy bounds across the room and nearly knocks me over in her exuberance. Banner grins from the kitchen. He's ravishing—clean and neat in a nice brown button-down and one of Mammaw's aprons thrown over it. "Hey, Babe," he calls. "I was beginning to think I'd have to come find you. How's your day been so far?"

I glance around, stupefied, still trying to determine whether or not I'm in the right dimension.

Banner's too busy tasting what he's cooking to notice. "You want to get cleaned up?" he continues. "And then we'll have a glass of this NA wine before we eat. It's supposed to be pretty good, though, I have yet to find one that's great. We can always scrap it." He lifts his head and his sweet expression morphs as he misinterprets what's going on inside me. "Oh. We don't have to try the wine. Was that a bad idea? I'll get rid of it." He moves to do just that.

"Stop!" I say and he snaps to attention. "What are you doing here? What is—all this?"

There's a slight pause. "Youuur birthday dinner?" he says.

"You left."

"Yeeeeah? I wanted to—" He waves around at all of the gifts and supplies. There's a framed photo of the two of us sitting on the table next to the flowers. "And I needed to answer about five billion emails. What's the matter with you?"

"Youuuu left. You took your clothes. And your toothbrush. And your dog. And—everything. You made your bed."

"Isla, I'm a son of the United States Army. I can't *walk* past a bed without making it. You're lucky I didn't make you up in yours. I actually did straighten the corners a bit." He tries to embrace me, but I step back.

"What about your clothes, your toothbrush?"

"My clothes are in the duffel underneath the bed. My toothbrush is in *your* bathroom now."

A sharp exhale punches through my lips. "You couldn't have just told me your plans?!"

"I left a note," he says defensively.

"That said you were leaving!"

"That said how beautiful you are to me!" Banner snatches up the notecard and scans it, the disconnect contorting his features. "How could you possibly interpret this to mean I was leaving for good?"

"How could I possibly not? Do you not know how to spell BRB?"

Banner laughs out loud.

"It's not funny," I snap.

"It is funny," he counters. "It's funny to me. I want to be with you. Have I not made that clear? I want to be with you here. And when you're done here, I want to be with you someplace else." He circles my waist with his arms, resisting my half-hearted attempt to push him away. "Stop it," he tells me.

"No, I will not stop it," I pout. "All day long I thought you were through with me and off to your next exotic location."

"All day long I was thinking about you. I've been planning this since I realized your birthday would be difficult for you."

I am not finished sulking. Though, clearly, what he is saying is true. He even remembered Pap's old guitar, which is hanging from a proper hook—that he has aesthetically attached to the wall—and sporting all six strings.

"Forgive me, Eesa," he purrs and sways me to the music. "Forgive me right now before another moment passes." He stoops to look me in the eye. "I love you," he says.

"You do?"

"I do. And if I forget to write it in the future—which I seriously doubt that I will—you can be confident that you have a standing BRB." He has his forehead resting on mine now.

I do enjoy the whole close-up dancing thing.

"Why in the world did you leave your necklace?" I ask.

There's a lull in which Banner examines me, and then he treks over to the counter to pick up the notecard again but instead of reading it, he searches for something else. "So that you could fix it," he says.

Next, he searches the floor on his hands and knees. "I explained that in the note." Between the counter and the wall, he procures something and rises to offer it to me. "On the *second* card. You didn't see it, did you? You *really* thought I was gone."

I nod my head in injured increments.

"That I had just abandoned you completely. And, what? Left the necklace as an insult?"

I shrug.

"Fuck, Eesa. I'm sorry. I would never do that to you."

"I didn't think so, but—" I interrupt myself to focus on the second notecard. The line about having to go is continued there. *I have to go…answer email and then grab some things for your birthday.* Next, I burst out laughing. "Is this true?!" The card explains that Banner's necklace came unknotted last night when I nearly strangled him with it.

"I now know you only put it on me to have reins." He tips his head so that I can see a bruise on his neck.

"Oh gosh!" I laugh. "I was too rough!"

"Please don't say that. You riding me like that is the best thing I've ever felt in my life."

Kind of makes me want to right now.

"Well, there is clearly a **BRB** on the second card. Wow. Sorry." I motion around. "Thank you. This is so thoughtful. It's a perfect birthday set-up."

"Apart from the large portion of the day when you thought—"

"Don't fuck it up."

"OK."

I grin at his ready submission. "Listen. I have things to tell you."

So, I tell Banner about my notes, my new bracelet, and how Jeremiah found me in the cemetery. "He said he killed him, Ban. He confessed it to me."

"Son of a bitch. Did he say why?"

I shake my head. "He looked like he'd been beaten." I feel very tired all of a sudden. I plunk myself down at the table.

"I threw out the whisky," I volunteer.

"You did?"

"But I drank some first. I'm sorry. I—"

Banner stops me. "You don't owe me an explanation."

"But I really am committed to being sober."

"I know. I'm not going anywhere. Why don't you get cleaned up, and then we'll eat and talk about what to do next."

"We should go to the police, right? Should tell them what Jeremiah said."

"You sound hesitant."

"I just wish I knew the whole story. He gave me these bracelets every year since then. He said it was to protect me. Was it just a guilt offering?"

Banner raises his brow to say he doesn't know, and I sigh before I rise to my feet. I'm overwhelmed by the turn of events.

"I *will* get cleaned up," I tell him, worming my way into his arms. "I'm glad you're here." My voice gets muffled by Banner's chest. I love it there.

"I want you to think about something," he says. "I want you to come with me when I travel."

"I told you I would."

"Not just to St. Lucia. All the time. You can write from anywhere, right? Stop editing other people's stories and finish your own. Give them to the world."

"Banner, I can't support myself like that. I can barely—"

"*I* can, though. I can support both of us if you're willing to live light. It's practically free, anyway. Everyone wants to give me stuff so that they can have a mention. Let's grow roots together. All over the place. When you sell your books, you can chip in if you want. Hell, a collection of the poems you wrote as a kid would sell a million copies."

"Poetry doesn't sell," I smile. "Do you really believe in me like that?"

"I absolutely do."

"The truth is," I say, "I could sell my share of this property and be a multi-millionaire overnight."

Banner's expression goes unexpectedly hard. "Don't you dare do that," he scolds me. "Don't you ever dare do that. This place is your lifeblood. Our kids are gonna sit at that table right there, alongside Wren's and all the others."

"*Our* kids?"

"Yeah," Banner smiles. "And you're gonna tell them about Jake and his wild schemes." He tugs on my braid. "While we untangle their hair."

Now, *that* is a happy thought.

"Banner, you can't say stuff like that if you don't mean it. Or if there's a chance you're going to un-mean it."

"I'm not going to un-mean it. But I'll give you some time to get used to it." He winks and swats my backside. "Go. I'll be here when you get back."

I STAND under that hot shower for far longer than a true environmentalist would dare. It feels so good on my neck and shoulders. The steam overtakes the entire bathroom. The body wash smells like gardenias. But when I do emerge and stand before my closet mirror, having adorned myself in a yellow sundress, I hear a vehicle drive up. I only just make it into the living room when someone knocks on the door.

Banner glances up from where he is placing serving bowls at the table.

"Miss Miller? Mr. Kirk? It's Officer Connors."

I open the door and ask him to come in.

"I feel bad you made the trip," Banner greets him. "I was just checking in this afternoon to see what news you had."

"I'm not here for that," he says curtly.

Yesterday, I had trouble deciding whether to call the man Kevin or Officer. I don't have that quandary today. I guess Banner doesn't either. "What's going on, Officer?" he asks.

In answer, Connors displays a photograph that looks to have come from a surveillance camera. It's black and white. It looks to have been taken at night, of a large man loading a police SUV with a heavy trash bag. Off to the side is a flowering bush I know quite well. The one Sissy planted on the spot where Jake's body lay after Jeremiah set him down. There's a stack of three river stones I put there myself.

"That is *this* house!" I say.

"That was one-fifty-two am, on Friday morning, the time you said Billy drove out. That is not Billy."

"It's Jeremiah," I say, and Banner says, "What's in the bag?"

The Last Will and Testament of Edna May Miller

"HOW IN THE hell was that picture taken?" Banner stomps past Officer Connors who is still holding the photo aloft. It's light out, but even so, Banner shines the flashlight of his cell phone into the shadow of the gutter. He goes along the parking pad until—"There!"

A shiny, black, barely visible ball reflects the beam. Seconds later, it is destroyed under the force of Banner's boot.

"We could have processed that," Connors says.

"Process the others. We only disabled them." Now he's rounding the house to make sure he hasn't missed any more.

"Mr. Kirk," Connors calls him back. "We need to find the sheriff."

"Yeah, I got that. Don't you have a tracking device on his truck?"

"It's not showing up. We're searching highway cameras in and out of town, but we have about as many of those as we have manpower. Which is not much. We're calling in more officers from around the state."

"What about park rangers?" I ask.

"I've put in the request. They'll be available tomorrow, but they want to scour the backcountry. Isla, will you take me around the perimeter of your property so I can get my bearings?"

I'd say *sure,* but it means Banner's perfect birthday dinner will go cold. He preempts my response.

"Let us turn some things off," he says. "We were going to have an early dinner."

"I'll wait." Connors doesn't mean he'll wait while we eat. He means *yeah, skip the dinner and let's go.* His voice is tight. He's worried.

As Banner turns off the oven, I cover the food. "Smells amazing," I lament. "I'm sorry."

He shrugs. "This is more important. It'll taste better once it's had a chance to soak up the flavor."

"You're pretty great," I tell him.

"You're pretty pretty. I like you in that dress." He tends to the stove again.

"Didn't you just turn that off?" I ask.

"No, actually, I turned it off before we ever went outside. I came back to make *sure* that I had turned it off. And now I am *re*-checking what I am already certain of. I do realize it's obsessive and compulsive."

"Because of fire."

"Because of fire," he confirms.

These moments are precious to me—when I get to see the inner workings of his mind. The attack that killed his friend scarred him in more ways than can be hidden by a beard.

"Come on." He offers his hand. "We've got our whole lives to mine that experience. Doubtless, you'll have to deal with it seeping out in ways I wasn't able to avert with a therapist."

He's heading for the door, but I tug him into the garage where my rugged, old Wrangler is waiting, no doors. The top is hanging from a hydraulic lift—best thing Wren and Sissy ever installed in this place.

When I start the ignition, Banner flinches.

"*Oops.*" The speakers are blaring until I punch the power button.

"Go on, Rockstar," Banner says. "I'll shut the door behind you." So, I back out to Connors, who climbs into the rear, and Banner takes the passenger seat. "We have a utility road," I tell them. "Such as it is. It runs the part of the property that borders the park. Everybody in?" Everybody is. I avoid what potholes I can while noting landmarks along the way.

"The barn is that way, where Pap's tractor lives. There's the garden. You can see how big it was when Pap worked it full-time. And you can see where our boundary is marked with signs every hundred yards or so."

A herd of deer mosey across the path and a few of them watch us from the cover of the woods.

"Who has driven this recently?" Connors asks.

"Nobody. The groundskeepers couldn't becau—"

"*Somebody* has. Stop here."

Connors is right. There are fresh tire tracks marring the soft earth that leads into the park's land.

Banner sniffs the air. "You smell that?" He turns to ask me specifically.

Smoke.

"Yes," I say. "It's really there."

Connors doesn't ask, but I catch his curiosity in the rearview mirror.

Banner must feel it. He says, "I smell phantom smoke sometimes. Mainly upon waking. A gift from Afghanistan."

"You told me you'd been in conflict." Connors is inviting Banner to say more, but he just flashes his eyebrows and turns his head toward his open door.

I depart the road to follow the tire tracks when Connors pipes up, "I'm not taking a civilian into a potentially dangerous situation."

"You're not taking me," I say. "I'm taking you."

Banner ends the debate when he points and says, "It's rising from there."

At first, I don't see it, but then the late afternoon sun filters through the leaves and creates a suspension through the smoke.

"OK, maybe just to there," Connors consents.

So, I drive us off my own property and into the woods of the national park, which I'm pretty sure is illegal. About a tenth of a mile ahead of us—I know because I've explored it—is a cliff's ledge where the whole side of the mountain plummets into a narrow ravine. Jake always maintained the drop was over a hundred feet, but we rappelled it once, and Asher said it wasn't quite. Anyway, it's close.

I stop the Jeep well short of the drop and hop out. There are tire marks, and there is a portion of underbrush that has been cleared as if by a tornado.

"Why are you stopping?" Connors asks.

"Why don't you come to see?"

The drop is deceiving. The way it falls, with the other side so close, it gives the illusion that there is no gap at all, and I almost don't notice that Connors has fallen for it—no pun intended. He takes one step too far when I realize his mistake, and I grab the back of his uniform to yank him back. We end up on the ground.

"What the hell, Isla?"

"Don't what the hell me. There's a drop-off. Were you not raised around here?"

When the officer sees his mistake, he turns white. Kids around here are taught to keep an eye on the trail as soon as we're taught to walk. Though, didn't I almost plummet into a snake pit recently?

Banner is staring down into the chasm without paying any attention to us. Connors and I flank him. I don't see any flames, but *something* is creating the smoke. At the bottom, upside-down, are the charred remains of a vehicle.

"Is that Billy's?" I ask.

"Has to be," Connors says.

"There are burn shadows along the rock." Banner's voice is uncharacteristically flat. "It exploded. Do you think it happened in the middle of the night?" he asks.

"You would have definitely heard an explosion that big at your house," Connors says. "Don't you think? Or felt it?"

There's a moment of levity when Banner catches my eye. During some of our romps, an atomic bomb could've gone off and we'd have been none the wiser. "Maybe not," is all he says. "This was an intentional dump. You'll need to send people down."

"Of course. *I'm* gonna go down. I'll be back as soon as I can."

"And make sure the fire is out," Banner says. "Everything's wet right now, but it won't be for long."

"Nothing mobilizes park rangers more." Connors is peering at the wreckage, chewing his lip. His brow is furrowed.

"You don't think you'll find Billy in there do you?" I ask.

When Connors turns to me, his eyes answer for him, but he doesn't say anything aloud. Just swallows.

"Jeremiah told me that he killed Jake," I blurt out. "He told me earlier today. I asked him point-blank and he said yes."

"Today? Where?"

"Here at the family cemetery. And then he beat a path back toward his own place." As an afterthought, I say, "He had been beaten. His face was bruised and he moved as if his ribs were sore."

"We're talking about Jeremiah Ridley?" Connors asks.

"I know. He's huge, but his father has a stronghold over him."

"You told me he stood up to his father on your behalf."

"Yeah. He did do that."

Connors forgoes the rest of the perimeter tour in order to drive between our outbuildings to make sure Jeremiah isn't hiding on site. Why would he be, though? If he's anywhere, he's in the tree huts.

I don't say this. I'm not sure why except that for some reason I feel I'm the only one who can extract from Jeremiah the real story surrounding Jake's death. And even though he told me he killed Jake —I just—I have to know why. At any rate, we don't see any sign of him. No tracks. Nothing unlocked or out of place.

Even things that ought to be.

"Alright," Connors says once we're parting ways. "If you see Jeremiah again, stay away from him and get in touch. He's a person of interest now. I'll be back to check out the wreck and depending on what we find, we'll likely search parts of this property."

We're watching him drive away. Banner has an arm around me. He says, "Well? Happy birthday."

"The barn door shouldn't be locked," I say.

"What?"

"No one closes or locks the barn. It's just an open place for the tractor and nothing much else. We never lock it."

"And you kept this from Connors why?"

"I don't know. Will you come?"

He will. He always will. I run to get the master key and then I drive over the ground too fast, turning hard in front of the barn so that the Jeep skids and tips for a split second. Banner looks impressed.

We fit the key to the padlock, and he asks, "Does Jeremiah have a key?"

"No, not that I know of. But the lock was already fitted. He would only have had to snap it shut."

I remove the lock, and Banner and I both roll the enormous door open by walking against it. Standing inside the yawning maw of the structure, we wait for our eyes to adjust. It smells like straw, and old wood, and grease from the part of the barn that was also a machine shop. I pull a string that illuminates five lightbulbs, hanging in a row above us from here to the other end of the cavernous barn.

"That is one big, beautiful, orange tractor," Banner says.

"We'll get to that," I assure him. There's nothing much else. Tools are arranged on the walls. Buckets. I cross the bare floor, which is hard-packed earth, and climb a ladder to peer into the empty loft. "I don't get it. We never lock the barn."

"Ees?" Banner calls up. The wary tone of his voice brings me to the rail. He's standing over a black plastic bag that is simply lying on the ground in the back corner. When I scramble down to him, he's waiting.

"It's the bag Jeremiah loaded into the police cruiser," I say and bend to untie it.

"You understand what could be inside, right?" he cautions me.

That makes me stand up and toe the thing, then give it a little kick. It's clunky. "It's something metal, I think. It's not a body."

"Are you sure? Should we report it? We're crossing a police line, here."

"It's on my own property," I retort.

"You do realize that doing something on your own property does not automatically make it legal, right?"

I shrug and untie the knot. Then I unfold the shiny plastic to reveal the head and neck of a giant, gaudy, yellow snake, the same one that was raised onto the cross near the snake pit. Or a lookalike. It's larger here on the ground than it had appeared on the cross. Other than that, there are some legal-looking papers. They haven't been bound neatly, but stacked haphazardly and shoved into the bag as if in haste.

Banner lets out a sigh of relief. "I am not gonna lie. I thought it was gonna be Sheriff Billy cut into pieces."

I look up at him. "Do you think Jeremiah meant for us to have this?"

"Don't you?" he says. "He stowed it inside here and then locked it up without having a key. He must not have meant to access it himself."

"Maybe he just needed a quick hiding place for it."

"In that case, who is he hiding it *from?*"

"Good question, Detective Kirk. Who do you think sent the photo of him loading it into the car?"

He makes a *hmm* noise that means he'd like to know. "Whoever put those cameras up on your house. Why don't we take this back inside to go through it?"

"Even the snake?"

"Ummm...maybe not the snake."

I glance around for a place to hide it, but when my eyes catch on one of the barn's load-bearing columns, I change my mind. The column is fitted with a crossbeam that makes a nice crucifix—if a device of torture can be described as such. "Help me get it up there," I say. "That's where it belongs."

Banner locates a crate which he then manages to jostle over to me. "Hop up, and I'll hand it to you."

So, I do, but when he hefts the golden serpent, he says, "*Whoa.* What is it made of? It's heavy as hell. Let me do it."

I shake my head, reach down for it, and nearly topple over from its weight before Banner has even stopped supporting it.

"Easy," he laughs. "Here. Let go." Banner sets the snake on the crate beside me and jumps up. After that, he hoists our snake into position but, even for him, it's a challenge. "Is that good?" he pants.

"I could've done that."

"But it's your birthday," he soothes. "And you shouldn't have to hang big, creepy rattlesnakes all by yourself."

We dismount the crate to observe our golden serpent-on-a-cross. "It's pretty cool," I tell him. "It's growing on me. Like some great, guardian of the barn."

I check for Banner's reaction. It is slight. "OK," he says.

We leave the plastic bag where it was but collect the papers. And while we wheel the enormous barn door closed, we ponder whether to lock it, but in the end, we just leave it as is.

Before Banner gets into the Jeep he searches the sky.

"You're looking for smoke," I guess.

"Just checking."

"It's hazy is all."

Back inside, while I deposit the papers onto one side of the table, Banner reheats our dinner. "Do you want to go through those before we eat?" he asks.

I kind of do, but I think it's going to take some time. They're legal-looking papers, from what I can tell, and Banner has done so much work to make this dinner special. Anyway, my stomach growls an answer before I do. "Let's eat. I'm famished."

He motions for me to have a seat.

"This is a fantastic birthday," I spout and my hands with glee.

"It is?" he laughs. "After all you've been through?"

"It's an adventure," I tell him. "People *pay* to get locked into adventures, and this one is real. Hey! Maybe you and I—when you need a break from more serious blogging—could write and sell adventures for people to play out in exotic locales." I nod at him expectantly. It's a great idea.

Instead of taking it up, though, Banner stares at me hard with one of those inscrutable expressions that makes me nervous.

"You know," I keep trying. "Like a who-dun-it. Or an escape

room. But bigger. We could hire actors to—" I can't believe I'm failing to persuade him. "This is a great idea. You don't like it?"

"Will you marry me?" he says.

Pause. "What?"

"You're my person."

"I thought you weren't spontaneous," I say.

"I'm not. But this needs to happen."

"Us to be married?"

"Yeah. You're my person," he says again. "And I'm yours. Like your blue jeans, right?"

"Right."

"I want us to work together. I want to get to joke with you and make love to you—all my life."

"How do you know?"

"I just know. I've never known before. And now I do."

I narrow my eyes at him to make sure he's serious. "If we did that, then you could only have me from now on. If you cheat on me, I'm out."

"Won't happen. But understood."

"What are *your* stipulations?" I ask. "Don't say drinking, because I'm not going to."

From where he sits, looking utterly sexy with one arm slung around the corner of his chair, he thumps his thumb with the weight of his nonchalance.

"None?" I persist. "You don't mind if I cheat on you?"

"Not worried. I will give you *every* reason to bring it home."

Oh, no. The immutable smile is spreading, the one I have no physical control over. Yep. There it is cracking my face in two. I use both hands to hide it from him, but Banner drags them down.

"Can I take that as a yes?"

"Stop gloating."

It's hard to concentrate after that. Hard to eat, even though it's delicious. Hard to converse about anything other than how well we fit and how it is we came to be together. But that leads us back to this wild adventure and the papers that lie at the end of the table, so I get to work trying to figure out what Jeremiah left for me and why.

Banner is clearing up. "What's that one?" he asks from the kitchen.

The envelope has been opened before. I reach in to procure a document that boasts the official state seal of Tennessee. "It appears to be a deed to the Ridleys' property. But—oh—Mr. Ridley has signed it over to the church! Jeremiah must be livid! I can't even imagine!"

"Or maybe not," Banner reasons. "His girlfriend said he lives to appease his father and God."

"Still! His property? His home?"

"Maybe they want to make a whole snake-handling commune." Banner dries his hands while I scan the next page in the stack.

"This one's an application for adoption."

"Anyone you know?"

"It seems to be for—Jeremiah."

"He was adopted?"

"It's news to me." I peruse the rest of it. "Maybe it's a rough draft. His mother's the only one who filled it out. It doesn't appear to be complete."

Setting that one aside, my eyes grow huge in my head, and I simply present the next to Banner without explanation.

"'The Last Will and Testament of Edna May Miller,'" he reads. "Mammaw?"

"Mammaw," I confirm.

"'Being of sound mind do hereby bequeath my estate in its entirety, in equal parts, to each one of my grandchildren.'"

"Why in this world would Jeremiah give me a copy of my grandmother's will?"

"Why would he even have it?" We're hunched over the table now, shoulder to shoulder. "Ees, why did your mammaw skip her own children with the inheritance?"

"It's all a bit hush-hush. Daddy and Aunt Rose had another sibling. She was troubled. She stole from Mam and Pap and skipped town—long before I came along. We learned not to ask about it, because it made Mammaw sad. But right after Pap died, I walked in on Daddy and Aunt Rose discussing her. I think maybe she had shown up trying to lay claim to things, but I missed that part because Daddy kicked me out of the room."

"Doubtless that didn't keep you from finding a way to hear them."

"Certainly not. Jake and I promptly climbed into the attic's crawl space to listen through the vent. They convinced Mammaw that skipping a generation would be the best way to keep the property safe and whole."

"Was your troubled aunt named Elsbeth?"

"How did you know that?"

In response, he hands over another certificate he's found.

This certifies that Elsbeth Loralei Miller and William Likely Banks were united in marriage on—

"Where do I know that man's name?" Banner asks.

"Sheriff Billy," I say.

"Ew. He could be her son, right?"

"Same name, different suffix. Billy's a junior."

"Your aunt married Billy's dad?"

I raise my hands in ignorance. "I've never met the woman. I don't even know where she moved."

"North Carolina." He indicates the state seal on the certificate.

The conversation is suspended when a sharp knock hits the front door. "Isla? It's Officer Connors. Kevin," he adds.

"That was fast." I throw a look at our papers as I travel to the door. "Will you snap pictures of those?"

Yet another document is thrust before my face as I open the door. "What is it?" I ask pulling back to see it better.

"It's a governmental contract between the national park and a towing company. We'll be crossing the property tomorrow with a crane. Will you sign this to give us permission?"

As I sign, he says, "Can I come in?"

"Of course."

I wave him in, and he skips the niceties. "You were Airborne, right?" he asks Banner. "You're comfortable rappelling?"

Banner ignores the question in anticipation of the request. "I'll go with you. Let me get changed."

"We don't have much daylight left," Connors calls after him. "And I probably shouldn't ask, but I've gotta know."

If Billy is in that car, he means.

"Well, he is *not* in the plastic bag," I offer. "Because that turned up in our garage—with these papers in it."

Connors quickly scans them. "That bag was bulky. What else was inside?"

"There was a big rattlesnake statue. We left it in the barn."

"OK. We'll go over it later."

Banner returns, tucking a brown Army t-shirt into his cargo pants, which are tucked into his well-worn boots. I think he gets hotter by the minute. "You've got the gear, I guess," he says to Connors.

"Affirmative."

"You coming?" Banner asks me.

"Yes." I turn to Officer Connors. "I am an excellent cliff dweller, *Kevin.*" I emphasize his name to let him know that he should have asked me too. "I mean, who can't rappel? All you have to do is fall."

I seek confirmation from Banner who licks his lips, and there's a bit of smugness to it.

"You doubt it?" I ask him.

"Certainly not. If your target is stable and large and directly beneath you. And if the thing you're tethered to isn't moving through the sky at a fair clip. Or being fired upon."

I frown at him. Who knows what all the man has done by way of falling from aircraft? Even so, I say, "I'll beat you to the bottom and back."

He snorts, but before he can condescend to give an actual reply, Connors says, "Nope. You are not trained. You are not doing it. You can race on your own time."

"This *is* my own time."

"Isla, I don't have the patience to discuss it," he snaps. "My friend could be lying dead at the bottom of the ravine."

I clamp my mouth shut before conceding with a, "K."

Connors stalks out the door, but Banner takes my hand. "We'll race when Wren gets back."

"Sure," I mutter. "After you've had a chance to *practice*."

He's chuckling under his breath. He likes me. But his mood takes a dive when we get outside, and more so the closer we drive to the ravine.

"The embers have caught on something," he says.

He's right. What I was able to disregard as haze before, is clearly smoke now, and the smell is stronger. Beyond the ledge, the wreckage smolders, but that's not what's causing most of the smoke. Off to the side, small fires are feasting on patches of undergrowth. Fortunately, it's mostly water and rock down there.

Connors curses. I feel for him. "Alright, well? We'll just..." He shakes his head and sighs into his next words. "Wait for the rangers to put all that out. Where is the rain when you need it?"

Banner watches Connors struggle. "No, we're gonna go make sure," he says and kicks into gear, walking several yards along the cliff in one direction and then the other. Finally, he points to a tree. "Tie off there."

Rummaging through the officer's large bag, he throws a rope down at his feet. Then, without waiting to see his order obeyed, he steps into a harness like it's a pair of shorts and tightens it around his legs and waist.

Connors lurches into action with half a smile. He rounds the tree a few times and makes a solid knot, tests it with a tug. Banner is tying off to a tree nearby while Connors hooks up a harness and turns his back to the drop.

"Stop," Banner says. "Old habits." He tugs Connors' harness and the knot around Connors' tree. Then he opens his arms to invite the officer to do the same.

"Good," Connors confirms and briefly clasps Banner's arm. I think it's his way of saying thanks. It's touching, the flash of understanding between them.

The two men rappel while I study the warm glow of the fires they'll soon walk among. Most are on the verge of extinction, but a few of them strike me as ominous. Not that I'd say that aloud to

Banner. I wonder what made him insist. The memory of Sayeed's charred remains must be forefront in his mind. I bet he wants to find Billy's body before Connors does—to try to spare him.

It doesn't take long before they're on foot and exploring the scorched metal. I didn't notice before, but the car is wedged in such a way that keeps it off the ground. They seem to be discussing how to proceed.

Banner pushes down on the back bumper—I think it's the back —before he climbs up and bounces on top of it to ensure stability. Now he's lying on the ground to scoot right under the damn thing. "What the hell?!" I yell from the top.

Only Connors raises his face. He puts a hand to his ear because apparently my *what the hell* wasn't loud enough. I just flag my hands in irritation.

Honestly. He's going to singe his own body under there, not to mention get squashed when the unstable ruin collapses on top of him.

"Banner!" I scold impotently from nearly a hundred feet up.

And now I grow extremely anxious with all the morbid possibilities assaulting my mind—that is the trouble with an over-active imagination. The car could fall or re-explode. There could be a mountain lion hiding underneath. Or a bear. A beaver's dam could break and a flash flood could come barreling through. Rocks could tumble down. A lightning strike—

I'm shifting from foot to foot, wringing my hands. How much could there possibly be to explore under there? But then I see Banner's boots and he reemerges whole. *Thank God.* He and Connors are speaking, gesturing. They walk further away from the car with flashlights sweeping from side to side.

It's getting harder to focus on them. Darkness has begun to impose itself. I look back to the clearing beyond the thick woods to where it's lighter when the ropes begin to groan under the tension of the men climbing up. Banner crests the top first, his handsome cheek smudged with soot.

"There's a lot of blood," he says, checking to make sure Connors is out of earshot. "A floor mat had been tossed out and it's covered. But there's no body. No bones. No clothing that we could find."

Connors reappears, climbs over the ledge, and lies on his back for a moment catching his breath. His face is turned to the treetops. His brow is heavy in thought. Finally, he rises to his feet, extricates the rolled floor mat from his harness, and says, "Let's go nail that son of a bitch."

By the time we get to the house, I'm worried Connors is going to stroke out. He paces back and forth convinced that Billy is dead by Jeremiah's hand, but he's so out of sorts, he can't string together a coherent plan. No reasonable advice will calm him. He just keeps saying, "We have to go right now. Tonight."

Finally, Banner seizes his shoulders and says, "Brother, nobody is going there tonight. You are not thinking straight. You don't know whose blood that is, or even if it's human. Jeremiah may be some-place close to this house, and there is no way I'm leaving Isla here alone." He kicks a chair from the table. "Sit down."

Amazingly, Connors complies. I think he needed someone to take charge. I bet Banner's dad would be proud of him.

"You're going to eat something," Banner tells him. When he moves toward the kitchen I motion for him to stay.

Connors is one lucky man. I pull out the leftovers from my birthday dinner while Banner assures Connors that he will accom-pany him to the Ridleys' in the morning.

"First light?" Connors asks.

"Sure."

"Will you take me to where you saw him last?"

"We can retrace our steps from right here. We'll bike there and approach the exact same way. Why don't you stay here tonight?" Banner glances my way to see if he's overstepped, but I show him it's fine.

"No, I want to be close to a working phone," Connors says. "Try to round up a search party and see if Jeremiah will just come in will-ingly. Not that anyone there has answered the phone yet."

"Come on, Kevin," I cajole him. "Stay here. The house is happier the fuller it gets."

"Thanks, guys. I appreciate it, but I'm OK."

He's calmer after that. He eats. Banner even gets him to tell some stories about growing up with Billy. I don't realize there's an ulterior motive until Banner says, "His folks were like family to you, then."

"His mom is like a second mom to me, to this day. She brings snacks to the office, makes me cookies on my birthday."

"And his dad?"

"Well, his dad up and left when Bill was in high school. He took up with somebody. Ended up moving to Raleigh. It's still a sore spot."

"Does Billy hang out with them?"

"Hell, no. I'm not sure he's spoken to his dad since the day he left."

Banner plunks down the marriage certificate.

"That"—Banner points to the woman's name—"is Isla's estranged aunt."

"Elsbeth," I say, and I get the queerest feeling when I say it like I've unlocked a door to a forbidden closet.

There Was a Pit Here Deeper Than a Man is Tall

BANNER'S POINT OF VIEW

I JERK awake in a panic because smoke permeates my nasal cavity, and I'm going to die. It's an illusion. I know that. A symptom of my PTSD. But it's all I can do to lie here while I feel like I'm suffocating. I force myself to breathe in rhythm. Inhale four, hold four, exhale six. Inhale four, hold four, exhale six. It's taken a hell of a lot of therapy and a number of panic attacks to get to this point.

Beside me in the dark, Isla slides her hand over my chest. "What is it Ban?" she mumbles.

Why does it always have to seem so real?

"Sorry, Babe. There's nothing."

She pushes to an elbow. "There's smoke."

"Yeah," I say flatly.

"No, I mean—there's smoke." She's out of bed and down the hall without another word, Lucy at her heels.

"Ees?"

When I catch up, they're on the front porch, and the smell's a lot stronger.

"It's too *wet* for the fire to catch," she protests.

"It's *not* that wet anymore," I counter and stalk through the house to survey the sky from the back deck. It's just beginning to brighten. I don't see any flames, but I am officially on alert. "Let's ride out and have a look."

"It could be that the wind has just changed and trapped the smoke."

"Let's ride out," I insist. We jog to the room to pull on our clothes, a feat which I fully manage to accomplish before the woman has selected the first item. I'm trying not to chomp at the bit.

"Should we make some coffee to take?" she asks. She's only just now clasping her bra. Normally, I would not rush this part.

"Are you kidding me?" I snap.

Her face softens in understanding. "I am. Sorry." Picking up the pace, she quickly pulls a tank top over her head and grabs the first pair of shorts she comes to.

"I just want to know if there's a problem," I say.

"I know. Come on." Isla tosses her keys to me, which sets Lucy's hindquarters to wagging, and it makes me feel better too. Driving is something I can control.

Connors is pulling up to the house as we're pulling out. "Where are you going?" he asks through his window. "We have to get started."

"Jump in. We need to make sure the fires aren't spreading."

"No, I called it in. They won't leave it to chance."

"Get in," I demand. "Ees, will you—" She's already crawling back between our seats to make room. "Thanks."

Connors lumbers into the passenger seat with an exasperated sigh.

Whatever. I'm not leaving it to chance.

There are already rangers on the other side of the ravine when we get there. Last night's fires are out, but others are burning further down, and one wants to crawl up the embankment.

"What do you think?" Connors calls across.

A ranger, who is rigging himself to rappel, lifts his head. His partner is lowering a bundle of shovels and picks.

"It'll be contained as soon we can get down there," he says.

"See?" Connors tells me. "Let's go."

It takes me a moment to concede, but I guess they've got it under control, so I reluctantly drive us back to the house.

I do not enjoy the idea of leaving Isla here alone. It's not that she can't take care of herself. She's absolutely capable. I think of the way she cocked that shotgun and yelled at a bear three times her size. Even so, I feel compelled to protect her—especially with all the blood we found. Who knows what's going on?

"What are you looking at me like that for?" she asks. I'm lingering inside the entryway. Connors is huffing on the walkway behind me—just to remind he's ready.

"I should stay," I tell her.

"No, you should go find Sheriff Billy. You want to as much as Connors does. Anyone can see that."

I reach for a strand of her hair. "What does your gut say? Is Jeremiah hanging out close to here or did he go back home? I don't want to leave you vulnerable."

A little hum means that I've pleased her. She pushes against me, her breasts beautifully plumped on my chest, and she's gazing at me like I'm all the shit. *Damn,* she gets me hard.

"I doubt he's anywhere near here," she says. "I'll be fine."

"What if you need me?"

"I'll find a way to call. Or I'll go get the rangers. They're practically in the backyard."

"You remember how to use the Sig?"

"No, Ban, you take it," she rushes to say and, for the first time, she betrays concern about me going. Her bare shoulder gives a half-hearted shrug, so I bend to kiss it. "I'll take it," I assure her. "But you don't need to worry about me. I won't do anything foolish."

"Oh my gosh!" Connors gripes. "Can we go?"

It makes me grin. "Keep her safe, Luce," I tell my dog. "Let her know if anyone comes around." I snap my holster to my pants, kiss her one more time, and reach over the door to smack the shotgun on my way out. "Keep this one in mind, Sharp-shooter. I'll be back as soon as I can."

She'll be fine. She can take care of herself. This is what I'm trying to convince myself of when Connors shoves a helmet into my gut.

"I don't understand."

"You didn't think I was going to *bike* bike did you?" he asks.

While I've been ignoring him, Connors has been unloading two dirt bikes, and suddenly I'm feeling better about how this whole situation is unfolding. I take the helmet to admire the bikes. They're powerful. "Do these belong to you?"

"I'm a total junky," Connors says. "You know how to get there?"

"I think so." I look at Isla. It's possible she's laughing at me for how easily distracted I've become by machines.

"Just stay on the trail," she laughs (*yep*). "When you reach the river, you can cross onto the Ridleys' property or climb up the falls as we did with Billy. You'll see where it's shallow enough."

"I remember." I squash my head into the helmet, flash my eyebrows, and rev up the bike.

"Hey, that one's mine," Connors protests.

"Not today!" I tell him and take off down the path, leaving him to process the disappointment.

I am *screaming* down the messy trail, wholly enthralled simply to feel the power of the engine underneath me when Connors catches up with a *whoop* like he's enjoying the hell out of it. He overtakes me where the path widens out, a huge grin plastered on the only part of his face I can glimpse beneath the helmet. For the next three curves, I try to slide past him, but he keeps skidding my way to cut me off.

So, I guess we're friends now.

It is only at this point when the speed of the chase has blown all the worries right out of my mind, that a new worry rushes to fill the void. Why didn't Isla push to come with us? It's not like her. She saw Connors unloading the motorcycles. She would have loved this. She would have had a great time, would probably have bested both of us. She's not shy. And she's not the type to sit things out.

The other day, when we climbed up the falls, she wasn't fearful. She was excited by the possibility of uncovering secrets. And later, though she was unnerved by Old Man Ridley, it wasn't as much as I was. And not at all by Jeremiah. Not really. You'd think she would have been more worried about the documents he left—but she treated them like clues in a game. And that huge, damned, yellow snake? Like a family heirloom.

"Why'd you stop?"

I'm standing with a foot on either side of the bike when Connors doubles back to check on me. My jaw's askew. My hands fisted around the handlebars. *What did she say she was going to do till I got back?* I search my memory. *Did I even ask?*

"Dude, why'd you stop?"

"Isla didn't so much as slow down when she thought I'd abandoned her yesterday. It tore her up, certainly, but it sure as hell didn't stop her from doing exactly what she'd intended to do all along."

"Are you saying something to me?" Connors asks.

I look up like I've only just heard him. "Coming." I twist the throttle and bound forward, but my mind spins faster than the tires. Did I not just get through promising the woman that I wouldn't do anything foolish? But *she's* the wild one. I should have had her promising *me*.

OK, well you just have to trust her. She's in her element. She's smart. She's bold. She's—maybe too bold. I can't think about it. I have to keep my head on the task at hand. The sooner we find Jeremiah and sort this thing out, the sooner she'll be out of harm's way.

"Is this it?" Connors asks once we reach the river.

"Yeah." I scan the pool where Jake drowned. "There are two ways to get across. That path to the left is easier. It's more of a hike than a climb. It leads directly onto the Ridleys' fields." I pivot a bit. "And that trail has a wall we have to scale. Good holds though."

Remember who told me that? The wild child. The one I cannot now imagine remaining in the safe, comfortable cabin when there are answers to be found.

"Where did you last see Billy?" Connors asks.

I simply gesture to the falls and we march. I'm keeping an eye out for the Ridleys, but that's about the only sense I can employ. The waterfall makes it impossible to hear anyone except for Connors, who is by my side.

My eyes wander up to where Jake had stood yelling his throat out while Isla worked to understand what he was saying—and she's been working ever since. It's no wonder she's so bent on finding out what really happened.

Before we begin our ascent, I ensure that my firearm is secure. I unload and reload. Connors waits for me. Doesn't ask any questions.

When we get to the top, clouds hide the sun. It's colder up here. Probably because of the way the rocks form a barrier around us. I lead Connors across the river and recall how Isla had slinked off by herself that day. I hadn't thought of it like that then. I'd been speaking to Billy about giving her some time to explore.

He had grown strange to the point of acting suspicious. He had towered over her and tried to rush her back home—even seemed to have demeaned Jake, calling him a wild son-of-a-bitch. But when I'd come to Jake's defense, Isla just blew it off. "He *was* wild," she'd said.

Must run in the family.

Why does that make me want to smile?

"Connors, have you ever been to a church where they handled venomous snakes?"

"That's been outlawed for ages."

"Yeah, but the Ridleys are hyper-religious. Apparently, Billy has had to warn them not to use snakes as a religious test on more than one occasion."

Connors shivers. "Well, I hope I never get the call. I hate snakes."

We find a way across the river and are dodging briars when we come to the place where I stood when I saw Old Man Ridley jerking Isla back by her hair and Jeremiah catapulting himself over the pit. But, though I am certain of my bearings, this is not the same place. There is no garden-like lawn. There is no pit. Instead of cultivated space, there are leaves and undergrowth that appear to have been growing here for years.

I fight a cold wave of unreality and spin on the spot like a dog chasing its tail. Behind me, the rock is as I remember it. I duck behind to re-establish that this is the correct way, the *only* way, and then I re-emerge to the same dizzying sense of insanity.

"Are we lost?" Connors asks.

I begin to kick the leaves. I jerk up undergrowth for a sign that I haven't lost my mind. "There was a pit here deeper than a man is tall," I say. "There were wildflowers. There was *grass*—like the kind you have to mow. This was all a garden not three days ago."

On the other side of what should have been the pit, I spot the straight pathway through the trees, the one that led to the crucifix. "*There*—you can't un-grow that." And yet, even that seems less obvious, less purposeful. For one thing, the focal point is gone, the crucifix, the yellow snake that—well, we know where that ended up.

"You've only been here the once, though, right?"

"Connors, this is the place!" At this point, I'm down on my knees using a sharp stone as a hoe. I chop and dig, but to no avail. "They made it disappear. The lawn. The altar."

"The pit?" Connors says.

The sheriff. I don't say it aloud, but I figure Connors must be thinking it too, because he says, "And this is where you last saw Billy? Where *was* this pit? They just filled it in?"

I swing my arms to demonstrate the circumference. "Right beneath me. Twice my wingspan. And over six feet deep." I flash my brow but keep my mouth shut. *A perfect grave.*

He gives me a quizzical glance and pats a spruce tree that stands where I've claimed the pit to have been. "This didn't spring up overnight."

"It—looks very old," I agree.

"*Years* old."

What the fuck is going on here? "I don't know what to say. This is the place. Maybe we could dig around?"

Connors seems to debate that. "We should go to the house," he decides. "I can serve the warrant and ask some of the searchers to dig here." He marks the ground with three orange flags.

"Let's get the dirt bikes up here," I say. "It's a big piece of property. I'd rather have speed on my side if we're going to be out in the open."

Once we get the bikes up the easier path, we ride over the Ridleys' fields, past the chicken coops, past the barn and the white pickup truck, and up to the front door.

"Ridley?" Connors pounds three times with his fist. "I'm here on police business."

Instead of an answer, the pickup roars to life, and Mr. Ridley races past, throwing gravel and dust behind its wheels and fishtailing until he catches traction on the main road.

"I have a warrant." Connors sardonically waves said warrant after the truck is long gone. Then he pounds some more. "Jeremiah?! We're coming in! Police!" The door is unlocked, but before he pushes it open, he says to me, "I don't know how long it will take more officers to get here. If Billy is—"

"I'm with you," I assure him and secure my firearm in front of me with both hands. I don't intend to use it, but I know what it's for.

When Connors swings the door open, I sweep the room with my gun as well as my eyes. From somewhere to my left, a man's voice can be heard, but only as if from a television. No other noises come to me.

There's a museum-like quality to the house as if no one actually lives here. I don't think it has seen any updates in a long time, maybe since the mom died. There's a couch. There are chairs. But I bet the last time they were employed—it's a weird thought, I know —was during the mourning period when neighbors brought food and sat in uncomfortable silence, fumbling for a way *not* to say that Ridley's loss was his own fault. Trying not to ask why he hadn't just taken her to the doctor. Trying not to lock eyes with the young son who would never feel his mother's arms again.

Or, hell, maybe there was a crowd of like-minded parishioners congratulating him on his remarkable faith.

Above the couch hangs a needlepoint verse from the Bible: *The prayer of a righteous man is powerful and effective.*

This screams irony to me. Either he wasn't righteous or he didn't pray. Or what he prayed for was not what I would have.

We clear the downstairs rooms: the kitchen, with its smell of burnt coffee, the laundry room, which is oddly pristine, and the office, from where the man's voice can be heard. He's a preacher (surprise) on a TV monitor. He seems to be practicing his sermon, though, not delivering it. There's a mirror in front of him, and he keeps pausing to consult his notes.

There are other monitors besides the one airing *Preacher TV.* In comparison to what we've seen so far, this room is strangely tech-savvy. A base for surveillance operations. I angle my body so that I'm not wedged behind the desk, nor caught with my back to the door.

Each monitor is labeled according to its feed. One of them spies on the congregation of a small, country church from behind the pulpit where the preacher would stand. Right now, it only shows empty pews and a few people standing or strolling around completing small tasks: turning on fans, opening doors... Two more of the monitors picture seemingly innocuous outdoor scenes. But *one* of them shows my Isla. She's gorgeous, standing in her bedroom in the window's natural light, holding a small mirror and stroking makeup onto her eyelashes. Absolutely naked. One of her curvy hips is thrust to the side. One of her breasts is spilling over her uplifted arm. And her smooth, firm stomach—

"Is that—" Connors begins.

"It is."

"Does she walk around like that all th—" He seems to realize what he's asking—or feels the weight of my attention—and averts his eyes. "Sorry."

I don't know whether to knock him in the head or brag that she *does* walk around like that—with me. I should probably just move on.

"I thought you disabled the camera," Connors says.

"I did. Jeremiah must have repaired it." *Why is Isla putting on makeup?*

"You think Jeremiah installed the cameras, then?"

I lift my palms. "Or his dad? I mean..." I motion around. "It's their house."

Connors indicates a different screen (thankfully, Isla has walked out of hers). "I want to know where *that* is."

The screen he has indicated is labeled "back deck," but it is clearly not the view from a back deck, making me think that the camera has been repositioned or moved entirely. Its subject is a gray room as if the space is fairly dark, but the shot is clearly live. There are lines of lighter shades that make me think there's a window or door off to the side, but no direct light is pouring in.

A flurry of wings bobs into view, and the room gets a bit brighter.

"It's in one of the chicken coops," I realize. "Is that a boot?" The way the camera is positioned, we can see one leg extending away and wearing a boot.

"I think we found the sheriff!" Connors says. He would have run out the back right then if I hadn't checked him.

"Hey! What about Jeremiah?"

We clear the rest of the house in a hurry and make our way to the chicken coops. I'd like to clear the barn and the other open buildings we pass, but Connors has become impossible to rein in. I can't blame him for wanting to rescue his friend, but I don't want to take unnecessary risks.

Bursting into the door of the first coop, Connors sends the chickens into an uproar—squawking, hopping, semi-flying—frenetic fowl everywhere. They're incredibly loud. They seek purchase on narrow ledges where there are small openings that let in light and air. Otherwise, they strut around our feet in choppy, spasmodic lurches, occasionally tilting their heads sideways to study us with one suspicious eye.

Connors has lost all sense of professional decorum. He races through the tall, narrow building with abandon. "Billy?!"

He's making me as nervous as he's making the hens. If someone is surveilling the chicken coop with a camera, then it may be under guard. They could be keeping tabs on it from somewhere other than the monitors in the house. Like right outside the door.

"Billy?!" Connors yells again.

This time I sling him against the wall. "Enough!"

It shocks him into submission. Wipes the excitement from his face.

"Do it right, or I'm out!" I snarl.

"Oh," he says. "You're right." He doesn't argue, doesn't bow up. Just accepts my rebuke and steps back into form. So, I relax the forearm I have pressed into his chest and then drop it altogether.

The rest of the coop, we travel in silence (except for the hens) and step out into the sunlight just feet from the next coop's door.

After we clear that one, there is only one more—the one furthest from the house. This one is different. It's wider, for one thing. It has a ramp up to the middle of it, and a garage door large enough for a wheelbarrow.

"This is the one," I say under my breath. "Ready?" He nods, and I motion us into action.

We're so quiet this time, we don't upset the chickens. We trek from partition to partition on opposite sides, always scanning the next opening before we duck through. Toward the center, while we're nearing the fourth narrow chamber of the coop, I see a man sitting on the floor. Well, I see the bottom of his leg and his boot. The rest of him is obscured. I chop the air with two fingers, then raise one to my lips. We travel the remaining length with firearms at the ready.

My own anticipation is building. I can hear my pulse, and I can only imagine how strong Connors' is. But he keeps it together, trudges as quietly as he can in this wobbly trailer of a hen coop.

Once to the room in question, we have crisscrossing views of the space. I shake my head to show him there is no one on the side that I can see, but Connors emits a little wail and dashes in. He dives onto the floor, while I instinctively jerk myself back to avoid an explosion that doesn't come. When I peek around, Connors is bizarrely tearing the boot from the leg. The leg is not fixed to a person. And it appears to be stuffed with straw.

"It is his boot!" Connors protests.

"Well, thank God it's not his leg." I'm still all systems go, scanning the room without entering. The camera is the same kind I crushed back at Isla's. I've got a bad feeling. "It's a setup. We need to get out."

"Who set it up?" Connors asks. He's not ready to leave. "How far into this boot can these pants possibly go? Did they superglue them?"

"Stop fucking around, *Kevin*." I got that from Isla. The use of his first name in her pretty mouth has a crippling ring of disdain. I don't think I did it right.

I'm trying to peer out the small row of windows for anyone lurking around the coop, first on this side and then the other. I can't see much detail through them.

"Holy shit!" Connors barks and simultaneously tosses the boot from himself. He half-scoots/half-jumps and nails the buttress of the wall with his head and shoulders. It rocks the whole coop, slamming two gates shut, one on the far side of the small space and one between us, effectively trapping him inside like cattle.

"Connors?" I seize the gate and give it a shake, but it's locked. I search for a latch and scan the walls for a lever or a switch, but there's nothing. From Connors' side, an awkward, sideways, coiling catches my eye, and a disgruntled rattlesnake begins to sound the *get-the-fuck-away-from-me* song of its people. I press my face to the gate's iron slats. "Was that in the boot?!"

Connors whines. He looks like he's trying to hold his head on with both hands.

"OK, don't freak out," I tell him. "It will calm down if you calm down. Look at me." He won't, or he can't. "I'm gonna get you out."

Connors is physically trembling. I think snakes might be for him what fire is for me. I keep talking. "Connors, I'm gonna get you out." I'd ram my shoulder against the thing, but I'm scared of what it would mean to the cranky snake. "Do you see a latch on that side?"

He casts a sidelong glance over the gate for about one-half-second before stammering, "N-no."

"Alright. It must be on the outside. It's made for livestock."

Connors doesn't appear to hear me. "Kevin? That means I have to step outside to see if there's a way to push open the gate from there."

He doesn't even nod his head. He's fixated on the rattlesnake.

"You know what? Just shoot the damn thing." I'd do it myself if

I could get the angle through the gate. It *is* pretty close to him. And it's a small, small space. He's paralyzed. "I'll be right back."

Moving as swiftly as I dare, for fear of causing more distress for the snake, I poke my head out the door to scan the area. I don't see anybody, but *anybody* could be hiding. There are somewhere between three and four *billion* excellent spots to make oneself invisible. Even so, it's good to breathe fresh air.

I jog outside the coop to its middle. "I'm here, buddy. How're you doing?" I can't see in, but it doesn't matter. I have to slide that gate. And there it is. From this side, you can easily unhook the catch. I pull, and the gate begins to slide. From behind the wall, I hear a whimper.

"I'm the one doing that," I grunt. "Hang in there." This part of the job was clearly meant for more than one man. "Is it open now?" I pant. "Can you walk out?"

Bang! Bang! Bang! I drop to my knees and cover my head as shots ring out, and then I hear footsteps smashing down the long hall of the coop and chickens protesting. The door bursts open. Connors tumbles down the steps and falls to the ground, where he writhes from side to side.

I rush to him and put my hands on him. "Are you hurt? Were you bitten?!"

He's groaning.

"Connors!" I search his ankles and arms. "Were you bitten?"

"Was I? I don't think so. Do you think I was?"

"What? No, I don't see anything."

"I shot that mother fucker," he says. "I shot him three times. He winked at me, and I shot him!"

"The snake winked at you?"

Connors nods emphatically. "I shot him right in his winky eye."

He's dead serious. I bark out a laugh and lean back against the coop with a big sigh that turns into more laughter. The more I do it, the better it feels, and I guess the release is so welcome, that I give it free rein. Connor's wide eyes are full of indignation, and that just cracks me up even more. I laugh until he laughs, and soon we're howling and I have to clutch my sides to endure it.

I'm sure we look ridiculous cackling on the ground beside these smelly, damn chicken coops, intoxicated on relief. We can hardly pull ourselves together long enough to figure out what to do next. I wipe my eyes.

"Goddamn snake winked at you," I say and help him to his feet. "And *that's* why you shot it."

"I hate snakes," he says.

"Really?"

"*Yeah*, really! When I was—oh, I see what you did there. Dude, I've been traumatized."

I can't help it. I wink at him now, nice and slow.

"Do not think for one second that I will not shoot your Army ass, you winkin' son of a—"

He's cut off when voices erupt on either side of the coop, and several forms appear wielding firearms.

"Police! Drop your weapons!"

I raise my hands and lower my gun to the ground, but Connors just rolls his eyes. "*Now*, we get manpower."

"We heard gunshots," an officer addresses him.

"That was me. The threat has been eliminated."

I snort.

"Don't you dare, Army," he warns.

Now that we're several officers strong, Connors delegates some to dig up the pit, some to clear the property for real, and some to give him more information on the surveillance system in the office of the house. That's where he sets up a command post.

"We'll organize a larger search if we don't find Sheriff Billy on site. When does the cadaver dog get here?"

I walk with the officers to the house and await news from the search. If Jeremiah is on-site, I'd like to ask him a few questions myself. When we get the all-clear, though, I want to get back to Isla. What if *that's* where he is?

"Son of a *bitch*," Connors says. "Are those fuckers just toying with us?" He's gripping the back of the office chair and staring at the live feed from inside the church. "Jeremiah Ridley is sitting right there in that pew!"

My thoughts immediately turn to Isla. *I doubt he's anywhere near here,* she'd said. That little *fox.* She knew *exactly* where he would be! Did his girlfriend not specifically tell us? I don't know whether to be pissed or to laugh. She's going to corner Jeremiah Ridley in his own sanctuary, the way he cornered her in hers. No police to intimidate him. No over-protective Army guy to remind him of Jake. And no easy escape without causing a scene. *Wow. I'm impressed.*

ISLA'S POINT OF VIEW

IT PROBABLY WASN'T the best idea to come. There are several reasons. Not the least of which is that upon entering the dimly lit sanctuary, worshipers gawk at me like they know good and damn well what kind of sinner I am. It's unnerving. I already spent fifteen minutes in the parking lot working up the nerve to come in. The steeple's pretty. There's a cross perched on top and a real, iron bell. The rest of the small building is whitewashed cinder block.

—Reminds me of something Mammaw said when Jeremiah's mother was dying. "Whitewashed religion." And she'd quoted Jesus. Something about the church being corrupted by its leaders.

I'm staring down a red-carpeted aisle and what should catch my eye but a chalice full of wine. The words, "Take. Drink," are chiseled into the wooden table upon which it stands. The irony is not lost on me. Today is my fifth day sober—not counting the debacle of yesterday morning—and right now I'd like to drain that thing dry. My eyes linger on the cup.

Aren't they supposed to offer grape juice to the *weaker brethren?* What the heck am I supposed to do during communion time?

I do realize that this is the least of my worries.

Sidling into one of the back pews, I peruse the place as

discretely as I can, but it's impossible to be invisible here. It's just the one room with about...twelve darkly stained benches on either side of a center aisle. None of them seat my bulky neighbor, but I'm confident he'll show up—also confident that he'll be loath to cause a scene in church. Maybe this will be the perfect place for him to get on with his confession about Jake—maybe let me know what happened to Billy.

I wonder how Banner is doing.

There's a Bible in a wooden pocket on the back of the pew in front of me. I proceed to look up the word *whitewashed. Whitewashed.* Here it is. *Your religious leaders are like whitewashed tombs. Clean on the outside. But inside, death and all kinds of impurity dwell.*

It probably wasn't the best idea to come.

"Good morning." I look up to find a plump woman with a kind face. "Is this your first time visiting with us?" She scans my yellow sundress, which I wore to blend in, but which I now notice is about four feet shorter than hers. I glance around at the other women. They take maxi to a whole new length.

Here are the ways in which I don't stick out: I'm white. Even that is up for debate. If I could see more than the ladies' hands and faces, I'd have more to go on, but I don't think any of these women expose too many skin cells to the sun. Now I'm worried about their levels of vitamin D.

The face of my greeter has morphed from kind to slightly concerned. She had asked me a question.

"Yes," I say quickly. "I'm just visiting. Hoping to see an old friend, actually. I heard he attends. Jeremiah Ridley?"

The woman makes an *ah* sound and then coos, "Jeremiah Ridley," as if he's the most eligible bachelor in the South. "That young man has the Spirit of God inside of him. I've never known anyone as righteous or as holy."

"Wow," I accidentally let slip. "That is quite a statement."

"You are looking for a good father and provider."

"*Huh?*"

"To start a family. You're sure to have loads of children. He is a *big* man."

I do not know this woman, but I am fairly certain, by the scandalous way she just drew out the word *big*, she is describing something other than Jeremiah's height. She blushes while I work to decipher what in the world she assumes I'm doing here.

Before she can divulge more, I dip my head to the open Bible in my lap, and I guess she decides I want to prepare myself for worship because she moves along.

I used to worship. Used to believe as Mammaw did. But going to church with a hangover sucks. Not just because of feeling vomitus and puffy and over-sensitive to light—those things I could possibly endure. It was the sharp point of my own hypocrisy that stabbed me. The whitewashed tomb of it. The cycle of confession, followed by the renewed commitment to live in clear-minded integrity, followed by the fuck-it-I-want-to-feel-better, followed by the blackout, and then the hangover. It's too hard to serve two masters. I gave my allegiance to the one who offered the quickest relief.

Take. Drink. This is my blood spilled for you. Do this in remembrance of me. It's funny that Jesus asks us to drink wine to remember him. And wasn't his first miracle turning water into wine? Honestly, the man was a little obsessed with alcohol.

I'm kidding, God, I think at the ceiling. *I'm the one with a strange, abusive relationship with something that should be a gift. But instead of smiting me, you gave me Banner. Please protect him. He's the best thing you ever did. Please let that lying, cheater Billy be OK.*

My prayer is cut short when the broad presence I seek settles into the pew a few rows ahead of me. As if he can feel my eyes upon him, he goes still and then slowly turns. I think it takes him a few seconds to believe I'm really there. He exhales an irritated huff, and honestly, he looks like he's been given a task that's too onerous to bear. His next move is to survey the room.

Jeremiah scoots out of his row and into mine while the plump, kind-faced woman watches. "Come on," he says and places a hand under my elbow.

"No." I don't stand up. "I'm not leaving. I need to talk to you."

"It's not safe for you here." He keeps his voice quiet and his hand on my arm.

"Jeremiah, we are in a house of God. *He's* not out to get me, is he?"

The sick look that crosses Jeremiah's face makes me wish I hadn't asked.

"I need to talk to you," I insist.

"Meet me in your cemetery."

"No." I lean in so that I don't have to raise my voice. "They're looking for you. They think you killed the sheriff."

"Is that what you think?"

"They found blood in his truck," I hiss. "You told me you killed —" A few of the congregants stir slightly. Jeremiah emits a low warning, so I get closer still. "I don't know what to think. I don't think you're a murderer. You left the papers for me, didn't you? I just want answers."

He can't reply because the piano begins to bang out a triumphant, royal-sounding hymn. It's energizing. Not creepy with every fifth note out of tune, and not played badly by some ancient practitioner as you might expect in an old, country church. The song sweeps the whitewashed tomb images from my mind and replaces them with thoughts of a military gala, the soldiers in formal attire, and their spouses dressed to the nines. Maybe all of the presidents are there along with—

The rest of the congregation rises to their feet thumbing through hymnals, so we both stand as well. From beyond the pulpit, a door opens, and a neatly suited man, the preacher I guess, steps out of a back room.

That's when I spot Mr. Ridley, mainly because the preacher spots him first, standing in the front row. I can't read his expression, but it is clearly not the joy of Christian fellowship. As everyone sings, Mr. Ridley scans the crowd. When his eyes snag on me, he seems stupefied, but then his lips begin to curl into a slow, malicious smile.

Jeremiah tenses. "Please, go," he says through his teeth, and the dreadful whine of his plea convinces me that I should.

I can't, though, because a tardy family hurries into our pew fumbling with hymnals and blocking my way. I'd push past Jeremiah, but the song ends, and everyone sits down, Jeremiah last of all. Stiffly. His eyes straight ahead. He tugs me down beside him and clenches the hard bench to either side of his knees.

Suddenly, he reaches over to roll the stones on my bracelets and gives my hand a quick squeeze before he returns to choking the bench. The kind-faced lady sends a smile and a knowing wink.

Once everyone is settled, the preacher greets us with a joke about the vacillating weather, how Randy Smith must be praying for rain on his crops, while his little Jimmy is asking for enough sun to play outdoors. A patronizing chuckle issues from the worshippers, and a man—I can only assume him to be Randy Smith—waves his hand accompanied by a loud, "Amen."

The preacher instructs us to bow for prayer, but a ballsy voice from up front calls out, "I have a word." I watch the muscles of Jeremiah's massive forearms strain as he grips the bench that much harder.

The preacher raises his head in what looks like mild curiosity, but I wonder if there is more underneath the expression than I can see.

"What's going on?" I whisper to Jeremiah. Only his eyes answer —*something bad*—by shifting my way and back to the man who has spoken. His father is standing now.

"Yes, Mr. Ridley?" the pastor says. "The Lord has given you a word? Please share it with us." Though the preacher invites Mr. Ridley to share, he does not sound that enthusiastic.

"From the prophet Isaiah," Mr. Ridley says and turns to face the congregation. "'When you pass through the waters, I shall be with you; and when you pass through the rivers, they shall not overcome you.'"

Well, that sounds nice. Encouraging even. Until Mr. Ridley continues with words of his own. "They are sinners whom God uses the river to scourge. Fornicators. Drunkards. Liars. Self-mutilators." Now his eyes land on me with all the judgment of doomsday, and several people turn to follow the track of his accusation. It is clear that he is singling out one hell-bound individual, and that individual is me.

I shake my head.

"You seduced your cousin, and God gave him to the river. Now here you are looking to snatch another young man to hell. But sinners who enter these sacred walls heap judgment onto themselves. Is it not written: 'No sinner shall live within my walls?'"

Jeremiah slowly stands, and as he does, murmurs arise. Though he's huge, he projects an air of humility. His shoulders slump forward like the last thing he wants to do is bring attention to himself.

"He's going to speak!" someone whispers. "The boy who took up the serpents."

"I didn't know he *could* speak," says someone else.

It occurs to me that Jeremiah isn't considered odd here. He's revered. He addresses the church at large. "You are my family. My sisters. My brothers. When my mother died, you took me in. You raised me."

"Yes, we did," a woman agrees supportively. "And you are ours."

Jeremiah gives her a small, grateful smile without meeting her eyes. "So, believe me," he continues, "when I tell you that this woman is a true child of God. Her heart is pure."

The preacher looks relieved. "Good. Well, I'm sure that is good enough for all of us."

Many voices attest that Jeremiah's word ends the matter.

"Bring her up, then," his father says, silkily. "And let this accreditation be confirmed."

"She has already been confirmed. I've witnessed it myself. During the worst of floods, the river could not overcome her. If that is the sign, then please know she is marked by God as his child."

"'And *these* signs shall follow them that believeth,'" his father answers. "'In my name shall they cast out devils; they shall speak with new tongues. They shall take up serpents; and if they drink any poison, it shall not hurt them.'"

Jeremiah strides to the front of the sanctuary and stands before the pulpit so that the arms of the cross on the wall behind seem to embrace him.

"The word of the LORD," he says.

The whole place inhales while Mr. Ridley's sour expression slides from Jeremiah to me—still in my pew—and back again.

"'You shall not put the LORD your God to the test,'" Jeremiah quotes.

"It's not the Lord I'd like to test," his father spits.

"Gentlemen?" the preacher says. "What is going on here? We haven't practiced public testing for many years."

But now, sounds are coming from Mr. Ridley that, at first, make me think he's having a seizure. Guttural popping syllables and groaning. The people lean in to hear what is being said. I don't know if he's sick, or possessed, or if he's playing a role.

"Is there an interpreter?" someone cries.

"Yes," Jeremiah answers briskly. "The Lord is telling me, through my father, to take Isla and go into the woods to allow the Lord to reward her faithfulness in the intimacy of his arms."

Wait. What? I'm not going to the middle of the woods with you.

"So, we'll go," Jeremiah says.

His father has suddenly ceased his fit and can speak in English again "Vengeance is mine! I shall repay!"

"Sayeth the *LORD*," Jeremiah adds.

"I shall send against them the fangs of wild beasts, the venom of vipers that glide in the dust."

"Sayeth the *LORD*," Jeremiah says again with emphasis. "Thank you, Father. We'll go fulfill the LORD's word."

"Surely not before you receive from the LORD's table." Ridley procures the communion cup, seems to add to it, and sweeps it through the air so that it is pointing across the room at me.

"Go on, child," a man encourages me. "And then you'll know the Lord's blessing."

I have no intention of moving up the aisle to Crazy Man Ridley, but all the saints begin to shunt me forward against my will. I catch Jeremiah's eye, but I can't tell what he's thinking.

When I'm face to face with Mr. Ridley, he holds the cup to my mouth.

"Oh, no thank you," I manage. I am pressed on every side, so I can barely do more than turn my head. "I don't drink alcohol."

"It's not wine," Ridley says.

"Let's do it right, Father," Jeremiah intervenes. "Reverend, will you allow me to serve the flock myself and to pray over them?"

Some of the parishioners gasp through surprised smiles and immediately find their way back to their seats. One of them actually squeals. What in the world has Jeremiah done to garner so much adoration?

Mr. Ridley has not budged. "Drink," he demands of me. "If you are a child of God."

It feels like a substantial threat. Not just, "If you don't drink, you'll look like a fool," but more, "If you don't drink, I'm going to toss you into an inescapable pit full of angry rattlesnakes, and you can prove yourself to them."

I flashback to how helpless it felt to be jerked back by the hair. I don't consider myself to be a weak or cowardly person, but inwardly, I cow to Mr. Ridley, and it fills me with as much pity as it does fear. *My god, what must Jeremiah have suffered all these years?*

My voice is unsteady. It barely comes out. "What is—" I have to swallow and begin again. "What is in there? Grape juice?"

"Do this in remembrance of me." He presses the rim of the chalice between my lips, uses it to tip my head.

"No," I say, working to keep my mouth closed. "I don't want it."

"You refuse the Lord's Cup?" Mr. Ridley thrusts a hand behind my head and the cup into my mouth, banging my tooth and bloodying my lip. Some of the liquid spills down my throat and I jerk away to cough and sputter. Meanwhile, Jeremiah knocks the cup out of his father's hand and sprays its contents across the carpet and onto the shoes of a man in the second row.

"Stop," he says, and his low tone rumbles through the room like an earthquake. "She is not at liberty to receive the Meal today. She is fasting, but she is too humble to declare that in front of the whole congregation. She protects you by refusing your advances. Would you tempt her to break a vow to the Lord?"

I never knew what a smooth liar Jeremiah Ridley could be! I'd be impressed if I wasn't suddenly dreadfully aware of how grievously I have underestimated him. He's not the backward little boy I took him to be. And he's not a gentle giant full of protective instincts like a sheepdog. He's something other. Something with the intellectual capacity to manipulate the twisted game his father has forced him to play. But to what end?

"Forgive me, Reverend," he says. "I did not mean to dishonor the sacred Cup. I will clean it up immediately. Allow me to go for towels, and please continue with the service."

The preacher nods in absolution and Jeremiah herds me to the back room, the same one the preacher came out of before the service began. Before the door has even closed behind us, he's cramming marble-sized objects into my mouth. My protest is stifled by his hand.

He bars the door shut with the clank of an iron bracket as I sputter and gag. And he flips a switch, a microphone maybe. I don't know, because I'm fighting him off of me so that I can get this stuff out of my mouth. I can't even bite down. There are too many hard lumps. My nostrils flare as I try to find oxygen. The substance turns globby and sweet. It inhibits my ability to form words. I'm smothering.

Jeremiah coils one snake-like constrictor of an arm around my rib cage, making it impossible for me to extricate myself.

"Swallow it," he demands.

I shake my head maniacally.

"Isla Miller," he seethes and pushes my chin upward the way we used to do Mammaw's dog to get him to take his medicine. "You had better swallow it down—right—now."

For the first time, I do believe he is capable of murder. I do believe he is capable of whatever it takes in this whole world to satisfy the requirements of whatever horrible god he is trying to appease.

Tears flood my eyes and fall onto my cheeks. I can't swallow. I can't breathe. It's too much. I choke and gasp for air, only to inhale the sugar and suction Jeremiah's hand to my lips. Some of the gunk oozes out of my mouth in a goopy slime, and he scoops it up with his thick fingers to stuff it back in. I'm going to die.

Finally, with a sneer of contempt, he fills a cup of water at a small sink and forces it into my hand. "Swallow it," he says again.

With the help of the water, I'm able to get it down. I spend a full minute coughing and fighting for breath. "Am I going to die, Jeremiah?" I manage to say. "Did you poison me?"

He scowls at me hard and then hands me a rough, brown paper towel with which I blow my nose and catch a glimpse of myself in the mirror, lips crystallized with sugar, mascara running from my eyelashes.

"No, I didn't poison you. My father did. The cup contained cyanide."

"I don't understand."

"'And if they drink poison, it shall not hurt them.'" He repeats that part of the verse his father said.

"Another test? It's a wonder any of you people are still alive."

"Well, you're not supposed to *drain* it."

"I wasn't trying to! You force-fed me sugar?"

"It binds with the cyanide in your stomach. Keeps it from being absorbed."

"And so, what? You keep it on you just in case?"

Jeremiah nods sincerely. "It's impossible for a human body to build up a tolerance to it."

I exhale a long-ass breath and look around. "I have to get out of here." When I turn back to Jeremiah, he's glaring down his nose at me with a double dose of *no shit.*

"Shut up, Jeremiah. If you had just come to talk to me to begin with, like a normal person, I wouldn't have had to track you down. Where are we? The preacher's office?"

"Yeah. And they won't give us long. They're being brain-washed right now into believing you should be put to the test."

"Well, isn't there a way out?"

"'Fraid not. But you know how to handle snakes. You'll be fine."

"No, I will not be *fine,*" I snap. "What are they planning?"

He glances at the door like he can see through it and takes a step that way.

"Jeremiah Ridley, if you walk through that door right now, I will *curse* you!"

That stops him in his tracks. He wheels around. "Don't say that, Isla!"

He's so sincere, I can see the little boy he used to be.

"You are such an enigma. Tell me you didn't kill Jake."

"I did though."

"You pushed him over the falls?"

"Yes."

My chin starts trembling. "Why did you do that?"

"I thought it was his only chance. He had trespassed into a— scene that he shouldn't have."

"Jeremiah, does your dad test you in that pit?"

He lifts his eyes but not his head. They are large and sad, and my anger surges against his father. "Did you feel humiliated that Jake saw what was happening to you? Is that why you pushed him?"

Jeremiah switches to a harder tone the way he'd done in the cemetery. "He was going to die anyway."

"Why was he going to die?" I push. "He was in his prime. He was—what happened to him that he was going to die?"

"He stepped in." Jeremiah lifts his face to the ceiling. "He took my beating. God help me. He took my beating and fell into the pit. I think he was bitten. I reached down and yanked him out. I had the strength of ten men that day."

"I know. You carried him all the way back."

"I felt like—"

"Samson," we both say.

I remember the character from Mammaw's Bible. He was strong like a superhero, but he was bizarre and cruel.

He continues, "Jake's blood, like Able's, cries out from the ground. I believe it. It changed my whole life. I was supposed to die. The fire said so. But Jake took my death. He took my curse, and I couldn't save him."

He sinks to his knees, and I'm not sure why, but I place my hand on his head. "I couldn't save him either, Jeremiah. I've been living with it too. Look, we have to let it go somehow. It was your father who killed him."

"No. It was my mother."

I feel awash with cold. "Jeremiah, what are you saying? Are you telling me your mom's alive? Or—is she a ghost?"

"My biological mother. Your aunt Elsbeth."

I sputter like I did when he was choking me with sugar. "Your mo— She was there?" Something clicks for me. All this time I thought I was seeing myself in memories and dreams about that day. But it was my aunt?

"My mom never told me," Jeremiah explains. "She just treated me like I was really hers. But that day, Elsbeth came to claim me."

"You're my cousin?"

Jeremiah tilts his head the way Lucy does when she's working to understand what's being asked of her. "Yes."

"She'd found out Mammaw had changed her will, hadn't she?" I ask.

"I think so. Why else would she come for me? I was nearly an adult. She never came around before that. But she learned things that day. Things that put your whole family in danger. And I don't know how much longer I can hold her off."

There's a knock at the door, more of a pounding really, and now I hear the unrest that is happening out there.

"There is only *through*," Jeremiah says. He mutters scripture to steel himself—or me—as he gets to his feet. "'When you pass through the waters, I will be with you; and through the rivers, they shall not overcome you; when you walk through the fire you shall not be burned, the flame shall not set you ablaze.'"

"Jeremiah? Get me out of here."

He goes silent, kind of bows to me, and throws open the door.

BANNER'S POINT OF VIEW

I **WATCH** on the screen as Jeremiah exits his pew to sit with a beautiful brunette a few rows back. Sure enough, my Isla has made her way to the church, and they are now speaking together—peaceably, as far as I can tell. The whole congregation stands to sing, and I lose sight of Isla, but Jeremiah's a full head and shoulders taller than everybody else, and he's plenty visible, moving his mouth along with the others, though he doesn't look that into it.

I watch for another few minutes. If he's going to play nice, then I'm going to try to find some answers. Church services are fairly uneventful, right? What could possibly happen in the middle of that crowd?

"She *knew* he would be there," Connors realizes out loud.

Of course, she did. I just shrug while Connors eyeballs me and then commands an officer to go wait outside the church to bring both father and son Ridleys back to the house for questioning. "I should have Isla detained as well," he mutters.

I'm chuckling to myself up the stairs to Jeremiah's bedroom. It doesn't have any of the normal stuff you'd expect. The guy is what? Twenty? Twenty-one? It's all old man stuff. In fact, I have to scout around a bit to make sure it *is* his room. But there's a picture of his girlfriend tucked inside a book on the nightstand. The book, by the way, is an anthology of Cherokee lore. *The Gods of Thunder and Flood.* There's a picture of several fierce deities wearing live rattlesnakes as jewelry and brandishing lightning bolts. The river beside them is raging and a boy is drowning, his head half-submerged, one arm waving wildly. The whole scene is eerily reminiscent of what happened to Jake. Even the shape of the waterfall and the way the rapids eddy out onto the shore. Creeps me out a little.

Beside the nightstand, is a long table made from a board laid upon two saw horses. A shop lamp with an extendable arm is attached, and there are cups of river stones, like the ones on Isla's bracelets. Hanging on the wall, there are beautiful depictions of celestial people rising from the water with arms outstretched to the rising sun. Words are written in what I assume to be the Cherokee alphabet. The symbols look like runes to me.

Other cubbies are full of tools and craft supplies. In one of them, I find a computer-generated map. I can't resist a map, especially this one, with the bend of a river I recognize well. I've been working to perfect it myself.

The map shows Isla's property joined to the Ridleys' by a solid border that includes the church, marked with a cross, but it excludes the small peninsula of national park which protrudes from the north.

There are subdivisions and roadways printed onto both family homesteads that do not exist in reality. *I could sell my share of this place and be a multi-millionaire overnight.* Isn't that what Isla said?

Another two paths are dotted onto the map by hand. In charcoal, I think. I can't say what they depict. I almost think they are symbolic. Or underground? They converge upon the river where the properties join, and they feed into the clearly defined representation of the snake pit.

I run the map down to Connors.

"What if we've been thinking about this all wrong?" I ask.

Connors, whose backside is the only visible part of him under the desk, stops searching long enough to take the map, still on his knees.

"How much is this land worth?" I ask.

"With all the rental potential? I can't even begin—there's what? Four hundred acres here? Whose plan is this?"

"It was in Jeremiah's room."

"OK, so maybe the Ridleys are plotting to take over the Millers' property and develop it commercially?"

"I can't see the Ridleys building a resort. Can you? Maybe a compound for a deranged cult or a private militia. Mr. Ridley signed this property over to the church. What if the map doesn't belong to Jeremiah? What if it's just another one of the documents he has managed to procure?"

"Whose is it then?"

I flick the watermark in the upper-left corner. *Banks Development.* "Remember the marriage certificate I showed you? Billy's dad and Isla's estranged aunt? There was also a will. Isla's grandmother left everything to her grandchildren. Billy might be able to make a case that *he* is a grandchild. He's ambitious. He's—"

"An officer of the law," Connors butts in defensively. "What are you saying? He's trying to lay claim to the Millers' land somehow? And the Ridleys' too?"

"I don't know what I'm saying," I backpedal. "I'm just trying to work it out."

Connors chides me under his breath. "Man probably bled to death somewhere and you're trying to implicate him in a crime that hasn't even been committed."

"No, I'm not. Look at this, though. See the waterfall there? That's where Jake died. Do you see the pit drawn above it?"

"I see a circle."

"Well, the circle is in the exact spot I witnessed the pit." I nod toward the screens. "Can we access this footage? Is it being recorded?"

"That's what we're trying to figure out."

The monitors continue to tell their stories in real-time. Isla's empty bedroom. The chicken coop with one empty boot and one dead snake. And the church, its seated congregants shifting from side to side like unsettled cattle.

My eyes wander to the room where we saw the preacher practicing his sermon, and I seize the monitor with both hands. "Connors, what the *fuck* is going on?!"

Jeremiah has Isla violently pinned to his side, cramming something into her mouth. She's struggling against him, but she's powerless. She looks tiny in his grip.

Connors screeches into his radio to command the officer at the church to intervene. "Get into that back room! Assault in progress. Jeremiah Ridley." He unhands his radio. "What the *hell?*"

I launch myself out the door. If I jump on the dirt bike right now, I can be to my truck within twenty minutes. Actually, it might be faster to bike to the church directly.

"Not you, Army!" Connors barks me back. "We're already going to catch hell for interrupting a church service. If I send a military guy in there, we'll have every right-wing nut from here to Virginia to answer to."

"Negative. She needs me."

"You won't get there in time to help. Let my guy handle it."

Fuck. I squeeze the back of my head in frustration and stare at him with growing alarm.

"He'll get the job done," Connors assures me. "Watch."

We position ourselves in front of the screen. It's all I can do to keep from screaming. Isla is coughing, but Jeremiah has unhanded her. He even offers a small cup of water.

Now he's handing her a towel, and he seems to be comforting her. If he weren't so odd, I'd be able to read him better. "This room had audio before," I say.

"It's gone." Connors shrugs to say he doesn't know why.

"It seemed like he was assaulting her," I say. "Didn't it?"

"It did seem like that."

Back on the screen with the sanctuary, a deliberation is taking place. Mr. Ridley roams the front of the church waving his arms. He's acting more like the crazed, old chicken man he'd been on the day we visited hoping to buy eggs. *Gah, that was an eternity ago.*

Isla smooths her face. She and Jeremiah are conversing. Is she getting her answers?

The officer enters the church, calmly but with intention, and moves up the righthand aisle. A man from the back rises to question him. Another man bars his way, and now the officer is waving them aside with his back to the wall, his hand on his holster.

Most of the congregation hasn't noticed. They are out of their seats, pressing toward the front as if they want to get a better look at Ridley or as if they want to take part in the action. The preacher is trying to gain attention, but no one is listening to him.

"This is not good," Connors says, and then into his radio, "Stand down." So, the officer presents his hands to the men and stops pushing to gain ground.

What that officer probably can't see from his vantage point is the box that Mr. Ridley removes from underneath his seat and places on the front table. The thought does cross my mind that there are poisonous vipers inside that box, but there can't be because that would be illegal and good church-goers would not participate in an exercise that is both illegal and life-threatening. Right? Still, I've lost too much to zealots to feel good about it.

Isla and Jeremiah have disappeared from the back room's feed.

The radio on Connors' shoulder pipes up, first with static and then with a voice. "I have eyes on the target." *Static.* "Jeremiah and a female. Advise."

"Do not intervene." Connors silently seeks my reaction. I don't give him permission, but I don't contradict him. I think that Isla and Jeremiah may have formed an alliance.

Mr. Ridley lifts the lid, and some of the congregants step back while others solemnly nod. Ridley is speaking to the room at large. He also addresses someone off-camera to his left. Now Jeremiah joins him from that direction. And Isla too.

"What's in the box?" Connors asks his radio.

Radio static. "The crowd is blocking it," his officer returns. "Do you want me to go find out?"

I feel Connors' eyes on me, but I can't take mine off of Isla. Her face is set. She swallows. Ridley slowly lifts the contents for the congregation to see. Several people clasp their hands. One woman waves hers up and down.

Whatever is in the box is causing quite a stir. Ridley spreads his arms to reveal two serpents, one draped from each hand.

"That man is a fucking psycho," Connors says. "I didn't know rattlesnakes could grow that long."

The radio breaks in. "You seeing this?"

"Tell him to stand down," I blurt out. "Don't create excitement. It'll make the snakes nervous."

"Stand down," Connors repeats.

"Copy that."

Instead of shrinking back from her testing, Isla steps up. Like some beautiful witch in old Salem, soon to be tied to the stake to let fire devour her flesh. I may grow to abhor snakes worse than flames. *Come on, Jeremiah, back her up.*

"What the hell is she doing?" Connors asks.

"Come on, Jeremiah," I whisper.

Jeremiah does *not* intercede. He looks half-pleased, half-impressed. I'd be impressed too if I didn't care whether she lived or died.

"She's got balls," Connors says.

"Yeah, she does. You should've seen her deal with an enormous bear the other day."

Isla slowly reaches for the tail of one of the snakes, but Ridley denies her, moving it away from her grasp. He speaks, and she looks vaguely pissed, eyes shifting to the side, but she offers her outstretched arms, palms up. Meanwhile, the preacher stalks to the back of the church to consult with Connors' officer.

Mr. Ridley places, first one snake across Isla's forearms, and the other around her shoulders. While the first explores the pulse point at her wrist, the latter flicks its tongue over her chest, which heaves once to betray her cool exterior.

You've got this, Babe.

Mr. Ridley's wearing a big, sneer of a smile. I'd give almost anything to punch it off his face.

"How long is this circus supposed to last before they decide she's holy enough?"

"I don't know," Connors says. "But when it's over, I'm gonna arrest every mother fucker in there."

It's good to hear Connors sound as furious as I feel. He senses me staring. "She'll be alright," he says. "Dispatch? I need you to find out where the closest timber rattler anti-venom is. Would we have to fly a patient to Knoxville, or do they have some at the clinic?...........No, there's no victim yet.......... Just find out for me. And put the air ambulance team on notice."

Isla's chest rises more rapidly now, and I can tell she's working to keep her brow from furrowing. I can hardly take it. The snake on her arms has decided to climb to her shoulder, and the other is sliding behind her neck, weaving in and out of her hair. I know the softness of that neck, how sensitive it is, how prone to chill, and I cannot bear for that goddamn animal to be slithering there. I inadvertently seize Connors' shoulder. If it decides to chomp into her jugular, I really don't think anti-venom is going to help.

I feel sick.

"Take a seat. You look like you're gonna pass out." Connors rolls a chair up behind me, and I comply, elbows on knees, hands tenting my mouth and nose.

Jeremiah says something to the crowd and presents Isla to them with a slow sweep of his hand. His face is damn near radiant. He smiles. He seems to make eye contact with every parishioner. Dude's a showman. Knows how to play the game. Or else he's just genuinely into it.

With another sweeping gesture, he moves toward Isla, his head wagging in pride. But his smile is a farce. As soon as it is out of the view of the congregation, he drops it. He looks lethal. I'm not sure who his anger is directed toward. Maybe it is simply disgust for this whole shit show. Or maybe I'm misinterpreting the expression altogether, and it is something else he feels.

"That is one scary individual," Connors says. "You trust him?"

"No," I scoff. "But Isla does."

Jeremiah approaches Isla while the first snake flicks its tongue in her ear—she shuts her eyes—and then muscles its way across her breasts.

Jeremiah gently hooks a finger under the snake's head and plucks it off. He holds it aloft for the crowd to applaud and then reintroduces it to its box. All of this is done only slightly faster than tortoise-pace.

Mr. Ridley gesticulates and I follow Jeremiah's gaze from his dad to the piano where an older woman begins to pound on the keys. Jeremiah glances back at Isla. The congregants begin to sing. It must be loud in there. Mr. Ridley is directing them to get louder still with large, rapid movements. What in the world would he have to gain by getting Isla killed? Does he actually believe she is deserving of death? Or does he just get high off his own power, like a serial killer?

Jeremiah moves more quickly now, and I can tell that the snake has tensed its body. "It's rattling," I say.

"I think so," Connors replies.

Jeremiah snatches its head into his fist and yanks a good deal of Isla's hair out in the process. He manages to extricate the animal and, just when I think she's safe, his father slaps the snake onto the floor at her feet. It rears its middle into a foreboding hunch, its head lowered menacingly, its rattle raised like a dagger—well within striking distance of the nearest bystander. Isla.

Jeremiah steps out front but his father blocks him like a defensive back in a football game, so Jeremiah physically shoves his father to the ground and takes two swift steps toward the snake—which propels its head upward and strikes.

I can practically see the collective gasp that issues through the crowd, their questions popping like corn. "What happened?" "Did it bite him?" "Did you see it?" "Is he not God's chosen?"

Jeremiah wrings his hand once, but otherwise gives no indication he was struck. He studies the animal, and I think he would wait for it to calm down, but it strikes again. This time he grabs it, gets bitten a third time, and deposits the snake into the box.

The piano player has ceased playing. The crowd has ceased singing. Even Mr. Ridley seems slightly stunned.

Isla alone moves toward Jeremiah. She takes his hand and tugs him down the center aisle. When she spots the officer, she jogs over to speak to him. The next thing we hear is his radio, but Jeremiah is lumbering toward the door, and Isla follows.

"Jeremiah was struck. Timber rattler." The officer heads to the exit too.

"Get him to the clinic," Connors says as the door swings closed and we lose sight of them.

No response.

"Officer? Repeat back." He bites his lip and awaits an answer.

Someone comes galloping through the front door of the Ridleys' house and yells at us, "Cadaver dog got a hit!"

"Fuck," Connors whispers. "I'm coming," he calls.

I wonder if this man ever thought becoming a cop in this small, mountain town would have him juggling such a strange series of events.

"I'm sorry," I say. "I have to go to Isla."

He nods uncertainly and then speaks on the radio. "Get Jeremiah to the clinic. Copy?"

Still no answer.

"Something's wrong," he says.

After a delay, the officer's voice comes back weakly. "He knocked me out. I think he drove away with the woman."

Accelerant

ISLA'S POINT OF VIEW

"GIVE ME YOUR KEYS." Jeremiah holds out the same hand he just used to punch an officer in the face.

"No, Jeremiah! Did you really have to do that?" I bend down to make sure the man is breathing. "You probably gave him a concussion!"

"Let's go," he says.

"Where to?"

"I don't know. Just give me your keys." And then he stumbles. So, no, I am not giving him my keys.

"Didn't *you* drive?" I ask and follow his gaze to a canoe that is propped against a small bridge beside the church. "Seriously?"

"I don't think I can paddle it right now."

"Jeremiah, that is because you were just chomped on by a rattlesnake. Three times! You could be *dying!*" A dried stream of blood demonstrates where, just minutes ago, there was a fresh rivulet seeping from his sleeve.

"I'm not dying," he says.

"I have to get you to the hospital. Get into the Jeep. Into the *passenger* side."

"Isla, I'm not dying. I'm a kingsnake."

"Lord, you've gone delusional. *Please* get into the Jeep."

Jeremiah obeys me, but only, I think, because he's growing too weak to argue. He can't even get the seatbelt secured, so I stretch over him to snap it myself. "What if we're too late?" I worry aloud.

"I'm not dying," he repeats. "I just feel sick. I need to sleep."

His last words slur and I can feel my throat clench the way it does when I'm about to cry, but a few people emerge from the church, and I sure as hell am not going to entertain them anymore, so I start up the Jeep and screech out of the church parking lot. If I can just get him to the local clinic, they'll know what to do.

I fumble with my cell phone while I navigate the curvy mountain road too fast, and I drop it to the floorboard.

"Well, I'm not going to die from the snake venom," Jeremiah mutters.

"Are you making a joke right now?" I ask.

We're speeding over the hills, through the patches of sun and shadows, and I'm still searching for the phone on the floor. After nearly wrecking us, I lay my hand on it and manage to dial 911, but the service is bad.

"Ma'am?" an operator asks.

"Yes! Can you hear me? My friend was bitten by a timber rattler. Three times. He—"

Jeremiah grabs the phone from me, ends the call, and physically shoves it under his immovable thigh. "I'm telling you," he says. "I'm a kingsnake."

That makes me mad enough to spit. I brake and skid to a stop to glare at him. "What do you mean you're a kingsnake?"

He closes his eyes and smiles, but he looks like he could puke. "I've spent a lifetime building up resistance to the venom. Though —this time is going to suck. I can feel that."

"You were bitten in the elbow, Jeremiah! And the wrist. And who knows where else." He points to his tricep. "What if this time the venom went directly into your bloodstream and overwhelmed you? From what I've heard, it is not a pleasant way to go!"

"If you take me to the clinic, I'll refuse treatment on the basis of religion."

"*Bull*shit!"

"I will."

"Then I'll knock your ass out, you freak, like you did that officer."

Jeremiah laughs. "I saw you punch Billy Banks one time."

"You did?"

"It was funny." He closes his eyes again. "You have a powerful left hook."

"Do you promise me you won't die?" I say.

"I promise. I just need to sleep."

"The police are going to arrest you."

"I know."

"If I take you to my house they'll find you faster."

"That's OK. If I can just sleep a while, I'll be able to think up a plan."

I'm pretty sure he's already got a plan, but for some reason, I throw the gearshift into drive, and now we're on our way home where this huge man will probably die, and that will be my fault. And they'll probably need a crane to get him out of my house. Why did this have to happen? He took those bites for my sake.

"Inola is going to be mad at me," I say, just to have words coming out of my mouth. "If you die, she'll hate me."

"No, she won't." With that, Jeremiah snuggles into the seat, inasmuch as a giant can snuggle into a small Wrangler's seat, and says, "Thank you, Cousin." After that, he remains silent, and I manage to get my phone out from under him.

When we arrive at the cabin, I'm afraid I won't be able to wake him up. "Jeremiah?" I nudge him. "Jeremiah? Come on. I'll put you to bed."

He doesn't budge.

"Please don't be super-poisoned," I plead. "How many times a year do we hear how harmless they are?" I mock the nature educators' know-it-all voices. "'Rattlesnakes won't bite humans except in defense, and even then they probably won't inject venom.' Well, you know what? I am just going to call a global bullshit on this whole thing!"

Car wheels spit gravel across the driveway behind us, and what a welcome sound!

"Jeremiah, look who's here." His eyes flutter open.

I left a voicemail for Inola along the way, and she must have flown because here she is to help. "What's wrong with him?" she asks.

"He was bitten by a rattlesnake—three times!—but he won't let me take him to the clinic."

"Dammit, Jeremiah!" she says. "I'm going to break up with you for good."

With Inola on one side and me on the other, we pretend that we are supporting the man, but really Jeremiah staggers to the door on his own strength. Lucy is ecstatic to have visitors. "Go pee-pee," I tell her. "You can greet everybody after that." Meanwhile, we somehow get Jeremiah to the couch where he immediately slumps over.

The sky outside is too close. I don't understand why the dark smoke is still so pervasive.

"Isla!" Inola must have been calling my name while I was distracted. When I turn from the window, Jeremiah is shivering. I stumble over to feel his forehead. He's burning up.

"I'll drive out," I volunteer. "I'll call for an ambulance. I should've gone straight to the hospital."

"No, he wouldn't want that. He'll be OK. Could we get him another blanket, though?"

The worried look in her eyes does nothing to convince me we're doing the right thing. I go for a blanket and some antiseptic.

After we get Jeremiah's wounds cleaned up, Inola encourages him to drink some water and strokes his head until he falls asleep again.

"We probably don't have much time before the authorities come," I tell her. "He decked a police officer, and that's the least of his worries. Maybe he can blame it on the venom. Inola, do you know what happened to the sheriff?"

"You mean Billy Banks?"

Heavy boots interrupt our conversation as they thud up the back stairs. That was faster than I thought.

Knock-knock-knock.

I open to the smudged face of a distraught ranger. "Wind changed and whipped the fire into more than we anticipated," he said. "We need to use your driveway to pull in trucks."

"Yes. Please do. Should we evacuate?"

"I would. I don't want to underestimate this thing again. It's like it's fighting against us. Springing up here and there with a mind of its own."

As he tromps away, I can make out a siren in the distance, and in my mind's eye, I see Mammaw's cabin burning to the ground. First, the fields, then the barn. It races like a monster to the house, bent on devouring the place. There's a moment when I want to stand my ground—flip that evil fire monster the bird and dare it to burn everything over my dead body. But Banner. It would *torture* him even to know the fire was still an issue.

"We have to get out," I say to Inola and scan the area for what I can take. *What, if only one thing? And wouldn't that be the essential thing I've been trying to blog about?* The pictures, the guitar, the *Cousins* poem, Mammaw's recipe books. The coffee cup, the quilt, the perfect jeans. The porch? The very walls? I don't think I can take the essential thing with me. Or wait, maybe the essential thing is already with me and I carry it inside all the time.

"Isla?" Inola, again, brings me back to the job at hand. Jeremiah's head and shoulders rest upon her lap, and I can see that he is her essential thing. How will we get him out?

"Jeremiah?" I say. He's snoring. "Jeremiah?"

Inola rocks him, nudges him, coaxes him to wake, but he only groans and heaves a breath. I feel his head again. *Help us.*

"To hell with this," I say. "I'll drive out to where I can call. Maybe I can flag down the fire truck and get some of those guys to come back with me."

Inola regards me with large eyes full of conflict. "He's so hot," she says, which I guess is her permission to get help on his behalf.

I grab my keys. "I'll be right back."

When I get to the river, though, instead of the bridge, I find a partially submerged firetruck lying sideways in the current. I jump out and say, "You broke my bridge?" Which, perhaps conveys the wrong energy, but they've obliterated my only means of getting help.

Several firefighters are working to free the driver through the passenger-side door. His own door is underwater. The whole truck is in danger of floating downstream. It rocks menacingly in the current.

"What can I do?" I ask the firefighters. Because I'm not an asshole. They're not paying attention to me, anyway.

On this side, an odd, silver sheen makes the broken bridge look wet, and I spin to follow a sudden motion that I can only see out of the corner of my eye. A mockingbird? A willow branch?

The firefighters get the driver and manage to scramble up the embankment on the far side. In moments, the whole truck shifts a few feet. It's setting up an alternate flow way, and I wonder if the current is creating enough pressure to force the thing further downstream.

"Hey!" I yell across. "My friend was bitten by a rattlesnake." I point back toward the cabin. When nobody seems to care because they're all pining over their truck, I add, "Three times!" That part's important to me. "And there's a fire!"

One of them looks up. "You need to evacuate," he says.

I close my eyes. "I know that," I manage. "But this is my only driveway."

"How many of you are on site?" he asks.

"Three."

And now I hear laughter behind my shoulder, tinkling like funhouse music and setting my teeth on edge. Again, I spin, but find nothing.

"We'll have to rope up a makeshift bridge," the firefighter calls to me.

"With what?" his co-fighter says and gives a meaningful look at the truck.

"My friend is very sick," I insist.

The man is compassionate. I can see that. And he's sympathetic. But he's also overwhelmed with difficulties, not the least of which is a forest fire he cannot now fight—one that could jeopardize thousands of acres, including the tourist attractions that are the sole source of income for this town. Not to mention a few precious, historic homesteads like mine.

He searches the river bank, but there's nowhere to cross for a mile. "The second truck will be here soon," he calls. "Their ladder will reach. If not, they'll have ropes."

I don't have the heart to tell him that someone will also have to follow me to the house so that we can lift Jeremiah. "Could you radio for an ambulance?" I ask.

Another look at his underwater truck. I guess the radio is waterlogged.

"I'll be back," I say and jump into the Jeep to speed back up the driveway. Then, right as I barge through the front door, it hits me that this may be the last time I ever enter this old place.

Inola turns as I come inside. "He won't wake up," she says.

"OK, here's the thing. The fire engine broke the bridge. There's no way to drive across it."

"But how will we get help?" Inola says. "And, *oh*, how will I get to my grandmother? I only meant to leave her long enough to make sure Jeremiah was OK. She's helpless without me. What if *she* needs to evacuate?"

How did I go from zero to three people to keep alive?

"A second firetruck is coming," I say. "You can drive to the bridge and wait for them to get the ladder across. Maybe they can radio for an ambulance and—I don't know—maybe you can hitch a ride to your grandmother's while I wait with Jeremiah."

She is visibly torn.

"I'll take care of him," I assure her. "You make sure to send one of those strong firefighters my way. I'll call you when we get out."

Considering me and then the sky, she says, "It shouldn't be this dark. It's not even two p.m."

"No," I agree. "It shouldn't."

We hear the second firetruck approaching.

"Go ahead," I tell her.

She nods like she's trying to convince herself and kneels to kiss her boyfriend—which is still just mind-blowing to me.

"Get better," she murmurs. "Come see me as soon as you can."

What Inola should probably know is that Jeremiah won't be able to come to see her because he's going to be in jail. And it will have little to do with him punching a cop in the face and everything to do with pictures of him in a missing sheriff's exploded vehicle. But I'm not going to be the one to tell her. Not right now, anyway.

She drives her old car away, and I watch her go. The siren is quite loud now. The second truck has probably arrived at the gap that used to be my bridge.

I've barely pivoted in from the door when I plant face-first into the hulking figure who is supposed to be passed out on my couch—which startles me half to death. "Jeremiah!" I scold him. "Do you do *anything* like a normal human being?"

He lumbers to the sink, fills his glass with water, and drains it.

"Thanks for getting rid of Inola," he says between gulps. "Makes things less complicated." He fills the glass again. Drains it. Fills it once more.

He doesn't seem to notice that I'm scowling down my nose at him, which is annoying. What good is it to have a great scowl of condescension if the condescended upon won't wilt beneath it?

"Jeremiah, what the hell is that supposed to mean? Honestly, I am getting really tired of trying to decipher all the cryptic nonsense you say. Nothing is complicated. You need medical attention."

Although, now that I observe him, he does look amazingly better. "Let me feel your head." He's cooler. "Why aren't you dying?"

"I told you."

"You're a kingsnake," I say.

"It happens when your paranoid father considers the regular testing of your moral fiber part of an appropriate parenting regimen."

That deflates me. "I'm sorry that was happening to you. I wish we had known. Wish we had put a stop to it."

I don't think Jeremiah is used to someone expressing sympathy. He says, "Jacob tried to stop it. And look what it got him."

I think of Jake yelling down at me, waving his hands, cupping his mouth to get me to hear him. Jeremiah is looking at me with sympathy now. "It's hard to escape this web," he says.

"But you've been keeping me from getting caught, haven't you? Who is the real spider, Jeremiah? Is it your dad?"

"No, he's just a stupid pawn. He really does believe all the things he says."

"Who, then? Not the preacher. He didn't want to—"

"It has nothing to do with the church. It started out as a simple land grab. Plain ole greed."

"But the deed your dad signed over…"

Jeremiah bites back an unexpected grin. "Yeah, well, that was my idea. I sort of convinced him it was what God wanted. But what my father doesn't know is that I own the church."

"How?"

"When I was born, the church was way more of a cult, and your aunt was part of it. She got pregnant, then wanted out, but she couldn't leave without signing me over to the church. I don't think she cared much, but it's why my mom could never adopt me. You know those bizarre state laws that give parents permission to marry off their young children? You can marry them off to God."

"No."

"Yep. I am truly, literally, legally a son of God. And it makes every holding of that church belong to me."

"Aunt Elsbeth fucked up."

"Yeah, she did!" Jeremiah laughs.

"Is *she* the spider?"

"Black widow. No doubt. But evil finds like mates." His tone changes the way it does when he quotes from the Bible. "'For there is no truth in their mouths; their throats are open graves; they flatter with their tongues. *They lie and they cheat.*' Sound like anyone you know?"

While he's speaking, he's moving from window to window along the back wall. "Do you smell that?"

I sniff and say, "Yeah. What is it? I've smelled it recently."

"I think we should leave. Let's hide in the tree huts."

"Jeremiah, if that fire gets more out of control, we'll be trapped in a burning forest. Why did you have to dump Sheriff Billy's truck like that? That's what started the fire, you know."

"I didn't dump his truck."

"We saw you loading the plastic bag into the back."

"I never did that. I may have propped it—"

A new sound gives him pause. A dirt bike. *Banner!* I can't get to the door fast enough. A fist pounds on it, and when I begin to pull, it flies open from the outside, nearly taking off my head.

"*Easy!*" I say. Sheriff Billy Banks pushes into the room, eyes darting from side to side. "Who is here with you?" he asks.

"Hi, *Billy*," I say. "It's good to see you're *alive*. Where the hell have you been? You've had everybody worried si—"

"Who is here with you?" he asks again.

I wave a theatrical hand to indicate the elephant in the room, namely Jeremiah. But he is nowhere to be seen. "Well, Jeremiah *was*."

Lucy is barking her head off. If she were a different kind of dog, Billy would already be on the ground.

"Hang on," I say and escort her by the collar to the boys' bedroom. Almost as soon as I return and get a good look at Billy's face, I wish she was loose again. And that she was a Doberman.

"You know he killed your cousin, right?" Billy asks. The same edge is in his voice as when we stood at the top of The Hydraulic. "Whatever lies he's been telling you are just that. Lies from a weirdo who makes love to snakes. And that's what he was doing the day Jake got killed. It was a *freak* show!"

"You were there?!" I ask. "Why didn't you tell me? Why did you go up with us the other day like it was a reconnaissance mission?"

"It was a reconnaissance mission. To see what you remembered."

It occurs to me that my childhood instincts about Billy Banks were spot on. "*Why* were you there when Jake died? Were you tracking your stepmother?"

"I thought I could catch her cheating on my dad, maybe ruin his life the way he had mine. But what I discovered was even better. Go to your room." Billy pulls a huge whisky bottle out of his shoulder bag. The very kind I drink.

Drank.

From the belligerent way he's acting, my guess is that he's already been tagging it.

When he lifts his eyes, he seems surprised that I haven't obeyed him. "I said, go to your room."

"Billy, what in the world makes you think you can order me around?"

"Oh that's right," he says and slams the bottle down on the counter. "You're a Miller. Too proud and privileged to take orders. You know what? Never mind. We'll have a few drinks while we wait."

"While we wait on what?"

He throws a look out the back window, and says, "I'm going for glasses. You sit. If you try to leave this house, I'll shoot you."

"Billy, what the hell is wrong with you? Nobody blames you for Jake's death. Should we?"

"Jake's? No." He pours us each a healthy swallow and throws his back before he even gets to the table. Then he smacks down the glasses, sloshing mine, and pours himself another. "Drink up."

"You know, this is the second time today I've been ordered to drink. But I don't drink. I'm a teetotaler."

Billy shoots his second pour and wipes his lip with one sharp movement. "Since when?" he scoffs.

I find that odd. He's never been around when I've been drinking. *Shit.* What if he has and I don't remember it?

"That's right," Billy says. "I know how you like it. Straight and hard. I won't tell your prissy new boyfriend."

"You better hope my prissy new boyfriend doesn't catch you talking to me that way."

"He won't," Billy says. "He thinks you were smart enough to take Jeremiah to the clinic. You Millers always did act like you were better than everybody else. Kings of the mountain. Such an old family. Such a respected name. So much goddamn land. Your trust fund must be enormous."

He eyeballs me for actual confirmation of that statement. When I don't give it to him, he says, "But that's over. I've been paying attention. Biding my time. Building my case since that very day your cousin died. And I know the things you do here by yourself. I've seen how far you ride your twisted fetishes, how much you get off on the pain. I've watched you drink yourself stupid until you can build up the nerve, and then tremble from the release of your own blood until you pass out with that razor in your hand. Sometimes, I watch it on repeat."

He slides his hand up my dress—despite my immediate reaction to block him—and fingers the series of raised scars on the inside of my thigh. "I bet you *literally* dream of the day you find the balls to get the job done." I grapple to wrench his hands off of me. The chair bounces and squeaks on the floor. Before he releases me, he pinches so hard I cry out and jerk myself to my feet—only for him to yank me back down into the chair.

My cheeks are hot with humiliation. "*You* set up the cameras?" I choke out. "The one that sees into my room? Why?"

"Knock that whisky back, and I'll tell you."

Is this really going to come down to a drinking game?

"You know what?" I say. "I don't really care why you're a pervert."

Billy pours more into my already full glass so that it spills onto the table. "What does the *priss* think about your cutting habit?"

Banner hasn't asked me about the scars. He has stroked them, has kissed them—I'm sure he suspects what I've done. I mean, he knows everything else, and his knowing is the opposite of Billy's knowing.

"Now," Billy says, "take a calming drink, and let's get you into that bedroom."

I can tell that the fire is closer than ever. The smoke is black at this point, and the realization of how very much danger I'm in is settling into my bones. I dare not risk a look at the shotgun, but I consider how quick I'd have to be. He's bigger, stronger. But he's also slowing down his thought processes with alcohol.

"Billy?" I ask. "What is that weird smell outside the door?"

"Oh, that? That is the fertilizer the Miller family groundskeepers use. Barn was full of it. Highly flammable."

The way he talks about us having groundskeepers makes it sound like we're the most ostentatious pricks in the world. And, you know, it is not unlike the way he sounded that day he stole the base-ball tournament.

"Billy, I always knew you were a big, lying cheater. I can't believe I prayed for you today! That barn wasn't full of anything. Is this what you've been up to for the past few days? Bringing in an accel-erant? You brought it that very day Wren called, didn't you? That's what we smelled. And then you dumped your own truck!"

"Yup. But Jeremiah followed me. I thought sending the photo of him to Connors was a stroke of genius. You may as well drink. You're going to die either way, and you're going to be on camera when you do, along with that empty bottle of your favorite whisky. Maybe if Jeremiah doesn't die from the snake bites, you two will go down in a lovers' quarrel. He set up the cameras and became jealous of the new guy. I haven't figured that part out yet. Maybe a murder/suicide. I'm sure everyone in your family can attest to how depressed you've been. They'll understand why you stayed away for so long. And why you had to come back to burn the place to the ground along with the man who killed your cousin. It's romantic, in a way. After all the tragedy, I bet your family will want to let the place go. Forget all about this cursed property. I've got big plans for it."

"You and *Elsbeth* have big plans, you mean. You partnered up?"

But when I mention my aunt, Billy practically balks. "I'm not afraid of her," he says.

'K. That's not really what I asked.

I think Billy is feeling good and buzzed now. He's chatty, and I'd like to keep him talking. Where in the heck is that strong firefighter who's supposed to help me? And where the heck did Jeremiah get off to? I risk a glance at the door and see a shadow pull out of sight.

Evacuation

BANNER'S POINT OF VIEW

"WAS he showing signs of a snake bite?"

Connors relays my question to the officer at the church while I stare at the screen of confounded parishioners.

"He was wobbling. Kept blinking like he couldn't see straight. I reached out to help steady him, and that's when he punched me."

"Take it easy," Connors says. "I'll send a bus."

"No, I'm alright. Give me ten, and I'll trail them to the clinic. Or do you want me to arrest some of these snake-handling yahoos instead?"

"You lost consciousness," Connors says. "You need to stand down."

My thumb is tapping a dent into the table. I'm too anxious to listen to the rest of this argument play out. "I'm going to find Isla." That probably would have sounded more resolute if I hadn't followed it up with, "How do I get there?"

"Just hang on," Connors says. "We'll take a cruiser. Let's check what they found where the cadaver dog hit."

I have no interest in anything other than being reunited with Isla, but I guess I'm at the mercy of whoever can get me there.

We're outside now, making our way to where we dismounted the dirt bikes. It pains me to ask but—"You smell that right? The smoke?"

"It's real," Connors says matter-of-factly—the way the friend of a blind man might assure him that the *walk* sign is lit.

Why has the smoke traveled this far from the ravine? I think about where the ravine lies on the map in conjunction with where we are now. The fire is spreading. Unbelievable.

When we reach the place where we parked the dirt bikes, one of them is gone. "These guys know how much I hate it when they do shit like that without asking," Connors says.

"This one's got a flat," I point out, and Connors mutters, "Perfect."

So, we continue across the fields on foot, and my patience is wearing thin.

When we finally reach the spot where I last saw Sheriff Billy— alive—the cadaver dog lies panting on a mound of un-interred dirt. He seems to be letting us know that his work here is done. The snake pit is being re-dug in careful scoops. Upon further inspection, there is a man's mud-caked hand and a forearm protruding from the earth.

"What in the world have the Ridleys done?" Connors asks.

"I've gotta get to that clinic," I say. "I am so sorry, man. I actually do know what it's like to see a friend in this shape. But I've gotta take care of Isla. There's no telling what Jeremiah is capable of."

Connors doesn't answer me. I'm not even sure he's heard me. He's kneeling in the dirt staring at the body while the gentle digging continues.

A minute ticks by. My jaw hurts from clenching it. I'll just have to ask somebody else where the clinic is. I'll fix the dirt bike's tire and head toward town.

"It's not him," Connors says. The dead man's head and shoulders are visible now, lying sideways in the dirt. "It looks like him, but it's not."

I think Connors is going to need a lot of therapy. He's in complete denial. The other officer must think so too. He says, "Who else would it be?"

"No, listen to me!" Connors insists. "I know this man. It's Billy's dad."

It's his dad. OK. Who killed his dad? I lunge toward the body and start digging myself.

"Hey! You can't do that!" The officer shoves me back. "We have to preserve the evidence."

"It looks like he's in a uniform," I point out.

That gets the officer wiping the dead man's shirt and cleaning off a metal pin. "He is. He's in Billy's. Here's Billy's badge."

"Does that mean Billy's alive? Have the results come back on the blood in the car mat?" I ask.

"Inconclusive. It seems like some of it was his."

Connors remains silent. He's troubled. I think it's for more than that Billy's dad is dead. I remember how he spoke of Billy's anger toward his dad for leaving him and his mom.

"Why didn't Billy want to be a big city cop anymore?" I ask. "Why did he move back home?"

The officer doing the digging answers. "The sheriff's job opened up. He wanted to be closer to his mom."

Connors is frowning. Suddenly, he stands and tugs my elbow to lead me away. "Let me know what you find," he calls back. "Especially cause of death."

Once we're into the open of the Ridleys' field, Connors says, "That's not why he moved back. He was caught using sensitive equipment for his own use. Told me it was a misunderstanding, but it raised flags—enough to bar him from the position he wanted."

"Which was?"

"Intelligence. Surveillance technician."

"Cameras, remote tracking, that sort of thing?" I try to keep the accusation out of my voice.

"Yeah," he answers darkly.

"Look, I know he's your friend, but—"

Connors shakes his head. "He always was a voyeur. Let's go search his place."

We take somebody else's patrol car and head out for Billy's apartment. There's a niggling worry in the back of my mind. What if the dirt bike wasn't borrowed by one of the folks working the scene? What if Billy's been on site this whole time, not as a prisoner, but as an instigator? He could have taken the bike, could have slashed the other bike's tire. He knows the way to Isla's house. We showed him the path ourselves.

"What about—" I begin, but Connors says, "Clinic's on the way." And he throws on the siren as we speed out of the drive—so that's kind of fun.

Meanwhile, fire is a growing concern. The radio dispatcher says that the rangers are issuing a limited evacuation. All available personnel is being asked to help organize routes.

"Well, I'm not available," Connors says.

A firetruck screams past us, heading in the opposite direction and I crane my neck to watch it go.

Now that we're on the main highway, I consult my phone, and it has bars. Two thoughts crowd my head. One, *Call Isla!* And two, *You don't even know how.* "Uh...do you have Isla's number?" I ask.

Connors keeps his eyes on the road. "I was under the impression you two were—"

"We are."

"How could you not have her number?" He slides forward in the seat to dig his phone out of his pocket and hands it over ready to use.

"We've never been apart." I find her number and type it into my phone. It goes to voicemail and her call-me-back message makes me smile for no reason. "Hey, Ees, we're on our way to the clinic, trying to track you down. Do you know that they're issuing an evacuation because of the fire? Let's figure out where to meet up. I have things to tell you. Let me know you're OK. I love you." I text her the same message. Then I text, *PS: BRB.*

As we pull into the clinic, I search for her tough, little Jeep, but no joy. So, I rush to the front desk while Connors parks the car.

"I'm looking for Jeremiah Ridley. Big guy? Snake bites?"

"Doesn't ring a bell," the receptionist says. "When would he have come in?"

"Within the last hour."

While he checks his computer, I scan the waiting room.

"Are you sure he wasn't directed to Knoxville's larger hospital?"

"No," I say. "I'm not sure of anything. Except that you guys really need to invest in some cell towers." My fist bounces compulsively on the counter above the guy's head, but I don't realize it until he glances up. "Sorry." I stick my hand into my pocket.

And then I see Isla. *Thank God.* She's across the room with her back to me, gazing out the wall of windows onto the parking lot. Her hair falls in waves around her shoulders. I practically lunge in her direction. "Ees?" She doesn't hear me. Seems to be tracking Connors as he walks from his car.

"Isla. Babe."

But it's not her. Of course, it's not. The clothes are all wrong, for one. Isla's wearing that pretty yellow dress. This lady's wearing business slacks, but in silver. I'm pretty sure Isla would not be caught dead in them. The lady's older too, and there is something very un-Isla-ish about the unfriendly slant of her eyes as she turns to the sound of my voice.

She quickly sizes me up, pursing her lips to the side, and it is clear to me that she had hoped to find someone far more impressive than I. I'm not at all accustomed to this reaction. Generally, my appearance wins a second glance from a woman, if not a smile. But this lady drops her eyebrows, and I half expect her to cut me off at the knees.

"You're Elsbeth," I surmise. "You're Isla's aunt."

Instead of confirming my statement, she sighs and says, "Haven't you heard that the Millers are monsters? Get out while you can."

I'm beginning to understand why there's a family rift. "Too late," I tell her. I wonder if she knows about her husband's demise. "What are you doing here?" I ask.

"Same as you, I suppose."

"Making sure that the love of your life isn't in harm's way?"

She laughs at me. Not the flirty kind of laugh that means she finds me attractive. The scoffing kind that means she finds me dense.

"You're aware, then, that Jeremiah has abducted the *love of your life*, my niece? She's the only thing standing in the way of him owning this whole mountain and all the power beneath it."

I do not like this woman. I do not trust this woman. But her words claw at me. And she knows it. She says, "You don't trust him either. You're smart not to. He was raised by backward imbeciles and tortured more days than not. It's interesting, though, how he learned to bear it. Interesting what happens when monsters mate. Maybe we'll let him *keep* Isla for a multi-generational experiment." She savors the words as if they're exciting to her, and now all I can see is that big oaf taking advantage of the woman I want to be my wife.

"You know, the Army offers all kinds of classes," I tell her. "I took one on psychological manipulation and, while it didn't give me mastery over a warped mind, it did help me to recognize one."

Connors enters the building. Elsbeth throws him a look. "Get out while you can," she says again. "Come nightfall, there won't be anyone on that property left alive." And she disappears down the hallway.

"Was that Isla?" Connors says.

"Her aunt."

"Why's she here? Is she looking for her husband?"

"I don't think so. I get the feeling she already knows where her husband is. Come on." I backhand his chest and jog down the hall after Elsbeth with Connors close behind. "She's here looking for Isla. She just threatened everyone on the property."

We get blocked by a hospital bed being wheeled across the hall and by the time we bypass it, Elsbeth is nowhere in sight. At the end of the hall is a door to the outside, swinging closed. "There!" I say, and we run out that door.

We don't see Elsbeth as we leave the clinic and, believe me, we look for her. "How did she know Jeremiah was hurt?" Connors asks. "Did she have access to the video feed? Was she there at the church?"

He wants to go back inside, search the rooms, search the property. But I convince him she has other plans. "She's not going to cooperate. She was squeezed out of the family inheritance, and I don't think she takes *no* for an answer. How unlikely is it that she and Billy became partners?"

"Pretty damn unlikely," Connors says.

Connors has a call into the hospital in Knoxville. They're supposed to let us know if Jeremiah checks in—or anyone who's had a snake bite. But what if Isla doesn't go there? What if Jeremiah isn't even sick and he really has abducted her?

I call her again. "Hey, Babe, I'm with Connors. We're exploring a lead, but I'd sure like to know you're safe. I ran into your aunt Elsbeth at the clinic. I think she's looking for you or maybe for Jeremiah. I do not trust her. Call when you can."

"You're worried," Connors says.

"I just don't understand who the real players are or how they're connected. I'd have thought the only real threat was Mr. Ridley and those damn snakes."

"Well, if we find video evidence, we'll know more."

We get to Billy's apartment. We knock. We look through the windows. "Please don't let anyone know what I'm about to do," Connors says. We break in.

There's nothing. Nothing to lead us to believe that Billy knows anything about surveillance technology. We go through cabinets and closets and drawers, but it's just a waste of time. "One more try," Connors says.

Now we're driving to Billy's mother's house.

"Kevin, is that you?" she asks with a sweet, country accent, and she steps onto the porch to give him a hug, but when she pulls away, her smile falters. "Have you heard from him yet?"

"No, Ma'am. I thought maybe we could search his room here."

"Yes, of course. Are you looking for something in particular?" She opens the door for us and leads us to Billy's old bedroom.

"Surveillance equipment? Cameras, laptops, digital file storage?"

"I don't think so. It's all things from years ago before he moved out on his own, but see what you can find." Concern darkens her tone. "Help him, Kevin. You know how secretive he can be, how ambitious." Poor woman's on the verge of a breakdown. She wipes at her eye and excuses herself.

In Billy's old room, there are bookshelves full of trophies. Football, basketball, baseball—probably thirty or more. I grin to wonder which one is Isla's. What would she do if she knew I had it within reach? There are other kinds of awards and plaques. She wasn't kidding. The man takes pride in winning. Or at least he did as a boy.

"*Ugh*," Connors says. He shows me a photo of a younger Billy with his arm around the man we were just digging out of the dirt. "What is going on here, Army?"

There's also a picture of Billy and his parents from when he was a boy. They must have married in their teens. They look young. "Did Billy's folks grow up around here?" I ask.

"Yeah. Both families go way back."

"Ms. Banks?" I call and hear her hurry down the hall to us.

"Did you find something?"

"No. Sorry. Your ex married Elsbeth Miller."

"So I've been told," she answers.

"Right. But before that, you knew her? You grew up around here?"

"Sure. Small town. The Millers were a prominent family. Elsbeth and I went to school together—well, when she went to school. She was so wild."

"How wild?"

She shrugs. "You know…there were rumors. She joined this cult one summer and disappeared. Got pregnant by one of the leaders there. It was said that she had to leave her baby with them when she wanted out."

"Was Mr. Ridley the father?"

"That's what people said. I could hardly believe it. He was so scary when we'd see him around town, at least to us high school girls. Grumpy, old recluse. But leave it to Elsbeth to get involved with the weirdest fringe group around."

"At some point, though," I press, "she moved to North Carolina, and then your husband moved there too? Your ex, I mean?"

"No, you were right the first time. I wasn't granted a divorce for over a year—and my husband *living* with his new lover. What does all this have to do with anything?"

"I'm not sure. What is it he did for work, your ex? Did it have to do with land development?"

"He better *still* be doing land development. He's been more successful than ever, according to my alimony checks."

I asked it in the past tense. That was a mistake because no one knows he's dead. "No, yeah. Present tense. *Does* he work in it. Not *did* he."

Connors clears his throat to shut me up. Ms. Banks probably wouldn't have suspected anything if I'd just let it go, but she does now.

"What aren't you saying?" She turns from me to Connors. "Kevin?"

Connors silently rebukes me in the form of a quick but sharp glance which I deserve.

"A man was found matching his description," he tells her. "Nothing is certain. Nope—hang on." He has to physically embrace Billy's mom to get her to listen because she has begun to grapple with the news by wringing her hands and interrupting.

"A body?" she asks. "Is it Billy?! They look just alike."

"Nope. No, it is not Billy. I promise. I saw him myself."

"Well, then you know, Kevin. Unless. Oh, the body must be—oh no." Ms. Banks presses a hand over her mouth. "She's killed him. I warned him. She's the craziest person I ever knew. What has she done with my Billy?" The question ends in a pitiful wail and Connors escorts her from the room.

My bad.

What if crazy Aunt Elsbeth *did* kill her husband? Still, she couldn't have wrestled him into Billy's uniform, could she? Or have wrestled Billy out of it in the first place? Not without his help. My eyes fall upon the trophies again.

Some of the words I've heard to describe Billy Banks are as follows: secretive, ambitious, voyeur, thief, and big lying cheater.

When Connors returns, he graciously skips mention of Billy's mom and my lapse in judgment. "Let's walk it through out loud," he says. "You left Billy at the Ridleys' in a situation that worried you for him. But it's his dad who ended up in the hole. You think his dad is the one who drew up the proposed development, so, what? His dad came to town to get the Ridleys to sell their property, and they killed him for asking?"

"Among the documents Jeremiah left," I say, "was an application for his adoption by the woman he called *mom* his whole life—the woman who raised him. She was the only parent named on the form. His dad wasn't mentioned."

"Because his dad was already the father," Connors says.

"I think so. Elsbeth had Jeremiah and then handed him over when she left the cult. It was long before her mother—Isla's grandmother—changed the will to skip a generation. I think Elsbeth must have found out about the change, and she came back to try to finagle a share of that property in her biological son's name."

"Is she that brazen?"

"She stole from her parents while they were still alive. And then she came back after her father's funeral to try to take more. That's why the will was changed in the first place."

"The map you found showed the Ridleys' property coupled with the Millers'," Connors says.

"She tried to make a deal," I suggest. "She'd use Jeremiah to get the Millers' property if the Ridleys would partner with her. Come to think of it, maybe she promised it to the church."

"How was she going to get it away from the rest of the grandchildren? Kill them all?"

"Elsbeth practically said as much to me," I say. "One of the heirs is dead already." *Jake.*

"By Jeremiah's hand," Connors reminds me. "And Jeremiah's the only one who has been skulking around the Millers' place. Not Billy."

"Jeremiah didn't send the picture of himself, did he? Someone has the damn feed recorded."

Connors empties a shelf and goes through its contents. Then he starts on the drawers while I search in the closet.

"I bet Jeremiah killed Billy and Mr. Banks," he says under his breath. "He's so strange. I mean, somebody had to get that snake into Billy's boot. I should arrest him for that alone. What are you mumbling in there?"

I stick my head out to say, "I do not trust Jeremiah."

"*Pff.*" I take that to mean, *Who does?*

"Isla," I say. "She does. And she's known him best for the longest. And you know what? He's her cousin. That will mean a lot to her when she finds out."

"So, what? Elsbeth is her aunt. And apparently, that doesn't mean shit."

That's true, I say with a head tilt. Aloud, I add, "There's nothing much in here. It's been cleaned out." I search under the bed and between the mattress and box spring.

"Look at this," Connors says. He's flipping through a scrapbook, page by page.

"What is it? Old photographs?"

"More like old grievances, and your girlfriend is among them."

I step around to view the book over his shoulder. "Looks like newspaper clippings about his sports triumphs. What high school jock doesn't have those?"

"Some of it is, but look at these. He's obsessed with the Millers."

He's right. He turns over notice after notice about what the Millers have received or accomplished or endured, affixed to the pages of his brag book. Obituaries. Weddings. Graduations. Community meetings. Job promotions.

And not just things that happened after his dad had the affair with Aunt Elsbeth. It's years before that too. Here's a picture of Isla and Jake with their mid-youth baseball team—in second place. And a much larger picture of Billy's championship team with a whole paragraph highlighting Billy as the hero of the day.

And here, a much, *much* larger picture of Billy holding the cup-shaped trophy like he's going to drink from it. I can see why Isla is sore. The trophy is huge and, even in the picture, Billy looks like a pompous asshole.

There are a few pages devoted to articles about Jake's death along with editorial markings penned in. *A private burial was held the next day at the family homestead*—has been underlined. *Questions surrounding the death*—has been circled. *Young Jacob leaves behind a long list of loving family members, including a matriarch of this town, his grandmother Edna May (Banks) Miller.*

The *Banks* has an exclamation point drawn above it, and the next pages have a handwritten family tree, some lines filled in, some left blank as if more research is required. Isla's mammaw was Billy's great, great aunt, which seems to have been news to him.

"So, after obsessing over, envying, and competing with this prominent family," I begin.

"And don't forget having his father stolen by one of them," Connors adds.

"He finds out he is actually blood kin—kind of. What does that do to an ego-driven young man who has been living in the Miller shadow his whole life and has just been denied the job he wanted as a big city cop?"

"I always knew he had this rivalry with them, but I had no idea it was so much more than that." Connors keeps flipping through the book.

"What did that say?" I ask.

He returns to the previous page, a schedule of dates printed off from a vacation rental site. "Connors, has he been *renting* the Millers' cabin?"

Connors throws a look at the bedroom door and quietly says, "Well, that would certainly give him unfettered access to install cameras."

I cast around the room. "Where did you put it?" I mutter. And then it hits me. I pace to the bookshelf to read the etched descriptions on each trophy. When I find the huge cup that matches the photograph, I remove it from behind the rest and present it to Connors with an expression pompous enough to match young Billy's when he held it aloft for the first time.

"You're kidding me," Connors says. Reaching in, he pulls out a flash drive. "How much information could it store? There has to be somewhere else where the bulk of the information resides."

"Maybe this is the highlight reel. Look at this." I display a small, metal box.

"Looks like a pet kennel for ants."

"It's a satellite terminal. There must be a transceiver on Isla's property. It was just too small to find."

"Alright," Connors concedes. "So, Billy is in deep. He partnered with Elsbeth? With Jeremiah?"

"Maybe Jeremiah is working against them. Maybe the whole snake in a boot thing was a lure for Elsbeth."

"Fuck, I don't know. Whole thing is—I don't know. The Ridleys allowed them to put those monitors in their house."

"The church is very important to Mr. Ridley," I say. "Maybe Billy allowed him to keep an eye on it."

We say our goodbyes to Ms. Banks without divulging what we've found. Connors swears to her she'll be the first to know when we hear from Billy, and he begs her to go to a friend's house for support in the meantime. "Keep an eye on the sky too," he says. "Several homes are being evacuated because of a fire."

We drive as far as a gas station, and Connors throws the cruiser into park to pop the flash drive into his computer. "They don't go too far back," he says. "The first saved video coincides with the rental dates. Jeremiah creeping around the house, searching for something."

"I think he's searching for the cameras," I say. "He must have found out they had been installed. I don't think he had anything to do with them. Look! He found one!"

"Damn, he's a scary individual. He's glaring right into it."

"That's the one on Isla's room. Is there a video for last Sunday?"

Connors searches and pulls up a video of Jeremiah tacking his snake art above the window. "What the hell is that?"

"I'm beginning to think it's a token of protection. Maybe he's defying the camera's operator."

"Look at this shit," Connors says.

The feed shows Billy beside his cruiser, and then Jeremiah comes into view. They have words. Billy draws his gun, but Jeremiah whacks him with what we now know is the heavy-ass golden snake in the black plastic bag.

A radio call alerts us to the fact that Mr. Ridley has been detained for questioning, and I ask Connors to drop me off at Isla's, but the closer we get, the darker the sky appears, and he begins to question whether or not to pull in—until he sees my face.

"I'll be in and out," I assure him. "I have to make sure she's not there, and I'll grab my truck. Plus, my dog's there. You can't make me evacuate without my dog."

Way before we get to the bridge, however, I fear the worst. A firetruck blocks the road. Firefighters are outside the truck, and they appear to be grappling with a decision. We pull up beside them and while Connors speaks to them, I dash to the house on foot.

But there is no bridge. I stop short and stare down into the water, dumbfounded. Another firetruck is wedged in the riverbed, lying on its side. One of the firefighters tells Connors that a woman was trapped on the other side, but they got her across and got her a ride to her elderly grandmother's house.

Inola was here. That means Jeremiah was here.

"We called for an ambulance," the firefighter continues, "but it's going to be a while, and if the man was bitten three times…"

I don't wait to hear more. "I have to get across. How did you do it before?"

"No, we can't let you go. We nearly dropped the woman. It's too wide. We have to wait."

Isla said there were ways to ford the river. I jog down the bank. Why didn't I just come back here in the first place? I'm fighting through the undergrowth, and I swear the river is getting wider and less possible to cross with every step.

I'll use the firetruck as a bridge. Why not? I can get close enough to jump onto the other bank and climb up from there.

I double back as fast as I can and jump before anyone can guess what I'm doing. I land squarely on the truck, which heaves sideways and I crouch to keep my balance. Water washes over my feet and hands, and nearly knocks me down. Firefighters are shouting at me and cursing. But I'm racing to the other side. I don't stop to think. I hit the end of the truck and leap for all I'm worth.

Landing in swirling water up to my waist, I get dragged downriver, but I manage to lay hold of a root, or a vine, or something, and I pull myself to the shore.

It's steep. And muddy. In fact, it's vertical. But there are roots protruding here and there, and I don't worry too much. They have to hold me. So, I climb.

When I get to the top—I run. I've never run faster. I can see fire now between the woods and the barn. Isla's Jeep is in the drive. She's here. I jump the steps to the front porch, but the front door is locked, so I start pounding. *It's never locked. Why is it locked?* I run around the back and drill up the stairs. But before I can get to the door, its window explodes in my face. The glass disintegrates and sprays onto me like a sandstorm.

And now I'm back in Afghanistan. The noise of a gunshot. Fire and smoke. I fall to my knees.

You train for it. You prepare for it. You visualize. But it's always a mystery whether or not your courage is going to show. I've gotta act. I can barely see. My eyes are watering buckets and stinging like hell. I don't have time to assess how bad it is. But it's bad. I muscle them open and hope my tears will do their thing.

Focus, Kirk. I force myself. Every individual thing you *can* see, and hear, and smell—I stop on that one. *Don't think about that one. You are here now. Sayeed is gone, but Isla needs you, and you cannot check out. Get up.*

They Shall Walk Through Fire

ISLA'S POINT OF VIEW

BILLY BLINKS his eyes hard from where he sits catty-corner to me at the table, and when he opens them, he doesn't seem able to focus. He glares at the whisky bottle, picks it up, thumps it down again. Or maybe it simply slips through his fingers. "What have you —" he begins and rises to his feet so fast his chair clatters to the ground.

That makes me jump up as well, startled by the noise and the abrupt shift in his mood. "Billy, what are you thinking?"

He has drawn his gun, and he waves it around like he can't figure out what to do with it.

At the same time, someone beats on the front door. "Isla?!" *Thump, thump, thump.*

I start to cry out, to tell Banner I'm here, to tell him to be careful, but Billy smashes his hand against my mouth, muting my reply.

The thumping ceases, replaced by the retreating sound of Banner's boots, which is *stomp, stomp, stomp*—and silence.

He jumped off the porch. He'll round the house next. Billy thinks so too. He spins around to aim his firearm at the back door, but he stumbles in the process and clutches his stomach. So, I run for the shotgun.

"Stop!" he bellows and swings the gun at me with a click that means all he has to do is squeeze.

Banner thunders up the back stairs. I see him racing for the door.

"Don't!" I cry out.

Billy fires. The window disintegrates. Banner drops out of view.

From somewhere below the deck, I hear Connors' voice scream, "Army?!" and I listen without breathing.

"Kirk?!" he screams again, closer now. I don't even know how I hear him. My ears are ringing from the shot and the same deafening fear that I suffered while Jake was drowning.

But I have to know. I trip over my own feet to get to the door when Billy catches my wrist. "Let *go* of me!" I shout in his face, and his response is to jerk me sideways.

I don't know if it's because he jerks me like that or because he's denying me access to Banner, but my inner monster roars to the surface. It explodes from my fist, torquing my whole torso to make contact with that son of a bitch's cheekbone. "*Fuck* you!" I yell at him. "Get out of my house!"

He's definitely drunk. Or I'd be dead. There's a ridiculous mixture of annoyance and confusion—and possibly nausea—on his face as he rights himself from my blow and touches his knuckles to his bloodied nose.

Connors comes into view. He dives as Billy shoots again. But it's Billy who staggers like *he's* been shot.

"The bridge," Billy says, and I guess he's sorting out how anyone else could be on-site if the bridge is broken, but all of a sudden—in this scary, absurd, unpredictable moment—it is Billy who identifies my essential thing. The bridge to this place. The bridge to home and family and all the things that give me life and inspiration.

I don't wait for another opening. I run to Banner, and I almost sob for joy when his form rises to fill the window's broken opening. His shoulders engaged, his eyes murderous, his weapon drawn. "Drop, Eesa!"

I'm mid-stride, but I fall and flatten myself. In the next moment, he discharges his firearm.

The sound I hear from behind me, from Billy—is not good. Like a muddy, bubbly, sinkhole. I don't look. I do take a huge breath, and I think maybe it's the first in a long while.

The door falls from its hinges as Banner busts through. "Ees?" he barks but stalks right past me. Connors is close behind.

I can't answer.

Billy is lying on his back, and blood is soaking through the side of his shirt. Banner kicks his gun away. "Ees?!" he repeats. His face is vexed. His eyes are squinted like he's weeping. There are blood smears on his cheek.

"I'm OK. Are you?" I worm my way into his embrace. "I thought he'd hit you."

He can't look at me straight. His eyes are swollen and red.

"What happened?"

He ignores that. "You're not hurt?" he asks hoarsely.

"No, I'm fine. Just worried sick is all. What happened?"

Connors intervenes. "Isla, get him to the sink and flush his eyes. The glass shot into his face."

"Come." I lead my love to the kitchen sink while he props his eyes open with his fingers. Connors tends to Billy.

"Here, bend to the faucet." I flip on the water and stick my wrist under the flow to test it.

Meanwhile, Connors lets out a deeply disturbed sigh. He kneels down to find a pulse and, even though his so-called friend just tried to shoot him, he says, "I'm here Bill."

"How is he?" Banner calls. He's bracing himself against the counter.

"Come on, Ban," I say. "Let's take care of you." When he does lean over, all kinds of tiny grains of glass pour out of his beard and into the sink. I try to help by combing through it, only to cut my fingers.

"Lord, help," I mutter. "That's what's in your eyes? You can see, though, right?"

"Not very well." His voice is measured.

"It must sting like hell. Your cheeks and forehead are pocked with blood." I cup my hands to bring the water to his eyes and face.

I do it again and again as thoroughly as I can. "Will you just put your whole head under?"

He obeys me, and I use the hose to spray out his hair and beard.

After he submits to my ministrations, he stays my hand, allowing the water to drip from his head into the sink. "Connors?" His voice is thin. I think he's scared he killed Billy. "I hit him in the shoulder, right?" he asks. "He's unconscious?"

"There's a lot of blood," Connors says. "But not enough to—I mean, unless the bullet hit an artery—and I don't think it did. I don't understand."

Billy is definitely unconscious. Connors has been putting pressure on the wound, and I'm sure he can see more blood than I can from here, but it's nothing like the amount you'd imagine if he were bleeding out.

"How are your eyes now?" Connors asks.

When Banner flutters them open, blood falls from one to join the water that's streaming from his face. I don't comment on it, but it stabs me with concern. "You need medical attention," I say.

"Yeah," he admits. "I think I do. Nothing's clear. Everything's —jagged."

From the drawer, I grab two dishcloths and towel dry his hair while he holds the other to his face. From there, he says, "Connors, how's his pulse?"

"He *has* one," Connors confirms. "I should get him to the river. There's more going on here than a gunshot."

"Yeah, he's also blitzed—" I begin, but someone's weight causes the floor in the back hall to creak, and Jeremiah appears, overfilling the doorway with Lucy happily jogging at his heels.

"He was walloped by Isla's left hook is all," Jeremiah says. "The woman can pack a punch."

"Where the hell have you been?" I demand.

He points a thumb back. "Resting. I got bit by a pit viper, remember?" He adds, "*Three times*," with a grin that means he's making fun of me.

"Jeremiah Ridley, you come over here and I'll show that left hook up close. Why didn't you save me from Billy?"

With a meaningful—and proud?—glance at the whisky bottle, he says, "I did."

Two robust seconds tick by until I gasp. Connors is listening, so I don't ask, but by Jeremiah's self-satisfied countenance, I can only assume that he means he added some of his father's special sauce to that bottle.

"You—He wanted *me* to drink that whisky!" I say.

"But you don't drink," Jeremiah points out. "Remember? Your manifesto?"

"But what if I *had?*! What if he had *forced* me to?"

Jeremiah shrugs. "That didn't happen."

I huff. "You *have* to be family. You're too infuriating to be anything else."

He makes a sound that means he likes this way of relating and asks, "Do you not have any sugar around?"—like I'm a dumbass.

"Oh, are you out of all of yours?" I say thickly.

He just laughs. I think he's going to stroll into the living room, but Connors says, "Jeremiah, don't you take another step until I say so. You're coming with me."

"No time," Jeremiah says. "This place is going to burn. I'm sorry, Isla, but it is. I'll do what I can."

"You have to save Billy first," I insist.

"No way. He killed his own father. This is justice."

"Please?" I ask. "He'll still go to jail, but his *life*, Jeremiah." Secretly, I don't want *Jeremiah* to go to jail. And I know that Banner will also suffer if this man dies, even if it wasn't his fault.

Jeremiah rolls his eyes and steps over the threshold, making Connors bolt to his feet.

"Leave him alone, *Kevin*," I say. "He can save him. Go on, Jeremiah."

With an aggravated glimpse at me, Connors steps back, and Jeremiah leans over Billy's barely breathing body. "Bring the sugar," he says, but he doesn't sound happy about it. Scurrying to the pantry, I'm back quick as a mouse, and Jeremiah pours the sugar into Billy's mouth—way more gently than he did mine, I might add.

While Jeremiah works on Billy, I lead Banner to a chair.

"No, we don't have time to sit, Babe. Go grab what you need for the next few days, and let's get out of here."

"I know. Just give it a minute."

Jeremiah pounds on Billy's chest one time. Billy gasps for breath and Jeremiah glares down into his eyes. He dies. Jeremiah pounds on him again. And he wakes. And he dies. Jeremiah lies on top of him, head to head, chest to chest, hip to hip, hand to hand. He says, "LORD, my God, let this man's life return to him."

We all instinctively bow our heads, even Connors, and I wonder if he's praying for a miracle.

Jeremiah finishes his prayer, and—nope. We re-bow our heads as he pipes up again. "Yea," he practically sings, "let this man's life return, so that before he enters the eternal torment of thy holy wrath, he may also suffer the full horror of an earthly judge, and live out the rest of his miserable, wretched existence in the bowels of some—"

"OK, that's good," I interrupt.

Billy is breathing. He doesn't speak, but he's focused on Jeremiah, and some kind of understanding passes between them.

Jeremiah gets up, drops all the fanfare, and says to me, "You have to go. Get off the property."

"What about you? Come with us."

"I have one more snake to trap." Jeremiah exits the back door, but Banner says, "Wait. Jeremiah?"

He turns to fix Banner with a look of suspicion.

He's just not good at human interaction.

"Yes?" he says warily. I lead Banner out to him.

"My eyes. Will you heal them?"

Banner's eyes are completely swollen shut at this point. Blood seeps from them like tears. They must hurt like hell. And he thinks that Jeremiah can heal them. But it's all tricks.

After some internal debate, Jeremiah says, "Do you believe that I can?"

Banner rests his hand on my shoulder for balance.

"*I'll* help you, Ban," I blurt out. "I'll be your eyes until you heal —or forever."

He squeezes me, but he answers Jeremiah. "Yes. I believe you can."

"Because of what I did for Billy?"

"No. Or, not just that. Isla believes in you."

"You're wrong about that. She sees behind the curtain is all." Jeremiah starts to walk away.

"She believes in *you*," Banner says with different emphasis, and Jeremiah stops. "When nobody else around her believed. You carried Jake's body all the way back here for her. And ever since then, you've kept watch over her, have surrounded her with protections. You do it invisibly, thanklessly. You do it because you're family." Now, Banner has Jeremiah's absolute focus. Jeremiah looks like the one who is being healed. "You've taken the punishment for sins you didn't commit," Banner continues. "You've foiled the plans of the wicked, the bloodthirsty. Because you're family."

"You read the Bible," Jeremiah says with a small smile. It's not a question.

"Enough to know you quoted the words of the prophet Elijah over Billy in there—you know, with some of your own added flair."

Jeremiah breaks into a real smile this time, as rare as it is bright.

"Please," Banner says. "I believe you can if you will."

Jeremiah wraps his massive arm around Banner's head and drags Banner's eyes to his mouth like he's going to kiss him. If it's awkward for Banner, he doesn't show it. He submits when Jeremiah blows huge, slow breaths into his eyes so fully that it puffs Jeremiah's cheeks. Over and over, slow breaths, and Jeremiah speaks words I do not understand.

I don't know what it feels like to Banner, whether it hurts or soothes, but the bloody tears that stream down his face soon run clear.

Then, Jeremiah cups his hands over Banner's eyes. Into his ear, he says, "You made her heart able to feel again. Who's the real miracle worker?"

Banner stands stock-still and accepts all that Jeremiah does and says, the last of which is, "Remember her." He clutches Banner's head like he wants to stuff the memory of me into the man's brain. "Remember her even when you can't call to mind her name."

The fact that Jeremiah Ridley is actually *family* kind of chokes me up. I gained a cousin. And he protects me. Kind of.

"I will," Banner says. "I promise."

"Open your eyes." Jeremiah pulls his large hands away, and Banner's beautiful greys are as clear and as brilliant as I've ever seen them.

The *how* that I'm thinking will not manifest on my lips, so I stand stupidly with my mouth agape. Jeremiah is already down the stairs and walking toward the barn.

"Jeremiah?" Banner yells down.

"Get her out of here!" is the response.

"Where are you going?" I call, but he doesn't answer. "Jeremiah?!"

Lucy is unhappy about Jeremiah leaving. She paces back and forth at the top of the stairs and whines for him. Then she stares at Banner. And Banner stares at me.

"I have to go with him," he says. "You go with Connors. Get across the bridge. Call Wren, and let him know what's going on."

"No. What? I'm not leaving you after everything that's happened."

"I feel like he needs backup."

"Into the fire?"

Banner raises his hands. "If that's where he has to go."

"Wow. He reached further into your head than your eyeballs."

Banner puffs out a laugh. "You may be right." We both watch Jeremiah, who is jogging now.

"Probably a hazard of being healed. You want to follow the healer."

He gives me a forlorn and conflicted look.

"Come with me first," I bargain, and he obeys.

Connors has been impatiently calling out to us, and now he breeches the back door. "We need to go! I've got the sheriff hand-cuffed in your Jeep."

"Ew, he's going to bleed on the seats."

He deadpans me. "You and your family have some very bad people skills."

"*We* have bad people skills?" I snap. "I'm the only reason that asshole is alive, and if you had any idea what he did to me here today, you would—" I swallow it down. I hadn't meant to allow the things Billy revealed to catch up to me yet, but they barrel in with surprising force. Who knows what all is recorded or how public it'll become? How am I supposed to endure *that* without drinking? How is Banner? How will he be able to stay with me? He's practically a celebrity. It's one thing for him to know I've been a cutter. It's another for his fans. And another still, not to just know it, but to actually *see* the desperate, drunken, tormented, display in living color.

Banner's watching me, but I stomp to my room where I throw off my dress and quickly find more suitable clothes. He follows me. I'm fuming, but trying not to, trying not to be a whirlwind of anxiety and fear and shame—and I say, "OK, I'm ready. I'm coming with you. Don't try to dissuade me because you'll just be wasting time."

"Stop." He catches my hand and speaks gently. "We're not going anywhere except to find a comfortable room someplace safe. We'll eat and rest, and when you're ready, you can tell me what you meant by what you just said to Connors out there." He wraps his arms around me. Aaaaand, now I'm crying.

"I feel like an asshole," Banner says. "Did he hurt you? Did he —" He can't make himself complete the thought.

"No. Not really. But he captured some of my—less glorious moments with that camera." I wave to the window. "It's my own fault. It's just—" I raise my eyes to keep the tears from spilling out. "Intolerable to consider anyone seeing them. Especially—" My face puckers as the sorrow punches me, and as I stare into his eyes, my chin trembles.

"Who? Me?"

"And your fans," I say in a thin, high, pitiful voice.

"First of all," Banner says, "it's not your fault. You did those things in private, right? It's that fucking voyeur who should feel regret. And secondly, we've all done desperate, shameful shit. Especially when we're hurting. Eesa, I want all of you. OK?"

"What if what was recorded is really, *really* disturbing, like near psychotic?"

"Like that time you got so wasted you couldn't remember stripping down for me, and then when I wouldn't sleep with you, you called me a—"

I cover his mouth to keep him from saying it, but it does bring a smile, and he nibbles my fingers.

"I'm not scared of *shit*," he says comically. "Pack a bag. I'll grab mine and meet you in the living room."

In the living room, Connors is admiring the amber color of a whisky freshly poured from Billy's bottle. "Shitfuckdamn!" I yell and drop my bag as I launch myself to smack it out of his hands. It clatters to the floor, drenching the coffee table on the way down.

"What the hell is wrong with you?" he asks.

"Drinking's not good for you!" I grab the bottle and race to the sink to pour the poisoned liquor down the drain. "Did you already have some?"

"No."

"Good. Come *on*. We have to go."

Connors mutters something about weird-ass mountain folk while we walk to the Jeep.

At the river, we help Connors get Billy out. The firefighters have finally rigged up a makeshift rope bridge, and Connors cuffs him to it.

I catch Banner gazing in the direction of the fire. He searches the sky before he feels me watching him. "Ready, then?" he asks as if he's not regretting the decision to leave Jeremiah. He holds out his hand to usher me onto the ropes.

"We should go get him," I say. "Or stop him. Or save him from whatever harebrained thing he has in mind to do."

"No, let's get out of here," Banner says. "It's what he wanted."

"He's family, though," I say as if that solves the matter.

Billy is halfway across the bridge. "Elsbeth's going to kill all of you if you stay on the property. She'll mess with your mind until you do whatever she wants you to. She's that powerful. She's some kind of a witch. She'll make the whole forest grow in around you and bury your bodies underneath."

"Hey, Asshole," Banner says. "Why don't you just shut up?"

"Where are you going?!" Connors yells after us as we head for the Jeep.

I honk twice in response and we tear toward the barn, which is now actually on fire.

Aunt Elsbeth

AT FIRST, we drive past the barn because, I mean, who's going to enter a burning barn on purpose? But the fire is spreading fast, eating up the grass, and when Jeremiah is nowhere in sight, I get a bad feeling, so I wheel around and double back.

On the horizon, Mammaw's cabin is lit from within, and it's so perfect, I gush with affection. *I love you, precious cabin.*

"There's still a lot of land between the fire and the house," I muse.

Banner doesn't measure it that way. He blinks sympathetically. "I know it hurts you, Ees, but we'll rebuild it."

Despite the dread I feel, his inclusion of himself in the effort comforts me. "I'm grateful for you, Mr. Kirk. I'm pretty sure there would be no rebuilding for me if you hadn't shown up."

He lifts my hand from the stick shift to kiss my knuckles and then places it back, leaving his hand on top. "I'm gonna get Wren a huge Christmas gift this year," he declares. "Maybe his own yacht. Where do you want to celebrate?"

"Christmas?" I laugh, but Banner says, "Yeah, it'll be here before you know it. Come to think of it, where do you want to live when we're not on the road?"

"Well? I kind of thought about building a little cabin right here. Out in the glen where the river runs smooth. All of my cousins have busy lives away from this place and they've been discussing the need for a resident caretaker. What do you think of that?"

"I think you know I'd love that."

"Asher could help us design it so that it was green and solar-powered."

"And I'll install the satellite communications to bring you into the modern era—whoa, little lady!"

I don't know whether Banner says the last to me, or to the doe that bounds across our path—or to Lucy who jumps to her feet in the back seat to keep careful track of the doe's progress.

"I guess everybody's being displaced," I say. "I can't bear to watch it all burn. Let's find Jeremiah and get out of here."

The huge door to the barn is wide open, so we leave the Jeep to peer inside. It's the wall to the right that is on fire. I say, "I wonder if the ceiling has caught."

Banner doesn't respond, and I think he's about to be sick.

"Are bad memories catching up to you?"

In answer, he just raises his eyebrows and takes my hand. "Stay close," he says. "Jeremiah?!"

No answer.

"This was a bad idea," he adds. "He didn't even want me to join him." He points upward. "Look at your guardian of the barn now."

The serpent Banner and I hung on the crossbeam is gleaming in the flames. It's not gaudy anymore, not that garish yellow. The paint has come off, and now the serpent's shiny tongue flickers in the light, giving it a dragon-like appearance.

"It's so *shiny*," I say. "It looks like real gold."

"It was *heavy* enough to be real gold."

While Banner continues to stare at the snake, I'm trying to ascertain if there is someone walking under it. I certainly don't want to enter if Jeremiah just ran for the tree huts or something.

"Nah," Banner says. "It can't be real gold." But his brow remains undecided.

Remember that question I had about the ceiling being on fire? It is. A piece of the roof falls to the ground.

"He's in there!" I take a step into what is becoming a fully-fledged inferno. The smell of smoke is tangible with particulates. I cover my nose with my t-shirt.

"What is he doing?" Banner asks. "Jeremiah! Come out of there!"

"Come out of there!" I repeat, but Jeremiah is too invested in his own activities to listen. He's pacing a circle around the floor of the barn, which also leads him around the snake. He's chanting something or praying, and sometimes he threads his fingers to make a single fist which he fervently presses to his forehead or to his chest.

When we get closer, Banner says, "Why can't you pray outside where there's more oxygen?"

"This is where the snake is," Jeremiah answers. "You shouldn't have come."

Something wooden splinters and cracks. Another part of the ceiling collapses. "Just grab it then, Jeremiah," I tell him. "And let's go."

Instead, Jeremiah gets to his knees, his eyelids clenched, his hands fisted, his head bowed. "That's not the snake I mean."

Banner coughs. He's still clutching my hand. "Bro, you have to come with us. Last call."

The light from the outside fades as the door behind us suddenly travels its track and bangs shut with a thump. "What the hell?" I sprint to reopen it. "It's locked!" I pound it with my open hands. "Someone locked it! Hey! We're in here!"

Banner comes to slam his shoulder against it. "Is there any other way out?"

I shake my head.

"We'll break it down," he says. "It's old. Let's find something to batter it." He's off to search while I yell, "Help us, Jeremiah! We're going to burn."

Jeremiah tilts his head to consider this and says, "They shall walk through fire and *not* be burned. The fire shall *not* set them ablaze."

"Jeremiah!" I spout. "You'd better get your Bible-quoting, miracle-working, prayer-offering ass over here, and I mean it!"

He obeys, joining me with supreme nonchalance. "How many more times do I have to say goodbye to you today?" he asks.

"Probably just one! What in the *hell* is that?"

He's gutting a rattlesnake with a wicked-looking boning knife. He tosses its carcass behind himself, and now I see that there is a whole trail of them.

"What are you *doing?*"

"Pissing off the gods of thunder. The last time I did this it rained for a week. We could use that right now."

Jeremiah has a sack slung over his shoulder, and it is from that sack he draws another damned snake. It's not rattling. It's not doing much of anything. Except now, it's dying. He reaches for another.

Slice. Drip. Thud.

"I think I could have saved Jake that day," he says, "if I'd known more about my potential and the power of this place."

I'm listening, but I'm also watching him murder the next snake.

"My dad was furious, but I think it was the thunder gods who sent the flood." *Slice. Drip. Thud.*

Jeremiah is more frightening than usual right now. "Your aunt showed up talking about re-joining the church. They're a pair, right? My dad and your aunt?"

Slice. Drip. Thud.

"You mean your *mother?*" I ask.

"I guess so."

I lift my eyes to check on Banner's progress, but I don't see him.

"Will you please bust the door down?" I ask Jeremiah.

He ignores the question. Instead, he says, "Jake yelled at my dad. Something I could never have done. He didn't recognize your aunt, but she knew who he was. The craziest part is that I'd *just* found out we were cousins, Jake and I. And that was precious to me. But your aunt was appalled. Said he was the enemy. Said we'd have to kill all of you. '*We,*' she said." *Slice. Drip. Thud.*

"Just for land?" I ask.

"Land with gold embedded for the taking. That's the day she found out. And Billy found out too."

"We have gold?"

He uses the bloody hand holding the creepy knife to tug the bracelets on my wrist. "You didn't notice?"

I stare at the golden beads up close. "Yeah, but—they're *gold* gold?"

"Where our two properties converge, there are veins of pure gold. They criss-cross the river. I found them by digging around the pit when my dad would leave me down there to rid me of my sorcery. I dug a whole mine, it seems."

"Jeremiah, is there no end to how amazing you are?"

He regards me quizzically.

I don't know whether to smile or to cry. He's so unused to being admired.

"My mom use to say stuff like that." He means the mom who raised him.

"Your mom was nice to me. I remember her. Break the door down, OK?" I cough. "Or we're going to die."

"It's not the gold, though, that your aunt wants. Not for gold's sake. It's what the confluence of the veins means about the site. There is power here, and it can be harnessed by the right person. But it can also ensnare."

Slice. Thud.

Slice. Thud.

"That's really gross, what you're doing," I say.

"Yep."

The fire is roaring, but another sound catches my ear. A rumbling old engine as familiar to me as the wind through the trees. Pap's tractor. While Jeremiah has been slitting snakes tongue to tail, Banner has been working on a way out of here. "Hop up," he calls from the seat, along with, "What the fuck?" when he sees Jeremiah's handiwork.

I scramble up beside him. There's nowhere to sit but on his leg, which could be fine on any other Sunday, but I'm just a little antsy right now. "Do you know how to drive it?"

"Not really. Is this the clutch?" He releases it and the tractor lurches forward, only to stall.

"Move, Jeremiah!" I call with a wave. "The roof may cave in when we drive out. You have to come with us."

Jeremiah has a bemused expression now, but he ignores my warning and steps further into the barn. I think he's gone back to praying.

I explain the clutch. "It's persnickety. You have to get a feel for where it engages."

"Well, we don't have time for that." Banner maneuvers me into his seat. "I'll follow you out." With that, he jumps down. I do not like this.

"Where will you be?" I ask.

He can't answer me because he's coughing, but he points to a load-bearing corner that is likely to remain, and he takes Lucy by the collar.

OK. This is good. This has to be done.

I start up the tractor, give her a little pat, and clunk her into reverse. I know the sweet spot. After I get enough room, off we go with as much might as I can draw from her, and *BAM!* through the door as its hinges detach from the beams. There is an almighty crash of things falling to the ground behind me, but the tractor chugs onward, and, for the moment, I am out of harm's way.

I spin in the seat to find the whole front of the barn collapsed. That crazy snake statue is now standing in the open above the charred rubble, and I swear it is glimmering more than ever. I guess it is actually made of gold.

"Banner?!" I turn off the tractor to listen for him as a new wind sweeps this way. It seems to emanate from the cabin itself, dragging my hair around my face. The sky grows darker and, at first, I assume it's more smoke, but it's not. It's real cloud cover. Jeremiah Ridley is raising a squall.

"That was clever," the low voice of a woman sings below me.

From my seat, I search for her. I can't tell if she's addressing the tractor stunt or if she knows that Jeremiah is summoning a storm. Either way, she's being sarcastic.

"Oh," I realize, though I've never met this woman. *"You're* the snake."

"Is that any way to address your aunt?"

I jump down, and I'll be damned if a bolt of lightning does not nearly blind me as it exposes all things visible and invisible—like the strange symbol on my aunt's forehead and an ugly expression that makes her appear decrepit.

A wave of energy rushes through me, and the dam of heaven bursts, releasing an ocean of rain. I've never seen anything like it.

I try to climb into the barn, but the rain is too hard and the rubble is too high. The fire is consuming its back wall now, and the ceiling is falling in chunk after burning chunk.

"Who is left in there?" Elsbeth asks over the deluge.

"Your son," I say. "Why don't you help me get him out?"

"Because he opposes me. So, he has to go." We're both soaked. We must be a sight.

"You are all kinds of crazy, dear Aunt," I yell over the rain. "Jeremiah's the best thing you ever gave this world."

"You always did let the notion of family cloud your judgment."

"How would you know?" I snap. Another sharp flash, another unbelievably loud clap of thunder, and I feel angry all over because it scares the bejesus out of me.

"There are stronger alliances," my aunt declares, unperturbed.

The cool tone of her last statement cuts through the din of the rain and raises the hair on my neck, turning my anger to fear. To whom does she owe her allegiance? I start to claw away at the debris.

"Jeremiah! Banner!" *Please answer me.*

The rain is quenching the fire. It's working. If not too late.

Aunt Elsbeth is frowning up at the snake. "How did the stranger come to be here?" she says—like we have time to chat. "I didn't anticipate that."

"I really don't understand what you're asking." And I really don't care at this point. *Maybe part of the wall has opened up around the side. Maybe they've already escaped.*

"No, really," she pushes. "How did he come to be here? The one who woke you up."

I wrestle a huge piece of the wall out of the way. She must mean Banner. "Wren invited him," I grunt. "There was a—storm where he lived. Wren told him to shelter here."

"*Wren.*" She quirks her lips to the side. I've seen Jeremiah do the same thing. "I don't think so. Do *you* call magic?" she asks.

"What are you *talking* about?"

Although...did I not just see Jeremiah heal Banner with nothing but his breath? I stop trying to force my way into the barn and face her full-on. "Do *you*?" I ask.

An eery moan of iron and wood wails and snaps, and something from inside the snaggletoothed opening of the barn comes flying out. The enormous, golden snake, atop its beam and cross plank, falls forward in a great, heavy arc. Like a monster attacking, it strikes from above. I dive out of the way, but the cross crushes my aunt Elsbeth where she stands. One moment, she is upright, and the next she is crumpled and broken, lying at odd angles under the snake, rain drenching her battered body.

Jeremiah emerges behind the cross like a buffalo. I guess he singlehandedly dislodged it from its mooring and forced it down. He observes Aunt Elsbeth, but instead of addressing the fact that his biological mother is crushed beneath a snake, he says to me, "Sorry about your barn."

Maybe we *could* use some work on people skills.

I crawl through the mud to clasp my aunt's hand—"Elsbeth?"—and feel for a pulse. I've never done that before, not for real, not when I actually had to discern someone's fate. I think I do feel one, though. "Elsbeth, we're going to get you help," I tell her.

Jeremiah *pffs*, but he's smiling up at the sky allowing the rain to wash his face. The fire is completely vanquished. Even the smoke has been knocked out of the air. In its place, is the smell of petrichor as happens during summer storms. Fresh. Earthy. Alive.

I try to heave the golden snake off of my aunt, but it's too heavy.

"Leave it," Jeremiah barks.

And I do. I have to. I'm panting from the effort. "Where is Banner?" I ask. "He got off the tractor. He was standing in that —corner."

Jeremiah regards what used to be the load-bearing corner of the building.

"Wait! Do you hear that? Lucy!" I slip in the mud to get through the new path Jeremiah has cleared. "Lucy?!" Clamoring into what's left of the barn, I halt and listen for more dog sounds.

Then Banner calls out, but I can't tell what he's saying.

"We're here!" I assure him. "We're coming!" *But where are you?* The heap of rubble is enormous. I don't know how he could have survived. I toss splintered planks of wood out of my way. "Are you hurt? Are you bleeding?"

His reply is muffled and impossible to decipher.

"Help, Jeremiah!" I squeak.

From the gaps in the roof, where there is no ceiling, the rain pelts and rebounds in puddles.

"Move aside, Cousin," Jeremiah says. With his own massive arms, he begins to heft impossible sections of the fallen building like he's a bulldozer. Every jagged, hulking remnant he removes fractures my heart. Banner is broken. He has to be.

Finally, Jeremiah clears so much of the rubble, I fear he's been digging in the wrong spot. The ground where we thought to find Banner is clear except for one flat metal board.

"We can't give up," I tell him. "Please."

I move to the next section, but Jeremiah touches my arm and gestures toward that metal, so I reluctantly give it my attention. It is sort of interesting, closed flat to the ground like it wants to be opened. I question Jeremiah and tug the thing upward—on working hinges! It reveals a perfectly preserved bubble of space below the ground.

"Ban?" I ask.

He blinks up at me from where he's sitting on a bench that has been carved into the wall of earth. Lucy raises her head and wags her butt. Neither of them appears to have been harmed.

"Are you OK?" I ask.

Banner's head nearly rakes the ceiling when he stands. "I could use a few days we don't have to ask each other that," he says. "But otherwise, yeah."

Upon further inspection, there are shelves stocked with bottles of water and jars of peanut butter—not enough for any real Armageddon, but still... I lower myself into Banner's arms.

"You're sopping wet," he says. It doesn't stop him from holding me.

"You wouldn't believe how hard it's raining. Jeremiah pissed off the storm gods. The fire is completely out."

"Unbelievable."

"Banner, is that invitation to St. Lucia still on the table?"

He chuckles into a kiss. "You think your pap had any clue his storm cellar would really save a life one day? I bet you guys used to hide in here all the time."

This *storm cellar*, as Banner has dubbed it, does not occupy any space in my memory. It's as if it popped into existence from sheer need, for this very event.

"I have no knowledge of this hole," I tell him.

A voice from on high descends. "You two coming out?"

We look up to find Jeremiah crouching over us, and I stare into his simple face. "How did you do this?" I ask.

"Do what?"

"Dig out this small room."

"This sinkhole?"

"It has a *door*," I annunciate.

"And peanut butter," Banner adds.

"I do like peanut butter," Jeremiah says.

It sounds like the peanut butter showed up by accident from Jeremiah's imagination when he invented a small bomb shelter to keep Banner safe. In an instant. During a fire and a building collapse, while murdering snakes.

"Jeremiah? Are you..." How does one ask such a thing?

"Come on," he redirects me. "Your aunt got loose."

"There's no way that's true."

"Step up, Babe," Banner says. He makes a basket with his

fingers to give me a boost. Jeremiah reaches down to haul me the rest of the way. Then, they do the same for Lucy, who joyfully licks Jeremiah's face, and lastly, Jeremiah tugs Banner up. *How is it possible to be that strong?*

Banner doesn't release Jeremiah's wrist where he's gripped it. "Whatever you did," he says. "Thank you. I saw it just in time."

Jeremiah averts his eyes. "You've suffered enough by fire," he says.

"How do you know that?"

"I just do."

When we step into the open, the rain is so heavy, that I have to shield my eyes. Jeremiah's right. There is no Aunt Elsbeth. In fact, there is no heavy-ass golden snake.

The warm lights from Mammaw's cabin sing to me, even through this rain. How is it standing as if nothing happened here at all?

"Jeremiah, you saved it!" I move to hug him, but he stiff-arms me. His eyes rove the grounds. As unflappable as he's been all day, now he's nervous as a cat. In a low voice that makes my skin prickle, he says, "Isla, sprint to your Jeep and get to the house as fast as you can. Lock it down, and wait for me there."

"I don't underst—"

"Banner!" he barks and, like a well-trained soldier who has received a direct order, Banner snatches my hand.

Before we've moved five steps, however, a bolt of lightning smashes into a huge, old oak tree, and it crashes to the ground, cutting off our path.

"Holy shit!" Banner yells. "Did you see that?"

"How could I not?" I'm staring at the smoking tree and pressing my chest to hold my heart in.

But Banner is not focused on the tree. He's whirling around with his eyes on the sky. "There!" He points to the only pinnacle of the barn left standing. "*She* did that! On purpose!"

I spot Aunt Elsbeth for one moment, and the next, she is gone. Now I'm the one whirling around to search.

"Leave her to me!" Jeremiah croaks. He's tracking a silver wisp of light that streaks toward the cabin where it disappears. And now my aunt Elsbeth is perched on top of Mammaw's house! She's had a costume change. Her long silver dress billows in the strong wind. The strands of her wet hair that don't follow suit, hang heavily around her face.

Elsbeth raises her arms above her head. Her index fingers meet and point to the sky, and her other fingers interlace. It looks like she's going to shoot something into the clouds, but instead, something shoots at her. She has become a lightning rod! The crackle of thunder follows the beam of light right into her fingertips. And now, she lowers her arms, straight as pokers, and aims at us.

Banner shoves me to the ground and dives on top of me. But it's Jeremiah who takes the blow. As if it has been coordinated, he strides to place his chest in the perfect position to receive the blast, his arms spread wide, his face relaxed, and his eyes closed. Instead of convulsing or falling or smoking or—whatever it is people do when they're struck by lightning—Jeremiah absorbs it.

I glance at Elsbeth who is studying Jeremiah with a wary scowl.

We wait.

When Jeremiah opens his eyes, they are glowing gold, like fire from within. His face is as placid as ever, but as he shifts his gaze, his eyes trail with the last vestiges of evening's light.

Inhaling a long, slow breath that makes him larger than he already is, his voice travels with an other-worldly rumble. "The house won't work. Get to the graveyard."

Aunt Rose

WE HOOF IT for the downed tree, hand in hand. Banner flings his legs over its massive trunk and slides across rodeo-style, pausing only long enough to make sure I get over too.

He throws himself behind the steering wheel. Doesn't ask permission. "Ees, where are the——"

"Ignition!"

Which he has already found.

Lucy barks a *let's go* from the backseat, and we tear out faster than the wheels can gain traction. Rain is pouring in on us because the Jeep's top is in my garage.

"Jeremiah's eyes!" I say, clicking my belt. "You saw that?"

Banner nods and swipes the water from his nose. "I have no categories to for it. Except that there was a book in his room about ley lines, and now I'm wondering if these properties hold a——I don't know——energy?——that is not usual."

"Like Stonehenge?"

"Maybe? Ees, your aunt is a witch——or something like. And Jeremiah is——something too. And they're at odds."

"Do they have to be at odds in my backyard? There! Take that right!"

The Jeep throws mud as Banner skids into the turn.

"Why didn't *I* get any magic?" I gripe. "That's not fair."

"You make people see worlds that you create ex nihilo," he offers.

"Out of nothing? That's not magic. That's just imagination."

"Then God just had imagination," he argues. "When he called the universe into existence."

I scoff, but Banner says, "All I know is that words carry power, and yours carry more than most."

"But I can't summon storms or make people *literally* able to see when they've been blinded."

Banner shrugs. "I don't think you *know* what all you can do. Anyway, if the magic is in this *place*—to be mined as you mine gold, you do that. I saw those little flowers reach for you like you were their mama. And the lightning bugs. They watched you for their cues."

The path opens onto a field where we soar for two full seconds before the Jeep bounces and slides onto the slick grass. "Left," I point. "Cross the clearing. Do you recognize it? The cemetery's round knoll? The tree that spreads over it from the middle?"

The crown of our family, Mammaw would say. *The source of our —strength.*

She didn't mean more than that our lives were built on the backs of our forebears, right?

"Hang on!" A bolt of lightning streaks down and Banner swerves to miss it. Its huge *boom* rocks the atmosphere, casting the Jeep onto its side.

Instinctively, I pull my arms in, and thank God I do, because as the vehicle topples, the ground comes up to meet me. My seatbelt does its job, though, and nothing of me gets mangled. Just sideways.

Banner cuts the engine and checks on me from where he's suspended above in his own seatbelt. "Are you hurt?" His eyes are sharp, his expression hard.

"I don't think so. You?"

"No." Bracing himself, so that he won't fall on top of me, he unclips our seatbelts, points through the open top of the Jeep—which is now the back—and I crawl out with him close behind.

The rain is hard as ever. The wind blows with such force, I fear it will tear the whole forest down. Another concussive blast threatens to knock me off my feet, but Banner stabilizes me. Then, a sickening clash of green and purple rumbles back toward the house. If I doubted it before, I do so no longer. Something far more than the weather is at work here.

Banner echoes my thoughts. "This is war."

"It's like they're *aiming* for us!"

"Lucy?!" Banner calls. There's a crater carved beneath the overturned vehicle, quickly filling with water.

"Lucy!" I shield my eyes and yell into the storm, but Banner cries out and falls to his knees. Lucy must have been thrown under the Jeep. Or she jumped at the wrong time. Banner lifts her from the crater, limp and dripping.

"She's OK," I say without knowing.

He cradles her to his chest, and I worm my hands underneath to feel her warm, wet rib cage pulsing in quick, shallow breaths.

I motion to the graveyard, which is oddly awash in an orange glow, though the rest of the world is drizzling grey. "Can you carry her that far?"

"Yeah, let's go."

Instead of seeking cover elsewhere—which would have been more tempting if there were any around—we dash the remaining seventy-ish yards to the graveyard. As soon as we breach its invisible boundary, the rain ceases to fall.

Let me be clear. The rain is still descending in buckets *outside* the boundary. I can reach across to allow my hand to fill, but then I draw it back into the cool, dry air that surrounds the gravestones like a dome.

The persistent din of the battle and the roar of the rain cease as well, replaced by the gentler summer sounds of bugs and frogs, along with the cozy feelings they summon. But the most amazing phenomenon is the warm light I'd noticed back at the Jeep. The sun reaches down with golden rays, and the whole of the graveyard is illuminated, sheltering us in the very eye of the storm.

Lucy squirms impatiently and lifts her head. "Easy, Girl," Banner soothes and stoops to set her down, but she won't wait. She jumps from his arms and romps about like nothing was ever the matter with her

Banner gives me a funny look and follows his dog a few paces before he turns a full three-sixty and looks back at me with his eyebrows raised. "It's a safe zone," he says. "Some kind of protective vortex. How? Did Jeremiah instate it?"

"No, it's been here." I realize. "Mammaw used to walk us around here on picnic days to tell us stories of the different family members buried here, all the names and whatever made them interesting. She said it was because of the dead that the living are blessed. But mostly, she made sure we understood that it was our job to steward the land, and in return, she said the land would listen to us, would protect us."

The strange enchantment that is guarding this graveyard creates a false sense of security, and Banner and I begin to wander. As we wander, we relax.

Banner says, "Tell me some of the wilder stories you remember. What's the story behind this grave?"

Although there are etchings on the small gravestone in question, they've been worn beyond reading. "Oh, she was full Cherokee," I lie. "She married my great, great, great grandfather, and when she died, only half of her was buried here. The rest of her is on the Cherokee grounds. Split right down the middle." I make a cleaving motion. "This is her left side because she gave her heart to the Miller family."

Banner studies the gravestone in awed silence until I start to feel guilty for making him believe such a thing. "I'm just shitting you," I confess. "I don't have a clue who's buried here. It's probably all of her, though."

The spark of a grin Banner bites back tells me three things: 1) I got him, 2) he knows it, and 3) exactly what he'd like to do to me for it. He traps my arm around my back and bends to kiss me. "You can't even help it, can you?" he teases. "You've just gotta make shit up."

It's not until Lucy begins to bark and whine, that we lift our eyes to the cemetery's one sprawling tree and remember how very bizarre our reality has become. Hanging like grotesque lanterns from the long, low branches surrounding Jake's grave, are multiple large, silk-like bundles as if a monstrous spider has been spinning its victims. Or laying egg sacks. I'm not sure which is worse.

We draw near.

"What are they?" Banner asks.

Then, from behind us, Jeremiah bellows, "Isla, step back." A few of the bundles writhe at the sound, and Banner immediately shields me with his body. "Come, Lucy," he commands.

"What are they, Jeremiah?" I ask. "They're not going to burst open and spill a billion fighter spiders, are they?"

Jeremiah's eyes are no longer lit from within. He looks exhausted. "I think they're your family, but they may not be."

"What do you mean you think they're my family?!"

"Or *our* family, I guess. Your aunt had them wrapped up by the bridge. I can't imagine who else they would be."

I emit an irritated grunt and bypass Banner to yank on the first sticky sack I come to. It squirms against me and lets out a muffled cry from within. It's a voice I know.

"Millie?! Banner, help me! It's my niece." I try to rip her out, but it's impossible. I can't even get the thing out of the tree.

Banner unfolds his Army knife and tells me to step aside while he slices the cocoon in careful strokes.

"Keep still, Mill," he soothes. "We'll get you out."

Though Millie is shy of thirteen and has never met Banner, she stops struggling, and he's able to free her to the point she falls out of the sack and into his arms. This does not appear to displease her. She looks up at her savior with wide, grateful eyes.

Banner gently lays her on the ground where I then dive on top of her, and maybe that does not please her as much.

"What happened?" I ask. "Are you hurt? How did you get here? Where's Sissy—where's your mom?"

Millie can't answer all the questions I spew. She blinks and swallows like she's waking from a dream. Silver silk sticks to her clothes in patches like cotton candy.

Silver. It must be Aunt Elsbeth's signature color. I think she's the reason the bridge collapsed. I think she was the one laughing just behind my back.

Along each tree limb, Banner—and now Jeremiah, with that disgusting blade he used to disembowel the snakes—works to release the rest of my family. When Millie's twin is revealed, I go to *her* and hold her face until I am confident she's truly conscious.

"Is your mom here?" I ask, but her unfocused gaze sends me seeking my sister elsewhere. "Sissy?"

"Here I am," comes a hoarse reply. When I find her sitting with her back to the tree, I cling to her. "My girls," she rasps.

"They're fine. They're here. We've got them."

Her puff of relief settles me like the wind outside our window on the first night of summer at the cabin. She regards me steadily. "You look beautiful."

"Really?" I laugh. "Soaked to the bone and scared out of my wits?"

"Your skin is glowing. Your eyes are bright like they haven't been in years."

A benefit of sobriety, I guess. I also suspect that being in love has something to do with it.

Banner is roving from bundle to bundle. "Wren's here," he calls. "Seems to be well."

"What about Asher?" I call back.

"Are you Asher?" he asks, though I can't see to whom he's talking. "Asher's good!"

"So, that's *him?*" Sissy says under her breath. "Sounds like sex on a stick."

I sniff out a laugh.

"*Uh,* Ees?" The caution in Banner's tone brokers my attention. He's holding the hand of a woman who is unnaturally stiff.

"It's Aunt Rose!" I cross the grass, which is strewn with sticky spider fabric, and fall to my knees beside the boys' mother. She happens to be lying right on top of Jake's grave "Wake up, Aunt Rose," I cry. "Jeremiah, what's wrong with her?"

"Mom?" Wren says. Like Sissy, Wren is recovering quickly, and he stumbles our way. "The bridge was broken," he tells me. "A horrible woman came out of nowhere and attacked us. But Mom fought back like she was expecting her. You wouldn't have believed it."

"That woman is our aunt Elsbeth," I tell him.

He's paying more attention to his mother than to me. "Mom?" he says again, but she doesn't wake.

Where the hell is my miracle-working friend-turned-cousin? I spot Jeremiah lurking behind Mammaw's headstone. Unfortunately, he has reverted to his brooding, lumbering, ghost of a self.

"Jeremiah! My aunt Rose—no! *Your* aunt Rose! Get over here."

"How is *he* going to help?" Wren mutters.

"As horrible as Aunt Elsbeth is? Jeremiah is good. And he's our cousin!"

Jeremiah shuffles over and stares at us from beneath his eyelids the way a zombie might—if that zombie were also a sheep. Even so, Wren makes room for him to kneel beside us. After that, Jeremiah takes Aunt Rose's hand and simply closes his eyes.

I purse my lips in a bid for patience and have to stifle the urge to knock him over for not doing more.

"Look, I think we need to—" Wren begins.

"Just hang on," I snap. "Trust me."

Two full minutes pass this way, while Aunt Rose lies there looking dead.

Please don't die. There are things I have to say. Please wake up.

Wren begins to speak again when, without more ado—no explanation, no sympathy—Jeremiah says, "Get up, Aunt Rose. Isla needs to make amends."

Aunt Rose opens her eyes, regards Jeremiah, and gets to her feet. "Jeremiah Ridley?" she says, followed by, "*Huh*," like she's figuring things out.

Jeremiah puts a bit of distance between us and mumbles, "Make it fast. I didn't throw Elsbeth that far."

This enigmatic statement does not shock me the way it would have before today. I assume cousin Jeremiah did actually throw his mother somewhere. Nor does it shock me that Jeremiah was able to awaken Aunt Rose. I'm pretty sure there are no limits to what the man can do. The thing that fries my noodle is that after so many months of pining for a path to Aunt Rose, she is finally standing before me. I have a strong desire to flee. Before I can act on it, however, she grabs me into a tight embrace—and I break open the way the clouds did, sobbing against her shoulder.

There are many things I need to tell her, but I can't think of a single one except, "I couldn't save him. I couldn't save him." And I sob that one over and over.

"I know." She touches my hair. "I knew it then. But you were too stricken to hear it." There are tears in her eyes too, but there is also love.

"I thought you blamed me. I overheard you arguing with Dad."

"No, Baby," Aunt Rose consoles me. "I was never upset with you. If anyone lost as much as I did, it was you."

Behind her shoulder, Banner offers me a sympathetic smile.

"Your father and I argued," she continues, "because I suspected Elsbeth. But he said I just wanted someone to blame." Aunt Rose shakes her head to convey the fact that she couldn't make him believe her.

"Why didn't you tell me?"

"I tried. I tried to get details to confirm my theory, but you were too broken."

"Enough," Jeremiah cuts in. He keeps gazing up and around. "Isla's return has made her frantic. She's beginning to suspect the truth, and she is here to cut every one of you down. Is this everybody?"

This is so weird. My aunt and her boys, my sister and her daughters. All standing with faces lit by the brilliant evening sun among the raised gravestones of our ancestors—with rain pouring, but only outside the perimeter.

Wren takes inventory of us and says, "This is all who could come this evening. More will arrive tomorrow, Isla's parents and my wife and kids. We're going to spend some time altogether the way we used to."

Aunt Rose speaks up as if to say that Wren hasn't answered the question accurately. "Yes, Jeremiah. There are no others."

He considers us.

"It'll have to do," he decides. "Two who call magic. One seer. One believer—and he is a soldier." He regards Aunt Rose. "As soon as it rains, get all the others back to the house. Or better yet, off the property.

"I will," she nods.

To Banner, he says, "You keep Isla alive."

I'm not sure whether it's an observation or a directive.

Banner says, "What can I do against things I don't understand?"

"You do understand. You understand war. The weapons are new to you, but the tactics are the same."

"But her weapons are *magic,*" he says.

"Earth magic," corrects Jeremiah. "It's as much a part of the natural world as you are. Elsbeth didn't create the lighting you saw. She just found a way to redirect it."

"How did you absorb it without being electrocuted?" I ask.

"I convinced the earth to receive it. It's the same thing I do with my dad, using the Bible's words to convince him to do better."

When it is painfully clear that I have no idea how one would do that, Jeremiah rolls his eyes. "You just imagine what the earth wants and you help it along."

"What does the earth want?" I ask.

"Oh, my gosh—Sunrise. Sunset. The change of seasons. The spread of seeds. The earth wants flowers to bloom. It wants life to flourish—to the point of using death to make new life. It wants you to take care of it. Just let it know what *you* want."

After a pause, he adds, "Though, if the magic isn't part of your every day, it's harder to coax—well, we'll just have to pray that Banner believes enough for both of you."

Jeremiah turns on his heel and stalks away.

"Jeremiah Ridley, where are you going?! Don't *leave* us."

Over his shoulder he calls, "She doesn't know about you yet, not entirely. I'm going to try to keep it that way."

"*I* don't know about me yet!" I almost sob it. I definitely whine it.

Jeremiah halts and turns to face me. He softens his tone. "Isla, do you remember the funeral we went to? The boy, Onacona?"

I nod.

"Remember how the men received ashes and the women chanted his name?"

"Yes."

"We were asking the earth to receive his body and Creator to receive his soul. Do you think it was an accident that you and I were invited?"

"And Jake."

"Think back. Was Inola sent to invite both you *and* Jake? Or was she just being polite because Jake was around?"

I don't answer. He already knows.

"You and I were born of this land," he says. "And that is why the Cherokee extended the invitation. I'm *going to water*, as we did then, to seek Creator. There is earth magic, and then there is upper-world magic. And that is the assistance we need." He twirls his creepy knife and says, "The *lesser* gods heard me." Now his eyes are smiling. He's pleased with himself.

"Jeremiah, are you *gloating* about getting the storm gods to put out the fire?"

"No," he responds abruptly and sets his features hard as flint. Honestly, can the man not just accept a little friendly ribbing?

He turns to Banner and—once again—entreats him. "You made her alive. You have to keep her that way."

Banner almost looks hurt. "Jeremiah, nobody wants this woman alive more than I do."

"Seal her in your heart." He actually thrusts a palm against Banner's chest.

"Yes," Banner insists.

My odd cousin nods once and crosses the invisible boundary of the cemetery, where the rain soaks him as he starts to sprint in the direction of the river.

"Nobody here understands what the hell you're saying!" I yell after him. "As usual."

Banner heaves an unsettled sigh.

"Don't listen to him," I say. "He's nuts."

"You know he's not. You're in danger. And I have a feeling it's not the kind I can hide you from, you know? I can't just stick you in a safe cell and guard the door—not that you'd have that. I'm afraid it's more of a *follow-the-queen-into-battle* scenario. And maybe that's the whole reason I'm here."

I want to comfort him, make a stupid joke. Thing is, I know he's right. That woman killed Jake. And while I'm no hero and certainly no soldier, I can't unseat the clawing demand it awakens. Anyway, she wants to kill the rest of us. And who knows how evil she'd be if allowed to occupy this land?

I slap my thighs and peruse the precious faces of my family. In lieu of a call to action, I decide to make introductions. "Everyone? This is Banner. He asked me to marry him, and I didn't say no."

Banner chokes on the greeting he was going to give and sweeps me into a headlock. "Because you were smiling too broadly to answer, *Sweetheart.*"

"True," I say laughing. And, just like that, balance is restored.

Is it my imagination, or do the twins both drop their heads in disappointment? "Forget it," I snap at them. "You're too young. And you're too late." I point at Lucy. "You can pet the dog."

Asher cuts in. "Does anyone want to explain why Jeremiah Ridley seems to be in charge, or what he means when he says that two of us call magic? Which two?"

"Aunt Rose calls magic," Millie says, and then at length, Wren agrees. "It's true, isn't it?"

"A little bit," Aunt Rose concedes. "Enough to anticipate a fight from Elsbeth. Our childhood was fraught with them. She was cruel and impossible to anticipate until—I didn't know what I was doing —I asked to see her coming, and the very air began to warn me. It rippled that way today right before she attacked. But it was Jeremiah who kept her from doing worse."

"Jeremiah's the other one," I say. "The things I've seen him do are incredible."

"If he's counting himself," Banner adds.

But then I gasp. "Or Wren! It's you! Aunt Elsbeth couldn't understand how Banner came to me. *You* made it happen. You made a hurricane?"

"It's not me," Wren says flatly. "I do not have the knowledge or the expertise to make a hurricane. Nor would I consider doing such a thing. If anyone in this family created a hurricane, I think we can all agree that you are far more likely than I."

I think back to the days leading up to Banner's arrival. I spent a whole lot of time wishing that that bridge would flood and trap me inside. I brought a shit-ton of whisky and a single-edge razor blade. But I also did a lot of pleading to be healed, to be free from the drinking, free from hurting. *Make me alive again.* I kept chanting it like a prayer. Ley lines don't carry messages into the ocean, do they?

Banner is watching me.

Aunt Rose is watching me too. "We probably all call a bit of magic," she says.

Can she read my thoughts?! I stare at her as hard as I can and think at her, *"Can you read my thoughts?"*

But she just frowns with her eyebrows and slowly shakes her head.

Wait. What? Did she just answer my unspoken question about reading my thoughts by saying no? And if so, is she just fucking with me?

Banner looks back and forth between the two of us. Wren blurts out, "What is going on?"

It's Millie who answers. "Isla wants to know if Aunt Rose can read her mind." When all heads spring in Millie's direction, she shrugs and says, "That's what it looks like to me."

Now, a curious smile spreads across my lover's handsome face. He says, "I think we found our seer."

Sissy gasps. "That explains so much."

Millie is beaming at Banner like his attention is a prize. "I know things," she brags. "One time Isla fed wild rabbits from her hand. And another time, she settled an argument between owls."

"Isla's the other one," Banner seeks confirmation. Millie nods.

"What are y'all talking about?" I say.

"You can call magic, Ees. Like I said before. You can call magic from this place. You're so bound to it, you don't even know that's what you're doing." He gestures toward Jake's grave. "And now part of your heart has literally become part of this sacred ground."

"Do you hear yourself right now?" I ask. "This is ridiculous."

"It's not," Sissy says. "Remember the gardenia you grew where Jake's body was laid?"

"I didn't plant that gardenia, Sissy. You did."

"No, I didn't. And you didn't plant it either. Because it wasn't planted. Remember?"

My eyes roam the ground like they expect to find the memory there. I can see myself holding Jake's lifeless body. I can feel the hard ground, the crimp in my spine, but I don't care because I'm no longer attached to my body. I've cried all the tears I can make. My lips are chapped. My eyes are swollen.

"I was the only one you'd let anywhere near," Sissy continues. "And only then because I swore I wouldn't touch him. You were like a wounded animal. It wasn't until you had nothing left to cry and that gardenia grew right up underneath him and bloomed around his head, that you passed out, and we retrieved his body."

I half wish to pass out now. I feel for the ground and take a seat, not even knowing I'm leaning against Jake's headstone, the same way I'd been yesterday when Jeremiah found me here. "Well," I say quietly, "I don't know how to do anything like that now."

"That's what Banner's for," Millie says. "You can't reach into the earth without feeling things. Elsbeth feels greed and the lust for tyrannical power. She feels hatred. And maybe you did too, or something like. And you tried to dull it because it hurt so much. But Banner makes you brave."

"How do you know so much?" I say.

Millie shrugs again and hums an *I don't know* melody.

"Are we all just supposed to sit around until the coast is clear?" It's Asher who asks.

"No," I answer. "The coast isn't going to clear. Elsbeth wants us dead."

"She'll want you dead first," Aunt Rose says pointedly. "When she finds out you're the one standing in her way."

"Surely she won't kill her own family!" Asher says.

"She killed Jake," I tell him. "She had just found out how much more the land was worth than the money it could bring."

Suddenly, Aunt Rose pivots and says, "Quiet!" At the same moment, Millie cries out, "She's here."

A heavy perfume settles among us. It's the moldy scent of too many flowers as they rot. And now, up from the dirt on Jake's grave, putrid roses begin to protrude, heads and arms reaching like ghoulish toddlers demanding to be held.

I search for Elsbeth, but if she's around, I do not see her. Even so, I defy her. "Elsbeth, this is one piece of earth you cannot command."

I may not know the least thing about magic, but I know that if that woman wants to desecrate Jake's grave, she is going to get my foot up her—I swipe at the disgusting roses reflexively, and they fall to the ground. In their place, a gardenia bush bursts forth and begins to grow.

Sinking, Rising, East & West

BANNER'S RIGHT. I've been collaborating with the earth since I was a kid, I just didn't know it. The earth teemed with life force and I teemed with imagination. But only here at the cabin. Only *this* earth listened. I used to get so frustrated with the plants and animals where we lived during the school year—and the people too—so, I put my imagination onto paper.

Over the top of my gardenia's mounding height, Banner is staring wide-eyed with delight, and I can feel my own eyes smiling back. *How?* I mouth.

He shakes his head, that sexy lopsided grin begging to be kissed.

"Careful," Aunt Rose says, and her eyes rove the graveyard all around.

But Aunt Elsbeth's sickening roses are receding. They appear skeletal and black, and they're being sucked into the dirt without a fight, overshadowed by my thriving king-of-a-gardenia bush—which is budding!

"This is so easy," I say. "What was Jeremiah even worried about?"

There are tens of bulging buds blooming—a hundred—more! Lovely, white flowers unfolding with an intoxicatingly fresh scent.

"*Careful,*" Aunt Rose reemphasizes. "You don't know what she's capable of."

"What could go wrong?" I ask, and maybe I'm a little drunk on the fact that the earth just partnered with me to magic this plant into existence. "We're all here together. We're family. And Elsbeth's just a misguided, mean, crazy witch."

It's funny how much I've forgotten about my recent encounter with my estranged aunt. How shockingly powerful she is, how murderous.

I fondle one of the blooming flowers, but instead of the soft, velvety texture I expect, the flower is crisp like the paper in my sketchpad. Indeed, now that I study them, I think they are less flora and more origami.

I pluck one at its stem and emit a surprised laugh. "It's paper!" And then I remember what I buried on this very spot. My manifesto. My goodbye-for-now to Jake and my commitment to the land of the living. *Unbelievable.*

Pulling at the pucker in the center of the bloom, the paper opens for me. It's a letter, but it is not my letter. It's handwriting—handwriting I recognize—but it is not my handwriting. The familiarity of the messy, haphazard slant of the letters is a gut punch.

"I'm confused," I say. "If this is my magic—or whatever you want to call it—then why aren't these my words? How did he—" I can't finish my question for fear of the answer.

"What does it say?" Aunt Rose asks warily.

"It says, 'How—'" My throat spasms. It's the strangest feeling, like somebody's fist is closing around my vocal cords, shutting off the sound. As soon as I stop trying to speak, I am released. I shake it off, try again. "It says, 'How—'" But there it is again, the squeeze, the invisible fist. I put my hand to my throat.

"What's going on, Ees?" Banner asks.

How dare you write your goodbyes to me? When did you turn into such a hypocrite? If you had just climbed up there with me, I'd still be alive. Do you know how long I've been trapped here? Don't you dare abandon me now, Eesa. Help me!

"Isla, drop the paper," Aunt Rose says.

I can't. I have to read it again. It's here on Jake's grave, written by Jake's own hand. Was he able to conjure it for me? Is he really trapped here somehow? Did *I* trap him?

Aunt Rose strides over to snatch the letter from me.

"Why did you do that? He's talking to me! He's trapped!"

"No. He's not."

"Ees, what does it say?" Banner questions.

"He's *trapped!* Jake is trapped. I have to find him. He may be alive in the grave underneath me right now! Waiting for me!"

"It's not Jake, Sweetheart," Banner says. He sounds like he's talking to a skittish stray. "It's Elsbeth. It's a trick."

"It's his handwriting." My voice sounds thin. I don't feel right.

When I glance over, everyone else in my family averts their eyes, and one by one they turn their backs to me.

Under her breath, Aunt Rose says, "I wish it had been you."

That snaps my eyes back to her. "What did you say?"

The letter is gripped in her hand. Her face is molded in torment, the way it had been the night Jake's body lay cold on the dining room table. "It should have been you. You were supposed to follow him."

"No, it wasn't my fault," I argue. "I told him. I *begged* him."

"He needed you and you just stood there and refused him. You were practically his *twin!*" Grief overtakes her. Sobs convulse in her chest. "My baby! My son!" she wails. "*You* die!" With that, Aunt Rose slashes at me with a bo-staff. Where it came from, I have no idea. I jump out of the way just in time.

"Aunt Rose, no!"

Millie, from under the straight line of her shiny, black bangs, is speaking to Banner, and he's leaning down to hear her, nodding in agreement. Meanwhile, Aunt Rose is attacking me!

"I don't want to *fight* you!" I yell, but I swing to protect myself.

My punch is redirected by Banner's forearm. "Stop it, Isla!" He swipes my arm so that I can't make contact and surrounds me—less hug, more restraint. "Look at me."

I do—full in the face, and it's like being doused with cold water.

"You're reacting to something that is not happening," he says. "Nobody here is threatening you, least of all your aunt Rose."

I search around, panting, and now everyone is facing me again, watching in awkward silence.

Aunt Rose is watching too. Not with a bo-staff.

I squeeze Banner's neck to sink into his protection. "They're gaslighting me."

"No, Babe. It's Elsbeth. Trust me. When I saw her at the hospital, she targeted vulnerabilities I didn't even know I had. It's psychological warfare."

"But—she would have had to read my letter," I stammer. "She would have had to write in Jake's handwriting."

"I'm not sure about that. Maybe all she needs is to turn your memories against you. Trigger your regrets. Trap you in your own imagination."

"But it's right there written on the paper!"

Aunt Rose is shaking her head. "The paper is blank."

I gape at her.

Right.

Mind. Fuck.

"OK," I say. "Wow. She could just use *me* to kill all of us for her."

"You good?" Banner asks before he lets me go.

"I'm learning. Millie?"

"Yes?" my niece chirps. She's the only one of us who doesn't look at all traumatized.

I ask for the letter back and display it for her without eyeing it myself. "Do you see anything written here?"

"No. Wait. No. That is...something wants to be there, but it's not. Like when the heat shimmers over the road."

"Is it setting off any kind of hallucination for you?"

"I don't think so." Her eyes wander from side to side to test it.

"Millie's a very practical, very concrete thinker," Sissy says. "We took her to a hypnotist once to get to the bottom of all the things she says she sees—"

"I *told* you I really see them," Millie interrupts.

"I'm so sorry, Mill. We didn't know. But the point is that Millie couldn't be hypnotized. The guy said she lacked imagination. And here, the whole time we thought she was *over*-imaginative. Or having hallucinations."

"That's perfect!" I say. "Will you check a few more of the blooms, Mill?"

Millie unfolds several, and with each one, she squints harder. I guess that each one is full of potential messages she can't invent.

"That's enough," I tell her. "Can anyone else see what's written here?"

Surely, my family thinks I'm insane, right? But they shake their heads as if it's a legitimate question.

"And not you?" I ask Banner.

"I'm not looking at that thing," he says.

"Alright. So, Millie can see *something*, but it doesn't wield the same power over her that it does me." I'm just thinking out loud here. I turn to my aunt. "What does it mean?"

Aunt Rose says, "I think her roses were a test. She probably thought that I would be the one to react, thus the use of spoiled roses, like my name. She used to do that sometimes. But when you revealed your magic instead, she flexed—hijacked your gardenia and used it against you. It's possible that she has now marked you as the greatest threat to owning this land and its energy."

"She can't be allowed to have it. She'll kill all of us. And who knows what she'll do after that?"

"Then I think you have to get control of yourself and follow her into that letter."

"Nope," Banner pipes up. "What the *hell* are you saying? She's being *baited!* You want her to play into the trap?"

"Isla's magic may prove stronger." Aunt Rose holds the paper up to my face, but Banner steals it away.

"And what if it's not?! You may not be aware, but while you were hanging around in a spider sack, Elsbeth was hurling bolts of *lightning* at us. Forgive me if I don't trust that lunatic's headspace."

"You can keep her grounded," Aunt Rose says. "Let her go and trust her imagination."

"It's her imagination that's playing into Elsbeth's plan!"

"I can do it," I interject. "If you'll help me. I can hear you through the illusion."

He starts to object.

"I *can*," I insist. "When I saw everyone else turn their back on me, you got my attention. I have to do this, Ban."

Banner hangs his head with a huff. He hates it, and it occurs to me what I'm asking him to do. To risk the home he's never had. The one he hopes to have with me.

My next words sound incredible even to my own ears. "Banner, you're here because, in answer to my deepest longings, the earth and sky conspired to bring you to me. You started my heart again. You already saved me. Please help me do this, and then we'll be free to live our lives the way we want. With a home. And kids. All of it."

"I do want all of it." He puts his forehead to mine and makes a contentious sound of surrender. "Are you sure this is the way to go about it?"

"I am. You recognize what she's doing. You and I can foil her."

"If I do this for you, Isla Miller, you are bound to me. You have to marry me, and I'm not joking."

"Yes. I will."

"Tomorrow," he adds.

"If that's what you want," I laugh.

He rubs a hand down his face. "Alright. Lead on, my queen."

"Millie?" I say. "I'm going to need you too."

"I know, *my queen*," she mimics.

"Smartass," Banner says. "I can really see the family resemblance between the two of you right now, I want you to know."

"Isla?" It's Sissy.

I cut her off from what I assume is going to be her protective motherly instincts. "Sissy, I'll do everything I can to keep her from danger. We have to try."

"I know. Just—you can't underestimate her again."

"I won't. Ban, I need to read the letter."

He hands over the abused piece of paper without regarding it, but he doesn't release it until our eyes meet. He's so somber, I get nervous. "You listen for me, Woman. And you come when I call. Don't trust your other senses. And for godsake, don't trust her. In fact, doubt everything in the world except that I love you and I am waiting for you right here."

I don't know how to answer that. I nod in agreement, and Banner draws back a few inches, which I take for permission to go ahead. I bow my head to read the dreadful words that are somehow written in my cousin's own hand.

But I'm sucker punched again, because instead of the letter, there is an actual photograph of Jake in his coffin, not as he was the day we buried him, but rather, as he must have been later, green, decomposing, his flesh turning to a butter-like substance, his bones showing through. Even so, his eyes pop open and a look of terror masks his face.

As soon as his eyes meet mine, the sky crashes. Banner calls me back, but all goes dim. Oppressive grey clouds descend in a low, solid ceiling above me and press down until I am kneeling to keep from being crushed. I'm pushing against it. I'm forced onto my back. I know that Banner is speaking to me, but I'm falling through the ground.

And now it is no longer the sky above me, but the solid lid of a pine coffin, and I'm lying in the silent dark of Jake's grave.

I scream for help. Actually, I just scream, and so hard that it feels like I'm scraping my throat raw from the inside out. The sound dies as it leaves my mouth. It has nowhere to go. I bang frantically on the lid, and I suck in a huge breath to scream again, but instead of letting it out, I hold it in. *How am I breathing? How is there air?*

The vision goes blank and now I am no longer stuck in a coffin. The episode isn't over exactly. It's more like when the end credits of a movie play out and there's that little bit of extra tape rolling blank and black. Something silver shimmers at the edge of my vision, and I think of how Millie said the paper looked like heat over asphalt.

"Elsbeth?" I ask.

I think she can hear me. Some kind of whirring that I hadn't even realized goes still.

I wasn't supposed to be able to assess my reality—that I wasn't actually trapped in that coffin. That was a victory. But now I wonder if I really can find out what is in there. I have to know that Jake's body is going back to the earth and that his soul is free and at peace. I can't bear to touch his body, but at the same time, I desperately want to. I *will* myself back into that small, inflexible space. *Jake?* My hand only finds the wall of the casket. There's no one here with me. Except for Aunt Elsbeth's consciousness. I crane my head to catch a glimpse of her. She gasps and then she is gone.

"Eesa?"

At first, I think it's Jake calling, but it's Banner's voice breaking through. The scene shifts as quickly as a dream and floods me with desire.

It's still dark. It's still cool. But the surface upon which I lie is soft, and the arm surrounding me is strong. My eyes grow accustomed to the shadows. Banner is murmuring into my neck. Undressing me. Smiling over me and undressing himself. Not in memory, but in the moment. Not in a coffin, but in my bed.

"Listen to me," he says. "And come to my voice."

"I'm right here," I tease him with a bite.

"It worked," he says, but he's not speaking to me.

And now I'm back where I began, in the fading light of the cemetery on top of the earth covering Jake's grave. Everyone is looking at me. I must have fallen. Banner is on his knees beside me, pencil and paper in hand.

With a flash of her eyebrows, Millie says, "That asshole"—she means Banner, and I think calling him *asshole* is a compliment— "can not only see what is written on the paper but can also *manipulate* it."

"Wait," I clarify. "Banner can read the paper?"

"*And* manipulate it. Which was my idea. I told him to try that."

"I couldn't get you to hear me," Banner says. "So, I took the letter to try to follow you—"

"And then," Millie interrupts, "when I realized he could see what was on the paper—"

Banner interrupts back, "I thought maybe I could just give you a different scene to enter."

"But who found you a pencil?" Millie asks. "I did. Look here, Aunt Isla. You made them grow among the twigs in your bush and I snapped one right off for him."

"Are you guys trying to one-up each other?" I ask.

Banner and Millie share a silent consult.

"Yeah," they both admit.

"But more importantly," Banner continues, "you made your gardenia to answer to *my* imagination."

"Elsbeth bewitched the thing somehow," Millie says, "but Banner's words actually show up and become the magic. I mean, you guys were practically *doing* it!"

"Millie," I reprimand her, but she just laughs and says, "Look! My words don't do that." When she scribbles on the paper, although words appear, they don't hold any more power over me than any normal thing I read.

"Can I keep this one?" Millie fans herself with the paper in a way that makes me hesitant to read it.

"Give it here," I say. "Oh, my. Yeah, that's what—" Banner's vivid description plays out. "Millie, you read this?"

"Of course not. I'm just a child."

"I wouldn't worry," Banner adds. "What she was able to see, she wasn't that impressed with. Kept barking directions at me—threw me completely off my game."

"Millie, that was inappropriate," I scold her. "Don't spy on people."

"I'm old enough to know stuff," Millie spouts.

"Oh, I thought you were a *child*," Banner says.

"You *are* a child, Millie," I chastise my niece. "And that was private."

"Whatever."

I grunt out a breath and throw my hands up to my sister.

"Oh, that thing you said about having kids?" Sissy asks. "Just think about it is all."

"OK, well, Jake's not down there."

"Down where?" asks...everyone.

"Down *there*." I point. "In the grave."

"What do you mean?!" Aunt Rose keens.

Yeah, I should have thought through the ramifications of that one before I spouted off.

"You can't know that, can you?" Aunt Rose asks. "You're seeing what Elsbeth led you to see."

"*Oo!* Take me down there, Aunt Isla," Millie butts in. "Banner, you try to send us down. I'll find out for sure."

Millie has really embraced this whole helpful seer thing. Or maybe she has just embraced the idea of Banner as her partner in crime.

"Absolutely not," he says.

"*Why* not?"

"You're just a child."

She gives him such a narrowed-eyed glare, I have to laugh.

Aunt Rose does *not* have to, and her worry sobers me up. "Isla, you didn't enter his grave," she says.

It sounds like she's both asking me and trying to reassure herself. "You were here the whole time. He's not missing."

"I felt something, though, Aunt Rose. Elsbeth knew when it occurred to me that I wasn't really trapped down there. I was left with my own rational thoughts. I tried to enter the grave to see for myself."

I won't say the rest, but Banner's resigned expression tells me he knows what I believe. Jake's body is not down there.

"Where is he, then?" he says quietly. "That's where we need to go."

With a jarring blast of wind and thunder, whatever was holding the eye of the storm over the graveyard collapses. The hole to the sky disappears, and the clouds crash into one another like skyscrapers tumbling to the ground. The force of rain that has been pelting the world outside of the cemetery now pelts us. Within seconds, we're as water-logged as ever, and it's impossible to remember the rays of sunlight.

I round on Aunt Rose to remind her what Jeremiah said. "Get them out of here, Aunt Rose. Get them to the house. Or if you can, get them off the property."

Millie nabs several flowers from my gardenia and stuffs them into her pockets. She snaps off pencils too. "Let's go!" she says, her black bangs dripping with excitement. "Write us into the play, Ban."

So, now it's *Ban.* She forces paper into his hand.

Banner is chewing his thumbnail in thought. "You write it," he says to me. "Ignore your aunt Elsbeth's influence. Ask Jake where he is. If anyone can find him, you can."

He tosses the keys to the Jeep—"Here you go, Wren."—and chops a hand in the Jeep's direction. "It's about a football field that way. Engine may be flooded, and the whole thing's lying on its side, so...good luck."

I don't wait for the nonessential members of this expedition to flee. I start to write as an artist throws paint—long strokes sweeping memories over the page—while we're all getting rained on in buckets. The words show up somehow. They don't get washed away. But all I can think to write are the impassioned prayers that pounded through my head while I still hoped Jake would survive.

"Are you writing me in there too?" Millie asks. "I have to come with you. I am the *seer.* Very important."

"I'm *trying.* I don't really know what to do and I don't really believe it's going to work."

"It's going to work," Banner says. "Keep writing. Where would he be right now?"

"Well, it's a flash flood, so he'd probably be swimming in the fucking Hydraulic."

What if I could find him? What if I could find him four years ago?

No sooner has the idea left my pencil than we're there, knee-deep in the swirling pool, the falls thundering down.

"There's Jeremiah!" I say. He's in deeper than we are. Sinking. Rising. East and West. Sinking. Rising. East and West.

"Banner, look at him!" I say. "Just like we did at the boy's funeral!"

But Banner is not beside me. "Banner?!" I scan the area wildly and finally spot him at the top of the falls where Jake stood before he fell. He's locked up, tense like he has to keep his feelings in check. Or like he can't make himself move.

Meanwhile, another man is rising from the water. A man as dear to me as my own heart.

You Can't Keep Him For Free

FOR FOUR YEARS I have longed for nothing more than to gaze upon Jake wearing that shit-eating grin.

He is chest deep, flinging his wet hair, now hip-deep, securing the drawstring of his shorts, now thigh deep, shifting from side to side as he uses his core to drag his legs through the water. His wet curls are plastered haphazardly across his head. "I knew that fucker would let me out sooner or later," he says.

It's not raining anymore.

"Millie, do you see him?" I ask, though my throat feels full of sand. "Is he only in my mind?"

She doesn't answer me. Or I don't hear her. I'm not even sure she's still beside me. Maybe she got separated the way Banner did. But I don't have the ability to focus on that, because...*Jake*. I gawk at my cousin until he frowns.

"You look different right now," he says.

"Jake?!"

I splash through the water and jump on him, knocking him to his ass. When he resurfaces, it's with an overwrought roar, and he hurls me down, thinking I'm trying to wrestle.

"No, stop it!" I sputter. "Let me hug you before you disappear."

"What are you talking about?" he says but consents to the embrace.

I lose it. I start to weep violently, and I squeeze him so tightly, that he does a better job of hugging me back. "You were scared," he says. "You thought I bit it, didn't you?"

I nod into his neck and start to ugly cry until I can't breathe for being wracked with grief. I'm paralyzed, cramping. He's so solid. So genuine.

"Eesa, what is wrong with you?"

"Why didn't you listen to me?" I manage to choke out.

"I'm sorry. I didn't mean to freak you out." He worms out of my arms enough to regard me. "I'm sorry," he says again. "Let's get out of the water."

He's shivering. His shoulders and chest are covered in chill bumps. He's just—so very alive. I take his arm and walk him to shore because I don't want him to vanish.

"You won't believe what I saw up there," he says. "I knew Old Man Ridley was fucked in the head, but he's got those damn rattlesnakes—live ones—crawling around the pit, and he was trying to force Jeremiah down in there with them. Man's a lunatic. I tried to stop him." He looks confused for a moment. "I half-think I got bit." He consults the side of his leg.

"How do you feel?" I ask.

"I feel great. Have you *seen* Jeremiah?" He looks up at the falls. "Did he jump? Who's that guy?"

At the top of the falls, Banner is the only person we see. I wish he'd move back from the edge. Or come down. I don't understand how he got to be up there at all. I wave at him, but he doesn't wave back.

"That's the man I'm going to marry."

Jake barks out a laugh. "Have you ever even seen him before?"

I smile and study Jake's happy expression.

"How's your head?" I ask.

"It's good. I'm more worried about Jeremiah."

"He's around. He's performing some kind of ritual."

"I think we should go get Wren," Jake says. "Maybe even the

police. You know who else is up there? That lying cheater, Billy Banks."

"You don't say."

Wow. He is entrenched in his very last moments. Did I do this? Did I wish to find him so hard, that I went back and wrote things the way they *should* have played out? What I wouldn't give for this to be real.

Jeremiah calls out to us from across the pool.

"Here we are, J," I answer him. I'm not sure what he's saying, but he seems cheerful as he makes his way through the water.

When Jake lays eyes on him, he nearly trips over his own feet. "What the actual *fuck* happened to you in the last three minutes?" he says. "You're huge!"

Jeremiah grins. He's wearing that old, white smock and since it's wet, his muscles threaten to rip right through. Around his neck is a strap of sanctified stones, like the ones the holy man gave to Onacona's family, like the ones Jeremiah gives to me. He unclasps them and secures them around Jake's neck. The fact that Jake submits to it says something. He and Jeremiah share a bond now.

"Welcome back," Jeremiah says.

"*Is* he back?" I ask.

Jeremiah considers the question and glances up at Banner, his usual solemnity returning. "I can't tell. I think that choice may be up to you."

"What's going on?" Jake asks.

Can of worms. How are you supposed to tell someone they're dead? I look to Jeremiah for guidance.

"You're dead," he says. "It's been four years since you went over that waterfall. You died, and you were buried."

I guess that's how.

Jake blows out a doubtful laugh. "I'm not dead." But he knows something is weird because he scans Jeremiah head to toe, and then he does the same to me. I'm not sure how different I appear, but four years ago, Jeremiah was still a boy.

"You *were* dead, though," Jeremiah continues. "It should have been me. And Isla thought it should have been her. In fact, for all practical purposes, it *was* her. Until about a week ago, when she came back and set into motion this whole cataclysmic chain of events—which has led us to this moment."

"You set them in motion too!" I protest.

"Well—yeah, I kind of had to. I mean, I could have let the rattlesnakes kill you, or the cyanide, or Billy Banks, and I could've let the whole place burn to the ground."

"Jeremiah Ridley, stop acting like a messiah. You've spent the last four *years* studying it, and magicking, and digging out goldmines, and uncovering family secrets. You haven't bothered to let me in on *any* of it."

"Well, that's hard to do when you're never here and you're always drunk."

"*Unh.*"

Jake holds up a hand for peace. "I'm not really used to being the voice of reason, and while it is kind of fun to watch Eesa get flustered by someone other than myself, I have a growing concern about *that.*" He points to the top of the waterfall where Banner seems to be held in suspended animation. Behind Banner, the woman I have identified as myself all these years in my dreams is brandishing a thin sword above her head. She waves the other hand at us in mock delight, but Banner doesn't appear to notice any of this.

I flail my arms. "Banner, she's behind you! Aunt Elsbeth is—" But it's like someone has pushed pause on him. "Jeremiah, don't you dare let Jake disappear!" With that, I sprint up the trail, and in moments, I stand below Banner and Elsbeth in the same spot where I watched Jake fall. I can't tell if Banner is under duress or if for some other reason, he is unable to communicate.

"Come up and talk to me," Aunt Elsbeth says. So, I climb, all the while hoping I don't get my head lopped off.

Once I crest the rock wall, Elsbeth says, "It's just like it was before, isn't it? Only, your boyfriend stands where your cousin stood."

Beside Banner, there is a hint of movement—just a shimmer, a ripple in the air.

I try not to sound afraid. "You were up here that day too. And you found out what Jeremiah had discovered. You killed Jake because of it."

Elsbeth shades her eyes—dramatically—to peer down to where Jake and Jeremiah are watching us. "Doesn't look dead to me."

Me either. I can't figure out what manner of alive Jake is. *Oh, I wish Aunt Rose could see him. And Wren and Ash. Before he disappears.*

"Why do you look ill?" Aunt Elsbeth asks. "Isn't this what you wanted?"

"If I could have it for real," I admit. I go to Banner, who has yet to move. "What have you done to him? Have you placed him in some kind of paralysis?"

"He just hasn't caught up. The real question is, *how have you?* It took me years to be able to straddle the timeline. It took me as many years as the one you've written us back into. Tell you what, I will establish you in this timeline. You can keep your cousin and continue on as if this is the first go-round. Just step over completely and allow me to bind you here where you cannot interfere. I'll even let this one live. He forgets you and goes on with his life. You keep your family intact."

Don't trust your senses, I hear Banner's words from before. *And for godsake, don't trust her. In fact, doubt everything in the world except that I love you and I'm waiting for you right here.*

Elsbeth shrugs. "It's up to you." She fixes a keen eye on Jeremiah and Jake. "You can't keep Rose's son for free. You have to trade one for the other. You think there's no cost for reanimating a body? Even upper-world magic demands a sacrifice."

"I don't think you have the right to make that kind of a deal," I tell Elsbeth. "You can't keep hijacking this family's story."

Elsbeth makes a forward motion that physically jerks Banner into a bow. He stumbles closer to the edge, the water rushing over his feet. The sword, which Elsbeth has allowed to rest against the ground while we spoke, she now raises to strike.

"Stop it! Why in the world would you harm Banner? He doesn't have anything to do with this."

"He does, actually. He holds your heart and while that is the case, he holds everything I want. I will kill him to keep you from being a threat to my plans." Her eyes flash, but then her tone softens as if she is now pleading for his life. "You can set him free, Isla. Commit to this timeline. Look!" She gestures toward Jake. "Jacob lives."

Banner is forcibly bent at the waist, but he also appears, in a stilted sort of way, to be writing with his right hand on his thigh, though there is no paper. And no pencil. He opens the other hand to receive something and even wags those fingers a bit, so at least his usual signs of impatience are intact.

The shimmer thing happens again—that translucent ripple in the air—and something even more curious. Where I had seen no paper before, now I do.

"What *is* it you want, Elsbeth?" I ask—more to distract her than to find out.

"I want to walk in *then* and *now* and *later* as I please. But not with you able to thwart me. Choose."

"That's not fair. Jake's body was already gone when I went to look. I never removed it, and I damn sure didn't reanimate it."

Well, now *that* was interesting to her. Elsbeth zeros in on my eyes like she wants to see into my brain.

I've messed up. I've inadvertently revealed something she hadn't counted on. But she reveals something too. She doesn't consider me a threat anymore, and I watch her draw new conclusions. Her focus shifts downstream.

Jeremiah. Who glares up at her with a smirk that says, *It took you long enough.*

No way. He was too scared to even set foot on Jake's grave. There's no way he dug him out. What was it he said? "There is earth magic, and then there is upper world magic." Maybe he didn't need to.

Having lost Elsbeth's interest, she flies down the falls—literally—and across the water where she collides with Jeremiah. They tumble onto the shore. I don't see Jake, and that worries me, but I can't think about it because Banner, still hunched from whatever Elsbeth did to him, makes contact with my hand, and suddenly I am lost in the memory of his grey eyes reflected in candlelight on that first night—of his strong arms flexing beneath his wet t-shirt—of the comforting thump of his heartbeat against my cheek. And now it speaks. "Jeremiah draws her away from you. It's time to write your ending."

Yet another shimmer disturbs the air, but this time it's as if Banner has only just entered the space, as if he's only just got up to the speed of life. Our eyes meet in the present—or whatever present we're in, and he shockingly thrusts a paper against my chest and shoves me to the ground.

Quick as lightning, he pivots to combat a man who comes rushing upon us with a roar—Sheriff Billy. But this is not Billy from today. It's Billy from four years ago. He takes a swing, and Banner blocks it, using his other fist to punch Billy in the gut. I'd cheer him on if I knew the protocol for such a thing. Really, I just want to punch Billy myself. That felt great earlier.

Billy doesn't give up. He swings for Banner's head, but he's no match. Banner grabs his hand and wrenches his arm behind his back, spins him around.

"Who are you?" Billy grunts.

"Not the man you expected to ambush?" Banner tweaks his arm so that Billy cries out. "You haven't met me yet. But I'm the one who's going to end you if you ever come anywhere near Isla or her family at any point in the future. Keep your voyeuristic, psycho self in check." Banner hurls Sheriff Billy—well, I suppose at this point, he's just Billy—into The Hydraulic.

I'd laugh, but Jake is nowhere to be seen. *He's gone. He's gone. He's gone.*

He's not gone. He comes barreling toward us and hits Banner, both hands to his chest, nearly knocking him into the flow of the river.

"Jake, stop it! What are you doing?"

"He attacked you!" Jake is glaring down at Banner, his posture daring him to rise.

"No, he didn't, you doofus. He kept me safe. Did you not see him fighting that big, lying cheater, Billy Banks?"

It takes Jake a second to process that. He slightly turns his grumpy head to find out if I'm being serious.

Meanwhile, Banner waits on the ground for Jake to confirm my story. I think he finds it slightly amusing. When Jake spies Billy where he surfaced—coughing and spitting in a desperate fit—he offers Banner a hand. "My bad." It's not really an apology. More of a way to create some space till he decides whether or not to do it again.

Banner is probably recalling our discussion about the time of great testing Jake would put him through if they ever met. "You're undecided about me," he says. "But I think you're perfect."

"*Who* are you, exactly?"

"I'm a friend of Wren's. And I'm in love with your cousin."

Jake gives me a silent, but flippant, *Is this guy for real?* And I confirm it.

"Where is Millie?" I ask Banner

"She's here," he says. "And she can see us, but I don't think she can step through the—time zone?" He ends it with a question. "She keeps rippling the air, and she was able to hand the paper through."

Jake tries to spot the person we mean. "*Little* Mill?" he asks.

"Well, she's not so little now," I say, "and she's quite precocious. But yeah. Little Mill. Oh, Jake, your mom's at the house! And Asher, and Wren!"

"Well...*yeah*," he says like I'm being dense.

He expects them to be here. They were all here on the day he died.

I stay silent, which makes him falter, and, for the first time, he looks truly shaken. "Eesa, what is happening? Is it really four years since I fell from here?"

I just nod. But with a burst of joy, I realize that—"Mammaw's here! In your timeline—She's at the house! She's still alive!"

"Mammaw *died?!*" he cries.

"Oh, Jake. I'm so sorry. Yes. A year after you. And now Aunt Elsbeth is trying to kill all of us and take the property."

"Fuck that."

"Yeah, fuck that," Banner agrees.

Jake turns on him in an instant and snaps, "You don't get to talk yet."

Just as quickly, Banner smacks him upside the head. "You just tell me when you wanna go, Jake. We don't have a lot of time here, but if I need to knock some sense into you in order to save your family, I'll do it."

This could go either way. I hold my breath, but Jake grins and nods a few times. "Respect," he says.

I guess that means the time of testing is over. Banner gives an upward nod to seal the deal, and I roll my eyes.

"Elsbeth's going to come for us," Banner says. "When she realizes that Isla had *everything* to do with you walking around right now, she's going to be ruthless. So, you and I have to buy Isla some time to write." He backs up to explain, "Her writing is magical."

Jake casts about for how those last sentences connect with meaning. "What does that have to do with anything—that she's a good writer?"

"No, I mean it is *actually* magical. She's able to tap into the— look, I don't know how to explain it, but it's why we're here—in this place and in this moment—and I'm pretty sure it's why you're not in your grave or swirling around the—"

"Stop," I say. "I can't bear to think about that, and honestly, Jake, I don't know if you *are* alive. I mean, are you *really* here?"

"What kind of fucked up question is that?" he spits. "This is already fucked up enough without you making me doubt my existence!"

"Sorry," I say, and I half-laugh through it. I pinch the bridge of my nose to try to concentrate. "Elsbeth thought I raised you, but now she thinks Jeremiah did. And that's why she's down *there* instead of up here killing us."

"*Did* Jeremiah—raise me?"

I shrug. "He's some kind of holy man. Banner, did you see what he gave to Jake?" The beads around Jake's neck are bright and smooth, and I touch them gingerly. "He means to protect him now that he's alive again. He means to keep him here."

"Well? He's family," Banner replies.

I think about how Jeremiah said I might have to make a choice. "Elsbeth says we can't have Jake back for free." A decision between Jake and Banner does not exist in my world. Jeremiah has to know that.

Down on the shore, he is kneeling with his back to Elsbeth. His hands are lifted in surrender, but not to her. She is ranting. Tossing her head around, moving her mouth nonstop. The sword, she wields freely as if it's just an extension of her arm.

"God bless him," I say. "The man prays at the most dangerous times."

"Isn't that when you *should* pray?" Jake says.

"It is when you really believe in the person you're praying to," Banner confirms. "Write your ending, Ees. I'll catch Jake up on the rest."

They walk several paces, Banner explaining that Aunt Elsbeth is Jeremiah's biological mother.

I set the twig-like pencil to the flower-like paper. No pressure. I'll just write an ending that keeps everybody happy, alive, on this property, and in the same timeline. Except for Elsbeth. She has to go. *I'm* not going to kill her. I could lock her underground in the mine for a prison. But she'd probably enjoy that, and anyway, she knows how to make the earth listen to her. She'd get out. What about locking her in Jake's grave? Whatever we do has to be final. Why can't *she* be the sacrifice that keeps Jake alive?

Words appear on my paper that I did not write.

I'm glad we had the chance to be family.

Where did that come from? I lift my head to glance around.

More words appear.

And I'm grateful that you were always my friend. Without your kindness, I think I would have chosen a different and darker road. I'm honored to have walked this one. Keep Jake in whichever timeline you can. Only, keep Banner too. He will safeguard you. This is good, Isla. Don't doubt it. And don't worry. Tell Inola I love her.

I scan the rest. "No," I say quietly and rise quickly. "Jeremiah?! I did not write this!" I scream in his direction.

"Ees?" Banner asks.

A sickening gleam flashes in my eyes, and Jeremiah, from where he had been kneeling, flops forward, face first into the pool, blood threading through currents of water that eddy around him. He convulses once, twice, and lurches so that I think he may try to get up, but then he is still.

Elsbeth, with some effort, draws her long blade from his back.

"No! This is *not* what I wrote! You pigheaded jackass!"

"We have to save him!" Jake rushes to the edge of the falls and when I realize what he has in mind to do, to get to Jeremiah by leaping into The Hydraulic, I spin so fast and clock him so hard my hand goes numb.

"*Sit* down, Jake!" Which he *has* to do because I damn near took his head off. "If you ever jump from here again, I will hate you for the rest of my life!"

On the other side, Banner is climbing down. His face is set, his emotions in check, but barely.

Elsbeth watches him, standing straight and tall, resting her hands on the handle of her blade with its sharp point in the ground. She reminds me of a chess piece.

The odd magical disturbance we've attributed to Millie happens at my elbow, and a sheet of paper floats freely, swaying this way and that, this way and that, to the ground at my feet.

As I watch, words appear like Jeremiah's spreading blood across the page: *Aunt Isla, Jeremiah told me to look up II Kings 2. It's a story about the prophet Elijah, how he got taken up to Heaven, and how his protégé, because he had witnessed the going to Heaven, inherited Elijah's power. In the end, this weird two-paragraph addendum is tacked on about boys who ridicule the newly empowered protégé by demanding he go up to Heaven too—like they don't believe him to be God's new prophet or to have any power. So, the protégé curses them in God's name, and they die.*

I remember this story. "Thank you, Millie," I say, though I don't know if she can hear me, and I don't know how the story helps.

There are many things I should do. I should climb down. I should protect Banner. I should finish the story. But how can I?

From under the water in the pool below, another gleam flashes in my eyes. Jeremiah's golden snake. Upon seeing it, I know that what I *really* should do is simply *go to water*.

Jeremiah sacrificed himself for his family. I have to release his soul.

I don't remember climbing down. Once I've made the decision, I feel very peaceful about it, and I almost think I simply *will* myself to the pool below. At any rate, here I am. Sinking. Rising. East and West. Sinking. Rising. East and West.

I don't know what I should say, but what I do say is, "Creator, take Jeremiah's eternal soul to yourself in love and light. Well done, Jeremiah. Be free, Cousin. Go with God."

"Stop it!" Elsbeth shrieks. "What are you doing? How do you know to do that? You still have to pay!"

Banner has hauled Jeremiah's huge body from the pool. He listens to his chest. I know he can't find a pulse. He's saying soft, low words, and I think he is praying too.

Jeremiah rises from his own body and smiles at us for a moment before a strong wind blows around and spirits him away. *I saw it happen.*

I consider dragging the golden snake from the water to honor him, but maybe it's happy there. I kind of think it betrayed Elsbeth, and that is how it ended up here where Jeremiah prayed and gave himself for us. So, I leave the snake and step onto the shore to be with Banner.

"Did you see that?" he whispers hoarsely. He's still looking to the sky. A tear falls to his cheek, followed by another.

"What are you staring at?" Elsbeth asks.

It flips a switch in Banner, who abruptly aims his firearm at her chest. "This is over. Drop the sword."

"Oh!" she cries in false alarm and tosses the sword over its end onto the ground. Then she laughs and puffs with scorn. "Looks like you and your little witch are alone now."

With a twist of the wrist, Elsbeth swirls a small cyclone into her hands. "He cannot stay," she says to me and releases the cyclone, whipping it in our direction. Banner shoots. His bullet should have hit my aunt dead in the heart, but it simply disappears in the swirl of wind, which is growing. Now it envelops Banner, making him appear blurry. He lets out a sharp breath like he's been punched.

"No!" I wave the winds away from him, but it's slow going like I'm dragging an eighteen-wheeler with a rope.

"It's too late for him, little witch," Elsbeth says with satisfaction. "Or…it's too early." She laughs at her own joke while Banner gazes down at his chest and arms and seems to be disappearing the way his bullet did. I bet that bullet finished its journey in another time-line. She's sending him somewhere else.

"There's nothing you can do," Elsbeth continues to goad me as I strain to direct the whirlwind away from him. "You don't have the stomach for killing, nor the power for getting what you want. May as well go on up with him. Go on up."

What does the earth want? What does the earth want? I rack my brain to come up with a way to convince the wind to let him go. Interest-ingly, the answer comes to mind in the form of an old hymn my mammaw used to sing. *God's voice wasn't in the earthquake—no! God's voice wasn't in the fire. God's voice wasn't in the whirlwind—oh! Listen for the still, small whisper. Listen for the still, small whisper.* Mammaw would get quiet at the end when she sang it. She would tickle our ears and our necks.

"*Shhhhhhh,*" I say to the wind. "Be still." I open my eyes to find my arms spread wide and the wind listening to me. It gently sweeps past Banner and roams up the rock face to Jeremiah's fields. Banner pants and turns his head to me with a mixture of remembered pain and obvious relief.

That hymn was about the same prophet from the story in II Kings and now it is worming through my memories. "Go on up, Baldy!" the kids had yelled. "Go on up!" They ridiculed the new prophet just the way Elsbeth is ridiculing me.

And do you know what happened next in that odd story? What manner of ruin befell the ridiculers?

"I don't have the stomach for killing," I agree with Elsbeth. "Nor do I have the right. Have you no fear of God at all? Did you know that Mammaw used to pray mercy on your head? Late into the night when she thought no one but God was listening. She told me once that your name meant *pledged to God.* But now I name you *rejected,* and I call down curses on you. I leave your pathetic life up to God. Let him decide. Or...her," I add lamely. I'd been doing so well up to that point. "Or..." I lift my head imperiously like I just mean to leave the thought hanging.

Elsbeth scoffs. She does have a great scoff. She makes me feel like an idiot.

"Um...Ees?" Banner says. He takes my elbow and begins to drag me slowly away from Elsbeth.

"You have nowhere to go," Elsbeth sings. "You might as well step up and take it like a man." But she is *not* who Banner is afraid of. We watch her impending doom stalk up behind her while she flamboyantly drags empty hands from the ground over her feet, shins, knees, thighs, hips—all the way to straight above herself with a flourish. And as she collects whatever energy or weapon she is forming, her arms are ripped from her body by two massive claws and a vicious maw.

A younger Sam, the bear.

Elsbeth screams and darts forward, her arms dangling by unfortunate sinews. I can't look away.

"Let's get further up," Banner says. We climb a free-standing rock until we're about eight feet off the ground—not high enough, probably.

Sam tramples Elsbeth and holds her down to roar in her face. She screams again, causing Sam to bounce up and down on her chest. He pauses, then sinks his teeth into her soft belly and feasts upon her while she is still alive—which is longer than you might expect.

We're sort of stuck here. I don't know how well bears climb rocks, but if this one is still hungry, we could be in trouble. "Hey," Jake hisses right behind my head.

I whip around and slap him. "Dammit, Jake! Stop sneaking up on me."

"You are incredibly violent today," he protests.

Now that I see his bruising jaw, I do feel slightly ashamed. "Sorry."

"Honestly, to have missed me so much, you'd think you'd baby me a little more."

"I'm sorry," I say again. "I love you. I'll make it up to you. If we survive. And you're able to come home. *Gah,* can you imagine how everyone will react?"

That seems to please him.

Elsbeth is very dead now. Sam turns his sights on the three of us and waddles over. "I do not want to shoot this bear," Banner says. "But I sure as hell will."

When Sam gets to our rock, he stands up tall on his hind feet. The fur around his black mouth is wet and there are gross, fibrous chunks caught there. Banner takes aim at his head, but I reach down to him.

"Isla," Banner cautions.

Sam sniffs the sanctified stones on my bracelet and returns to his front feet.

"Thank you, Sam," I say.

"Who's that?" Jake points at a human form slinking through the shadows. Even Sam turns to notice.

The form gives a frightened chirp and stops moving. He stares in our direction. Billy Banks.

Without warning, Sam charges at him on heavy steps that cover the ground with thundering speed. Billy tears out of the shadows, and streaks into the woods—even faster than he tried to steal home plate. Sam chases him for a few more yards but stops without exerting himself too much. He stretches his neck to look back at us, and I swear he chuckles before he saunters away.

"I guess we're free to go," I say.

"What about Jeremiah?" Banner asks. But Jeremiah's body has disappeared, and in its place, a great, black kingsnake is winding its way toward the Ridleys' field.

An Unexpected Guest

THE SUN HAS SET. Stars are coming out. And the three of us perch on top of this rock. I'm ready to go home. But what if Jake can't follow?

"Was I buried on the property?" he asks. I think the fact that he has been dead is finally sinking in.

"Yes. But first, your body lay on the dinner table all night."

"Who's idea was that?!"

"Not mine. I wanted to tuck you into bed."

"You can tuck *me* into bed," Banner yawns. "I am bone-tired."

"Wait. Are you two *sleeping* together?"

Banner snorts.

"*Please* shut up," I tell Jake.

"This morning you'd never even had a real boyfriend," he protests.

"This morning I was your age."

"Right." He hangs his head.

"Oh, don't be sad," I tell him.

"It's just...a lot."

"Look at it this way," I offer. "You got your gap year."

"Apparently, I got four. And nothing to show for it. What

happens now? Are we stuck in the year I died while everyone else moved on? Or do we get to skip ahead?"

Banner and I exchange an uncomfortable glance.

"I don't know," I admit. "But Jeremiah told me to keep you both, so I have to believe that's possible."

"Let's go find out." Jake hops up and brushes dirt off his shorts. "I'm going to starve if we don't try."

Banner doesn't say anything. He's waiting for me.

"What about Millie?" I ask.

"Millie!" Jake hollers. "We're going to walk home. Can you follow us?"

"She'll follow," Banner says. "Kid's got horse sense. And she's a seer."

It's getting dark for real. "Being a seer doesn't give her night vision."

The three of us climb down. As we pass the spot where, four years ago, Jeremiah threw me to the ground repeatedly, I can almost see the ghost of myself struggling to get into the water. "Jake hasn't come up!" I'd said. "He hasn't come up!"

Impotent. Horrified. Now, I squeeze Jake's hand. *Please don't disappear.*

The clearing around the pool ends where the trail begins. Jake starts to take his hand back, but I don't allow it. "No, hang on to me," I command. We step into the woods, and now I take Banner's hand too.

Nobody seems to hate this *Follow the yellow brick road* type camaraderie. I can guarantee that Jake wouldn't be traveling hand in hand like this on any other occasion.

I say, "We need light."

And there is light. All of God's fireflies burst onto the scene like ushers at the theater illuminating the aisle.

"Did you do that?" Banner asks against my temple.

"I honestly don't know."

We walk for several minutes. Occasionally, the trail narrows and we have to go single file, but we remain physically connected—until a while later, when, in order to proceed, we really have to maneuver in an awkward sort of way, and Jake says, "OK, Eesa, I'd rather just disappear than hold your hand anymore. No offense."

"No, I'm too scared, Jake."

"We can't hold hands every second from now till the end of time. I already have to pee."

I take a breath and release it through pursed lips. "I love you."

"I love you, too." Jake, despite his commitment to a tough guy persona, says to Banner, "Take care of her. She can get lost inside her own head."

"Understatement," Banner responds. "You have my word."

With the hand he's not using to hold mine, Jake hugs me, pulls back to meet my eyes, and lets go.

The whole world goes dark.

"Jake?" I whisper-yell. "Jake?!"

"I'm still here," he says—in that way that means I'm overreacting. "It just went dark."

Ten seconds is probably all it takes, but to me, it feels like an eternity spent in a dreadful void. But then the lightning bug ushers blink back to their jobs and Jake grins. "Come on," he says and jogs down the trail.

As we progress, it occurs to me that we must still be stuck in the old timeline. The path is soft, but it isn't flooded with the torrential water that the storm gods released this afternoon. "Banner, what if we're stuck four years ago?"

He hasn't let go of my hand.

"You needed a bear," he says. "You were given a bear. You needed light. You were given light. How much do you need me?"

His eyes are not on me but on the trail ahead. Maybe it's a rhetorical question. At any rate, he doesn't wait for me to answer. He says, "Don't let go of me, Ees."

It's beautiful tonight. Every time the fireflies take a break, we take one too. Jake keeps hollering from further ahead to let us know he's alive. I start to breathe easier. I even get excited. "If we stay in this timeline, Mammaw will be home. You'll get to meet her."

Banner doesn't find this as exciting as I do. "How does it work, do you think? Do we stay ourselves? With all of our experiences intact? Or do we lose them? Do you have your college degree? Do I have my blog? Before, when Elsbeth swirled me into that cyclone, I started losing my memories. Of you."

The man may not have known me for long, but he can read me like a book, so when I instantly—and viscerally—begin to panic from want of answers to his very legitimate questions, he's ready for me.

"Nope. Do not freak out," he says. "Kiss me, though." He leans over and kisses me with all the passion he's been using to spoil me this whole time.

"Do not forget me," he says, betraying his own fear. "If I fall away... If we have to wait four years..." His hands cup my face. His eyes are burning.

"I won't. I promise."

"And don't lose faith. OK? Same rules apply. Doubt everything before you doubt me. I will be waiting for you."

"But just stay here," I plead. "Just stay with me."

"Eesa!" From up ahead, Jake sounds terrified, and Banner and I run to the sound of his voice. When we reach him, he's staring across the last length of the trail at his own dead body. And at me—holding his head and shoulders, vocalizing, wailing, groaning, unable to bear the reality that he is dead.

Banner grabs my arm and points out another onlooker: Jeremiah, four years ago, from behind a tree, his back to us. He must have stayed to guard us after he'd deposited Jake's body. Sissy, also from *then*, comes out the door. When she spots the me on the ground, she cries out and rushes to my side.

Upon seeing my sister, Jeremiah abandons his post and turns toward his home. His face is heavy with sadness. As he advances to where we stand, the space around us shivers like a curtain. He stops and listens. He looks through us, past us. I think he senses us. When he proceeds, I put out my hands to keep him from colliding with me. But the shiver that happens between us envelops him, and he enters the space I occupy. He stops again—inside of me, and doesn't speak, but sighs in relief before he plods down the path to his home.

At the same time, I am shoved out into the open yard by some invisible force. Wren blasts through the front door, followed by my mammaw, and I gasp when I see her. She sees me too. Not just the me from then, with Jake in my arms, but the me right now. Her thoughtful expression allows for the mystery. Maybe she knew all along.

"I love you, Mammaw," I whisper because I'm not sure if I'll get to tell her.

She puts her fingers on her mouth, blows me a kiss, fixes her eyes on Jake, smiles, and does the same. Then, with arms outstretched, she circles the space in front of her from knee height to chest, index fingers pointing, and she mouths the words, "Hold on."

As soon as her fingers touch, a tremor shakes the ground, and Jake and I fall to our knees. From behind us, a girl says, "I found them, Mammaw!"

"Millie!" I scoop her up as she tries to dart past me.

"You can see me!" she squeals. "You can hear me?"

"Yes! But you're—"

Younger. Am I younger too? Did Mammaw just consummate this new ending to that horrible night? I wheel around to locate Banner. I can practically still feel his grip upon me. But he is nowhere to be seen.

On the ground where the eighteen-year-old me sat in shock with Jake on her lap, Sissy is pacing back and forth rubbing her bare arms. We're not there anymore. Because we're here.

"Mama!" Millie runs into her mother's ready embrace.

"*There* you are!" Sissy says. "Where in the world have you been?"

"To help Aunt Isla. Jake is alive, Mama! Aren't you so glad he's alive!"

"Yes, of course, Sweetie," Sissy answers. She must think Millie's words are merely a child's fancy. She lifts Mill onto her hip, but Millie is craning her neck every which way. "Where is Banner?" she asks.

I stare at her. *I don't know.* If she can't see him, he must truly be gone. I can feel the fear building.

Sissy gives me a curious smile. "Happy birthday," she says.

"Come, eat. Everyone's ready."

"In a minute," I manage.

Jake regards me.

"Just go," I say.

Mammaw lays a hand on him, guides him inside.

I collapse in the very spot Jeremiah laid—*didn't* lay—Jake—and mourn a different kind of loss.

After a while, Mammaw pads from the house like a cat on bare feet. She doesn't speak—just sits beside me, and I lean against her as I did when I was little.

After a while, she says, "Gardenias were Pap's favorite too."

The whole time I've been crying, I've been growing one. I've made it gargantuan out of spite.

"Is that why there are so many around the property?" I sniff.

"Probably." Mammaw tilts her head to look up at what is becoming a gardenia monstrosity. "This one is ridiculous."

That makes me laugh, but then I start sobbing again. "Is becoming an adult going to exact a price every time I give my heart away?"

"'Fraid so. You know how the old oak tree reaches over our graves? You're not the only one who waters the earth with tears."

"Jeremiah sacrificed himself so that we could keep Jake."

"Did he?"

"And Mammaw?" I search her face. "Aunt Elsbeth was mauled by a bear."

To my surprise, Mammaw just nods her head.

"Come in, Little. We're going to celebrate your life over cake."

"I really don't want to."

"Well, we really do. Your life is precious to us. And maybe after that, you can begin to work out where your heart got to."

I allow Mammaw to cajole me inside. Along the way, I ask, "Do you think he'll remember me?"

"I'm not sure. But I think he will love you."

"I don't even know where he is. He may be in the middle of a poppy field. Or drunk in some dive bar in Florida. Hey, why didn't you ever tell me about the magic?"

"What was there to tell? You always knew."

"Well, I forgot."

"Well, I was dead."

"That's a good point." Before we break the threshold, I hug my mammaw. "I am incredibly grateful to have you for now." And I am. I try to compartmentalize the heartache I feel over Banner in order to celebrate with my family. My lost cousin is found, and this is the last summer I get to spend with Mammaw—if things go the way they did last time.

For the next few days, the bridge is underwater, and there's not much I can do except mope. I try to ask Wren about Banner, but he hasn't met him yet, and maybe he never will. Millie has all but forgotten him. I think the fact that she's so young, coupled with the fact she sees so many invisible things, makes it hard for her to determine what memories to keep.

Jake gets downright ornery with me. "Eesa, you have to snap out of it. We have the whole summer ahead. I'll help you find him. Wait until the bridge is passable."

But I'm lovesick. Everywhere I turn, there are beloved family members making the house noisy and small. And all I can think about are the moments Banner and I made love or laughed or danced when nobody else was around. I fear that if I quit obsessing over the memories, I will lose them. Already, I'm beginning to feel them only as one does a story about someone else.

When Jake died, the whole house changed. Everyone grieved. Everyone understood that there was a before and an after that horrible day. The house was eery with the hum of living humans who were missing a piece of themselves. But now, I'm the only one who hurts, the only one who lacks, the only one who is raw with loss and want.

As soon as the bridge clears, Jake loads me up in his truck and drives us to the coffee shop. Although I search for Banner online, I can't find information about him. I do find his dad, General Kirk.

Am I supposed to lobby a US general for the whereabouts of his handsome son whom I have yet to meet? I'm not above it.

Banner's blog doesn't exist, at least not publicly. I consider buying his domain name so that he might contact me for it. In the end, I bite the bullet and call the number for General Kirk, which is being answered by an assistant—who probably doesn't even know the man or ever see him—and I fumble through an exceedingly disjointed explanation about how I'm trying to locate his son, Banner, while Jake makes faces every time I sound like an idiot. Which is nonstop. I finally just end the call.

But I do get a follow-up. The general's son is in the middle of a tour in an undisclosed location. We're not a liberty to divulge more than that.

The last straw for me is coming face to face with the Hall of Heights, which I had yet to consider, and which is devoid of our happy contributions. I start to panic. I can't remember what's not there.

We made a mark of us, Banner had said. *Now we exist.*

There was a dog. What was its name?

I'm standing there, struggling to believe that we do still exist, when Sissy brings my sketchbook over. "Isla, is this just your imagination, or do you have a boyfriend I don't know about?"

The *entries* still exist. I flip through the pages. Banner's handwriting. His maps. All the vivid memories I chronicled when I thought he'd left on my birthday. "Lucy," I whisper. I hug that precious book to my chest and my sister around it. "Thank you, Sissy!"

For the next few days, I go off by myself. I lie in the sun at the swimming hole and read all the things over and over. I sit on that tall rock at The Hydraulic. I walk to the cemetery.

Jake's grave isn't there anymore, but my gardenia is.

"Why don't you write to him?"

It's Jeremiah. For some reason, it amuses me to see him walking around in sandals and shorts. I've thought about visiting him several different times, but he's sixteen again, and I couldn't bear to go over only to have him stare at me blankly. He plops down beside me.

"Jeremiah! Do you remember all of it?"

"It's a little hard to forget."

"But you are your younger self."

"So are you."

"No one else remembers," I say.

"Billy Banks does." Jeremiah withdraws a silver-plated cup from a bag he carries. "He told me to give this to you."

I laugh out loud. "That stupid, fucking mid-youth baseball trophy."

Jeremiah smiles like he's accomplished something. "He was too scared to come to give it to you himself. He's never going to install cameras. I know that much."

"Banner actually threw him into The Hydraulic!"

Jeremiah leans back with his eyes closed, the sun shining on his face. "It was glorious," he says.

"You were something, Jeremiah."

"You were too, Cousin."

We sit for a while, and it is the first real connection that has felt natural since I returned to this timeline.

"What if he has forgotten all about me?"

"*Nah.* Love is as strong as death. Haven't you ever heard that?" Jeremiah plucks one of my gardenias and flicks it open. "Write to him."

When I accept the paper, I lean over to kiss his cheek, and do you know, he just smiles like he is *finally* getting used to human affection.

"Have you talked to Inola?" I ask.

"That's where I'm headed after this. We didn't start going out until after your grandmother's funeral, but I miss her so much, you know?"

I deadpan him.

"Yeah," he laughs. "You do."

"You know you're welcome at the house, right? Any time. Mammaw wants to get to know you better and Jake won't be an asshole to you. Especially now that he knows how huge you're going to be."

That makes him grin. "I'll come."

"Bring Inola. Bring her grandmother."

"OK." He stands up. "If you get to writing."

"Deal." I snap off a pencil.

"See you soon, Cousin," he says. I like how he relishes calling me that.

"See you, Cousin." I watch him out of sight before I set pencil to paper.

Dear Banner, It's the bridge, I write. *My one, essential thing. I mean, if it's not a person. If it's not you. And, to be clear, it is you.*

I miss you so much, my heart hurts all the time. I tried to find you, but all I know is you're serving in an undisclosed location.

Your poor mother! She has all three of you to worry about!

I worry too. I worry about what you have to endure. I worry that you won't remember me, that things will play out differently, and you'll move on. Or worse. That you won't make it home at all.

Nobody here understands, except Jeremiah a little. He's here, Ban. He's alive. I hope that means he always will be.

So, the only one I'm missing is you, my love.

Please don't let go. Please don't forget. I love you.

He's nine hours ahead, assuming he's in Afghanistan. I looked it up. Time is strange. It's the middle of the night there, no magic needed. I hope he's sleeping soundly someplace safe. *You asked me if I needed you,* I write. *And I do. As much as light. As much as family. You're my home. And I am yours.* I make my way back to the cabin with the paper in hand. It didn't carry me to him, didn't allow me to see into the world he inhabits.

Tonight, I think about drinking, which surprises me. But I have no alcohol. In this timeline, I've never even been drunk. I pull the covers over my head, but peep out when Jake pushes the door open and says, "Want me to spend the night?"

"No, it's OK."

He enters anyway, his blanket trailing behind. "Well, I'm going to. Ash is snoring." Jake lies on top of my covers and goes to great lengths to conceal himself with his own cover, feet to shoulders.

"OK. Thanks." I lay my extra pillow on top of his head, and he shoves it underneath. We lie side by side, like when we were little, but without the giggling. He rolls a few times and adjusts his blanket. It's comforting. It is. His breathing evens out. I fall asleep to the steady, purring proof that he is truly alive.

It's a peck on my huge window that rouses me. I don't think I even open my eyes, but I'm looking through the glass just the same, and my breath catches in my chest when I see Banner. I hurry to push the window outward so that he can slide into my room.

"How did you—" I begin, but he's kissing me. I lose myself to him. At some point, he puts his forehead to mine, and I wake.

The room is lit from the outside by the bright morning sun. It was a beautiful dream. I don't even feel too sorry or sad to know it wasn't real. Jake is already up. His blanket is here, but I hear him joking with Wren in the kitchen.

The paper I'd written yesterday lies next to me on the bed. I almost don't look because I don't want to overshadow the memory of the dream by reading my own tortured words, but I do look, and other words are being written without my say-so.

Hey, Corn Maze, You're not really going to make me live out these four years again just passing notes back and forth, right? Straddle the damn timeline and come find me.

We did it. We connected over space—and time. I just have to figure out where we are in four years, right? I just have to want to find him as desperately as I wanted to find Jake. I just have to look ahead, have to recreate the hurricane, have to find my place on the front porch in the rocking chair with the quilt, with the rain from the roof and the thrashing branches, and even though we haven't met, I have to write it all down the way it was, have to—

Scream. Because about seventy pounds of soaking, yellow hair is panting in my lap, and I instinctively wrap the quilt around it.

In response, the dog works to rub its face dry on my tank top.

"No, Lucy!" a deep (and deeply mortified) voice shouts.

The dog's father drops his massive duffel and rushes onto the porch, bypassing the steps the same way his dog has. He wrestles the friendly beast off of me and scolds her, not harshly, more out of embarrassment, I think, with, "No, Lucy. No, Lucy."

When he turns his attention to me, he raises his hands in a silent apology. Lucy barks a proper hello, wagging her whole backend enthusiastically.

It feels like déjà vu. I cautiously rise to my feet. "Um…your bag's getting waterlogged," I tell him. "You should bring it up."

He sees the sense in this and once he has retrieved his bag, he draws a stabilizing breath which also draws him to height. I can't help but appreciate the contour of his broad shoulders beneath the sopping t-shirt. I swear he looks like Jake. Now that Jake has let his beard grow thick.

"This is Wren's place, right?" the man asks and, for the first time, he looks me full in the face—harder as the moments pass like he's working to place me.

I know the feeling. The grey of those eyes causes me to stammer. "Yes. Well. It belongs to all of Mammaw's grandchildren. Wren is my cousin. Did he rent it to you?"

"No. I've been slogging through the evacuating traffic from the coast. He called to check on me. Told me to shelter here." The man backtracks to explain that—"There was a hurricane in the Gulf."

"I'm aware," I assure him. And now I'm beginning to smile.

"I've been driving in this for over twenty-four hours." My mystery guest looks over his shoulder, but when he feels me rub the beads along his collarbone, he quickly refocuses on me.

"The br—" he begins. His brow furrows. "The bridge back there is—I barely made it across."

"Well, you're stuck here now, Banner Kirk," I tell him.

"How did you—" He allows me to cup his cheek, and he fumbles with my bracelets when they catch his eye.

"Ees?!" He crushes me to his chest. "You found me! You found me! I knew you would." He says other things, but they're lost to my neck and his breathlessness. And now he puts me down to stare at me. "I kept losing the details. I couldn't even remember your name." He grabs my hand and fits it to his chest. "But I kept you right here. Always. Is this real? It's not like the dreams, right? It doesn't feel like the dreams."

"Come inside, Man, and I will prove to you how real it is."

He smiles as broadly as his face will allow. "Yes, Ma'am," he says, and I think he'd like nothing better.

Lucy barks her congratulations, and Banner stalks me to my bedroom, where we peel him out of his wet clothes and fling them on the floor—and, do you know?—that neat freak of an Army man just lets the wet clothes lie where they land.

All night long, we keep waking each other. When we're not making love, we're just putting our hands on each other to stay connected. By morning, we are delightfully spent.

The whole week goes by this way: laughing, loving, eating, playing. We read the sketchbook curled up together in a blanket, and then enact our recorded memories to re-establish them. We visit Jeremiah and the treasure tree. We restore our marks in the Hall of Heights.

On Sunday, the whole family comes for our annual reunion. They don't remember meeting Banner, all except Jake, who has memories of that one day. As soon as he bursts through the door, Banner, who has been lying in wait, dives upon him and pummels him until he submits. "Welcome home, Jake," he says with overwrought pleasure. And Jake, wide-eyed in the most hilarious stupor of his adult life says, "What the hell just happened?"

"Jake, you remember Banner, right?" I ask.

"You found him?!" Jake jumps up and—he's bigger now, you know—he jumps up and confirms his own comment. "You found him!" And he hugs Banner. He hugs him so tight you'd think Banner was *his* lost lover. Then he informs us that he is not alone and waves the others in.

Jeremiah and Inola brighten the doorway, and soon the whole house rings with music and life, as it should.

"Mammaw?" I say because I feel her somehow. Millie waves to no one I can see.

"It's not only Mammaw," she tells me and her smile breaks wide. "It's *all* of them."

I intuit the message, that the bridge, from God's own land to the humus of Earth, connects us to Home. Creator calls us to create— not just on paper, but onto the hearts of those with whom we've been entrusted. Family. And that is the essential thing.

Amen.

Author's Note

Thank YOU for taking the time to read this. Please consider leaving a review! They help authors more than you may know.

Susan Holland, you have been such an encouragement. Thank you for your keen eye and your timely suggestions. And thank you for couching them in kindness.

Susan Neder, thank you for immediately grabbing your calendar to schedule time for me and for your morning prayer.

Jess Theune, thanks for reading it and making me laugh. Thanks for back deck visits and just generally being your awesome generous self.

Thank you, Jeff Neal, for the book cover and for listening in the middle of rain storms to the baby ideas for this story—not to mention for reading many, many, many chapters.

The beginning scene of this story came to me on a mountain walk between cow pastures on a foreboding and cloudy day. Storms were moving into the area from a hurricane that hit the gulf. It always surprises me how far hurricanes continue to travel over land. Isla and Banner were already friends of mine by the time I got home from that walk, so I invited them in, and opened up all the doors to welcome the first whispers of rain.

About the Author

Jennifer Daniels Neal is a performing songwriter, author, and teaching artist. She and husband, Jeff, have released nine music albums, a picture book, two novels, and two human children into the world. They live on Lookout Mountain in Georgia, where hurricanes occasionally flood their basement.

Visit JenniferDaniels.com to learn more.